C000217304

The
Mystery
of
Yew Tree
House

ALSO BY LESLEY THOMSON

Seven Miles from Sydney
A Kind of Vanishing
Death of a Mermaid
The Companion

The Detective's Daughter Series
The Detective's Daughter
Ghost Girl
The Detective's Secret
The House With No Rooms
The Dog Walker
The Death Chamber
The Playground Murders
The Distant Dead
The Runaway (A Detective's Daughter Short Story)

The
Mystery
of
Yew Tree
House

LESLEY THOMSON

An Aries Book

First published in the UK in 2023 by Head of Zeus,
part of Bloomsbury Publishing Plc

Copyright © Lesley Thomson, 2023

The moral right of Lesley Thomson to be identified
as the author of this work has been asserted in accordance with
the Copyright, Designs and Patents Act of 1988.

All rights reserved. No part of this publication may be reproduced,
stored in a retrieval system, or transmitted in any form or by any means,
electronic, mechanical, photocopying, recording, or otherwise,
without the prior permission of both the copyright owner
and the above publisher of this book.

This is a work of fiction. All characters, organizations, and events
portrayed in this novel are either products of the author's
imagination or are used fictitiously.

9 7 5 3 1 2 4 6 8

A catalogue record for this book is available from the British Library.

ISBN (HB): 9781804546161
ISBN (E): 9781804546147

Cover design: Ben Prior / Head of Zeus

"Advice to Young Children" by Stevie Smith,
from *Collected Poems of Stevie Smith*, copyright ©1972 by Stevie Smith.
Reprinted with permission of New Directions Publishing Corp.

"Advice to Young Children" by Stevie Smith,
from *Collected Poems and Drawings*, copyright ©1942 by Stevie Smith.
Reprinted with permission of Faber and Faber Ltd.

Printed and bound in Great Britain by
CPI Group (UK) Ltd, Croydon CR0 4YY

Head of Zeus Ltd
First Floor East
5–8 Hardwick Street
London EC1R 4RG

WWW.HEADOFZEUS.COM

With much love to
Mel and Alfred.

Advice to Young Children

'Children who paddle where the ocean bed shelves steeply
Must take great care they do not,
Paddle too deeply.'

Thus spake the awful aging couple
Whose heart the years had turned to rubble.

But the little children, to save any bother,
Let it in at one ear and out at the other.

Stevie Smith, 1942

Prologue

11th August 1940

Hastening home after work on the path across the common, zig-zagging between bushes of gorse and tufted grass and always watching for shrapnel, Greta Fleming hadn't seen the man until he was upon her.

'We know each other, don't we?' He grinned. 'You're at Dales' Bakery, you sold me an apple turnover. You have a lovely smile.'

'Yes.' Greta didn't remember him from the shop but, flattered – although she wasn't smiling – she forgot to hurry on.

Greta's mum didn't want her taking the shortcut through Esher Common, even in daylight. If she knew Greta had done so – in her best shoes – she'd kill her. Hitler had made her mum a bag of nerves. Greta's older brother, Phil, stationed at Newhaven with no leave, could face Hitler any day. Greta had promised her dad to be a proper help to her mum. Now look at her.

'My goodness, you are in a hurry. Have you a rendezvous with a beau?' The man touched the brim of his hat.

'I've been at work.' Baffled by the question yet suspecting it was what Phil called 'dirty', Greta prayed she wasn't blushing. The birds had stopped singing. She could only hear blood pounding in her ears. Quelling an urge to run, she minded Miss Manners. 'I'm going home.'

'You shouldn't be out here alone.'

'I'm fifteen and it's quicker, see.' Greta caught herself talking as if she was at home and justifying being late.

'Nevertheless, it's not safe. Inebriated Tommies on leave, damned conchies, all sorts of men about. No fifteen-year-old girl should be here all alone.'

Without it being agreed, the man accompanied Greta along the path. He was handsome, and his voice was like what she heard on the wireless, which must make it all right.

He cupped her elbow. 'And you are?'

'Greta.'

'Garbo?' He gave a strange laugh.

'Fleming.' Greta smelled cigarette smoke. 'My mum loves her, which is why. Stupid name for a shop girl, as if I'm better than I am.'

'Nothing stupid about you, Greta Fleming,' he said. 'We need shop girls.'

'I suppose.' Greta told herself her name sounded nice said that way.

'Has anyone said you are beautiful?'

'I have to get home.' Greta tripped. The man moved his grip to her upper arm.

That hurts. Politeness getting the better of her, Greta said this only in her head.

'You could be Garbo.' He leaned in and teased a lock of hair from Greta's forehead. After a day in the bakery, it had lost its curl. 'Baby-soft skin.' He brushed her cheek with the back of his hand.

'Don't,' Greta shouted.

The ground blurred as she ploughed forward, pumping the air with her fists, pushing onwards.

Away. Away. Away.

*

2

A heron poised on a post might gladden the heart. Or, like the albatross, signal doom.

As night descended, lime trees along the common's edge lost definition. One tree, felled by an army lorry that had skidded off the road two nights before, lay gashed and splintered.

Chapter One

28th August 1940

Beyond the graves, one of the chimneys at Yew Tree House seemed to shimmer against the blue sky. No clouds or bombers' contrails; it could be a normal summer's day. The house was empty: the Strides' nanny and their cook had been invited to attend the funeral and the interment with Adelaide and the children.

Reverend Smart's reedy voice faded and rose across the churchyard, audible only to those at the graveside. But everyone knew the words. Over the last months, too many had been buried.

Beside Smart stood his curate. Michael Snace was only twenty, but a stern manner and apparent charm had carried him beyond his years and engendered an unusual level of trust and increasing responsibility as well as devotion in those who Snace liked to call his flock. Until he had come to assist the Reverend Smart in Sussex, Snace's most devout follower had been his mother, with whom he had shared a Peabody flat in London's Old Kent Road. Blessed with fervent ambition – a greater cause of worship than the Almighty – with velvet step, he must nimbly ascended a ladder towards a bishopric and beyond. Today, keeping close to the creaky old cleric, whose every breath appeared a struggle, sleek of cheek and cool of brow, Michael Snace saw not mourners around the grave, but his future. Amen.

Snace was not the only one paying scant attention to the vicar's graveside service. Adelaide Stride and her two daughters – one in her arms, the other as close to her as Snace was to Smart – stood, their faces blank and drawn. Only Rosa, aged two, merrily chortling and flapping at the chasm in which lay her father's coffin, was finding the whole thing a hoot. Adelaide and fourteen-year-old Stevie Stride gazed off into the middle distance to the chimney of Yew Tree House. Each wishing themselves far, far away.

There were those who Pat Jordan called 'downright nosy parkers' that made a business of weeping into handkerchiefs at funerals. Adelaide had said, 'It's easier to cry for our own dead at other funerals. Many will be in fear that it will soon be their loved one they mourn.' She imagined the new and constant fear of death had killed idle curiosity.

'...Captain Rupert Stride made the ultimate sacrifice serving our esteemed leader...' Rather florid for dry old Smart, Adelaide thought.

The sermon had seemingly defeated the elderly vicar. Adelaide assumed an expression of concern as Pat Jordan and Old Hobbs, the only verger too old to enlist, led tottering Reverend Smart away. Poor man, if not for the war he would have retired.

Perhaps after Smart's rambling it was the clarity and confidence of Snace's rendition that caused Adelaide to pay actual attention to the eulogy.

'...his valiant service in the Great War set the scene for his courage in this one. Captain Stride stands for all that is marvellous about the indefatigable British spirit. A pillar of this community, he will live on...'

A pillar of the community. Adelaide set her face at the meaningless term. When war was declared, it was the destruction, the dead and injured which pierced her heart like an icicle. Adelaide was less afraid for herself, were it not that if she died it left Rupert to care for their daughters alone. At thirty-one, she was eleven years younger than Rupert so it had always been assumed he would go first. But not now and not this way.

'...a wonderful husband and father... irreplaceable.'

Snace spoke with more feeling than Adelaide, numb and removed, could summon.

Later, Pat Jordan would remind some of the 'hankie sniffers' who remarked on Adelaide's frozen features that, *the likes of Mrs Stride prefer to keep feelings to themselves and no harm in that.*

'...Thou knowest, Lord, the secrets of our hearts...' Mr Snace, prayer book half closed, intoned the words as if they were his own.

Now Snace was giving a potted history of the Strides' 'long and illustrious presence in our beloved Bishopstone.' How Rupert's grandfather opened his law practice, Stride and Son – *before he had a son* – and Rupert was the last of a long line of worthy solicitors. '...many of you have bought your home or sold off farm machinery at a Stride auction in the Bishopstone Arms...' Snace was an orator. His thin-lipped precise speech might be extoling the virtues of a rich man at an auction snapping up the spoils from another man's failure. Rupert had disliked Snace; jumped up, he'd said. Snace was now making ever more frequent visits to Yew Tree House. *Did he have his eye on Stevie?* Fat chance – Stevie referred to the scrubbed cherubic curate as 'Snake'. Adelaide thought it apt, but said it was rude.

She should leave the village, but with the war, where could they go? At least, Adelaide told the coffin, Stevie and Rosa would not follow their father into his hated life of conveyancing contracts and processing probate for the greedy.

When they arrived, Snace had called Henry 'Master Stride'. Seeing Snace flush with shame for his mistake, Adelaide almost felt bad for correcting him. 'Henry is our evacuee,' she'd replied. She felt far worse for seeming to put Henry in his place. But

Snace had been eerily perceptive: Adelaide did treat fifteen-year-old Henry as one of the family.

Since Snace had brought the news about Rupert – assuring her 'I am walking by your side' – Adelaide's vague dislike for him became revulsion.

In silk and astrakhan, hand in hand with Stevie – at fourteen already looking like the lovely young woman she would soon be – and clasping Rosa, Adelaide surveyed the mourners. Rupert had indeed been loved; many in the churchyard would be wishing it was she who had died, leaving Rupert a widower in need of a wife.

'...earth to earth, ashes to ashes...'

Adelaide felt Stevie's fingers grip hers. The service was over. Snace's eyes rested on her if he were reading thoughts.

Although it was summer, as if God was made angry by Rupert's untimely death, the skies darkened and rain pelted down upon the mourners and fell with a rapid tapping onto the polished oak coffin. The handfuls of soil Adelaide Stride and her girls scattered into the void dissolved to runnels of mud and obliterated Rupert's brass nameplate.

Rupert Stride 1898–1940

'Will Daddy get wet?' little Rosa whispered.

'No, darling.' Adelaide spoke as if the thought was new. 'A person can't get wet when they're dead.'

Chapter Two

On Street View, Yew Tree House, double-fronted with a stolid porch and walls clad in grey flint, had looked foreboding. But the view had been shot on a rainy winter's day so Stella had held out hope. It was the second to last house on Church Lane. The last being the Old Rectory, a severe red-brick affair that she'd think was haunted had she believed in ghosts.

Yew Tree House had not jumped out as the perfect holiday home and Stella had suggested they find somewhere else. But Jack said it was the only holiday let in Bishopstone, he'd been lucky to get it. *Besides, they had to be in Bishopstone.*

As they drove through the village Stella had noticed an Old Post Office, an Old Bakery and a gift shop with the signage Old Dairy. At least Chrismas and Son, family butcher, and the ubiquitous Co-op were in operation now.

Stanley, Stella's poodle, flew out of the car as soon as Justin, second born of Jack's seven-year-old twins, undid the dog's safety harness. The diminutive dog raced about Church Lane barking with excitement, before pausing to lift a teetering leg against a gate pillar engraved with 'Yew Tree'. Stella climbed out of the passenger seat and arched her stiffened back. The other pillar said 'House'. Dirtied rendering on the boxy porch was scribbled with cracks and was water-stained. Cobwebs dusted frizzled leaves of what Jack had called 'quintessential ivy around the door'. On Street View the ivy had been alive.

All the same, Stella told herself that, in sunshine with birds tweeting and not a cloud in the sky, Yew Tree House seemed less grim than on Street View.

'I'll get it.' Trailing her bright blue rucksack from one strap, Milly scattered up the path to the house. In the porch, she crouched down and tossed aside a brush mat. 'What a silly hiding place, any *burg-ellar* could have found it.'

Two minutes older than her brother and self-proclaimed boss of all their dual activities, Milly had reason to take prisoners of all who would have obeyed her. Lucie May dubbed Milly Godzilla but thought Justin, on the other hand, had the patience and sweet nature of a saint. Stella had yet to make up her mind.

'Only if a burglar was looking.' Although when Stella had read the instructions for the house – *keys in plastic bag under mat by front door* – this had occurred to her too.

Yew Tree House reminded Stella of the simplistic picture of a house she'd done at primary school which, after her parents separated, her dad had kept. Two chimneys each end, one missing a cap, three windows up, two down, with two dormers in the roof. Miss Stride's instructions had stipulated they not use the attic. The grimy glass suggested Miss Stride never went there either. Stella had been nervous of Miss Stride. The name implied a strict no-nonsense attitude with no leeway for noisy, messy children. Although dogs and children were, Jack had assured her, welcome.

The terracotta brick path suited Stella's vision of rustic, but in wet weather would be slippery. Stanley was nibbling experimentally on a clod of moss that had fallen from the roof. Stella darted forward and prised it from his jaws. Brave, because Stanley, a champagne-coloured toy poodle with teeth to rival a Rottweiler, was unpredictable.

'Doesn't the house look adorable?' Jack called from the car.

'Yes, it *really* does.' Justin would be concerned to reassure his dad. Milly was struggling to get the key into the lock and, for Stella, the jury was still out. Glancing across to her left, she spotted the Old Rectory beyond a tree in their garden. A yew tree, she guessed.

Stella wanted to think Yew Tree House adorable – not a word she used – she wanted everything to be adorable. She recalled the uncompromising advice her best friend, and Clean Slate's operations manager, Jackie, had given when Stella had baulked at spending August with Jack and his children in the country.

'Commit to Jack once and for all or end it and let him find someone else – which, since you're the love of his life, will never happen.'

Before Jack, Stella had ended relationships with texts and broken hearts at the slightest whiff of contention. But Jackie wasn't here now and nor was Stella's other friend, Lucie May, her father's erstwhile ex and an indefatigable crime reporter with a loose grip on ethics. Lucie could drive her mad, but she was great in a crisis.

This wasn't a crisis, it was a holiday.

Her gaze resting on ragged grass, rife with weeds – wasn't Great Willowherb a wild flower? – and straggling buttercups and dandelions, either side of the path, Stella saw her situation as binary. Were the holiday 'adorable', she'd live with Jack and the twins and, as Jack had said, 'be a family'. If the holiday proved a failure, they could not return to their status quo, which Stella had liked. They would be over. The sightless window and eyebrow gables of Yew Tree House seemed to challenge her not to turn tail.

Commit to Jack once and for all...

Twelve years ago, when Stella Darnell met Jack Harmon, then in his late twenties and a driver on London Underground's 'dead late shift', Jack had long had been intent on catching 'True Hosts'. This was Jack's term for psychopaths who killed in cold blood or had blood on their hands. Jack had maintained he could spot one at first sight. It was then, sneaking into their homes, that he had become a secret guest and they his unwitting host.

Stella, now fifty-six and soon to be fifty-seven, had come late to murder. Resentful that her detective father's job had meant he'd cancelled birthday visits, or just visits, aged eighteen she had torn up the police recruitment form he'd given her and started a cleaning company. After Terry Darnell's death his daughter had become engrossed in the case papers for a murder that had eluded Terry, by then retired, and which he'd been investigating when he died. Along with meeting Jack and solving the case, their unofficial investigation dredged up long-lost memories of times Stella had spent with her beloved dad which, perhaps because it hurt to remember, she had blocked out.

Cleaning had equipped Stella with transferrable skills – like her dad she delved into the darkest corners; her motto was *stain by stain*. Her ability to muster facts and express data in multicoloured spreadsheets, combined with Jack's fanciful thinking – reading signs in number plates, hearing ghost voices in foot tunnels – allowed them to solve Terry's cold case and then many more murders.

Eventually, Jack and Stella influenced each other. Jack took stock of facts while Stella opened up to feelings she'd always battened down. They fell in love.

Now they needed this holiday to tell them if they could live together.

As she went to help Milly unlock the door, Stella faltered. To how many seven-year-olds would the issue of security immediately occur? Wouldn't a typical little girl treat it as a treasure hunt and be gleeful to find the key? Detective Inspector Darnell's bedtime stories, if he was home in time, had featured crime and murder so Stella wasn't best placed to define typical. She knew no other small children with whom she could compare the twins. If Milly and Justin saw crime around every corner, it was her fault as much as Jack's. At least this holiday wasn't about investigating a murder; she would be The Sensible One.

'I can *do* it.' Milly flapped Stella away.

'Let Stella try.' Jack was hauling the box of groceries from the boot of his battered Mercedes. Although he was being helpful, obliquely Stella was annoyed – she could manage Milly.

'I'm jolly good with locks, I'm always opening other people's doors when I clean.' She went to take the key.

'*You have not opened this door.*' Milly flung Stella a thunderous look.

Patently true. The twins' mother, Bella, had allowed Justin and Milly to stay for August after she'd asked Stella to make sure Jack 'doesn't get up to his old tricks'. She'd meant Jack's penchant for walking night-time streets – Bella knew nothing about True Hosts.

Bella had not been swayed by Jack's saccharine-soaked point that the holiday would make sunshiny memories the children could treasure all their lives. A phrase Jack never used and to which Bella had retorted, 'You don't make memories, you either remember or you forget.'

Thankfully Jack persuaded Bella not to come and settle the children into Yew Tree House. After Milly's talk of burglars and now Stella's hasty capitulation, losing faith in Stella's childcare abilities, she'd have taken the twins back to London.

Had Bella known Jack's reason for choosing Bishopstone, she wouldn't have let the twins leave home.

With a deep-throated shout and, as if on a police raid, Milly crashed into the hallway. Stella supposed it was educational to let children work things out for themselves, but with Stanley she had always established boundaries. A streak of champagne fur and a volley of barks as Stanley cantered in after Milly. So much for boundaries.

Stella saw that had she done a hundred-and-eighty-degree turn on Street View she'd have seen the churchyard. Yew Tree House being on Church Lane was a clue. A Madonna and several angels peeped above the low wall; one looked almost human. Unlike Jack, she didn't believe in ghosts. Jackie lived opposite a graveyard in London so graves and monuments had good associations. As well as this, Stella had scrubbed up a few epitaphs for elderly clients mourning their dead in her time.

Miss Stride's letter had ended with a promise that Yew Tree House would be an escape from the hurly-burly. So far so true. *But what if you were the hurly-burly?*

Stella stood aside for Jack to stagger up the path with the groceries, followed by Justin, weighed down by his own rucksack and a five-litre container of washing-up liquid. Stella resisted offering to help either of them.

'Doesn't it remind you of the house in *The Railway Children*?' Jack grinned as he backed through the front door.

'I hadn't thought…' It didn't and nor was it a good comparison. When Jack had read E. Nesbit's story to Justin and Milly, he had fought back tears. Milly had wanted more about the train, and whatever Justin felt, he'd got out of bed and fetched Jack some kitchen towel '…*be-cos you've got wet from crying.*'

Returning to the car, Stella got her suitcase and grabbed a couple of pillows – Miss Stride had stipulated they bring bedding. As she wheeled the case under the curved iron archway she noticed the elaborately wrought gate. Taller than the twins, it depicted boxing hares within a wreath of flowers. The design offered footholds. However, since Milly's performance with the door, Stella doubted a wall or a locked door could deter her from breaking out. Jack had assured her Yew Tree House was dog-proof, Stanley would not escape. He'd said, being situated on the edge of the village, it was perfect for children. Craning along Church Lane, Stella saw that after the Old Rectory, it petered to a track which ended in a field.

One tractor was enough.

Regardless of birdsong and sunshine, as Stella made certain to latch the gate, she felt growing unease.

'Dahdee *dah… day.*' Justin hopscotched back along the path towards her warbling a tuneless and mostly wordless attempt at Madonna's 'Holiday' which Jack had played relentlessly on the trip down. He took the pillows off Stella. 'I can help.'

About to protest, Stella recalled Milly's shouty response. She was in a foreign land without a translator. She said instead, 'Thanks, Justin.'

'Looks like Miss Stride and her sister are rewilding.' Leaning in the porch, Jack waved at the overgrown garden. He'd be pointing out the 'good things'.

'Or they don't like gardening.' Reasonable. But for saving the planet Stella was just a blade of grass short of preferring Astroturf.

Jack preferred darkness and the solitude of his London Underground cab. The last time they'd stayed in the country – in Gloucestershire, where a recent body had been found in a Neolithic burial chamber – he had grown to love the unremitting darkness free from street lamps. Stella, used to restoring order from mess, had taken longer to adapt. How long would it take her now?

A droning caused them all to look up. A small plane cut across the sky, the contrail fluffy white. For a second, it caught the sun and glinted like a jewel. They watched it bank westward and, with a throaty bass note, roar out of view beyond the yew tree.

'That's a Spitfire.' Justin entwined an arm around Stella's waist. His sudden gestures of affection always floored her. In her family they hadn't gone in for hugs.

'It can't be. They haven't been used since the Second World War.' Slipping into teaching mode, Stella doubted Justin knew what the plane was. Nor, for that matter, did she.

'Maybe it *is* the *Wore.*' Justin could be fanciful like his father. 'Maybe we've gone to then.'

'Yeah, let's imagine we're in 1940.' Jack generally joined in with his children's games. 'There would be air raids. We'd have to take cover from bombs. A lot of people were killed in London. Everywhere, in fact.'

'And lots of people were unhurt,' chipped in the Sensible One.

'*I'm a soldier.*' Milly rushed out of the porch and, gripping an imaginary rifle, ducked headlong into the grass. 'Bang bang bang, *you're all dead.*'

So much for Bella refusing to allow her children to play with guns.

Back in the present, Stella set up a chain gang for unloading the car. At the tail end, when everything had been brought in, she remained alone at the front of the house. She cast a wistful look at the cemetery. Away from the hurly-burly.

She caught a movement. The Madonna, her shawl pockmarked and chipped, smiled. There was no one there. Priding herself on calling a banister brush a banister brush, Stella was annoyed she'd let her imagination play tricks.

From a stand of trees behind the church, as if disturbed, rooks cawed.

The statue that had looked almost human was *human.*

An elderly man stood by one of the buttresses. He was staring unblinking at Stella. She put up a tentative hand.

'Hi there.'

The man continued to stare.

'We're here on holiday.' Stella thought suddenly that the man might not welcome visitors. Persisting against her better judgement, she took a step towards the gate. 'I'm Stella.'

The man remained silent. Stella saw he wore a dog collar, so he must live at the Old Rectory. Thoughts tumbled incoherently... *old meant no longer used... the rector looked old too, very old, in fact...* She was lighting on the notion that the old rector was a ghost when, with a series of jerks, he executed a turn and with clockwork steps angled between the headstones and vanished.

'Stella, *Stella,* come and see! Me and Milly found a huge thing. Daddy says it's a pump for water.' Cheeks red, hair mussed, his usually contemplative brown eyes bright, Justin grasped Stella's hand and tugged her into the porch.

Passing through the hallway – doors either side, staircase to the right – Stella let herself be pulled along a stained and scuffed whitewashed passage, around a corner and into a kitchen which, with Aga, geyser above the sink and a twin-tub in one corner, could, like the ghost shops in the village, be called The Old Kitchen. Not a historian, but used to cleaning kitchens that reflected eras of decor, Stella put the wallpaper of bright red teapots with yellow cups and saucers in the nineteen fifties. A deal table, the top undulating with use and pocked with grooves and dents, looked even older.

'It's as if the occupants are still here, cooking, chopping and chatting over steaming pots and pans.' Hovering by a yellowing plastic microwave, Jack was a fervent tour guide.

'Or scrubbing at stains and dripping with sweat.' Where Jack saw ghosts, Stella saw grease.

'Don't start talking to Daddy.' Justin grasped Stella with both hands. 'Come and see. We're going to have *real water without a tap.*'

'Wow.' Stepping onto a patio and tripping over a stalk of groundsel straining between the bricks, Stella followed. She always found Justin's hectic delight infectious.

'It has to be over a hundred years old.' Joining them, Jack sounded sheepish. 'I actually assumed Yew Tree House was connected to the mains.'

'I'll pump the water.' Justin let go of Stella's hand and ran at the rusting iron pump as if into battle. He flung himself over the handle and hung there, limp as a rag doll.

With a prolonged groan, the handle lowered an inch. Flapping his arms and legs, Justin coaxed it downwards. After what seemed ages, a trickle of orange liquid splashed onto the patio.

'I expect it hasn't been used for a while,' Stella said. 'Didn't you say Miss Stride lives in that annexe around the corner?'

'Shall I ask her to come and pump?' Hand on knee, Justin posed as if about to start a race.

'*No*. Rosa Stride and her sister are at least in their eighties and anyway, we can do it,' Jack said. 'And listen, Justy, we are not to bother Miss Stride so we must stay away from that side of the house, OK?'

'I'll try, but Milly might not be able to.' Justin's stern expression suggested it would be nigh on impossible for Milly to avoid the annexe.

'Where *is* Milly?' Stella said.

'Milly will have to.' Jack rubbed his hands on his trousers and grasped the handle. 'Now for water.'

'If all else fails, we'll buy water at the Co-op.' Meaning it kindly, Stella realised she sounded as if she doubted Jack would get the pump working. Unfair, as his father had been a civil engineer and Jack could drive a train. Returning to The Old Kitchen, she called back, 'Can't wait.'

Following a scent, Stanley's claws clipped on the tiles as he nosed around the room, under the table, into cupboards. Stella hoped he didn't find a dead animal. She finger-tested the deal table. Positive for dust. Rosa Stride had put out four plates, four cups, and a milk jug and a teapot. The cups were tannin-stained. A loaf of bread in an enamel breadbin smelled fresh, as did butter in a dish decorated with orange poppies next to a jar labelled *Honey*, with a recent date and the word *Blunt*, which looked home-made. In a Smeg-like fridge which was too rusted to be fifties-retro, Stella found a litre of milk and six eggs from the Co-op. There were no knives with which to spread the butter and honey.

With no more confidence in the Aga than the water pump, Stella supposed the four-ringed Belling hob connected by a rubber hose to a cylinder of Calor gas was the only cooking option. *They were on holiday, they could have takeaways.*

Milly. No one had said where she was when she'd asked about her. She flew back along the passage and in the hall, took the stairs two at a time, Stanley in her wake.

'Milly, where are you?'

'In my room.' Milly poked her head out of a doorway along a corridor off the landing.

'We all have to choose rooms together,' Stella panted. *They had left a little girl to roam in a strange house alone.*

'I *have* chosen. Anyway, Justin is sharing with me.' As if this explained the executive decision. 'I can't open that door.'

'That must be the attic, we're not allowed up there.'

'We *must* find a way.' Milly did that thing with her chin. As a Terrible-Two she had thrown explosive tantrums, but Stella had only met Milly at the tail end of them. Nowadays Milly had developed more sophisticated methods of achieving an objective.

Stupid to be nervous of a child. Yet even as a child she'd been nervous of children; they were chaotic and unpredictable, sometimes plain rude. Stella channelled her mother who, perhaps because she'd lived with Stella, had been a stricter parent than Stella's every-other-weekend dad. 'We will *not* find a way.'

Deciding to pick her battles – preferably she'd be Switzerland – Stella proposed they visit 'your bedroom'. To her surprise, Milly instantly caved in.

'It could be yours.'

Two points of interest were a dead beetle on the window sill and a collected mound of fluff and dust which Rosa Stride must have forgotten to dustpan up.

'This is the very best bit.' Milly swooped across the room to the wall behind 'her bed' and jabbed a finger at some marks. 'There were children in here before us. Perhaps they'll come back.'

Stella examined pencil lines ruled at intervals up the wall. Each set of two was dated starting with '5th January 1940' where the marks carried the legends 'four feet one inch' followed by 'Stevie'. The other was four feet five inches and said 'Henry'. The other set was dated 26th June 1941 when Stevie was four feet eight inches tall and Henry exactly five feet.

'These were done during the Second World War so we won't see them, but you're right, there must have been children. Perhaps Miss Stride.'

'That's something to check.' Milly sounded like Bella, who talked as if ticking off items. A trait Stella put down to being a parent and always running to keep up.

'That reminds me, you missed when Daddy said to keep away from the annexe where Miss Stride lives. We must respect her privacy.' Another *Don't*. Stella was becoming the kind of adult which, as a child, she'd viewed with a dull sense of disappointment.

'The children are probably dead from bombs, that's why there's no more lines,' Milly told the wall.

'I'm sure not,' Stella said.

'I'm sure they *are*,' Milly said cheerfully and began bouncing on the side of the bed which made the springs squeak.

Stella wandered over to the window. The room was at the back of the house and overlooked the garden. Preoccupied by the horror of the rusty pump Stella had looked no further than the patio. Now she saw that here too the lawn had been given over to weeds and wild flowers. At the bottom was a thicket of brambles which would indeed be Stanley-proof. Beyond, Stella saw more fields and then, as she knew from the Ordnance Survey app she'd downloaded and because the name had given her pause for thought, the trees merging with the sky on the horizon marked the start of Beggar's Wood.

'We have water.' Soaked from head to toe, their heads swaddled in towels, Jack and Justin filled the doorway. 'We'll buy plastic bottles from that pound shop we passed and amass supplies.'

'Stella doesn't want this room so we'll have to have it. You're sleeping there,' Milly informed her brother, pointing at the bed nearest the window, then, as an aside, 'Dead children have lived here.'

'No, they haven't.' But Stella bet they had.

'What?' Jack looked more excited than interested. *Like daughter like...*

'Show me our room.' Stella changed the subject. Jack would have chosen too.

'It's at the end of the corridor, by the attic. I've put your stuff in there. Hope that's all right? It's on this side of the house so we have a lovely view of the garden.'

'Lovely,' Stella repeated absently.

There was no danger of Jack's possessions taking over their room – he'd brought two books, three T-shirts and some underwear. Jack travelled light. Actually, dark – all his clothes were black. A trait that in other men Stella found creepy. Once, this had included Jack.

'Daddy, how can we get in the attic?' Milly said. 'It's important.'

Milly had been biding her time. Stella unzipped her bag. As an adult she should not mind that Milly had appealed over her head.

'We can't, Mills.' Jack sounded as regretful as Milly.

'Where's Justin?' Stella asked.

'He's hiding.' Milly flapped a dismissive hand.

'We should look for him.'

'He hates to be found straightaway,' Jack said.

Stella watched as Jack folded each T-shirt and laid it in the top of a chest of drawers. Stella appreciated that his need for order matched her own.

'This does this when you step on it.' Arms akimbo as if walking on a tightrope, Milly trod back and forth across a floorboard beside the bed. Creak. Creak. Snap.

'Maybe don't? You might damage it,' Jack suggested as he shut the drawer.

'Whah-sis?' Milly crouched down and heaved at one side of the board.

'Milly, careful—' Jack warned.

Too late. Milly succeeded in prising up the floorboard and, with more strength than Stella would have expected given her age, plonked it to one side.

'It's a secret hiding place.' Milly appeared to be familiar with the concept. 'Ooh and there's a dagger here.'

'*What? Don't touch it.*' Jack stayed his daughter's hand and with the other reached down and lifted out a leather sheath in which was encased a knife. As if it was a live creature, he carried it in both hands over to the window and gingerly laid it on the window sill. Stella joined him.

'Don't forget it's mine. I found it.' Chin on elbows, Milly, at the other end of the sill, gave a peremptory sniff.

Jack unclipped the leather holster and drew out what did indeed look like a dagger. Made entirely of steel, the handle indented for a firm grip, it morphed into a sharp two-sided blade and tapered to a fine point.

'That's for mur-dah,' Milly said.

'It most certainly is *not*.' Jack glanced at Stella. Like her, she guessed he was wondering what else the dagger could be for. 'We are putting this out of harm's way.'

'But—' Milly's eyes went fiery.

'But nothing.'

'Didn't you say Justin is hiding?' Stella asked. 'We'd better go and look for him.'

'He always comes out in the end. OK, if we must.' Milly did a twirl of largesse. 'Actually, I think he's in the attic.'

'Nice try, Mills.' Jack grinned.

'Fine... I know where he is. He always hides behind doors.' Milly raced out of the room.

As soon as she had gone, Jack wrapped the knife in one of his T-shirts and pushed it to the back of the drawer.

Stella, still at the window, looked again at the back garden. It was wide and long, at least a hundred metres, she estimated. Stanley was trundling along a massive bush of brambles at the end; he'd be snouting for an illegal exit. Justin – now found

– chased his sister through the grass, both of them whooping towards Stanley. Soon all three of them were dancing about, leaping and jumping. The crazy capering caused Stella's mood to soar. Was this what it was like living with children?

'The house looked perfect on paper,' Jack said. 'I know it's not up to scratch.'

'Once I've deep cleaned it, Yew Tree House will be perfect. It'll be a palace.' Some holiday-makers, faced with dirt and dead insects, would be warming up to demand a refund. Stella saw only the happy prospect of diving into her portable cleaning kit.

She pulled up the sash and filled their bedroom with the scent of harvested corn and shouts and barks from below. 'I'll do it with Justin.' Two years before, aged five, both twins had been enthusiastic helpers. Now Stella had no chance of enlisting Milly. *Fair enough.* Stella liked Milly as she was. 'It'll be grand to be away from the hurly-burly.'

This thought recalled the churchyard. 'Did you see that vicar by the graves? An old man. Bit strange actually, he was staring at me.' Stella's optimism left her as suddenly as it arrived.

'No, but I expect the village is stuffed with old vicars,' Jack said. 'You're worth staring at.'

'Stop it.' Stella biffed him. As she did so, it dawned on her with a shock that she wasn't the only one taking a risk here. Jack would be all too aware the holiday was make or break. *They were in this together.*

'We'll have walks, swims, get fish and chips...' Stella put the old man to the back of her mind. They were new on the block, of course he had stared.

'We shall.' Jack whisked Stella into a jig.

'And we'll visit your mum's grave,' Stella murmured into his neck when falling into a hug. They came to a standstill.

Jack's mother, Kate Rokesmith, had been murdered in the summer of 1981, her body found by the Thames, her little boy on the other side of the Great West Road, rendered as mute as the statue against which he sat. Kate was buried in Bishopstone.

'There's a woman with flowers.' Red-faced from playing in the garden, Justin frowned around the door jamb. '*She stole them.*'

'*Justin,*' Jack sssh'd.

An elderly woman, dressed in an open man's shirt over a T-shirt, the fabric of her trousers busy with a pattern of orange and yellow petals, stood on the path. She grasped a ragged bunch of flowers that, while surely not stolen, Stella reckoned had been hastily picked. 'Good afternoon. I'm Rosa Stride, your host.'

'Host rhymes with *ghost.*' Justin sniffed the flowers which, inexplicably, the woman thrust at him. 'They don't smell.'

'Ah, Miss Stride, hello, *hi.*' Leaning over Justin, Jack stepped onto the path and put out a hand.

'Call me Rosa or I'll feel ancient,' the woman said. 'Welcome. We left provisions to start you off.'

'The kids love honey.' Stella brought it back to specifics.

'*I* love honey.' Jack beamed.

'What is "we"?' Milly appeared from behind Stella with Stanley on his lead. Stella would have to have a chat about Stanley not needing the lead indoors.

'What do you mean, Mills?' Jack said.

'I heard you say "we" about the honey. My teacher who is Miss Barnes says if it's you then it's "me".' Hands on hips, gripping the lead, Milly addressed Rosa Stride.

'We're in the annexe.' Rosa Stride appeared not to have heard Milly. She gestured to the side of the house. 'If you need anything tie a hankie on the pump, I'll keep a lookout for it.'

'Or we could ring?' Stella suggested.

'Ste— I hate the telephone.' Rosa shook her head violently. 'It was Eric's idea.'

'*Fabulous.*' Jack liked secret signals.

'Who's Eric?' Milly said.

'Not our business, Mills.' Without Bella, it seemed Jack could keep tabs on Milly's manners.

'It was our secret signal.' Rosa looked wistful. 'He let me keep the handkerchiefs. I have a drawer full.'

'I saw a person when I looked through your window, but she didn't see me,' Milly declared.

'Milly, what did I just say?' Jack said.

'You said, "I love secret signals."' Jack had not actually said this, but clearly Milly knew her dad.

Logic and fact trumped the instillation of good behaviour. Stella resolved to consult Piaget. A client of Stella's had lent her a book by the French child psychologist. It was written in 1966, the year Stella was born, but surely, apart from toys, children didn't change much. When she'd asked her mum if she'd read it, Suzie Darnell had said action spoke louder than words and revived her refrain on what a wonderful mother Stella could have been. Having given up on Stella and babies, Suzie was spending more and more time in Sydney with Stella's brother Dale's children.

'Goodness, I have to get off on my round. I deliver the *Bishopstone Bugle*, our little magazine.' Rosa Stride gave a start. 'When you finish the honey, you can buy more from outside Colonel Blunt's house, five pounds a pot. The colonel's long dead, his daughter-in-law does the bees. Mrs Colonel started in the war when you couldn't get anything. I was allowed to put the pennies in the old Oxo tin. It went to the WI garden for seeds. There, I'm chattering on... remember, just tie a hankie on the pump!' With the poise of a ballet dancer, Rosa glided to the gate where she heaved up a satchel bulging with paper that was propped against the pillar. Stella noticed she turned left along Church Lane. Perhaps she had already posted a magazine at the Old Rectory.

'She pretended not to hear me cos she said a lie.' Milly sniffed the flowers in Justin's fists. 'Ugh.'

'Don't say "she",' Jack said. 'We call Rosa, Rosa.'

'What window did you look through?' Justin said.

'The little house round there.' Milly pointed towards the annexe.

'We're not allowed there.' Justin looked horrified.

'I didn't know.' Looking astonished, Milly pulled Stanley's lead taut.

'Pass Stanley to me, please.' Perhaps Milly recognised Stella's command as the tacit bargain it was. Stella wouldn't tell Jack she had in fact explained to Milly they must not go near the annexe if Milly released Stanley.

'We'd better put them in some of our water.' Justin's concern for the flowers was typical, he was a kind boy. 'Or they'll die.'

'What a shame Rosa Stride and her sister are exiled to the annexe. I suppose they need the rent.' Stella said to Jack when the children had gone inside. 'Especially when they've lived here all their lives.'

'Rosa said in her letter she was brought up in Yew Tree House with her mother and sister. Her father died in the London bombing. She called him a hero.'

'The house doesn't really look fit for renting.' Stella added hurriedly, 'Obviously it's OK for us. It's lovely.'

'We're Rosa's guinea pigs. It was empty until now.' Jack ruffled Stella's hair. He'd know she was up for giving Yew Tree House the benefit of the doubt. 'Sounds like Rosa is the younger sister.'

'That must mean her older sister is pretty old.' Stella thought again of the old rector. 'Why the hankie on the pump when we could just tap on the door or drop a note through?'

'More fun for the kids?' Jack shrugged. 'We're making a mystery out of a molehill. Let Rosa have her secrets. We're on holiday.'

'Yes, we are.' Their relationship didn't need a murder to work. 'Time for bread and honey.'

About to close the door, Stella gave a last glance across to the churchyard. She was relieved to see only the angels and Madonnas. *Ridiculous.* Why had the elderly man so unsettled her?

The sun had gone, casting the nearest statue's features in shadow. Dark clouds massed over the church spire and the air felt damp. *It wasn't supposed to rain.*

Chapter Three

September 1940

The sound had come from the drawing room directly below her bedroom. The ARP wardens had no reason to go in there so Adelaide crept along the passage and checked the girls' bedroom. Rosa and Adelaide were asleep. She felt intrusive looking in on Henry but she was his substitute mother, so it was only right that she did. She was reassured by a mound in his bed. The dining room was the post for their sector of Air Raid Precaution so a sound from there had an explanation. She would see for herself. Downstairs, Adelaide let go of the newel post and made for the drawing room door. She had lived in Yew Tree House since she married Rupert at seventeen, but the blackout made it strange. Darkness coiled, pressing on her chest and playing games with her inner compass.

The piece about the missing girl – for weeks now – in Surrey had become rather an obsession, not only for Adelaide, but for the country. Newspaper editors splashed their front pages with the face of the timid, dark-haired girl; it was a diversion from air raids and rationing. Greta Fleming was prayed for in church services, her fate discussed in queues for meat. Police had scoured Esher Common although Mrs Fleming was clear, her daughter would not have taken the shortcut.

Revolted by Snace's unctuous prayers for the girl – the curate was fulfilling Smart's role frequently now – Adelaide had resorted to the superstition which had dictated her hopes and fears since the bombing started. If Greta Fleming was found safe and well then Stevie, at nearly fifteen, little over a year younger, would survive the war unharmed. *Greta held their hearts in her hands.*

From the dining room, she could hear Blunt hectoring poor Ridgeway and Merry, who were on tonight. Adelaide found the handle and crept inside the drawing room. Light on. Then off. Henry, self-appointed blackout monitor, had been assiduous. On again. *No one behind the door.*

Whatever had woken her must have been in a dream. Immediately after his death, Adelaide had dreamt that Rupert had come back. Always the same, *'I thought you were dead,' 'You thought wrong, Addie.'* Since her parents' deaths – her dad of TB twenty years earlier, her mother after contracting diphtheria two weeks before Rosa was born – no one had called her Addie.

It was only then that it occurred to Adelaide that if an intruder had got past the ARP wardens, she might have shut herself in with him. She scoured the room. She dared not approach the thick velvet curtains. Absurd. There were three men just down the passage who could rush to her aid if she called for help. But she didn't want their help.

Perhaps she had heard one of the wardens, going to the kitchen or to the lavatory. Or one of them was in the room right now. Adelaide didn't trust either Blunt or Snace – who, apart from being quasi-vicar, also led the Home Guard – not to poke about her things. Blunt, for one, presumed carte blanche to treat her home like his own while she and the children slept above. Anything to do with Snace made her skin crawl.

'What the—' She spun around.

'I didn't mean to frighten you.' Henry's hair was flattened on one side where he had slept on it. 'I heard something.'

'You should have called me.' Adelaide lacked conviction. For all the boyish sleepy-headed look now, Henry could pass for older than his age, although like Stevie, he was only fifteen.

'Perhaps I heard you?' Henry said.

'Perhaps.' Now keen to leave the drawing room, Adelaide was conspiratorial. 'Henry, let's make Ovaltine as a treat.'

'OK.' Henry looked doubtful. 'What if... Colonel Blunt catches us?'

'This is my house and I shall tell him so.' Adelaide was gripped with fiery determination. 'However, we will be quiet as mice or he'll want some.'

While Adelaide tried to hide her dislike of the colonel, chief warden since Rupert had been called up, for some reason she made no secret of it with Henry.

The dining room opened onto a passage beside the staircase. A drift of light from the gap under the door appeared ethereal. At any minute one of the wardens might come out. Adelaide's brief bravado had gone, she felt unaccountably afraid. They were Air Raid Precautions, not Nazis. Or looters. Her jaw ached from clamping it shut.

She could neither hear nor see Henry and dared not stop or they might bump into each other. Her fingertips walked the chill whitewashed wall until she felt nothing. She was at the corner of the passage beyond the dining room. Letting herself breathe, just once, Adelaide made for the faint light spilling from the kitchen. Why was there a light? Although she wasn't touching Henry, she felt him tense.

'I assumed I'd ambush a burglar.' His voice silky smooth as fresh cream, Michael Snace pushed off the Aga door and strolled around the deal table to within two feet of her. 'Master Henry too, quite the party.'

'I heard a noise.' Her tongue stuck to the roof of her mouth.

'You should have called us.' Smiling Snace treated her to his cold gaze. Doubtless he shared Colonel Blunt's evident disapproval that Adelaide was an independent widow, had joined the ARP and kept on the evacuee from London *'who you hardly know'* after Rupert's death.

'Perhaps it was you, Reverend,' Henry said.

'He's not a Reverend.' Adelaide just stopped herself saying he was a mere boy. Twenty and daring to confront her in her own kitchen. With pointed politeness, 'It's rare we get visits from the Home Guard.'

'I am trespassing.' His lips were pink and moist.

Although not the official leader of the Home Guard, Snace ran rings around Patrick Dean, the actual Captain.

'Did you see anyone prowling about?' Henry said.

'Only you, Master Henry.'

'Henry was looking for an intruder.'

'That's not your responsibility, Master Henry. Men like myself will keep Mrs Stride safe.'

'Can I make you an Ovaltine?' Adelaide swiped the tea towel off the Aga, refolded it and put it back. Glancing up, she saw Snace had observed the pointlessness of the action. She felt suddenly violent towards him. *If Rupert was here...*

'I'm going on duty, I have a flask.' A stigmatism had kept Snace from fighting. However, he had turned the local Home Guard platoon into what amounted to his private army. This was – unfortunately – stationed in a 'pill-box' in the Strides' garden. Snace was all too often an unwanted visitor to Yew Tree House. 'This is the perfect time for you and I to have a chat, Henry. Follow me, please.'

'Could it wait until tomorrow?'

'I'm afraid not, Mrs Stride.'

'What is this about?' Adelaide's creeping fear had returned.

'We are enlisting Henry and that Chrismas boy into the Home Guard. It should keep them out of trouble.'

'They're not in trouble and Henry's far too young, surely. Good God, he's only fifteen,' Adelaide protested. 'Isn't young Jimmy about twelve?'

'Thirteen and perfectly able to be a messenger.' Snace would be enjoying her dismay.

Last week, playing football in the garden with Jimmy Chrismas, the butcher's eldest, Henry had accidentally kicked the ball through a window in the annexe. Snace, who had the knack of silently appearing, almost as if he had always been there, had an absurdly overblown response. Without actually losing his temper he had confiscated the ball and told Adelaide to send Henry home to London.

'Most evacuees have left and you have enough on your plate.'

'Henry came from a Hammersmith tenement. Perhaps you remember that at Rupert's funeral, you mistook Henry for my son. He is indeed one of the family and, as such, this is his home.' And for good measure, 'How awful it would be if we were punished for every mistake.' From Snace's closed expression, Adelaide knew she had hit home.

The day before the football incident, Michael Snace had rammed the Reverend Smart's car into the gatepost of the field at the end of Church Lane. The only witness, Adelaide had made a production of asking if Snace was hurt then exclaiming over Smart's twisted bumper. Her triumph had been pyrrhic. She had made a fool of him and now Henry was paying. Snace recruiting the boys into the Home Guard would increase their risk of injury, of facing air raids and imminent invasion.

'Follow me, Morrison.' Michael Snace unbolted the kitchen door and ushered Henry out into the garden. He gave Adelaide a thin smile. 'We won't detain Mrs Stride.'

As she moved after him, Snace closed the door.

Adelaide had been careful not to share her dislike of the curate with many people. Women in the village regarded Michael Snace as a literal godsend. His popularity owed more to his pale baby-faced looks and bachelor status than to his tireless good works.

The one person who did know of her dislike was Snace.

But it was not just that Adelaide disliked the curate. He physically repulsed her.

In the passage, Adelaide could hear Blunt talking on the telephone to HQ in Lewes. Under cover of the colonel's peremptory verbal firepower, she moved into the hall. Though glass in the front door only diluted the darkness, she could see enough to mount the staircase.

In her bedroom, Adelaide kicked off her slippers and, appreciating the tangibility of the ice-cold lino on her bare feet, pattered to the window. Gingerly she revealed a gap in the blackout. She left the window open to catch the siren at the other end of the village. No raids tonight, cloud had kept planes away, but it was ideal cover for parachutists.

Smoke. With a shock she saw the firefly glow of a cigarette, right under her window.

'...don't want to stay out of the army.' Henry sounded distressed. Adelaide felt an uprush of anger.

Like Rupert, the curate smoked Kensitas which, irrationally, always upset her.

'...follow orders... *official secrets*...' With a chill down her back, Adelaide could tell Snace was smiling. So kind, people had said of Rupert. Now they said it of Michael Snace. '...*answer to the man himself.*'

A complete silence.

What orders? Who was the man himself?

The only 'man himself' Adelaide could think of was Winston Churchill, but Snace could not mean him. On one of his trips up to London, Rupert had seen the prime minister being whisked to Whitehall. She had thought that, him being too old to sign up, Rupert was comparatively safe although he'd warned her that his day would come.

It had come on the emergency stairs in a tube station where he was battered to death for his wallet and a packet of Kensitas.

Or did Snace mean Colonel Blunt? She would ask Henry when he came upstairs.

However, when Henry tiptoed along the corridor to his bedroom and paused outside Adelaide's room with no intention of knocking, dwelling on Rupert's pointless murder, Adelaide had fallen asleep.

Chapter Four

'Let Justin help,' Jack suggested to Milly.

'I can do it by myself.' Milly bit her bottom lip with the effort of lugging the overfilled watering can, water splashing her bare legs, from a tap on the church wall.

'That's not the point, this is something you should both do,' Jack said.

'I don't want to both do it.' Knee bent, Justin was fiddling with the buckle of his sandal.

'Here, let me carry it.' Having resolved only to observe, Stella fell into the trap of the day before.

'*I* am *carrying* it,' Milly puffed.

Sitting back on the bench by Kate Rokesmith's grave, it occurred to Stella that Justin was usually *too* keen to help. Ever willing, he was everyone's little helper. Maybe, like her, Justin wanted to be anywhere but in the churchyard watering the grave of his grandmother, murdered when his father had been half the age he was now. Quite a lot for a seven-year-old to grapple with.

'I am doing it by my own,' Milly added for good measure.

Up until now Stella had been easing into holiday mode. The night before, they'd unpacked and gone into Seaford for a fish and chip tea. This whisked Stella back to meeting Detective

34

Superintendent Darnell at Hammersmith police station, when they had gone along Shepherd's Bush Road for, in her case, a small plaice and chips. Her dad would cut off an illicit bit of one of his two battered saveloys, which Stella's mum forbade her because they were full of fat. Perhaps her mum had been right; months after Terry retired, he'd had a fatal heart attack.

Coincidentally, he'd collapsed at the Seaford Co-op just metres down the road from the fish and chip shop, but last night Stella had been able to put this out of her mind. Now, watching Milly careering across to the grave, spilling water onto her flip-flops, it rushed back to Stella. While Jack was so set on introducing his children to their grandmother, he hadn't once acknowledged that Seaford was the last place on earth Stella's father had known. *And actually, the last place she wanted to come for a holiday.*

When they had got back to Yew Tree House Stella had suggested they have a walk to 'see what happens on Church Lane after Street View ends.'

This had proved to be a field of corn and a five-bar gate. On the left the graveyard continued, making the field L-shaped.

'An old lamp-post?' Justin had been taken by the 'old' things in the village.

'It's too short.' Milly had leapt up and nearly touched the top of a brown rusting iron support close to a sturdy-looking wooden upright.

'It's the old gatepost.' Jack pointed at iron loops at the top and the bottom of the post. 'The original gate would have slotted into these.'

'Someone has bashed it.' Justin had peered at a faint dent midway down where the rust was a lighter brown. He was an observant child. Stella would have missed it.

'It must have been a long time ago, the new post is in front of the dent.'

'Are we being detectives?' Milly, bouncing her football between hefty kicks, showed interest.

'Stella is being one.' Jack grinned at her.

'It was Justin who spotted it.' Stella had not actually noticed the dent. Jack would be trying to include her, which was nice. And irritating.

'Is the person who bashed it dead now?' To Bella's frustration, Milly had taken to asking if anyone who came up in conversation was 'dead now'. Jack said this showed it was a good time to introduce the twins to his – dead – mother.

'Possibly. It looks as if it was done a good while ago.' Stella hedged her bets. 'Nevertheless they might still be alive.'

'It's like the Post Office.' Justin had been intrigued by his dad's concept of ghost shops where signs were the only footprint of shops long gone.

To one side of both posts was a kissing gate. The last time Stella and Jack had been in the countryside, whenever she climbed a stile she would end up, absurdly, perched on the top facing the wrong way. Jack said it was a sign of being a Londoner. He'd gone to boarding school in the country and, besides running away, had been sent on freezing cross-country runs.

'Bedtime,' Jack fanfared as he headed back along the track.

'Watch, I'm scoring a penalty.' Milly planned to play for England as soon as she could.

'Be *caref*—' Stella didn't want to be one of those adults who, as Milly had once said, spoiled stuff. What harm could she do out here in the countryside?'

A moment later, as they all watched the football sail over the wall of the Old Rectory followed by the sound of breaking glass, Stella got her answer.

Stanley, whose barking rent the quiet twilight air, tore after Jack up the path. Stella was close behind.

'I am so sorry, sir.' Jack hurried to a patch of the flagstoned path lit by a pool of light from the window above. 'Of course, we'll get it mended.'

A man was standing at the window. From his stillness Stella sensed he had been watching them before Milly's football hit the glass. The football lay at Stella's feet. There was no glass on the path although the frame was empty. Milly had a strong kick, but Stella guessed that the putty was loose so the pane had dropped into the room.

Beyond the line of fire, she took note of a roll-top bureau on which sat a carriage clock. A lawyer's lamp and booklined walls lent the room a cosy aspect.

'I'm sorry, er...' Bless Milly, Stella thought, she could dig out her manners when most needed.

'*Send her back.*' Cold yet reasonable.

'Sorry, who—' Jack moved closer to the window.

'Send her back to London.' The man turned and Stella saw the dog collar.

It was the man from the churchyard. Skin as leathery as a reptile's, hands like claws. Although upright with swept back grey hair, he looked very old.

'How did you know we came from London?' Unfazed, Milly said, 'Are you a detective?'

'Go away.' The man flicked his hand with a knife-like gesture. 'Leave my house now.'

'We're in the garden.' Justin would mean to reassure.

'About turn, everyone.' Jack hustled them back onto Church Lane. 'We'll sort out the window tomorrow, sir.'

Sir. What century was Jack in?

'He is the Old Rectory.' Justin read a tarnished plate on the gate.

'Rector.' Stella absently corrected him as she was assailed by the fear that Stanley had gone off foraging in the rector's garden. But he was sitting obediently outside Yew Tree House.

'The Reck-Tor looked frightened,' Justin decided.

'He had a shock,' Jack agreed. 'We'll call a glass mending place in the morning. I won't try to patch it up now, he wanted us to leave. At least it's a warm night.'

Stella was astonished. Jack never saw the effect of a broken window as likely to let in the cold. It was an opportunity for a True Host to find their prey.

'I saw the rector yesterday when we arrived,' Stella had confided to Jack the previous night when they were in bed. She didn't add that the man had given her the creeps. Or that she disagreed with Justin; the man hadn't looked in the least frightened.

Now, sitting on the bench by Kate Rokesmith's grave, Stella made herself reflect that, on holiday, there could be worse places to be than a churchyard, warmed by dappled sunlight, the air chirruping with birdsong. From her vantage point Yew Tree House was picture-postcard. The actual yew tree in their front garden blocked a view of the Old Rectory. When he'd knocked on the door that morning, Jack had got no reply. He'd gone ahead and measured the window frame, collected a pane of glass from a place in Lewes and fitted it without encountering the rector. Although the second time, Jack had suspected the rector was not answering the door. They would ask Rosa Stride when they next saw her. It wasn't important enough, Stella had told Milly, to tie a hankie round the pump.

'Are you crying, Daddy?' Justin strode across to Jack, who was kneeling at the foot of the grave.

'It's hay fever.' Stella had heard somewhere that parents shouldn't express feelings in front of offspring or, like Justin, the child might – inappropriately – attempt to soothe them rather than the other way around. OK, so Jack had taken his children to see where his mother was buried, but it wasn't OK for him to grieve openly.

'Yes. It's from the combine harvester.' Waving at the field where a combine harvester was threshing the corn, thankfully, Jack had got the message.

'If that was Mummy, I would cry.' Justin was scrutinising the headstone. *So that was it.* Justin was fretting about Jack's mother being dead. He had hated it when Babar's mother was shot.

Stella sat up. It was as plain as day that if Bella knew Jack had her twins weeding and watering his mother's grave she'd have forty fits. Stella should never have let it happen. She made a cack-handed effort to deflect the children's attention to nature. 'There's a skylark.'

Ignoring Stella, all eyes were on Milly, who was dragging another can of water over to the grave.

Stella took refuge in that they had at least spent the morning on the beach at Seaford. She had snapped pictures of the twins bobbing in the shallows in their plastic rings for Jack to send to Bella. There would be no photos of how they had spent their afternoon.

At the Seaford Co-op, grabbing orange juice, snack-boxes of raisins and a bouquet of alstroemeria, Jack had described the visit to the grave where, forty years ago, Kate Rokesmith was buried, as, 'a happy thing, we'll have a picnic.' Milly's response was to demand two boxes of raisins and now, Stella remembered, Justin had said nothing.

Piaget didn't cover taking children to visit graves, nor did death figure in the index. Resisting the Agatha Christie that she'd borrowed from Jackie, as a fan of hard facts, Stella had skipped to chapter two in Piaget – *The Construction of Reality* – which was at least informative on relating to small children.

On the subject of death she'd resorted to the internet to find out that, by seven, children might conceive death meant a person would never come back while still not quite grasping that never meant *never*. Stella could see it was Jack who was processing 'never'. Having *never* met Kate Rokesmith, the twins were more intent on soaking her grave (Milly) and pulling up weeds (Justin).

Last night Stella had resented Jack for not mentioning her dad's death and now she fervently hoped he would not. Justin and Milly should deal with only one dead person on this holiday.

There was nothing in Piaget about murder.

Milly had transferred her attention to sedum spreading over the adjacent plot. Allowing herself to relax, Stella 'put her face in the sun', as her mum used to say. Since Suzie Darnell had taken to spending half the year with Stella's brother in Sydney, nowadays she only warned that the sun killed. Stella could be exasperated by her mum, but right now was deeply grateful it was not Suzie's grave that they were visiting.

A snorting sigh broke into her thoughts.

Stanley, chin on Mr Ratty, his first ever toy, and paws outstretched, lay in the slatted shade beneath the bench. Somewhere around nine – a rescue, so Stella didn't know Stanley's age – the little dog knew nothing about death. If Stella died before him – the odds hopefully long – would Stanley lie on her grave and howl like dogs in stories? A horrible idea. Pulling herself round, Stella reassured herself it was good for the kids to face the concept of death in a tranquil churchyard rather than due to a road traffic accident, illness. Or murder.

'Shall we water that person too?' Justin was reading the sedum grave's headstone. Haltingly he said, 'What. It. Mean...'

'Meant.' Milly was good at reading.

'...*meant* to lohse.'

'Lose,' Jack said. 'What it meant to lose him, no one will ever know.'

'That's a funny secret,' Justin said. 'If no one knows, it can't be a secret someone has to know and keep it secret.'

'Spot on, boychick,' Jack crowed.

'Good point.' Stella too felt pleasure at Justin's ability to work things out.

'What's a secret?' Probably cross that Justin had pipped her to a possible post, Mini-Bella dumped her can and, marching over, scowled at the epitaph.

'No one will ever know.' Justin rubbed at a bloom of lichen at the end of the phrase.

'That's silly,' Milly said. 'Why won't they? What if *I* know.'

'You don't know.' Justin was peaceable.

'It means those who loved Captain Rupert Stride were sad that he is dead.' Jack showed no annoyance that the children had seemed less interested in 'Granny'. 'It means no words can say how much he was missed. Rupert Stride died over eighty years ago, forty years before—'

'That's not what it means.'

They looked to where the voice – silky and reasonable – had come from.

'Oh goodness, *hello*.' Jack leapt up. The old rector, with Rosa Stride on his arm, stood a few metres away.

'I hope we didn't startle you, Jack.' Rosa looked concerned.

'In a good way,' Jack said.

From closer and in daylight, Stella saw less a reptile than boyish good looks. His skin had a waxy patina, the eyes were blue, his hair more of a blond-grey than it had looked in the twilight shadow of his study.

'Do let me introduce you to the Very Reverend Snace.' Rosa smiled up at Snace, who was a good head and shoulders over her. Snace himself didn't react.

'What does it mean?' Perhaps seeing Rosa notice the watering can, Milly curled a possessive arm around it.

'It means one's depth of grief never ends,' Snace said.

Rupert Stride was Rosa's father.

'We should get going.' Stella stood up. *Too late.*

'Thank you for watering my father's grave, dear,' Rosa told Milly. 'I was two when he was killed.'

'I'm seven.' Milly looked affronted.

'Forever mourned.' Jack echoed the words on the headstone. Reverend Snace shot him a look. Stella tended to think that when in an awkward situation – they'd smashed the old man's window the previous evening so this was awkward – it was wise to say very little.

'What is mo*rrrr*ned?' Milly growled the 'r's.

'It means I shall always miss my daddy,' Rosa told her.

'My daddy shall always miss his granny after lots *and lots of time*.' Milly puffed out her chest.

'She's *your* granny and my mummy,' Jack mumbled.

'Jack mended your window.' Stella spoke in spite of herself.

'Does Stevie miss her daddy?' The rector tightened his arm around Rosa's.

'We both do,' Rosa sounded agitated.

'Who is Stevie?' Milly pounced.

'I haven't yet told her you have come to stay,' Rosa chirped.

'She'll be pleased.' Were the rector not a rector, Stella would have thought him sarcastic. His manner confused and unsettled her.

'Would Captain Rupert like some of our flowers? We got them from a shop,' Justin ventured.

'I have to go,' Rosa said suddenly, appearing not to hear. 'Stevie will be wondering where I am.'

'Do thank her for my little gift.' Snace curled gnarled fingers around Rosa's twig-thin wrist.

'We must go too.' Stella wanted to rescue Rosa, but didn't know what from. At the least they should get out of the graveyard.

Sensing action, head tossing, Stanley smacked Mr Ratty on the grass with jubilation. Used to this, Stella found the sight of what was ultimately a mock killing the final straw. Events can switch on the turn of the sixpence, her dad would say.

'Why was your daddy a hero?' Justin regarded a dandelion clock growing on Rupert Stride's grave.

'He went to fight the Nazis. They were horrible people who made you do anything they wanted,' Rosa said. 'Daddy never got his chance – he died in London.'

'Max is a Nazi, he made me turn my light off before it was bedtime.' Milly's tone suggested she understood the issue in the round.

'Milly, no. You mustn't say that. Max is *not* a Nazi.' Jack snapped to attention. Max was the latest in a string of unsuccessful relationships for Bella. Max had lasted a year so perhaps there was hope.

'He did turn it off.' Red and hot, Milly smacked her forehead with her arm. 'Anyway—'

'Yes, but—'

'Who cares, Mummy made him go be-cause he wanted to make her marry him.' Milly's cheeks dimpled with satisfaction. 'Mummy doesn't do that.'

'She's dump— parted from Max?' Jack's horrified expression was well done considering he'd never taken to the perfectly nice botanist.

'We went on the beach this morning,' Justin said.

Grateful to Justin for attempting to change the subject, Stella gave him an encouraging smile. The feeling didn't last long.

'Will Stevie be pleased when you tell her about us?' Justin asked Rosa.

'Oh yes. Delighted.' Rosa looked actually frightened.

'It's time you all went back to London. There are no more bombs,' the rector said.

'It's not the war any more, Reverend. We are at peace.' Rosa tapped the claws on her wrist.

Astonishingly, for little floored them, neither of the children had an answer for this. They all watched Rosa and the Reverend Snace slowly move to a gate in the low wall on Church Lane.

'Jack, tell us about your mum, it is why we're here.' Stella launched into a diversion with the very subject she longed to avoid. Equally, she knew that Jack hoped his children would give Kate Rokesmith's grave more attention than they had. 'All the nice things.' *Hint.*

Milly abandoned the Stride plot and hurled herself beside Jack on the grass by Kate Rokesmith's grave.

With Stanley on her lap, Stella relaxed back on the bench. Jack's voice mingled with the skylark's twitter and steady growl of the combine harvester. Warmed by the sun, paying half an ear to Jack's – limited – memories of his beloved mother.

'...she was born here in the village, not far from Yew Tree House...'

Reassured, Stella drifted into a doze.

'*...played the piano after putting me to bed... sent me to sleep. When I hear piano music at ... favourite... Beethoven's Pathétique, that CD I play you guys at bedtime... Mummy, I called her Mummy, like you do... could be with me.*'

'*I don't say Mummy.*' Milly's voice was faraway. '*She is* Isabella. *I'm really* Amelia.'

'*Yes but, you don't call her Isa—*'

'How did she die?' Milly asked, loud and clear.

Why hadn't she seen this coming? She *had* seen it coming, but she had trusted Jack. Why had she trusted him? Bella had said she was The Sensible One.

Feeling herself slide down a slope, Stella willed Jack: *Say she fell peacefully asleep...*

'She was murdered.'

'*Jack.* We are leaving,' Stella shouted. With a volley of barks, Stanley belted about the graves, scouring the churchyard for the enemy it was his job to vanquish.

'Was there lots of blood?' Milly was on her feet.

'Stella said we should leave.' Justin was pale.

'No.' Staring beyond his mother's grave Jack seemed in a fugue state. His mother was strangled, so no, there hadn't been blood.

'Time for tea,' Stella insisted. 'Where's Stanley?'

Behind them, the combine harvester, a vast machine, billowed a cloud of threshing dust. Stanley had once tackled a tractor, dancing and leaping in its path, the driver unaware. Stanley believed his enemies included anything that moved: lorries, tractors, *combine harvesters...* Stella wished herself in a London park where enemies were skateboards and joggers.

'He's under your bench all tired out.' Milly pointed as if at a far horizon.

'He's staying out of the sun.' Justin was being reassuring. Stella wanted to reassure him that as an adult she didn't need reassuring. Except it wouldn't be true.

'He needs to recharge his batteries,' Stella said.

'How did your mummy die, Daddy? What happened?' Milly kept on point.

Stella was numb as Jack told them about the day when his life had changed for ever.

'Did you cry?' Justin had been drawn back in. 'You were very little.'

Justin and Milly regarded anyone under seven as 'little'.

'No. I'm told I didn't speak for weeks.'

'Did they catch the murder-*rah*?' Milly did a circle with her head as if for dramatic effect.

'Not for a long time.'

'Tea time.' Stella cleared her throat. Jack would be heading towards the – hardly romantic – tale of how, decades later, Stella and he found Kate Rokesmith's killer. Theirs wasn't one of those 'how we met' stories that travelled well.

She was saved by the bells, or rather wind chimes. In fact, a ringtone.

'It's *Mummy*.' Milly leapt on Jack's rucksack and pulled out a phone.

Bella had been the one to insist the twins have a phone; it had been Jack's turn to be aghast. They were too young to go off on their own, so had no need to let Bella know where they were. However, Bella's intention was that Jack keep custody of the handset. It had quickly emerged that Bella intended the phone for when Justin and Milly were with their dad so she could keep tabs. Were there the slightest point, Stella would get Stanley a phone for when Jackie minded him.

'...we've been to the sea, me and Justin went in. My costume was the *best* there. I found a fishing net and Jack said we could keep it.' Stella saw Jack tense. He wouldn't like 'Jack'.

'...you want to speak to Justin? We're watering flowers and doing weeding. Jack's telling us a story so I have to go.' And Bella wouldn't like her daughter cutting short the call.

Stella gripped the edge of the bench as if hanging from a cliff. She knew the precise second when Milly told Bella that they were watering Jack's mother's grave and hearing how 'Granny' had been murdered, the holiday would be over.

Never mind that. *Jack might lose custody of the twins. Bella might stop him seeing them at all.*

'Tell Mummy I love her, but we're busy.' Nestled back against Kate Rokesmith's gravestone, Justin appeared impatient for Jack to resume the story.

'We've got our story to have.' Milly was official. Stella was pleased, for Bella's sake, that she'd omitted that Justin was 'busy'.

'What story is Jack telling you?' Bella's voice was faint through the handset. Stella saw Jack freeze. *This was a definition of suspense.*

'Oh, about flowers, a man called Rupert and we went to the Co-op.' Milly ended on a squawk. Bella must question that Milly sounded excited: she used to have tantrums in supermarkets.

It should have been a relief when the call ended with Bella none the wiser. It was not. Stella had seen that, to keep a secret, Milly and Justin had no trouble twisting the truth.

'That was over the top.' Gathering up the picnic things, Stella watched the children chase around the gravestones. 'What were you thinking, telling them Kate was murdered?'

'They would have found out in the end.' Jack's distracted air must mean he regretted it.

'When they were fifteen, perhaps, but not at seven or on holiday. I wouldn't have agreed to come here if I'd known what you planned.'

'I didn't plan to tell them... it came out,' Jack said. 'It's their past too.'

'It's their family history, it's not in *their* past,' Stella fumed. 'You and Bella are not going to be murdered. It made Milly lie to Bella, so she knew it was wrong.'

'Milly tells lies.'

'Oh, and that's OK?'

'No, but it's a phase.'

A phase from which Milly's father had never left.

Stella checked the lane before letting Milly and Justin, champing at the gate, burst through. They charged up the lane and in at Yew Tree House. As she and Jack passed the Old Rectory, Stella couldn't resist a glance at the mended window.

She went cold. Reverend Snace was there. He stared back at her. Taken aback, her own face a mask, Stella didn't manage a nod in greeting. Instinctively, she moved closer to Jack.

'He's a True Host,' Jack said.

'How do you know?' *Jack always knew.*

'Everything. His eyes, his demeanour, his utter command of the situation.' Jack spoke in a monotone. 'Did you see how he had a firm hold of Rosa?'

'What I did see was that he seemed to enjoy giving away that Rosa has a sister.' Feeling in her jeans for the key, Stella hurried along to Yew Tree House. 'Why didn't she want us to know?'

'Maybe her sister is a Mrs Rochester.' Jack grimaced.

'It's not funny, Jack.' The foreboding was back with a vengeance. 'Promise you won't do anything about Snace? Whatever, he's a harmless old man now.'

'You're only harmless when you're dead.'

'Can we have fish and chips for tea?' Milly ran literal rings around them on the path.

'Not two nights in a row. It's bad for you,' Jack said. 'Too much stodge.'

'It's not as bad for you as getting murdered.' Milly uttered an undoubted truth.

Chapter Five

Present Day

'Why didn't you tell me you were inviting a family of strangers into our house?' Despite the hot day outside, Stevie Stride's thin frame was huddled in an Aran jumper that had been her mother's.

'If I had, you would have refused,' Rosa called from the kitchenette. 'We need the money.'

This conversation between the sisters was taking place in the annexe of Yew Tree House while the family of strangers were eating bread and honey, spread with the back of a spoon until they remembered to buy knives, at the kitchen table with just a wall between them.

'Mother would have welcomed them, like she did the evacuees,' Rosa added.

'That was different.' At the mention of their mother, Stevie hugged further into her jumper. 'Mother wouldn't have wanted people stomping about her house. She hated Colonel Blunt.'

'Everyone hated Colonel Blunt, especially me.' Rosa remembered the Colonel as an even more unpleasant man than he had been during the war. 'He pulled my ear once.'

'Was that all?' Stevie tugged at her sleeve.

'I got away,' Rosa said.

'Mother would hate strangers poking through her things.'

'What things?' Rosa plonked a mug of tea on the little table beside Stevie. 'You've given away most of them.'

'I certainly have not.'

It was rare that Rosa took issue with her sister, who was twelve years her senior. Perhaps disadvantaged by taking a holiday let and despite glaring evidence to the contrary, she knew that now was not the time.

Chapter Six

Present Day

Since Jack and Stella's confrontation the afternoon before, they had operated a speak-when-spoken-to rule with each other. After breakfast the 'family' scattered. Justin and Milly, showing no ill effects from Jack's murder story, had gone into the garden with Stanley.

Jack was in the dining room staring at the heaped – thousand – jigsaw pieces of Ravilious's Newhaven lighthouse. With a bit of sea (or sky) between finger and thumb he hadn't moved for ten minutes.

Jack had been jubilant when he spotted the jigsaw in a hospice charity shop. Newhaven was just up the coast from Bishopstone so it was a sign that Yew Tree House would be a success. *Not so far.*

Across the hall, in what Rosa's instructions referred to as the drawing room, battling with Piaget, Stella sat by the fireplace. Progress was slow because she must keep clicking to Kindle's dictionary for the meaning of almost every word. If her eye did make it down a page this was because she hadn't absorbed a single fact.

One bit she had taken in was that a child's sense of obligation was dependent on them being willing to accept 'orders' with no time limit, like '*don't tell lies*'. This only worked when the child had learnt to respect the person issuing the order. Kids were less likely to take on board requests from a younger sibling or from an adult they considered 'unimportant'. Did Justin and Milly think any of the adults in their lives important enough to accede to requests with no sell-by date? Justin being a fraction younger than Milly might explain why she rarely listened to his requests.

A fresh new day had given Stella a happier perspective. They were staying in a twenty-first-century village, there was no Mrs Rochester in the annexe, and if Reverend Snace was crabby – she would be if a football had knocked out a window in her house – so what? Stella frowned as her internal devil's advocate swooped in. Was it that Jack couldn't cope with 'ordinary' life? There must always be a drama around death. *Could she live with that need full-time?*

In the past when she had been estranged from Jack, she had lost herself in cleaning. Indeed, Stella had scrubbed the kitchen down, and the children's bedroom, but all the time she felt weighed down by Jack's presence. This time there was no Jackie to pick her up. Not even Lucie May, who could drive them both so mad they were propelled into an alliance.

But whenever Stella considered making it up with Jack, she remembered what happened and got cross all over again. If they had been playing chess, Jack and Stella would be at stalemate.

Jack and Stella had faint comfort that they'd kept the fallout from the twins.

They were wrong. Rendered anxious and miserable by the chilly atmosphere, which no amount of manic cheeriness had disguised, Justin and Milly had Jack's absently given permission to play outside.

That had been an hour ago.

Justin and Milly had long since given up encouraging Stanley to fetch Milly's football, which, not fitting his jaws, was a challenge he was now done with, and were ambling about at the bottom of the garden. They were stopped in their tracks by a shrill barking.

Had Stella torn herself from Piaget – she had reached a bit on telling lies so was glued to the screen – and looked out of the French windows she would have seen a sight that, were she with Jack, they would have found comic.

Leaping the tussocks and molehills, a rabbit tore across the uneven lawn with Stanley giving chase. The animals had several metres on the twins who, slow to react, were now pell-mell in pursuit.

'*Stan-ley*. Stop. Being… *naught…*' Milly gasped as they ran.

'Milly, please don't let him kill the bu-ah-nee,' Justin panted.

In reality, at no point was the rabbit in danger. Stanley had never yet caught a live creature and when the rabbit ducked into a thicket, Stanley lost valuable seconds storming back and forth by the brambles. Then, as Milly reached him, no doubt overtaken by the possibility of being put on his lead as Stella would have done, Stanley nosed into the undergrowth and he too disappeared.

Head down, elbows and feet scrabbling, Milly crawled in after the rabbit and the dog.

Justin knew better than to follow. Milly might be a few minutes older than he was but his mummy had said that when Jack and Milly were being 'silly', Justin must take charge. Now he slumped onto the grass, clamping his hands over his head as if held at gunpoint. Alone in the sprawling garden, all Justin had charge of was two cabbage white butterflies flirting in the sunshine.

Idyllic countryside sounds.

Gradually, Justin became aware of a baby crying. He felt afraid.

'Mill-ee.' No sound came out. It was like something was squeezing his neck. Justin knew he should get a grown-up. Stella was sensible but she was cross with his daddy so might not like being bothered. Besides, wherever she was, he couldn't leave Milly.

The branches moved.

Justin pushed himself away on his bottom.

'There's a house in there.' Milly peered out from the brambles. Her hair was stuck with dried leaves, a scratch across her cheek smeared with blood.

'With a baby?' Justin leaned on his knees.

'What baby?'

'There's crying.' Justin put his finger to his lips.

'That's Stanley, silly, he always does that, remember?' It was one of Milly's attractive qualities that she was mindful that her brother could get scared. 'He found who lives there.'

'Who?' Unlike Milly, who questioned anything she was told, Justin was inclined to take information at face value and see where it went.

'I took a picture, see?' Milly pulled their mobile phone from her jeans pocket, swiping with a dexterity that had alarmed Stella when she saw it earlier, then thrust the screen up to her brother's face. 'Stanley was sniffing so I went and pulled off that blanket.'

The image, lit by a pale shaft of light, showed a human skeleton propped against a brick wall. A crumpled tarpaulin lay beside it.

'Whose house is it?' Justin said.

'This skeleton's, I s'pose.' Milly tutted. Justin lit upon a seemingly less important fact.

'It doesn't show from here.' Justin stepped back a few paces, looking at the thicket and, for all the difference it could make, stood on tiptoe.

'It's not a proper house. It's small.' Milly's declared facts rarely stood up to scrutiny. 'Anyway, that's a skeleton.'

'He's got a crack on his head,' Justin said.

'So what?' Milly reacted as if her brother had pointed out she'd been done. '*She*. It's a girl. She's called... *Mary*.'

'How do you know her name?'

'I called her by it.' Milly's stare dared Justin to argue.

Justin peered more closely at the photograph. 'Mary got murdered.'

'Murdered.' Milly widened her eyes. 'That's *fantastic*.'

'Why is it?' Justin looked horrified. 'It's sad.'

'We are *detectives*. We will solve the murder.'

'Let's tell Daddy and Stella, it will make them friends again.' Justin was suddenly jubilant.

'No.' Milly rounded on him. 'It's *my* secret. I will find out the murdering person by myself. You can help if you want.'

Stella might have felt chagrin to have it confirmed that she had played a part in making a detective out of Milly and a sidekick out of Justin. Stella already knew Milly was capable of lying to keep a secret from Bella. Not just from Bella, it seemed.

'S'pose,' Justin considered, 'we find the mur-drah, Stella and Daddy will be so happy they'd be nice to themselves again.'

While sharp-eared and gimlet-eyed, neither Stella nor Jack caught the twins creeping exaggeratedly along the side of the beech hedge before scampering to the blind spot at the side of the house and out of the gate.

Chapter Seven

Present Day

'Our mummy is in that shop. She said we must wait here,' Milly informed the woman who accosted them on the high street. Then fiercely, 'And to *not* talk to strangers.'

'Milly, that's not— *ow.*' Justin winced when Milly, who had made them hold hands to look 'busy', dug her nails into his palm.

'Goodness, all those cuts and scratches. What have you been up to? Your mummy should put a plaster on that nasty one.' Martine Barratt, fervent volunteer for any local initiative, be it the annual summer festival or the WI, and mindful of the Jamie Bulger tragedy thirty years before, would not pass unaccompanied children without establishing the whereabouts of their parents. *What mother left her children alone on a busy village high street?* Anything could happen.

'Mummy is getting a plaster.' Milly was inspired. 'We're minding our dog. *Don't* stroke him, Stanley will bite you.'

'He should be trained.' Disapproval mounting, Mrs Barratt snatched back her hand. Her sixty-five years had made her impatient less with children than with their adults.

'He is trained to within an inch of his life.' Milly channelled Bella, who believed Stanley was spoiled.

Martine Barratt also had views on dog owners – used poo-bags hung from trees or dropped on paths, dogs off leads near sheep – but laden with shopping and the pressing task of securing a last-minute speaker for the literary society evening, she had no time to share them. Mrs Barratt hastened on her way, full to the brim with the sense of duty done as a responsible citizen, the unaccompanied children now her past. She had not taken in that they had been not outside the chemist as the girl implied, but by the Old Post Office, now a flower shop.

'*Is* Mummy in there?' Squinting between ferns and tall-stemmed flowers in galvanised pots ranged on the pavement, Justin tried to see through the window. From experience, he knew Mummy could magically appear when he and Milly were with Jack and Stella.

'Don't be silly,' Milly said. 'I said that so she didn't want to solve the murder too.'

'You do need a plaster.' It dawned on the little boy that if his mummy was in the flower shop, she could take them home.

Jack and Bella had split up before the twins were born, so their children were long adept at slaloming the rapids of their thorny interactions. While Milly took arrangements in her stride, Justin didn't think himself lucky to have two bedrooms and dreaded the waving goodbye and saying hello to Jack or to Bella. Nevertheless, it was a routine of sorts, and today was in freefall. Stella and Daddy had stopped being friends and Milly was on an 'investee-gayshon', a word she'd got from Daddy which, while Milly was hazy on detail, Justin was sure they shouldn't do by themselves.

Several passers-by on the high street vaguely noticed the little girl and boy with a small poodle on a taut lead – pulling towards a discarded hamburger bun in the gutter – but no one else intervened.

'We'll start to investigate in shops about a person who knows the skeleton,' Milly told Justin. 'Don't say "skeleton", see what face they make when we say "murder". Then we'll know it's them.'

'I'm not talking to strangers.' Justin was firm.

'You have to if you're a detective. You can't only talk to murder-ahs that you know.'

'I won't.' Justin stamped his foot, which made Stanley bark.

'This is my new plan.' Milly was nothing if not quick on her feet. 'We'll search for clues. You look out specially for nasty people.' Milly had an inkling from overhearing Jack and Stella that her father kept on the alert for 'nasty people'.

'How will we know they're nasty?' Justin sniffed – he'd been delegated a more minor task.

'Like that woman who said about a plaster.'

'She seemed nice.'

'How wrong can you be?' Milly had a string of prepared phrases gleaned from Bella. 'She didn't get a plaster for us, did she?'

'For a start you said Mummy was bringing it.' Justin cast a wistful glance at the flower shop from which he still hoped Bella would emerge.

'*There!* He's a murderer.' Grabbing a break in the traffic, Milly dragged Justin across the road. A few metres away, by the village pond, sat an elderly man, gaunt cheeks bronzed by the sun. His hair was combed back from his face, in the timeless style that conferred instant dignity.

'You didn't say "go".' Justin pulled free of Milly.

'It's not a game.' Milly gave a sigh. 'Justin, you could go back to Yew Tree House. But don't tell Stella and Daddy what I'm doing. *It's top secret.*'

'I'm doing it too.' Justin capitulated. 'You said we're not asking people any more, we're hunting for clues.'

'We will look for clues under that bench.' Seeing success within her grasp, Milly's plan flip-flopped.

The bench was set back from the pavement, only visible to passers-by should they look. On that warm summer's day, going about their business, the few walking on the pond side of the street didn't as much as glance across.

'Hello, we're investigating murdah. I'm a *please* detective here to ask you questions.' Many times in bed at night, Milly had pronounced this to Sultan Duck, her stuffed platypus.

'A *please* detective?' The man's voice resembled a bee in a jar. Smiling. 'I'll be *pleased* to answer anything you ask, young madam.'

Generous mouth, cheeks creased with laughter lines and a dimpled chin suggested the man, still attractive, had once been much more so. Considerable age had scrabbled his features which were sketched with grey stubble. Had any of the three adults with responsibility for the twins been there, his keen appraisal of Milly, who was blocking his view of two swans, would have got alarm bells ringing.

'Do you live here?' Milly knew from Lucie May – who was Daddy and Stella's reporting friend – that detectives were friendly to murderers before they arrested them to stop them running away.

'All my life.'

'Is that a very long time?' Milly moved to the edge of the pond and for a moment was distracted by her reflection in the water. The man's gaze shifted to the swans gliding around an island of reeds in the middle.

'Seems like yesterday,' the man said. 'In my head I'm your age.'

'We're seven,' said Justin as he stood on one leg.

'*Both* of you are seven?' The man mouthed an O in exaggerated wonderment. 'You're twins.'

'How did you know?' Milly said, then, as the man put a hand down to Stanley, 'He bites strangers.'

'So do I.' The man laughed. Both children stared in fascination at the gap where he was missing a front tooth. As if the idea was dredged from far back in his mind he said, 'I am a stranger, we shouldn't be talking. Where's your mum?'

'She's in London,' Justin said.

'In that shop.' Eyes narrowed, Milly pointed at the flower shop as if firing a gun.

'Are you evacuees?'

'I don't think so.' Milly hedged her bets. 'I'm Milly, he's my brother. He's called Justin, which is the same as our daddy, but he's called Jack.'

'Jimmy Chrismas, pleased to meet you.' The man appeared to be about to shake hands then changed his mind.

'Are you Father Christmas?' Having recently reduced several classmates to tears insisting there was no such person, Milly was wrong-footed to find that there was.

'I actually was Father Christmas for the Rotary Club, until the vicar stepped in. Going back a bit now.' The man's face darkened. 'No T in my Chrismas. Plenty of us in the churchyard. Butchers here for four generations.'

'We have our granny in the churchyard. I've been watering her,' Milly said.

'I did too.' Justin found a way to join in. 'But our daddy is still sad.'

'Do not neglect the dead.' Jimmy waggled a finger at the swans. 'Where are you billeted?'

'What? I mean pardon?' Justin said.

'Who's got you two? Which house?'

'Yew Tree House.' Milly drew out the vowels.

'We're not supposed to say where we live.' Justin nudged her. 'We say our mummy and daddy are watching us.'

'That's a lie.' Milly was finding Justin a hindrance.

'You'll be well looked after there. Mrs Stride is an angel. Stevie will show you the ropes.'

'She stole flowers for us.'

'That wasn't the one called Steee-veeeh.' Milly ogled.

'I'm talking rubbish, you'll have to watch me. The past is so much more real than today.' Jimmy Chrismas frowned.

'We saw her with a man yesterday. The old rector.' Milly tore herself away from her watery image. 'Do you know him too?'

'The old rector?' Jimmy looked puzzled. 'There isn't one. Just the vicar the other end of the village in the new house.'

'He was a ghost,' Milly decided.

'You said ghosts aren't real.' Justin got frustrated by Milly's ever-changing opinions. 'Anyway, I saw Stevie taking him a present to the Old Rect-ory.' Intending to trump his sister, Justin had given away a secret he'd meant to keep until everyone was happy.

'You did not.' Like Bella, Milly tended to deny the reality of anything she hadn't herself witnessed.

'From the stairs window, I did,' Justin held his ground. 'I was going to rush downstairs and say hello, but Stanley stole my sock.'

'You've got that wrong, lad.' Jimmy's tone was rough. 'Rosa nor Stevie would *ever*—'

'What do you know about a murder?' Milly fixed on Jimmy Chrismas.

'My days! Where did a seven-year-old learn that word?' Jimmy Chrismas glared at her. 'You both listen here, don't be putting your fingers in the fire. Let sleeping dogs lie.'

'Stanley plays and then he goes fast asleep.' Justin considered.

'Don't be asking questions of strangers.' Jimmy Chrismas's hands bunched into fists. He struggled to his feet.

'We're detectives.' Milly sounded less certain. Whipping around, she set off along the perimeter of the pond back to the pavement. She called back to Justin, 'Race you.'

On the village pond the swans had retreated to their nest. The sun had gone behind clouds and a cool breeze riffled the surface of the water.

In Yew Tree House, Stella and Jack remained unaware that Justin and Milly were no longer in the garden. Jack, stirring the puzzle pieces with a finger, had made no headway with the jigsaw. Stella had grasped one point. Children's games were not imitations of adult reality. Children adapted props, dressing-up clothes and toys as signs and signifiers to construct a situation they could control, a constructed reality without 'coercions or sanctions'. Stella's dad had given her a police officer's helmet for her sixth birthday. She had a vivid memory of walking her 'beat' in the back garden. She could be sure it had been that birthday because by the time she was seven, her mum and dad had split up.

She wandered over to the French windows. At some point it had become cloudy. Her app had said there was 35 per cent chance of rain. If it rained, they wouldn't go to the beach which, Stella realised, she had been relying on to engineer a truce.

The garden was empty.

Disbelieving the expanse of grass leading to the end of the garden, Stella burst through the French windows and wheeled about.

'Milly. Justin.' *Where was Stanley?* 'No. No no, *no.*' She yelled the last no.

They were hiding. Relief flooded her system. *They were hiding.*

'What's happening?' Jack rushed out. 'Where are the kids, you were looking after—'

'*Stop.*' Stella blazed. 'They're great kids, but they're *your* kids. We did not agree I would mind them this morning while you did a *stupid* jigsaw.' Sick with panic, Stella didn't recognise herself.

'They must be hiding.' Jack was one step behind her.

'I thought that, but there's no way they could stop Stanley from giving them away when I called.' Stella paused. 'Unless they knocked him out.'

'They would never hurt him,' Jack stormed.

'I didn't mea— they'll be here somewhere.' Stella was far less certain than she tried to sound.

'Who put that there?' Jack pointed to the water pump by the beech hedge.

A handkerchief had been tied to the handle.

Chapter Eight

November 1940

Over the months, Adelaide had come to think of their gas masks hanging above the row of oilskin cloaks as standing for the dead. While it had been Rupert who had volunteered the dining room of Yew Tree House for the Bishopstone's ARP HQ, it was not Rupert who had to deal with wardens there every night. Wardens which, to the simmering fury of Colonel Blunt as chief warden, included Adelaide. She was on duty tonight.

'Here we are.' Adelaide nodded thanks to Nigel Ridgeway, who had leapt up to open the door for her. 'This will warm everyone up.'

The grandfather clock in the hall struck ten. Adelaide knew it was fifteen minutes slow; it had been Rupert's job to keep it punctual. She had refused Blunt's offer to correct it although he had stopped the casement rattling with a wad of lint from the First Aid cupboard. *'With Captain Stride no longer... it falls to me'*, was Blunt's favourite phrase.

'It's very kind of you, Mrs Stride.' Mr Ridgeway cleared a space for the tray among the training leaflets and plethora of forms scattered on the dining room table. Jotting in his notebook, Colonel Blunt glanced up without comment.

'I had a word with young Stephanie at the post office this afternoon. She was with those tykes, that evacuee and the butcher's oldest. They were pushing a barrow laden with junk and yelling like the rag and bone man.'

'They are collecting salvage for Spitfires.' Adelaide watched Blunt stir two teaspoons of sugar into his drink. Mr Ridgeway's usual show of unwrapping his twist of sugar was lost on Blunt. He never brought his own ration.

'A woman gave them the contents of her cutlery drawer.' It was rare for Mr Ridgeway, a conscientious objector who Blunt hated having in the patrol more than Adelaide, to throw in his pennyworth.

'Damn fool thing – her husband will have something to say.' Blunt's brick-red complexion darkened.

In his late fifties, with a gammy leg, Blunt wasn't in this war. After Rupert's funeral, Blunt, already self-appointed as chief warden after Rupert had left for France, informed her her husband had 'tasked him to keep an eye on you and your girls'. Adelaide had initially been furious with Rupert. Now, when there was nowhere to direct her anger, she'd realised Rupert would never have asked any man – and not Blunt who was a *bloody charlatan* – to look out for her and their children. In addition, Rupert had believed himself invincible, he had not expected to die.

Or, more specifically, be murdered.

'Stevie wants to do her bit. We all do.' Adelaide fixed on the man's great slab of a face, his moustache coated with foam from the Ovaltine. 'And as you know, the boys have been recruited into the Home Guard.'

'What? Damn fool of a man, what was he thinking?' Blustering, Blunt began packing his pipe. As Adelaide had suspected, Snace had not told Blunt. The colonel made no secret of his disgust that Snace – 'too young to lead and old enough to fight' – was gaining ground in the village. That both men despised each other hadn't led either to form an alliance with Adelaide. Nor would she want it.

'Frankly, my bigger concern when it comes to the children is that, like Greta Fleming, they go missing.' Adelaide returned to the grim subject never far from her thoughts. 'Her poor mother must be worried sick.'

'Who?' Already wrong-footed, Blunt would be feigning ignorance to make the point that the missing girl was chaff in the wind compared to 'Hitler's ruddy show'.

'The girl who disappeared on her way home from work.' Ridgeway would be making sure to spell it out. 'A terrible thing indeed.'

'For God's sake, there are people dying every day.' Expostulating, one eye shut, Blunt lit his pipe. 'I'll lay my last shilling she's not the good girl her mama thinks. Which brings me back to Stephanie—'

Far off, they heard the siren.

'Moaning Minnie's woken up.' Mr Ridgeway drained his cup. For the abject coward Blunt preferred to paint him, Nigel Ridgeway was always first out of the door.

They paused at the gate to do up their coats. Adelaide glanced back up at the house, solid black against the not quite dark sky.

The front garden was given over to allotments either side of the brick path. It was tended by the WI. Washed with moonlight, the cane wigwams were so many spires and the cold frames miniature mausoleums. The clear night, stars shining brightly – the moon would be full tomorrow – shone with open arms for the Luftwaffe.

Adelaide lived with the parallel emotions of constant fear spiced with pure happiness. She loved being an ARP warden and becoming proficient in the fire drills and first aid. Her girls were blossoming, Rosa learnt new words almost every day and Stevie was turning into a friend. The only fly in the ointment was that Henry had somehow changed. He was moody and watchful. He did long hours with the Home Guard, sometimes staying out all night, so she put it down to exhaustion. Everyone was tired, no one was at their best.

Bombs had fallen to the west, Shoreham perhaps. Women who lived in the cottages before the pond stood on their doorsteps. Mr Ridgeway urged them to take cover, but as Adelaide expected, no one listened. From that distance the bombing felt unreal.

The night before, a light was reported in a window of a house in Jackson Lane. Mr Ridgeway had been on duty with Mr Merry and seen nothing, but they had to check tonight to be sure. Adelaide hoped they would find nothing because Blunt would relish berating Ridgeway.

'It was the moon, I bet,' Ridgeway whispered when they arrived. A silvery sheen glazed a window where the light had been reported. 'Last night a cloud must have been covering it.'

'We can't pluck the moon out of the sky,' Adelaide said.

'I would imagine you could, if you tried, Adelaide.'

'Who's that?' Mr Ridgeway flashed his torch downwards in the direction of the voice. 'God, Snace, you should have warned us you were there.'

'A Nazi won't warn you,' Snace said. 'It's good to keep on our toes.'

With the all-clear, Snace took it upon himself to escort Ridgeway and Adelaide home along the high street. At Snace's insistence and despite his and Adelaide's reluctance, Ridgeway parted from them at his house next to the chemist. This left Adelaide alone with the young man.

Snace kept close to Adelaide and when she moved to her left, he closed the gap. Aware of the ditch, she had nowhere to go.

'I said a prayer for Captain Stride tonight,' Snace said after they had walked without speaking past the pond around to Church Lane.

'Did you?' Adelaide was on alert. 'Thank you.'

'What a needless and brutal death.' His arm touched hers. 'Have they caught that deserter? The soldier who killed him?'

'No.' Adelaide paused, her hand on the gate of Yew Tree House.

'Silly question. If they have, he's back out there. We need every man we can get and the wretch might as well kill a few Germans before taking a bullet.'

Adelaide was left aghast at the young man's confident belief. The colonel was blunt by name and nature, but even he utilised a modicum of tact, and patriotism would prevent him voicing anything that suggested the British were anything less than gentlemen.

'Rupert would perhaps have approved.'

'Rupert believed in justice.'

'Of course. Of course.' Snace crooned. 'But war means different rules.'

As Adelaide stumbled up the path to her front door, what stayed with her was not the horror of Rupert's murder. It was that Michael Snace had spoken for Rupert and used her husband's first name. As if they had been friends.

Chapter Nine

Present Day

The sisters stood in the cramped kitchenette clearing up after breakfast. Stevie washed while Rosa dried. A little window high above their heads and a cheerless strip light lent the little room the look of a prison cell. Perhaps worse, as the glazed glass gave no view of the sky beyond a filtered colour, which today was grey. It also allowed little light. However, as if a prison officer herself, Rosa limited them to only using the strip light in the evenings.

The window overlooked the back garden of Yew Tree House where Milly and Justin had been playing with Stanley, but the dimpled glass offered no view.

A tall woman, Stevie had to bend low over the butler sink. Washing up was the least attractive of the two chores, but as the elder sister, Stevie insisted on doing it.

'There's no sense in us living here instead of the house if we don't make it pay. And since you won't sell, renting it out is the obvious choice. That, or shivering in our beds while Yew Tree House falls down around our ears. Is that what Mother had in mind for us?'

This was, Rosa knew, a trump card. As much as Rosa, her elder sister knew how anxious for their safety their mother had been. Stevie put it down to the war. However, mention of their mother also took Stevie back to the entire point of all that had followed.

'I promised Mother that we would not sell.' Stevie sluiced out the sink and pulled off her washing up gloves. 'You will not make me break it now.'

Faced with the usual impasse, the sisters lapsed into silence. Rosa went through to their tiny sitting room and, gathering up *Sussex Express*, a weekly treat she allowed herself, sat in her armchair facing the door into the garden.

Stevie had been about to go up the narrow staircase leading to their sleeping quarters – little more comfortable than when it had been the billet of their grandfather's chauffeur – when Rosa let out a wail.

'*He's dead.*'

'Snace?' Stevie, in the doorway, was immediately animate.

'You don't waste a moment to be nasty about poor Reverend Snace.' Rosa rattled the paper. 'Dear Eric. It says here he has died.'

'I would have thought him long dead.'

'How silly. He is – was – only four years older than me.'

'Why is it in the paper? Did he die stealing from someone?' Stevie was acid.

'Please don't.' Rosa shot a warning look that untypically – for Stevie was used to being in charge and being right – silenced her. '"Jarvis, Eric Louis, aged eighty-nine, died peacefully at home in Newark surrounded by his loving family." It says he had three daughters and four grandsons. *He got married.*' Rosa threw the newspaper onto the carpet and slumped back.

'Why are you surprised? If he couldn't have you, he had to take his spade and dig for gold elsewhere.' Despite her acerbity, Stevie came in and sat down. Her tone softer she said, 'He never meant he would wait for you. And if he had, he'd still be waiting.'

'You *ruined* my life and you act as if you had nothing to do with it.' Rosa pointed a trembling finger.

'You're being dramatic.' Stevie began kneading at a blanket on the arm of her chair with fretful fingers. 'For the hundredth time, I saved you from making a fool of yourself and worse, from bankrupting us both. This is precisely why Mother told me not to sell. Have you conveniently forgotten Jarvis had Reynolds value the house on the sly to assess your worth? When I refused to sell, the man threatened me with violence. *Still*, you blame me.'

'*We* wanted to know what my share was worth. Eric was a solicitor – like Daddy – he didn't need my *money*.' Rosa retrieved the newspaper and smoothed out the births, deaths and marriages page. 'We *loved* each other.'

'Will you stop saying "Daddy"? You were two when he died,' Stevie said. 'Never mind that he hated me calling him that. It was always "Father".'

'I'll call him what I bloody well like. Those little children next door call the nice man – Jack – daddy.' Rosa pushed back a lock of grey hair with an elbow. 'It says Eric had a "loving family" – that's not the obituary of a gold digger.'

'I saved you from a lifetime of misery. Besides, we all know that obituaries, like epitaphs and eulogies, lie. What was his family meant to put?'

'We could go into a sheltered flat in Lewes, you like it there. We could afford taxis so it wouldn't matter about the hills. Think of never being cold or worrying about what we eat. This house is killing us. Most old people live in poverty through no fault of their own; we have a choice.' Rosa rammed the paper into a rack decorated with roses that sat beside her chair.

'Now we have strangers in our house who could steal our valuables, change the locks and take it over. You know that happens.'

'What valuables? You've given them away to the church.'

'*Enough*. Mother's will stipulated we both have to agree to sell. This house has been in the Stride family for generations, that's why she couldn't sell.' Stevie straightened objects on the table beside her chair: a spectacles case, throat lozenges, a Barbara Pym paperback and a packet of tissues.

'I shall go to Eric's funeral.'

'Rosie-Posie, that is not a good idea.' Instinctively protective, Stevie used Rosa's age-old nickname. 'It would hurt—'

There was a violent knocking on the door. The sisters froze. Putting a finger to her lips, Rosa moved first.

'Hello? Hi there?'

'It's that fellow, Jack.' Rosa motioned for Stevie to stay where she was.

'Come in.'

'*Where are they?*'

'Where are who, dear?' Stevie asked.

'You put a hankie on the pump. We thought it was to tell us the children were here.'

Stevie stared at the woman. Choppy dark hair, black trousers with a considerable number of pockets, extraordinarily tough boots such as a workman might wear. And so tall. However, it wasn't any of that which made Stevie catch her breath. Something indefinable had brought back Stevie's mother Adelaide as if she stood before her.

'Did I really?' Rosa looked astonished. 'Goodness, I must have sensed Eric had died.'

'We looked away for a second...' Trailing off, the man clasped the back of his head. While believing his anguish genuine, Stevie knew an untruth when she heard it. From her expression, so did the woman.

'Do you mean the girl on Esher Common?' Rosa said.

'Rosa, you're getting mixed up,' Stevie said. Rosa's past and present often became one. 'You are too young to remember poor Greta Fleming.'

'Mummy told me about her.' Rosa pouted. Then, with a rapid shake of her head, 'Oh your lovely twins of course.'

'They've gone.' The woman was half out of the door.

'They'll be exploring. I was out from dawn to dusk as a girl, Jimmy led us into terrible scrapes.' Too late Stevie knew she hadn't reassured but really, as her mother said, kiddies must be allowed to get dirty.

'Now Jack dear, do not fret. They will be right as rain, Bishopstone is a jolly safe village,' Rosa told them. 'Goodness, we've never even had a murder.'

Chapter Ten

Present Day

'For *pete's* sake. Murder?' Stevie Stride said. 'Rosa, even saying the word will scare the parents.'

'I'm not...' Stella felt precisely like a scared parent.

'Now, I don't mean to scare you, but Rosa tells me your children are young. Have you phoned the police?' Stevie looked at Stella. She was surprised that Stevie was being so helpful given the elderly rector had said she would be very angry that Rosa had invited strangers to live in their house. Although older, Stevie struck Stella as more switched on than Rosa.

'No, we saw the hankie and came here.'

'That was plain daft, if you don't mind me saying, er...?'

'Stella. This is Jack.' Stella flapped a hand in apology that they had crashed into the elderly women's home without introduction. Her mum said there was no crisis so large that you forgot your manners.

'Milly has been angling to come here.' Jack said. 'Forbidden fruit and all that.'

'We'll call them now.' *Stupid not to have done so immediately.* The flipping hankie had diverted them. 'Wait, Jack, you installed that location app on their phone.'

'They're not allowed to go anywhere alone with their phone so it's pointless.' Jack's monotone voice betrayed terror. If something had happened to the twins, Jack would never be able to live with himself. *He would not be able to live.*

'They're not allowed to go anywhere *alone*, yet they have.' Stella's own terror made her brutal.

'I never put it on, you said it was spying—'

'*For crying out—*' Stella had said it intruded on the children's privacy, but she'd assumed, given Jack's surveillance propensities, he'd downloaded it anyway.

'Mother said war makes people turn on each other and then the worst happens,' Rosa said. 'It's vital we stay together.'

'I'll try ringing anyway.' Stella stabbed her own phone and put it to her ear.

'This is Stella, if you're not both busy, what about a chat?'

Everyone stared at Stella.

'You said that without moving your lips,' Rosa Stride gasped.

Stevie was on her feet. 'It came from outside.'

Stella felt a horrible crawling in her stomach. She walked around Jack and Rosa and stepped through the open door onto the path. She redialled.

'This is Stella, if you're not both busy, what about a—'

She strode back to the lawn. Amidst a clump of dandelions lay the phone Bella had bought her children. The case – emblazoned with a photo of a rarely smiling Bella and the twins – lay face up.

'Max, the man that Bella was seeing, made Bella's laugh his ringtone for when she rang him. Milly and Justin made me do one.' Stella snatched up the phone. 'That's the first time I've heard it.'

'How unnerving.' Stevie Stride was propped against the wall of the house in the sunshine. Not as unnerving as Stella was finding the elderly woman's eyes, which seemed fixed on her. Almost as if Stella was a ghost.

'They must have dropped the phone.' Jack took it from her. 'When they were being chased.'

'Jack. You absolutely don't know that,' Stella stormed at him. 'I'm going to call the police. They're not adults, they'll put out a search immediately.' Stella knew it was pointless not to voice her suspicion that the twins had been communicating with someone who had lured them away. Jack was right there. Lucie said, '*It's a foolish adult who assumed seven-year-olds were not expert navigators of Google.*' She paused to confirm there was no breaking news on the BBC news app; summer had long ceased to be journalists' silly season. It was the time when children died in accidents or were...

'Wait, I found something, what is that?' Jack was peering at the phone, a hand shielding the screen from the sun.

Cavity eyes, grinning teeth. The photographer had caught the skull from an angle. A lozenge of greenish light filled the top right-hand corner.

'Where is this?' Stella snatched the phone off Jack to show it to Stevie Stride.

'I've no... how would I know?' Stevie pushed the phone away. 'That background is a wall.'

'I agree, but it's not in Yew Tree House or our annexe, if that's what you are suggesting.'

'I'm not suggesting, I'm *asking*.' Stella zoomed in on the pinkish brickwork.

'She's asking if we recognise it because we've lived here all our lives,' Rosa told her sister. 'This is a den. I had one in the churchyard when I was their age, between the Blunt mausoleum and the cherry tree. Depend upon it, any moment they will appear, crying *boo*.'

Yesterday, when Stella had wished that Lucie May were there, it had been a symptom of homesickness. Now it was because the seasoned crime reporter would cut through the panic like butter. With Jack's kids missing Stella could not be the Sensible One. She couldn't think straight.

'Let's check the details.' Jack leaned in and tapped the photograph.

'When was the photograph taken?' Stevie moved to one of the garden chairs and lowered herself into it. 'They all say it nowadays, I understand.'

Facts. Stella felt her mojo returning. 'Here we are, it was at three minutes and twenty seconds past ten. The location is Bishopstone.'

'It looks like a cellar.' Jack's voice was strangled.

Stella homed in on the pin on the map and gasped, '*It's here.*'

'They're in the house after all.' Jack rushed to the open French windows into the drawing room.

'Stop. *Wait.* I heard something.' Stella heard it again. *A bark.* Deep and throaty. Once. *Twice.* 'It's Stanley's "come here" signal.'

'It came from down there.' Jack was already running towards the thicket at the end of the garden.

Another bark.

'We're coming.' Stella kept pace with Jack, leaping and swerving over molehills and tall weeds.

Stella and Jack were brought up sharp by a wall of brambles that, up close, towered over their six-foot heights.

'He's in there.' Like a caged animal in distress, Jack ran to and fro along the brambles. He stopped and grabbed at a branch but snatched it back, his hand scratched by thorns as sharp as knife tips.

'That's where they must have got in.' Stella crouched down. 'See those broken branches, I think there's enough room— *Whoa.*'

Stella was flung backwards as Stanley, shooting out of the makeshift tunnel, launched himself at her and slathered her face with frantic licks. Then, before she could put a hand in front of her face, he had belted back into the brambles.

Head down, fearsome thorns ripping his shirt and snagging his hair, Jack plunged in after Stanley. With no hesitation, Stella crawled in after him.

Gifted with acute olfactory powers, Stella registered a bass note of rotting flesh beneath earth and parched vegetation. Her head rang with a silent plea.

Please let them be alive.

Chapter Eleven

November 1940

An owl hooted somewhere across the field beyond the hedgerow. Adelaide, returning from fire practice at the village hall, paused. These days an owl could be a Nazi parachutist signalling to another Nazi. The man wouldn't have been shot down, there had been no raids tonight. Good at orienteering in the dark, Adelaide was sure she was only about fifty yards from Church Lane. Two minutes from Yew Tree House.

Winston said Jerry would be invading any day now. It was imperative to stay alert, Blunt had instructed them. Adelaide suspected he'd taken particular delight telling the wardens a parachute can land without sound, allowing the enemy to sneak up and slit their throats. Snace had dared upbraid him. 'Remember you're talking to a lady.' *A lady.* Adelaide was quick to say she'd have no hesitation in slitting his throat first. Which, she'd noticed, had rather disappointed Ridgeway who – obviously – hated violence, but if her children were threatened, she wouldn't waste time talking to the enemy.

Blunt might enjoy putting the wind up them, but he hadn't invented the danger. Last night, when Brigadier Parsons arrived at Yew Tree House with medical supplies – her supplies since the kindly retired officer considered her entirely competent to be in

77

charge of the medicine cupboard – he'd told them Seaford had taken a hit. The bomb had missed the railway by yards and left a crater the size of a railway carriage in the middle of the water meadows.

That evening, rather rattled, Adelaide had accidentally called the curate Mr *Snake*, which had greatly amused Brigadier Parsons. Blunt had guffawed. Snace merely dipped his head with a gracious smile. But when, later, Adelaide caught him gazing at her in his strange contemplative fashion, she reminded herself it wasn't only the Nazis she should fear.

Once upon a time, when the darkness had swaddled her, it had been an escape to be alone. Before the war, she had found companionship in the insubstantiality of gravestones, fences, bushes and grazing sheep. Seated on a memorial slab in a corner of the churchyard with only the dead for company, she had felt at peace. The night-time of war was different. It spelled danger.

Distracted by these thoughts, Adelaide lost track of where she was. She stopped and tried to separate the greys and black of the hedge, the ancient oak tree out of which Stevie had fallen two years ago and knocked out a tooth. Just as well, it had turned out, or her mouth would have been crowded. Rupert had been furious. He'd never lost his temper with Stevie before. 'He's just worried, darling, it could have been much worse,' she had explained.

Adelaide wasn't concentrating. It was, Blunt told them, when they lost concentration that Jerry would get them.

Were these darker outlines fabrications? No, the sketched shape was the butterfly bush. In the day the purple blossom was alive with bees. Yet in parallel to this, Adelaide saw the huddled monster which, after the '38 village Christmas show, Rupert had told Stevie was lying in wait for them. Rupert said the odd scare toughened them up. *'The war is one big scare.'* She winced now at the memory.

Chill crept through Rupert's overcoat. Each step could take her home or to oblivion. Cold air numbed her cheekbones. The owl had not hooted again. Was the enemy leaving an interval before responding to put her off the scent? She couldn't tell how long it had been since the first one. Since the war – everything was 'since the war' – time was both specific and amorphous. A minute was a lifetime, an hour measured by raids and sirens. Adelaide rather regretted refusing Nigel Ridgeway's offer to walk her home. *She was being silly.*

The village Christmas show had been a Stride family tradition. Rupert's father's Widow Twankey had become a legend. Rupert, unwilling to play a woman even for fun, had broken hearts as the prince in *Cinderella*. The phoney war had put a stop to last year's production. When told Rupert's death meant another cancellation, Adelaide had insisted it must go ahead this year. Jimmy Chrismas was to be the genie, which was fitting as there was something mercurial about the boy, and Henry had persuaded Stevie to be Aladdin. It was only November, but already the children were champing at the bit. Never had Adelaide been so grateful to the – usually dreaded – Christmas show.

Pat Jordan called it a cheek that Snace had put himself forward, he was only a curate and he'd been there five minutes. Adelaide hadn't yet dared pursue if Pat shared her view of Snace.

Another step. Adelaide became conscious of slowing her pace. It reminded her of being a girl and seeing how far she could walk with her eyes shut. She'd start off fast and then, her confidence ebbing, would eventually stop. Stevie had tried it and got a lot further. Stevie was a warrior at heart. It was Rosa, the spit of Rupert, who worried Adelaide. *Did she protect her properly?*

Adelaide had overheard Henry telling Stevie to stay still if she ever heard something when she was outside. *'Don't hardly breathe, kid the Nazi you don't exist.'* She guessed it was his Home Guard training. It concerned her now that Henry was out almost every night.

Another hoot. Surely too long to be an answering signal. It was what it sounded like, an owl. After the night she had encountered Henry in the drawing room, Adelaide had told herself her imagination was a fifth columnist. It undermined her courage and common sense and offered up demons and ghosts.

Mrs Hall had seen her son William outside the ironmongers, even though he was lost when his ship was torpedoed off Norway. When she rushed outside, full of joy and relief, she found the high street empty. Puce with shame, Mr Hall had followed Adelaide from the shop and assured her his wife was not losing her mind. Adelaide said it was grief. For good measure she said she sometimes felt Rupert close and she was perfectly sane. Perhaps because Mr Hall had disliked a woman witnessing his distress he'd said it was all right for those who had their loved one's remains and a place to pay their respects. His boy was at the bottom of the sea. Grief could be caustic. War had brought people together and it had driven them far apart. Still, Adelaide decided, the owl was an owl.

She smelled Rupert's hair oil. She was still wearing his coat. Reverend Smart had told her smell was the last sense to evoke the memory of the dead. More cogent than the mind's eye or ear, it could last years.

Adelaide inched forward, one foot in front of the other; each step, she told herself, must be given due attention. Her rubber-soled boots were silent on the newly metalled lane.

A branch of blackthorn snagged her shoulder. To avoid the ditch, Adelaide moved into the middle of the lane. She must soon reach the churchyard wall.

Smoke.

Not the comforting scent of burning cedar. A cigarette. There was someone on the lane. Without waiting to find out if they were behind or in front of her, Adelaide hurled herself into the hedge and pain shot across her chest. Something had hit her in the midriff. Winded and gasping for breath, Adelaide felt smooth wood. Reality resolved. She had slammed against the gate into Salmon's field. Hugging the top, Adelaide gathered her last strength and hoisted herself over. She stumbled to her feet and raced into the darkness. The field had just been cut and, almost immediately, her boot caught on stubble and she fell headlong.

At last Adelaide dared lift her head. She strained either way, trying to get her bearings. The breathing was her own. Supporting herself on her elbows, she flattened her palms on the ground and pushed herself to kneeling. She had the distinct and definite feeling there was someone out there and they too were waiting.

Adelaide struggled to picture the field in daylight. The gate at one end of Salmon's field which led on to Church Lane. If she had run straight, then it should be far to her right. If she crossed the field diagonally, it was a shortcut. Some way along she should encounter the flint wall of the jutting section of the churchyard.

But not if she had run in a circle.

She got gingerly to her feet. Breathing. *In. Out. In...*

Adelaide took too long to realise it was the sea. *If Blunt and Snace could see her now.*

Adelaide risked crossing the field to the gate. Trying to keep one foot in front of the other – very difficult in the dark – she came up against the flint wall. She was wide of the gate, but now she had a guide. She felt along the wall until she reached the iron post that Snace had dented driving the vicar's car. She finally found it. She pushed through the kissing gate and out onto Church Lane.

She paused by the rectory and imagined, with some affection now that Snace was as good as the vicar, Reverend Smart would be behind the black fustian in his ground-floor study, cataloguing his plant specimens and dreaming of immortality by way of discovering a new species.

'Didn't Ridgeway walk you home?'

Adelaide recoiled, her heart beating like an express train.

'I could have attacked you,' she told Snace.

'How?' Snace murmured. 'Do you carry a weapon?'

'This torch could do you – could do *anyone* – damage.' Her dry mouth had made an alien object of her tongue.

'Ridgeway should have escorted you back.'

'He offered, but I know the way.'

'Why are you coming from the field?'

'I took a shortcut,' Adelaide said.

'A dangerous precedent. We don't expect anyone to be out there at night. Please stick to the road.' Snace stuck close to her as they walked around the house and in at the back door.

Adelaide grimaced as it screeched on its hinges. Blunt forbade them to be oiled because it would warn of intruders.

Snace stood to the side to shut it, which meant Adelaide had pass him to go into the passage. Once they were inside, he switched on the light in the hall. The bulb was dull, but after the pitch black, the light hurt her eyes.

'Good grief, what happened to you?' Snace touched her cheek with the back of his hand. Adelaide whipped away as if stung. 'Your face is streaked with mud.'

'I slipped.' Adelaide couldn't bear to start a drama and have Snace summon the Home Guard to look for the smoker on the lane. Besides, she had already lied to him. 'Good night, Mr Snace.'

Snace took out packet of Kensitas and withdrew a cigarette.

'Goodnight, *Mrs* Stride.' *He emphasised 'Mrs' as if the formality was her affectation.*

Although she left him in the passage outside the dining room, Adelaide felt sure Snace had glided after her in the darkness and was watching her ascend from the foot of the stairs.

Adelaide shut her bedroom door and locked it. She moved towards her bed and stopped. Cigarette smoke. It was Snace who had followed her on the lane. She hugged herself.

He had wanted her to know that he was there.

Chapter Twelve

Present Day

'She's been mur-der-did,' Justin told Jack, his voice squeaky with what Stella had to hope was excitement and not pure fright. That a small boy could even wrongly pronounce 'murdered' with such confidence was the stuff of horror stories.

Dizzied with her own fright, Stella took in Justin and Milly, cross-legged on the concrete floor of what Stella quickly recognised as a pillbox. Not a country person, she had noticed one on the road out of Lewes and had been grateful that Jack had been able to answer Justin's question about it.

'Mills, my darling.' Jack was on his knees in front of his little girl. 'Who has done this to you?'

Belatedly, Stella saw that Milly was covered in scratches.

'I'll get the first aid box from the car.' Stella hesitated at the opening beyond which lay the wall of brambles. She too was scratched.

'I'm busy. It's a meeting like you have at Clean Serrlate,' Milly informed Stella with a staying hand. With the other she splashed what looked like water into a folded leaf. In another context such ingenuity would have impressed Stella. Someone – Justin probably – had used a clutch of twigs to sweep up dead leaves and other best-not-examined detritus.

'A meeting about cleaning?' Stella said.

'No, silly.' Milly tssked. She jabbed a thumb at the skeleton. 'About who *murdahed* Mary.'

'It must have been a very long time ago,' Stella said.

'You found a very old murderer once,' Justin reminded Stella. 'He was dead.'

How did the children find out this stuff? Stella suspected Jack of having told other bedtimes stories – their closed cases.

'Ours is alive,' Justin said.

'That's not true,' Milly said.

Jack was running a hand over what Stella had instantly recognised as the brick wall in the photograph on the twins' phone. The greenish light – creating a horrible effect on everyone's complexion – which Stella had supposed was from a cellar window, filtered through an aperture opposite.

'There's a hole in Mary's skull.' Stella wasn't sure about naming the skeleton, but it wasn't like Justin and Milly could get attached. From their expressions, she saw that the twins considered themselves several steps ahead.

Covered from the waist down by a filthy tarpaulin, the skeletal remains of a human body were propped against the wall. Rotted rags clinging to the torso were all that remained of the clothes.

'She was bashed on the head,' Milly said with relish.

'Milly, don't frighten your brother.' Too late, Jack was being a responsible parent.

'I'm not frightened.' Perhaps to prove this Justin shuffled closer to the skeleton.

'Nor am I,' Milly said. Not that for a minute Stella or Jack had thought she was.

'Justin, you're quite right, the skele— Mary has been hit with something.' Jack was peering at the skeleton. 'The injury, were it being reported by a pathologist, which we know is a scientist, would describe it as "blunt force trauma". That means it was caused by being hit with a solid object.'

Stella had surely been right about the bedtime stories. If she lived with Jack, could she put up with him telling the twins about murder and not report it to Bella? Did her own relationship with Jack work because she didn't know the half?

'The hole is at the back of her head so we can guess she was facing away from her attacker.' Another kind of father would be explaining the laws of gravity or showing them the Milky Way at night.

'She probably never knew a thing,' Stella steamed in to try and distract the children from the grisly scene.

'Maybe she was looking out that window.' Milly pointed at one of the embrasures.

'It's not a window, you fire a gun through it.' Jack was prompt. He went on to remind them about his explanation of the reason for pillboxes on the way out of Lewes the day before. From the twins' expressions, it appeared to have gone in one ear and out the other.

'...by the Director of Fortifications and Works. The five sides with an internal Y-shaped blast wall meant this one was a DFW3/24, or a pillbox... shelf supported a Bren gun. It's bulletproof and if a bomb was dropped the men – and women – inside were protected by that Y-shaped blast wall...'

Stella wandered to the other side of the blast wall. It was slathered with graffiti. Three numbers were clear, though: '945'. A code? The dying woman's attempt to send a message? Above was what must have at some point been another letter, possibly an R or an A. Or neither.

'Nineteen forty-five.' Jack was beside her.

'Oh yes, of course. Maybe that dates the murder.'

'Could do.' Jack frowned. 'When the Nazis invaded Russia in 1941, the threat of invasion here was as good as nil. Although Churchill stood them down in 1943, it wasn't until after VE Day in 1945 that pillboxes were decommissioned. Mary must have been murdered after that or her body would have been discovered. Milly – and Stanley – broke down a barricade of that nasty rusting corrugated iron to get in, so the box had been sealed.'

'By the murderer?'

'More than likely. Although rather a risk at the bottom of a garden.'

'Not so much since Milly only just found it,' Stella said.

They had researched the war when they were investigating a murder in Tewkesbury three years ago. But while she'd mugged up on the same subject, she remembered little now. Jack's photographic memory ensured he could pluck out a long-held salient fact at will.

'This is a crime scene, we must leave. *Now.*' Stella came to her senses and, snatching at a straw that might convince Milly, said, 'We are destroying evidence.'

'Everyone out,' Jack said.

'This is *our* crime scene. *You* go,' Milly said. 'We already have evy-dence.'

'Milly *behave.*' Jack was terse.

'What did you find?' Justin hissed at Milly, but they were already crawling out of the pillbox, and Stella didn't hear her reply.

Stella paused at the opening, tangled with thorny branches, and looked back at the skeleton of the dead woman. Although she had likely lain there, undisturbed, since the nineteen forties, Stella felt unwilling to leave her all alone.

'I'll call the police,' Stella said when they were settled in the drawing room of Yew Tree House with the children seemingly distracted by *Peppa Pig* on Jack's laptop.

'We don't need the police.' Jack had been keen not to frighten the sisters with news that a murder victim had been found in their garden and Stella had agreed to that.

'There's no need for pleese,' Milly piped up over the lid of the laptop. 'I've solved it. We are sending him to prison.'

'No one is being sent to prison,' Jack said.

'He is. He is. He *is*.' Stella hoped Milly's 'Terrible-Two' temper wasn't about to make a comeback.

Stella waited for Jack to explain it wasn't a game, that murder, even committed long ago, was serious. He might perhaps point out that in this country people didn't get sent to jail without a trial.

'Great you've solved it, but do you have proof?' Jack was all approbation and pride.

'He *said* he did it.' Shutting the laptop with a bang, Milly muted *Peppa Pig*.

'He did-*ent*,' Justin said. 'He said how do we know about murder.'

'Who said what?' Jack asked.

'Jack, we have found a murder victim. OK, so we didn't tell Rosa and Stevie, but I am calling the police.'

'Let's think this over.' Jack put up a hand.

'Think what over?' Stella glared at him.

'Maybe hold off for a bit, just to see what we can find out ourselves? It's a very cold case and cold cases are us.' Jack looked excited. 'This could be a busman's holiday.'

'A what?'

'It means you go on holiday and end up doing your job—'

'I *know* what it means. Except my job is cleaning and this place certainly needs it so that's me sorted. You drive a train so how's that going to work?'

'You also solve murders.'

'Not any more.'

'Since when?'

'Since *for ever* – we haven't solved a murder since before the pandemic,' Stella said. 'Never mind this was supposed to be a holiday without murder or death.'

'Why did you take us to see the Murdered Granny then?' Milly looked at them with beady eyes.

'Why indeed.' Stella fixed her eyes on Jack. 'I thought the point of the holiday was to see if we could all get on. To leave all of this kind of stuff behind.'

'I thought the holiday was to have fun.' Justin looked betrayed.

'Yes, of course it was and it is. We shall have a ton of fun,' Stella gabbled. 'Which is why we must call—'

There was a rap on the door.

Perhaps because they all welcomed any kind of interruption, everyone crowded into the hall. Stella got to the door first.

'Stella Darnell?'

'Yes.'

It was a woman in black jacket and trousers, a foot shorter than Stella and the man next to her, dressed in a powder-blue suit and tan pointy shoes, who topped Stella and Jack's six foot. However, it was the man's haircut – more *Wolf Hall* than *Peaky Blinders* – that caused Stella to shield the twins. *Jehovah's witnesses? Charity chuggers?*

The woman's boots were identical to her own. *Stella's were police-issue.*

'I'm Detective Inspector Toni Kemp, this is Detective Sergeant Malcolm Lane.' Following Stella's gaze, Kemp glanced at Stella's own boots. 'Your son called us.'

'I don't have a—' Stella felt small fingers entwine with hers. Justin gazed up at her.

'Your son called us to report the discovery of a body on your premises.'

Chapter Thirteen

November 1940

Beggar's Wood was opaque dark. What little light there was as the night moved to morning was obliterated by the canopy of trees. A breeze rattled recently bared branches. Scurrying creatures, from burrow and sett, stirred the first fall of autumn leaves. At this hour, rabbits and badgers might have expected to have the wood to themselves. However, such creatures were not the only living beings dwelling underground.

A faint light speared the darkness, outlining, as if etched with metal, leaves, twigs and exposed roots on the woodland floor. It grew in brightness to take in the nearest oak tree. A casual observer – after 1939 there was no such thing – would have been forgiven for supposing they were prey to a vision as a tree stump rose to one side, flooding the area with lamplight.

However, any idea this was the work of the Almighty must have been extinguished by the appearance of a silhouetted head, shoulders and then a yelp of pain. Whoever was responsible was made of flesh and blood.

It was raining when, mission accomplished, in silence, Jimmy and Henry followed the path over the Downs to Bishopstone. It wasn't entirely dark and the chalk track showed treacherously pale against the grass. From somewhere came the ripping and snuffling of sheep cropping. Every now and then the boys veered off the track and then back to it, careful to avoid a predictable path.

Henry and Jimmy didn't risk speaking until they reached the wall of the churchyard in Salmon's field.

'He didn't think we'd do it,' Jimmy muttered.

'God help us when he finds out we did,' Henry said. Both boys knew Snace would be angered by their success; he would have preferred them to be hurt. Or worse.

'He's not as nice as old Reverend Smart,' Jimmy said.

'When he's a vicar he's very nice,' Henry reminded him. 'He shows his best side and then behind closed doors, he's... evil. My dad was like that. So was...'

'So was who?' Jimmy said.

'Nothing. He's the devil, I reckon.' Henry sighed.

Jimmy had grown to understand that Henry avoided talking about his home in London.

Both boys had seen the kindness with which the young curate treated his parishioners. Henry had learned what Adelaide and Stevie Stride had instinctively guessed: Mr Snace was a cold ambitious man.

Supposing themselves recruited into the Home Guard, the boys soon discovered they were part of a highly secret operation answerable only to Winston Churchill. Snace had them sign the Official Secrets Act and threatened them with a charge of treason if they told anyone.

Auxiliary Units had been set up months earlier when a German invasion looked likely. 'Stay-behinds', they were essentially a terrorist army trained to sabotage and act on instinct, answerable to no one. Confined to secret underground bunkers, they were to emerge after dark, blow up key targets and 'butcher and bolt'. Neither Jimmy – trained as a butcher – nor Henry, relished using the sharp daggers Snace had given them. Snace said Jimmy's ditch-by-field knowledge of the countryside qualified him for the unit, and Henry his brawn. The others were the village blacksmith, the foreman of Salmon's farm and his two labourers, a poacher and a convicted sheep rustler. Auxiliary Units required men capable of confusing right with wrong. Foremost of these was Michael Snace.

Snace's actual reason for recruiting Jimmy and Henry was that he was bitterly jealous that Adelaide Stride welcomed them into Yew Tree House while she had made her dislike of him perfectly clear. He would change that.

Tonight's training mission was to chalk a cross on a Canadian jeep a mile beyond the village of Southease and return undetected. The cross stood for an explosive device. The device might be symbolic, but the danger was real. Had Henry and Jimmy been caught in the act they risked being shot by a scared trigger-happy soldier.

'That was a close-run thing. That guard heard me drop the padlock.' Jimmy stopped by the corner of the flint wall about fifty yards from the gate onto Church Lane. 'Lucky for us he wanted a nose at that raid to the west; stupid bugger'll pay for dereliction of duty tomorrow.'

'We won't be telling that to Snace.' Henry biffed Jimmy on the shoulder.

'Thanks, mate,' Jimmy said.

Silence. Then both boys gave a start, each nudging the other.

'*Enemy. There*,' Henry breathed.

As if at a silent signal they bent low and, hugging the wall, crept closer to where a figure so insubstantial as to be a possible trick of the light was moving through the tooth-pale monuments towards the new graves. Only yards from where the boys were.

Henry and Jimmy, who had become adept at trusting no tricks of the light while being such tricks themselves, dared climb the wall and move swiftly to the dappled darkness of a chestnut tree.

Neither need call on the training that had covered observing mannerisms and gait to know who was moving about by Rupert

Stride's grave, now dominated by a gigantic stone headstone that had been erected the day before. Henry had helped Mrs Stride plant the plot with winter flowers with Stevie and Rosa.

Cleaving to the rules of silent warfare, Henry and Jimmy conferred with glances that said they should go, unwilling to witness a private moment.

The boys were on the fringes of Beggar's Wood, still some metres from the observational bunker, when they stopped again.

'You see what she was doing?' Jimmy whispered.

'Yes,' Henry said.

'Could she have gone mad? Like that Mrs Hall?"

'No.'

'Then why—'

'Forget you saw her,' Henry hissed at Jimmy.

'What are you doing here?'

The boys gripped their knives. *Butcher and bolt.*

'It's me, for God's sake.'

'*Stevie*, Christ. We could ask you that, more like?' Jimmy forgot to whisper. 'We was just saying—'

'*Shut up,*' Henry said.

'You were spying on me.'

'We never.' Jimmy was too quick.

'We saw you leaving the churchyard, that's all.' Henry opted for a sliver of truth.

'I heard you.'

Jimmy and Henry, so skilled at blending in with their environment, had not been able to stifle surprise when they saw something so awful as to make no sense.

'You still haven't said why you're here,' Stevie said. 'Why would the Home Guard wander about in the wood?'

'We do,' Jimmy mumbled. 'Which is why *you* shouldn't be here.'

'Mind your own business, Jimmy Chrismas.' Stevie's vehemence caught them all – Stevie included – by surprise.

'We heard a plane came down Southease way. We was looking for it, there's been talk of a parachutist.' Thinking on his feet, Henry stepped back onto a twig. *Crack.*

'You didn't think to ask me?'

'You're not in the Home Guard.' Desperate to avoid giving anything away, Henry was answering tit for tat. He tried to soften the response. 'Honestly, if we could we would of. It would all be better if you was in the unit too.'

'What unit?' Stevie said.

'He means the Home Guard,' Jimmy said.

'That's not a unit.'

'No, it isn't.' Jimmy pulled a face as if to suggest Henry was daft to get it wrong. Jimmy and Henry knew that the Home Guard, never mind the secret Auxiliary Unit, was a hot potato. Stevie had asked to be a messenger.

'That Snake enjoyed telling me I couldn't join the Home Guard because I'm a girl. So what, I said.'

'You said that?' Henry looked horrified.

'Of course. He makes me sick, the way the he looks at my mother. He's young enough to be her son.'

'He's twenty, I asked one of the blokes in the platoon.' Henry lowered his voice. 'You mustn't make him cross.'

'We shouldn't be here, there might be Germans,' Jimmy hissed.

Both boys knew the Germans were the least of their problems. Several metres into Beggar's Wood, they were close to the OB – the Observational Base – close to Snace.

'I'm going to bed now, that's because I'm a girl. Tell Snake from me to keep his slippery hands off my mother.'

'I will,' Jimmy was more than ready to do that.

Stevie melted into the blackest shadows as silently as she had come.

'He'll put Stevie on the blacklist,' Henry said hoarsely.

'Not if we don't tell him,' Jimmy said.

'What if Stevie tells him? She's not afraid of him and she doesn't know the truth.'

'There you are.' A smile in the pitch-black darkness. 'What are you doing?

The boys shrank away from the voice. Mr Snace was even more scary when he was being pleasant.

'Doing a last recce before report in, sir. Like you said.' Jimmy clutched his Sykes knife to stop himself using it.

While she knew it wasn't their fault, Stevie Stride was very upset that Jimmy and Henry had left her out. When she had asked to join the Home Guard, Snace had said how he was *so very sorry because what an asset she would be*. Despite these words, his expression said he was enjoying every minute of what he made a grinding humiliation, ending with an invitation to run his Sunday school.

Stevie had got only a few paces when she resolved to go back and find them. They could take her to Snace and explain that she wasn't scared to be out at night by herself. Perhaps actually being there would make him change his mind.

Stevie was fearless as she crept back into Beggar's Wood. She dared flick on her torch and found her way back to the spot where she had found Jimmy and Henry.

Stevie flicked the beam around, keeping it low. Tall tree trunks, like sentries, seemed to crowd in on her. Not far from where she stood was a tree stump covered in moss. No sign of Henry and Jimmy. Yet Stevie sensed she was not alone.

Chapter Fourteen

'We have to come too.' Milly folded her arms stoutly. 'Daddy and Stella don't know about the murder. *We* are the detectives.'

'We will talk to you too,' Toni said. 'But this is just for grown-ups.'

'Grown-ups never know about murders,' Milly asserted. 'Stella wants us to stay, don't you?'

'I'm in charge, so I'm afraid it's not up to Stella,' Toni said.

'Why don't you tell me instead?' Without seeming to, Sergeant Lane hustled Milly and Justin into the drawing room.

'They were playing detective,' Jack explained when they were seated around the dining room table.

'Beats hopscotch.' Seated at the head of the table, Toni opened her notebook. 'I gather you're here on holiday with your children.'

'We're here for a month.' Jack beamed.

'A *long* break.' With raised eyebrows which could mean 'nice for some', Toni Kemp switched to Stella. 'I gather your kids discovered the skeleton in the pillbox during a period in which they had gone missing. Is that right? It's not reported.'

'We didn't realise they were...' Stella went hot. 'We assumed they were playing with my dog in the garden.'

'You're not the children's mother, you said.' If by this Detective Inspector Kemp meant to suggest Stella felt less attached, nothing in her expression implied it.

'Their mother lives in London.' *Was* she less attached? If Milly and Justin were her kids, she would never take her eyes off them. She had taken her eyes off Stanley so maybe that wasn't true. *She did care about the children.*

'You found Justin and Milly in the pillbox. It's well hidden, how did you know it was there?' Toni Kemp pulled out a chocolate bar and, ripping down the wrapper, took a generous bite.

'They had dropped this in the garden.' Jack handed Kemp the children's phone with the photo of the skull. 'I could see that it was a wall—'

'We heard Stanley bark, Jack, remember?' Stella had forgotten about the phone.

'They have a phone?' Kemp enquired. 'What are they, five, six?'

'Seven. It's for their mother to chat with them when they're with me,' Jack said. 'They don't keep it themselves when we're not with them. Milly took this picture of the skeleton. When she showed it to her brother, he knew immediately the skull had been hit. That it was murder. Look.'

'Yet, they did have it or how did they take this photograph?' Toni Kemp took the phone off Jack.

Eye sockets, crazed fracture lines converging to a jagged hole in the back of the skull. Stella waited. While examining the picture, Kemp must be thinking to tell Sergeant Lane to get onto social services without further ado.

'I will have questions for the children,' Toni Kemp said at last. The taming-a-wild-beast intonation confirmed Stella's guess that Kemp wasn't a seasoned parent. Although, as a seasoned detective, she must have handled kids before.

'You can both be present. I'll be asking if they removed an object from the scene or disturbed the body. No more than that. Is that all right? We don't want to upset either of them.' Kemp's concern must be put on because by now she might have known that Milly was only upset at being barred from the room.

'I am sure they disturbed nothing.' Stella remembered the tea party and felt less sure.

'We'll never know.' Toni crushed the Snickers wrapper between two palms.

Bathed in afternoon sun, the cliffs were brilliant white, cut with grey strata of flint. A lush carpet of grass was draped like a vivid green shawl over Seaford Head; above, there was not a cloud in the travel brochure blue sky. Holiday-makers on the beach or floating upon inflatables on a sea as smooth as glass could congratulate themselves for choosing this staycation.

They had come to the beach, not to continue their holiday but because Yew Tree House was a crime scene and DI Kemp had asked Stella if she could take her family out for the afternoon. The sisters had remained in their annexe although Justin had it on good authority that nice Toni Kemp with the same boots as Stella had gone to visit.

Why did Justin think Toni Kemp was nice? Stella put her own doubt down to guilt rather than evidence to the contrary. The officer must take a dim view of Jack and Stella's ability to look after the twins. First, they had gone missing, then Justin had dialled 999 without them knowing. When Kemp asked them about the skeleton Milly had piped up that 'Daddy didn't want us to call you'. Asked if this was true, and if so why, Stella had been astonished when Jack said, 'Milly misunderstood, I wanted to get my kiddies settled, then of course I was going to phone.' *Since when?*

Kemp expressed bafflement that they were holidaying in such a dilapidated place, adding doubtfully, 'Great for kids, I suppose, not much to break.' Stella wondered now if Kemp suspected they had an ulterior reason for choosing to stay there. If so, she hadn't said. After Stella had transferred Milly's skeleton photo to Kemp's phone, she had bundled everyone into the car and made for Seaford.

This beach expedition wasn't the carefree experience of the morning before. Stella and Jack were again frosty with each other. Milly, fed up with Justin for telling the police, and 'sucking up to them', was treating him with hauteur. Justin was torn between being pleased that Stella had praised him for doing the right thing – *as had the nice policewoman* – and hating that he'd upset his sister and father. Everyone was sad and it was all his fault. Unknown to either of them, Justin and Stella were feeling exactly the same thing.

Set against garish props of the seaside – ice-cream cornets, animal blow-ups, bucket and spades – and despite the sunshine, the makeshift family was shrouded in gloom.

Even Stanley, swaddled in a towel after being smacked by a wave when he'd chased his ball into the sea, was flumped in a despondent heap beneath a Kia Motors golfing umbrella, a random gift to Stella from a grateful client.

Stella was adamant that she wasn't interested in investigating what Kemp had conceded was a murder, but lying on a beach in the sun had lost its allure. Who was the woman? Who had killed her and why? How long would the police be there? And at the top of her mind: had the Stride sisters known all along? From his expression, Stella knew that Jack was thinking the same thing.

This last question bothered Stella the most. She wondered if she would get a chance to talk to them. Rosa at least might tell her something. Did the hankie on the pump – there to stop them revealing themselves to Stevie – still hold?

It was Stella who heard the shout. She jumped up and, shading her eyes, scoured the sea, a glittering band of gold. At first she could see nothing. Two arms against the sky. She yelled, 'That person's in trouble.'

Others were racing to the shoreline, one man with a child on his shoulders; several were holding up phones. *Unashamed rubberneckers.*

'We need to get help.' Stella scrabbled for her phone.

'It's OK, love, don't call the coastguard.' A woman in one of the vast towelling tent-robes which turned people into triangles flapped a hand.

'Someone's drowning,' Stella hissed hoarsely to avoid the children hearing.

'Does that mean they will die?' Milly squawked.

Could today really get any worse?

'It's Vera Jackson's party piece.' The woman was watching the sea where now there was nothing but a buoy.

'She's been under for ages.' Stella went with the woman to shoreline.

'Two minutes and thirty seconds.' The woman was checking her watch. 'Vera does it on her birthday, been at it for years. Big day this year, she's ninety.'

'Does what?' *Try to drown herself?* Stella fixed on the distant buoy although dazzling sunlight kept blotting it out. *No arms now.* Why had she gone along with this?

'She swims to the marker then down she goes. She can hold her breath for four minutes. She reckons it's why she's so fit. Dad used to bring us to watch and now I bring my own kids.' A girl a bit older than Milly was peering through pink binoculars.

'It's four minutes.' Stella was looking at her own watch. 'What if she doesn't— Perhaps I should call the coast—'

The beach erupted with cheers. Two arms and a head had surfaced. Lined along the shingle, people were leaping about, fists pumping the air.

Someone was using a Bluetooth speaker to boom out 'I Will Survive'.

Jack and Stella caught each other's eye and grinned.

★

'Don't either of you *ever* try that,' Jack said. The aroma of pizzas eaten by the sea lingered as Stella drove them back to Bishopstone. 'Not everyone could survive. Never mind that it frightens people.'

'I could do it.' Milly was on cue. 'I wasn't frightened.'

'What did I just say?' Jack wheeled around in his seat.

'Eyes on the road,' Milly tootled. 'Just saying, if I did do it, I would sur-*vive*.' Milly relished the new word, as if it were a sweet.

'It's not clever or impressive. It's bloody stupid.'

'You *swore*.' The twins were back in unison.

'Will the plees be there when we get back?' Justin asked.

'Probably.' The not-drowning incident had successfully distracted Stella from the murder victim at the bottom of the garden.

'The one called Toni was nice,' Justin said again.

'She was rude,' Milly decreed. 'I said we'd solved it and she pretended she didn't hear. Be-cause she wants to find the murd-rah herself. That's it now, I'm not helping. Or you.' She nudged Justin.

'I will,' he said. 'She's nice.'

'You will *not*.' This was an argument that, through sturdy persistence, Milly was destined to win.

'You must both *always* help the police.' Jack would be saying it as an olive branch to Stella.

'We will not,' Milly said.

The police were not only still at Yew Tree House, but Church Lane was choked with a dog-handler van, a mortuary van, two police cars and a glossy black Jeep Wrangler. Two cordons had been set up. A red-and-white-striped one at the opening to the lane delineated the inner boundary where police expected there to be a greater amount of forensic evidence. Although, seriously, after what must be decades, what evidence could there be? The second cordon, of blue-and-white tape, was slung across the road which became the high street. This had meant they had to park near the village pond, a good five minutes' walk away from the house.

Stella coveted the Jeep, but since most of her driving was done in her Peugeot Partner van to clean in a city, she couldn't justify it. Stella bet the no-nonsense, booted Toni Kemp owned the Jeep. She caught herself wondering if it would be OK to check in with Kemp and ask how things were going. *No, it would not.* Glancing back at the sleek black Jeep, for the first time in her life, Stella found herself wishing she had joined the police when her dad gave her the application form. She wouldn't mind being on Toni Kemp's team.

Toni Kemp was standing on the porch like a welcoming host as they were ambling back to the house. 'We're off, we've sealed off the pillbox, but the rest of the house is yours.'

'*We* know the murderer.' Pushing Jack aside, Milly glared up Kemp.

'Nice one, mate.' Toni put out a hand, perhaps to ruffle Milly's hair, then wisely reconsidered it. 'You'll see us about for the next few days and I'll be visiting the Ms Strides again. It's possible they might remember something or know something but don't recognise its importance.'

'CID speak for "we think Stevie and Rosa are hiding something",' Jack said as soon as they closed the door.

'*I bet they are.*' Milly scampered through to the drawing room.

'So do I,' Jack muttered to Stella.

'I'm sure not.' Stella's response was knee-jerk.

Had Stevie known that would happen? That there was a murdered woman in the pillbox? She needed some normality. 'I'm going to give the dining room a clean.'

'I put out the puzzle there, I'll box it up.' Jack came with her.

'Don't.' Putting away the jigsaw was admitting they had lost the holiday spirit.

The dining room had a melancholy air, faded dark green walls, there was nothing on the mantelpiece and the walls were marked with outlines of where paintings must once have hung.

'Can you imagine what it was like for Stevie and Rosa eating in here, with Rupert Stride's chair empty and their mother trying to be cheerful for her children's sake?' Jack stood in the doorway.

'Maybe they ate in the kitchen.' Stella stopped at the one picture still remaining. A photograph, it showed a black rock with a baby perched on it who, given that the girl standing beside the rock was definitely Stevie Stride and July 1939 was printed on the bottom of the frame, must be Rosa. 'Besides, maybe their mother was cheerful.'

'That's a hidden-mother picture.' Jack came over.

'A what?'

'I was going to show you earlier, but we weren't speaking – anyway, it was a Victorian thing studios did so parents had photos of kids alone without them crying for their mums.' Jack tapped the glass. 'Rosa and Stevie's mother will be under that rock.'

'But it says 1939, so why do it then?' Now Stella could see that what she had supposed was a fake rock in the foreground of a painted garden scene was thick black fabric.

'Precisely. Very strange. By then cameras had faster shutter speeds, a picture could be taken before children – Rosa in this case – began to cry. Not that she looks remotely tearful.'

'It takes my mum ages to take a photo with a mobile phone,' Stella murmured. Suzie insisted on using a selfie stick even when a stranger had offered to step in.'

'Your mum is a one-off.' Jack loved Stella's mum. Stella did too, but it was a love mixed with ambivalence. Her mother's anger towards Terry had influenced Stella to think him a bad father. He had been an attentive dad with a demanding job.

'...tantamount to obliteration,' Jack was saying. 'Rosa and Stevie's mother is also missing from her husband's headstone. Strange, don't you think?'

Stella did think it strange. She had resented her mother for the barrage of criticism Suzie had levelled at Terry in Stella's presence over the years. Resentment that sometimes became anger. Time had mellowed Stella's feelings towards her mum and her dad. But some offspring got so angry with their parents it drove them to murder.

Was it the body of Stevie and Rosa's mother in the pillbox?

Chapter Fifteen

November 1940

'May God punish you and send you to Hell.'

'Ouch, *ow*. You don't know noth—'

'What is going on here?' Adelaide heard the shouting as she rounded the buttress of the church. Further down the grassy slope of the graveyard two figures struggled. She grasped the scene in moments. *'Leave him alone.* Get your hands off.'

The curate met her gaze and slowly – too slowly – let go of Jimmy's ear. He made a washing motion with his hands as if to clean off dirt. All the time he continued to look at Adelaide.

'What did I just say?' Adelaide pulled Jimmy free of Michael Snace.

Every single flower that she and the girls – with Henry's help – had planted had been ripped from the grave and strewn about on the grass. She let out a gasp. 'What has happened?'

'Need you ask?' Snace sneered.

Rupert's grave looked as if a tractor had ploughed through it. Clods of soil still with grass attached, like ripped scalps of hair. Now Adelaide saw that the headstone itself, erected with ceremony last week, was smeared with mud, Rupert's name obliterated.

'Who would do this?' Adelaide cleared her throat.

'Are you seriously asking?' Snace's face was red, his skin smooth as a mask. 'He did. I caught him red-handed. Once a hooligan always a hooligan. I won't forget this.'

'I was tidying it.' Jimmy wiped his sleeve across his mouth. 'You saw me doing that.'

'Do not answer back.' Snace spoke without feeling. The effect made Adelaide go cold.

'Were you perhaps tending the grave?' Adelaide fought her way through the fog.

'Yes,' Jimmy said.

'He's making a fool out of you, Adelaide,' Snace hissed at her.

'It was me.'

Everyone turned to the voice.

Henry came up the path from Church Lane. Fleetingly, Adelaide thought two things: Henry had seen them from his bedroom window; and that meant he was lying to protect Jimmy.

Ever since she had watched the convoy of London buses roll up to the pub last year and seen Henry climb down from the last bus, Adelaide had felt a connection with the boy. Lost, socks pulled up, shirt tucked in and his hair combed. With no one to look after him, Henry had looked after himself. People talked about love at first sight after giving birth or meeting their sweethearts, but Adelaide had had the feeling about Henry. Ever since then she had treated him like a son.

'Did what?' Snace looked suddenly triumphant. 'You and your friend need to get your stories straight.'

'Messed it up, smashed the flowers.'

Why had the grave needed tidying up? Adelaide saw Jimmy's warning look to Henry, who couldn't know what Jimmy had told them. It had been vandalised. Why would Jimmy do that? Or Henry?

'I had a fit of temper—' Henry began.

'I find that extremely unlikely,' Adelaide told him. Henry had the patience of a saint. Rupert had been concerned that having evacuees in the house would taint his daughters with their accents and 'grubby language'. If he had been alive, he would have been proved wrong. *Until now…*

'It was me,' Jimmy said. 'It was all me.'

'I don't care who it was,' Adelaide said. 'Mr Snace, would you leave us please. The boys and I will clear up this mess and then we will forget it ever happened.'

'If Captain Stride were here—' Snace fixed her with his stony gaze.

'Yes, well, he's not, is he?' Adelaide snapped. 'As I said, I will deal with this.'

'They are under my auspices, this is a quasi-military matter, if two of my men—'

'They are not men. Yet. That you have recruited them into your little platoon has no bearing on this… business. It is a private matter. Please go.' Adelaide rarely played the imperious 'class' card, but she didn't hesitate to do so now.

An hour later, it was as if nothing had happened to the grave. The headstone gleamed. Alone, at last, Adelaide looked up at the wintry sky. A single seagull wheeled above the church spire.

Neither boy had convinced her that he was telling the truth. It made sense that, good friends, they had sought to take the blame off the other. Yet Adelaide felt something about this didn't ring true. No amount of quizzing Henry after Jimmy had gone home made her any the wiser. She was sure that there was something Henry was not telling her, but whatever he was keeping secret, it seemed that he had no intention of giving it up.

'Where's Henry and Jimmy?' Although at their end of the village the siren was barely audible and certainly not deafening, Adelaide, ushering the girls into the Anderson shelter, caught herself shouting.

'Don't you worry, they'll be in that pillbox with the Home Guard.' Pat Jordan, caught by the siren when visiting Adelaide, settled herself on the opposite bench, by the entrance. 'Snace'll have them bang to rights for what they did.'

'You heard.' Adelaide hugged Stevie close.

'Rum do, ask me. I've known young Jimmy since he was a baby, it's right out of character for him to do that.'

'Henry, too.'

'What's happened?' Stevie drew away from Adelaide.

'Nothing, chickee, only boys being boys.' Pat shook her head. 'Look at baby Rosa, as if she ain't a care in the world, bless her.'

After Rosa's nanny had left to earn twice as much in a munitions factory, Adelaide had become reliant on Stevie to look after her little sister. Now, gifted with Rupert's fearlessness, two-year-old Rosa was by turns reaching down to grab one of the wooden bench slats or trying to pull Adelaide's hair.

'Are Jimmy and Henry in trouble?' Stevie asked Adelaide.

'Home Guard business, that's all,' Adelaide whispered in Stevie's ear. At all costs she did not want her to know what had happened to Rupert's grave.

'Nothing to worry about, ducky,' Pat Jordan shouted over the churn of engines above their heads. *What would she do without Pat?* Since Rupert's death, she had become a true friend.

The Anderson shelter, set between the Home Guard defence pillbox and the house, was Rupert's legacy. Improving on the basic kit, he had hired men from Salmon's farm to dig it deeper than the guidelines said and put in a concrete floor. Rupert himself had raised the benches which doubled as beds. Even in heavy rain, unlike other Andersons in the village, theirs remained dry. Rupert had warned Adelaide that the curving corrugated iron wouldn't stop a direct hit. For that Adelaide relied on superstition. *It would not be today.*

Crushed by the terrible roar above, Adelaide hoped the pilots were as scared as she was. *Please God make them die.*

Adelaide drew Stevie close against her body, Stevie thrilled with fear as if with an electric current. She wanted to stop this childhood from haunting her daughters' lives. But perhaps a baby that gurgled happily at the sound of German bombers would let life ripple over her.

Pat Jordan was saying a prayer. Adelaide had received all she could hope for from Him. While for so many the last year had been a nightmare, she had found a new kind of peace.

'God bless you, Adelaide.' Pat touched Adelaide's hand. Perhaps He had listened to Pat, because Adelaide became aware of the whistle for all-clear. She ducked out of the shelter into the sunshine.

'I didn't say when we were in there, but did you hear that lovely Alvar Liddell on the news this morning?' Pat put a hand on Adelaide's arm. 'He said they've found the missing girl, Greta Fleming.'

'Alive?'

'No. The blighter had hidden her in scrub on Esher Common. How the police missed her, beats me.'

'I see.' Adelaide looked down towards the bottom of the garden. Snace was leading his patrol out of the pillbox to the footpath that ran behind the garden up to the village pond.

'Not that she'd have been alive if they'd found her sooner, he'd strangled her.' Pat was bitter. 'Makes you think, doesn't it.'

What did it make her think?

Although the sun was out and it was warm for November, Adelaide felt as cold as ice. It made her think that if she could find Greta's killer, she would strangle him with her bare hands.

Chapter Sixteen

Present Day

From the oak tree at the bottom of the garden, a pigeon trilled against the background hum of traffic on the A259 coast road. As if a vestige of the setting sun, the pillbox was luminous pink. Stripped of its thorny protection, it was revealed as a squat hexagonal structure.

'Now they've beaten down that old footpath it won't be long before it's smothered in graffiti and littered with poo-bags and syringes,' Jack observed gloomily.

'It's on private property.' Stella took a sip of wine, soothed by the mellow liquid.

They sat on the old garden furniture on the patio outside the drawing room. Behind them, through closed French windows, shut against insects as it grew darker, the room with one light glowing had gained a cosy aspect that it lacked in the day.

Stella wasn't a great drinker, but tonight, with the children finally asleep and the police gone, she was relishing the Merlot. It had been a day from hell. Instead of battling with Piaget's theories on parenthood, Stella should have been putting it into practice and noticing the children had gone missing, that they were finding a skeleton. It was possible that their landladies were killers. Even if they weren't, they now knew there had been a body in their garden for a lot of the time they had lived there and likely knew the murderer and the victim.

'What worries me the most about today is that Milly and Justin – Milly really – kept the skeleton secret from us,' Stella voiced her next thought.

'It was a one-off, it's not every day they find skeletons.'

'Seriously? Honestly, Jack, all the more reason to have told us. How many children do you know who would hide that from their parents?' Piaget had nothing to say about secrecy. Stella suspected that the children Piaget had encountered were less interesting than Milly or Justin. 'And yesterday they didn't tell Bella they were at your mother's grave either.'

'...so, shall we?' Jack was looking at her.

'Shall we what?' she snapped.

'Call Toni Kemp tomorrow for an update?'

'Were you even listening?'

'Yes, but it's OK. They would have told us eventually.'

'Milly gets that from you,' Stella huffed. 'You didn't want to tell the police either.'

'Let's not fight.' Jack could be annoyingly reasonable. Especially after having been incredibly unreasonable. 'We found the skeleton on our property. We have a right to know.'

'You know the police don't tell the public stuff, not even relatives of victims.' Wine, a warm summer night, the scent of threshed corn wafting on the air was putting the skeleton into some kind of perspective. 'This isn't our property. If it was, we don't have the right to know.' After a childhood of trying to block out her parents' rows, Stella had always shunned conflict, but since arriving yesterday, she was going for it, sleeves rolled up. She quite liked her new self.

'Not to mention you and I didn't find the body, it was your seven-year-old twins. Best we keep our heads down and act like we're normal.'

'We are normal.'

There was no answer to that.

'We can't act like it didn't happen.' Jack poured himself another glass of wine. When he tilted the bottle at Stella, she covered her glass. Faced with a murder in their midst, she wanted a clear head to think.

'Stella, you and I are the perfect team. We are wasted lolling about by the sea. Let's do an investigation of our own.' Jack nursed his glass. 'I think the Stride sisters have something to do with it, and so, I bet, does Toni Kemp.'

'We have no evidence for that.'

'Ah, so you think so too.' Jack pointed at her.

'It's crossed my mind.' So much for a clear head, Stella reached for the bottle on the flags at their feet and poured herself a glass.

'Rosa told us they had both lived in Yew Tree House since birth. We don't need a bones expert to know that woman was murdered nearly eighty years ago. Going by the hidden-mother photo in the dining room, which was taken in 1939, Stevie was about eighteen when the war ended, and Rosa was a baby, which makes her about seven. Same as the twins now. Stevie at least was old enough to know something. How can they *not* have known the body was there? It could be why they've never moved. If they did, the body would be discovered.'

'We both have to resist jumping to conclusions.' They were both out of practice at detection. A state of affairs that, until that afternoon, Stella had been happy to continue. It was a good while since she had asked herself what her father would do if he was her. He would definitely have wanted her to call the police. Yet he had tried to call Stella on the last day of his life for help with Kate Rokesmith's murder. Terry Darnell would not want her to sit on her hands.

Jack's phone rang.

'Bella,' he mouthed.

While Bella had accepted Stella would be in her children's lives, she wouldn't like her listening to Jack's side of their conversation. Stella was getting up to have a nose at the pillbox when she caught what Jack was saying.

'...they're fine. It's no biggie, if anything they're excited to have their own murder—

'No, we are not investigating it, credit me with some sense, Bella. It's a matter for the police. You seem to forget they're my kids too, I would never— Oh seriously? This is an excuse, you never wanted them to come away— Don't hang— *Bella.*' Jack snatched the phone from his ear and looked at the screen. 'She's hung up.'

'She knows then?' Stella stated the obvious.

'It's in the *Evening Standard*. She's spitting feathers that I didn't tell her.'

'You would have, it's been hectic.' Stupidly, it hadn't occurred to her the murder would have made the news. Stella could spin it however she liked, but it still ended with the fact that they should have told Bella.

'She's taking them home tomorrow.'

'Did you explain that the body was only a skeleton, not a decomposed corpse?' *Idiot.* How was a skeleton less upsetting? A woman had still been brutally murdered.

'She hung up on me,' Jack fumed.

'We don't know they're OK, they could still have nightmares about it. Justin hates Hallowe'en, doesn't he?' Stella knew that nothing Jack could have told Bella would have changed her mind. Her children had discovered the body of a murder victim, she had to clap eyes on them.

'Justin hates masks and pumpkins and screams, not skeletons per se,' Jack said. 'We'll head out early tomorrow so she'll find the house empty and have to leave.'

'Jack, we *cannot* do that. It would be cruel, never mind you'd be risking custody rights,' Stella said. 'Anyway, the house won't be empty, the police will be here. If she doesn't get an answer, Bella would try the annexe and Stevie will then tell her that before we found Justin and Milly with the skeleton, we were about to report them missing. Is that what you want?'

'She's spoiling our holiday.'

'The skeleton spoilt our holiday.' Absently Stella poured herself another glass. 'But even if Bella takes the kids, you and I can stay on.'

'You'd prefer that?' Jack rounded on her. 'We came here to see how you would get on with my children.'

'And we have been getting on fine.' Stella hurried to neutralise her careless remark. 'I just mean it could be a differently nice time.'

'I won't see the kids for weeks.'

'You didn't mind when it was Bella who wouldn't see them.'

Stella's fair-mindedness wasn't always timely so perhaps it was lucky that her words were drowned out by a terrific roar. Thinking it an aeroplane, Stella scoured the darkening sky. Above were only twinkling stars and a nearly full moon.

'It's from the lane.' Jack leapt up.

'It could be reporters.' *A helicopter.*

'An aeroplane is going to land right on us.' Milly pushed open the French windows, her bumblebee dressing gown like a cape behind her.

'It is *not*.' Stella forgot that a moment before that had been pretty much her own impression.

Clasping Milly's hand, Stella followed Jack around to the gate. Not a plane, an ocean liner, light blazing from the windows. *The Dieppe ferry.* Stella blinked. The noise was from a tractor. It was towing a gigantic camper van, interior lights blazing.

Silence.

The driver jumped out of his cab and detached a rope that had been towing the vast van. He gestured to the front of the cab where someone gave back a thumbs up. The driver climbed back into the tractor cab, gave a final wave, and the machine thundered off along Church Lane towards the field at the end.

'Where's Stanley?' Stella let go of Milly's hand and flew out of the gate.

'I've got him.' Justin stood at the front door in his pyjamas with Stanley in his arms.

'It must be TV,' Jack said to Stella.

'In which case we are sitting ducks.' Towing Milly, Stella was about to turn away when a door at the side of the van slid open. A figure clasping a bag and what Stella took for an umbrella – a cut-out Mary Poppins – stood in the lit interior. A voice called out, words lost in the receding engine roar. Corncrake cackle, yellow hi-vis jacket and trousers, a marigold yellow bucket hat tipped over one eye.

'...Jackanory, Sherlock... bezzie mates... had to be at Ground Zero... and I have to read about Arsenic and Old Lace in the effing paper.

'I ignored a stupid sign that said not to go down that lane that runs into yours and got wedged. I'll need a new skirt.'

'You're not wearing a skirt,' Jack said.

'Not mine, Prunella's.' Lucie flapped a hand. 'That nice Farmer Salmon rescued me.'

Never had Stella been so pleased to see Lucie May.

Chapter Seventeen

Present Day

Stella slipped out of the gate and around Lucie's gigantic motorhome – she had ticked Stella off for calling it a camper van. Thankfully the blinds were down. At half past six in the morning after a late night, even Lucie would not be awake.

Stella opened the gate in the low flint wall and stepped into the churchyard.

She had chosen to leave the house and come to Kate Rokesmith's grave to be sure that, were Jack to glance out of the window or the twins to come downstairs and look out, they would not see her there. Stella wasn't a believer in ghosts, yet she hoped for tacit support from Jack's mother for her plan.

The one person who would be up and soon heading along the M23 towards them was Bella to fetch home her twins. Stella had resolved to head Bella off at the proverbial pass. It was the least she could do for Jack and, indeed, for herself. Yew Tree House would not be the same without Justin and Milly.

Already the sun was becoming hot and Stella was grateful to see that Kate's bench was partially shaded by the oak tree. From somewhere in the branches came a blackbird's song so loud it might have been electronically produced.

In the field beyond, giant cylindrical bales lay dotted amidst the stubble. With dull shock, Stella saw that the wall had been mended. Ten years ago, literally following in Terry Darnell's footsteps, she had found his lens cap behind the flint wall. Proof that he had been there – later she had developed what was one of the last photographs Terry had taken – and that she was on the right track. Bishopstone was full of memories. Now there would be more. Stella wiped a hand down her face and dialled Bella's number.

It rang. Once. Twice. Three times. Click. *Nothing*. Then Bella spoke.

'It's too late to change—'

'That's not why I've rung,' Stella said.

'They're not up yet,' Jack told Bella when she walked into the kitchen ahead of Stella.

'I'll wake them, it will be a *fantastic* surprise.' Bella, a botanical illustrator who worked in black ink on white parchment, dressed like her drawings. Today she wore her trademark man's shirt over a long black skirt, dyed black hair in an untidy bun.

'You know Milly hates surprises.' Jack was munching on a slice of toast. Yesterday evening, as well as wine, he had drunk two of Lucie's nippets – double gin with what she called shadow tonic. Not a drinker, Stella had expected Jack to feel wretched now, but the only state he was in was fury.

'Jack, I've talked with Bella.'

'Stella and Bella, great double act.' Jack waved the toast.

'If you're going to be like that...' Bella examined Rosa's now wilting flowers, perhaps thinking to draw one.

'Why don't you go up and wake them, they'll be very pleased to see you,' Stella said. 'They have missed you.'

'What was that about?' Jack demanded after Bella had gone upstairs. 'I thought we were back working together as a team then you ring my ex?'

'Bella has agreed not to take the children.'

'So why is she here?'

'I rang to make a suggestion to her, but she was just pulling up in Church Lane. We met on your mum's bench.' As if that would mollify.

'Typical.'

'Give her a break, Jack, we'd be the same if the roles were reversed. She's worried. It's only three days,' Stella said.

'What is three days?'

'I invited Bella to stay and she accepted. She has a meeting back in London in three days.'

'Three whole days?'

'What would you prefer – Bella takes the kids now or she stays and then leaves them with us?'

'Incredible, you are so generous,' Jack conceded. 'But still this is meant to be —'

'It's a *fantastic surprise*.' Justin flew into the kitchen, jigging around them.

'Yes, popsicle, *Mummy* is here.' Stella's news had made Jack magnanimous.

'No.' Justin paused for breath. 'Not that. There's people, all outside and shouting to come in.'

Stella marvelled how, in three days, she had grown used to both Lucie May and Bella Markham staying with them. At Milly's suggestion Bella had cancelled her meeting and booked herself more holiday. In the past Stella would have minded this, but Bella's company was growing on her. Ensconced in Prunella the Motorhome, Lucie wasn't literally staying with them. She had invited Bella to sleep in her motorhome. Not the sacrifice of comfort suggested by a camper van. The motorhome had a double bedroom and another bed in the front where, up late working on her story, Lucie would sleep. The twins had piled in there too, leaving Jack and Stella with Yew Tree House to themselves. Stella was surprised to find that she missed the children not being upstairs in their bedroom. Jack, on the other hand, welcomed their privacy.

What had been difficult was the posse of reporters, bristling with microphones and lenses, that had been camped at the end of Church Lane, milling around the graveyard and sitting on Kate Rokesmith's bench. Thankfully, Prunella the Motorhome blocked a view of Yew Tree House.

Whenever anyone emerged from the house or Prunella, they were hit with a barrage of questions about what it was like to find the skeleton. A photographer had sneaked down the back footpath and taken shots from inside the pillbox. After that, Lucie bought a coil of fearsome barbed wire from the hardware store, which Bella promptly took back. It was better to have trespassers than a lacerated child. However, by the second day, with only the news that the skeleton was not a woman called Mary (and never had been) but a nameless man, possibly homeless, the story was overtaken by other events. Now the only reporter still camped outside was Lucie.

Stella did appreciate that Bella was now in charge of the twins. Bella and Jack were united parents in keeping Milly in particular on a tight rein. Especially after Lucie had caught a man reaching over the gate to give Milly a clutch of fivers for her story. 'Disgusting, bribing kiddie-winks,' Lucie, no stranger to paying for a story, had admonished him.

Stella did not relinquish Piaget; she might be temporarily off duty but it was all grist to the mill. Not least for when Bella inevitably found out that Jack had told them about their grandmother being murdered.

It was now nearly midday and, at Stella's suggestion, Jack was going to the beach with Bella and the children. Stella wanted time alone with her cleaning kit. It would stop Jack pestering her to call Toni Kemp. The police had been back and although Stella had spotted Kemp warding off reporter's questions at the gate, Toni hadn't come to see her or Jack. With Lucie May here, Stella imagined that Toni, like any detective, did not appreciate being ambushed by a reporter.

When she refused Milly's request to take Stanley with them, Stella got full understanding of how Bella had felt faced with a month away from the twins. Absurd, Stanley would be gone only hours, but given all that had happened, Stella wanted him where she could see him. Risking Milly's wrath, Stella said that Stanley could not go to the beach. What if Jack, taken up with defending their graveyard visit, took his eyes off Milly when she was minding Stanley? It wouldn't be the first time the poodle slipped his lead and wandered off.

She held Stanley in her arms, and they both watched the family head down Church Lane from the landing window.

'You sure you don't want to go too?' Lucie appeared beside her.

'Quite sure.'

'That's my girl.' Lucie patted her shoulder. 'Bet you'd rather come into the village with me and meet some locals.'

'You're all right, I'll stay here.' Stella did not want to meet anyone from the village in the company of Lucie May. Watching the reporter wheedle her way into their confidence would be like pulling teeth.

Stella had put the kettle on and was ferreting about for teabags when there was a rap on the window.

'Stella Darnell.' Detective Inspector Kemp, her face pressed to the glass, gesticulated at the mug on the counter. 'Can you make one for me?'

Stella opened the back door and then took a mug from the draining board.

'You didn't say you were *the* Stella Darnell.' Inspector Kemp wandered into the kitchen, touching surfaces and peering about. She was casual in jeans and shirt, sunglasses pushed up her fringe into a plume. Puffing out her cheeks, she planted herself at the deal table.

'I didn't know I was. There must be lots.'

'The Detective's Daughter? Dash of milk, no sugar, thanks, mate.' *Mate.* Toni Kemp rested against the kitchen table. 'You've got a rep. I read about that murder in some cathedral a while back, never made the connection.'

'Tewkesbury Abbey,' Stella murmured. 'I just happened to be there.'

'And you just *happen* to be here.' Kemp pulled a chocolate bar – *another Snickers* – from her shirt pocket. 'Want one? I've got two.'

'No thanks.'

'I didn't steal it.' Kemp widened her eyes and laughed as if it was a joke.

'I'm sure you didn't. OK, thanks.' Stella looked for a knife to cut the chocolate. Cutlery in Yew Tree House was haphazard, plenty of forks and spoons, but no knives. They'd resorted to plastic picnic cutlery from the Co-op, but the knives wouldn't do for chopping. So far, they'd eaten takeaways, but Stella was working up to cooking something healthy. She'd need a knife then.

'Martin Cashman says your pa was the business, that they broke the mould after him. God knows, the Met was lucky to have a decent bloke.' The detective sliced across the chocolate bar and handed the wrapper end to Stella. 'Martin is one of the few good apples in the Met. I couldn't leave fast enough.'

'For that reason, maybe it's a shame you didn't stay,' Stella said. 'Martin was my dad's best friend.' Stella remembered Cashman's response to her as less complimentary. *What was Toni Kemp leading up to?*

Dislodging a wad of chocolate from the roof of her mouth, Stella invited Toni to come with her along the passage to the drawing room. She took an end of the sofa thinking Kemp would take the other, but she chose the fireside chair that faced Stella. It was upright and higher and put her at an advantage. Stella was now sure that Toni hadn't come for a Martin and Terry praise-fest.

'I worked for Cashman as a CID rookie at Putney, I owe him. He rang out of the blue and gave me the gen on you. Said he let you in on his Kew Gardens case and you were gold. I've been digging and found that you used to run a detective agency coupled with cleaning. Kind of garlic to a vampire for us lot.' Kemp finished her Snickers. 'Martin said if you'd joined the Met like your dad wanted, they wouldn't be in such a mess.'

'That's debatable.' Nevertheless, Stella felt pleased by the comment.

'I have to ask again.' Kemp leaned forward. 'Did you know there was a murder victim in the garden when you hired this house for your holiday? Is that why you're here? To solve it?'

'No!' Stella coughed. 'Clean Slate just does cleaning now, as we said before. We had no idea about the body. Nor, I think, did Jack.'

'You think?'

'I *know*. Jack chose it because his mother is buried here and he wanted to show her grave to his children.' *Hardly better.*

'Different than because the beaches are lovely and there's lovely restaurants, I suppose.' Kemp smirked. 'So, the skeleton was a happy coincidence?'

'Hardly happy.'

'For me, I meant.'

'I don't see...'

'Like Martin and no doubt your dad, I'm strictly by the book. Rules offer opportunities not restrictions. But Martin did say I might capitalise on you being here. He said you might be OK if I run things by you now and then. Informally, as it were.'

'What about Sergeant Lane?'

'You would be a bonus not a substitute. Never mind that you're staying at Ground Zero.'

'I'm not usually alone.' A flood of excitement made Stella wary. She knew suddenly that helping Kemp was just what she wanted. But not without Jack. *Never mind Lucie.* They had always been a team.

'Where are the stepkids? Have you lost them again?' Toni let out a laugh.

'Not funny.' Stella balled her chocolate wrapper into a pellet and rolled it between a thumb and forefinger.

'Yeah, no, sorry. That was rude.' Toni pulled a face. 'Thinking more of me, I guess. I'd have trouble with one child, but two...'

'I noticed you were wary of Milly.'

'Do you blame me? What a girl.' Toni drained her mug. 'She would run rings round my boss.'

'They're at the beach with their mum and dad.' Stella returned to Toni's question. With a shock she admitted she was enjoying chatting with no one to interrupt. Could she really live with the twins racketing about, even on a part-time basis? She shoved the thought to the back of her mind. 'My dad's... er... ex-girlfriend, Lucie May, is here. Lucie's a crime reporter for a west London paper. She's in that RV outside.'

'O-kay, yes, I know of Ms May.' Toni nodded. 'Will you tell her what we talk about?'

'I won't say we've talked at all.'

'No problem then.'

'But I want to tell Jack, we're kind of a team.'

'Would he tell anyone?'

'No.'

'Let's do it.' Toni slapped her knees. 'First off, we've tracked our skeleton.'

'You've found out who she was?'

'He. The body is a man, thought you knew that, and no, we haven't.'

Stella realised that she had thought the skeleton was a woman because – as with all her toys – Milly had decreed it female.

'The big news is DNA. We have a match.'

'You've ID'd Mary— him?'

'Not your skeleton, although, through partial DNA from bones, we can date his death to around the mid-forties. Otherwise, nada. What we have got is good, though. Strictly hush-hush, we

THE MYSTERY OF YEW TREE HOUSE

haven't told her family yet.' Toni shot a glance at the French windows. 'The Lady in the Van must *not* know.'

'Lucie won't hear it from me.' Knowing Lucie's uncanny ability to snout out information, Stella had little doubt that Lucie would be ignorant for long. 'I don't see how I can help.'

'Like I said, you're staying on the spot with Stevie and Rosa Stride right next door. We've talked to them, but got nothing. I think Rosa, the younger sister, is genuinely ignorant. But I'm not so sure about Stevie. Could you invent a reason for a chat, maybe a leaky tap or borrow a tin opener, whatever, and get her talking?'

'I can try, but she never wanted us here so she's hardly likely to want to pass the time of day with me,' Stella said. 'Wait, you said *her* family. You said the skeleton is a man?'

'He is. I'm talking about the victim.' Toni produced another Snickers. She waved it at Stella. 'Halves? Seems I had three.' As if it was usual to carry three bars of chocolate.

'It seems your pillbox murder victim was a murderer himself.'

Chapter Eighteen

Shop Girl Found Slain

Police say there is still no clue as to who murdered a young bakery assistant missing since August. Tremendous violence caused the death of sixteen-year-old Greta Fleming, who was found on Esher Common. Her clothes were disarranged and ripped and bore signs of the most brutal handling...

'Greta was the apple of our eye,' said her mother, Mrs Enid Fleming. 'She's left a gaping hole in our lives.'

Greta's older brother, Philip, is stationed at Newhaven in Sussex where the Royal Engineers have been shoring up coastal defences. Captain Alexander said, 'Private Fleming is devastated by this news. He loved his sister dearly.'

This is a terrible reminder to mothers and fathers all over the country that Hitler and his cronies are not our only enemies. For every family, but the Fleming family in particular, this is the worst possible ending to a story which has kept readers gripped for months...

On their way back to Yew Tree House from Newhaven, the swing bridge had opened and now they were stopped in a queue of traffic, engine off, while they waited for it to reopen. Not great at reading in a moving vehicle, Stella had taken advantage of the forced stop to read out an article she had found on the murder of a girl in Surrey nearly eighty years ago.

'I agree with your Toni Kemp – the brother took revenge on his sister's killer.' Jack tapped the steering wheel.

'She didn't absolutely say it was Philip Fleming, it's only that he was stationed here at the time that Greta was murdered in Surrey. It's a clear link to Bishopstone where her killer has just been found.'

'Her killer can't have been in the pillbox when Fleming was stationed here. Greta was found in November 1940, and at that time the pillbox was occupied by the Home Guard.' Jack frowned.

Stanley, strapped into the back, emitted a low growl.

'He agrees with me.' Jack grinned.

'As it says here, the Royal Engineers built the pillboxes, meaning Philip Fleming knew about the one at Yew Tree House. He could have come back after it was abandoned. Toni and her team are relying on circumstantial evidence, and obviously Fleming had a motive. This man – aka the skeleton – murdered his sister in 1940. If Philip knew who had killed Greta, he might have lured him to the pillbox and killed him.' Stella caught the echo. 'And she's not *my* Toni Kemp. Martin suggested she talk to me, that's all.'

'Martin effing Cashman.' Jack wrinkled his nose.

Stella and Martin Cashman had once had a brief relationship. Cashman had been separated from his wife and Stella single. Soon afterwards Cashman had considered Jack a murder suspect. When Jack had heard that Toni had visited Stella at Martin's suggestion, he had been miffed.

'Are you sure Kemp said you could tell me?'

'Positive. We just mustn't tell Lucie.'

Their reason for going to Newhaven had been to see the police. Events had begun the evening before when Milly, having waggled out a front tooth, had raced to bed to await the Tooth Fairy. This had been something of a relief because it had diverted her from insisting she and Justin arrest Father Christmas. When Jack had tried to get her to explain, Milly had ostentatiously clammed up. When Milly had finally dropped off, as she was sliding a twenty-pence piece under the pillow, Bella pricked her finger on something sharp. Feeling about carefully, Jack had retrieved a badge, the pin open. Fashioned in metal, the royal crown at the top, the letters ARP were beneath. These, Lucie informed them, stood for Air Raid Precautions and must, she insisted, belong to the murderer. Lucie need proof to launch a story.

Quizzed over breakfast, Milly would only say that 'twenty pence was *rubbish* for a big tooth'. It was Justin who had told them that they'd found the badge in the pillbox. When Milly was told it must be given to the nice detective, she had stormed out. Jack made it outside in time to see her clambering into Lucie's motorhome.

When Bella had gone to say that she and Justin were going to visit Eastbourne pier, she returned with the information that Milly would only go if they would see a person drown.

'*Care to explain, Jack?*'

Jack had related the thankfully anodyne story. So far, he had not had to explain watering Kate Rokesmith's grave. Stella knew that the holiday still hung by a thread.

Stella and Jack had taken the badge to the police station in Newhaven. They had to see Toni and perhaps learn more about Pillbox Man, as the papers were calling him. However, the DC who met them, Sheena Britton, informed them Kemp was busy and ticked them off for withholding evidence. Just as Stella was deciding if it was best not to say that it was Milly who had withheld the badge in case it reminded Britton that the twins had wandered off in the first place, Jack had told her.

'*You got off lightly, my nephew expects a couple of quid for a tooth. So would I.*'

'She was so young,' Stella said now. She showed Jack the pixelated photo of Greta Fleming on her phone. The article, dated 30 November 1940, was captioned, *The World Was Her Oyster*. 'Had Greta Fleming lived more than only fifteen years, she would be in her nineties now.'

'He may have known about the pillbox, but it was in the Strides' garden. They could have found the body any time afterwards. Fleming would have been as much a suspect then as now,' Jack mused. 'Rosa would still have been a child when the man was murdered; it might have occurred to her that it was the perfect den. Milly wants to make one in there now, it's only the police Do Not Cross tape that deters her. Why not dump the body at sea? If it didn't sink, it might have drifted along the coast.'

'Fleming was stationed in Newhaven when *Greta* was murdered, not when someone murdered the man in the pillbox,' Stella reminded Jack. 'If it was him nearly five years later, he'd have had to have done it when on leave from fighting in France. I think fixing on Greta's brother as the killer is clutching at a flimsy straw. I did suggest to Toni it might be Greta and Philip's father. Or someone else entirely.'

'Bet you driving a truck through her key suspect was more than welcome.' Jack was watching a tanker laden with aggregate following a pilot boat to the harbour mouth. Not having become a civil engineer like his father, Jack had been transfixed by the Newhaven bridge opening. 'Whoever hid the man there chose well. Our kids found it some seventy-odd years afterwards.'

Our kids.

'I'm glad whoever did it paid the price.' As the tanker passed, Jack turned the engine back on. 'Greta's killer deserved to die. He stands for all those murderers of women in the war who got away with it.'

'In those days her murderer would have been hanged.' A police officer's daughter, Stella could never justify murder, state or otherwise. Capital punishment had not deterred men from killing women, and life imprisonment, going on year after year, was punitive. If it meant life, Stella held little store in rehabilitation. Jack had been prepared to kill his mother's murderer himself. She wouldn't have wanted him punished.

'Perhaps Greta was killed by her boyfriend.'

'There's no evidence that she had one.' Swishing around Google Chrome, Stella found another picture of Greta. Taken outside the Flemings' home in Esher, the small terraced house reminded her of her dad's childhood home. Hands clasping each side of the door frame, head to one side, Greta was grinning into bright sunshine. The image was slightly blurred so Stella couldn't properly make out her features, but it told her more about the dead girl than the studio portrait that had been commonly used. It was easy to see that, as Greta's mother, Enid, was quoted saying, 'Greta was the life and soul in our family.'

'Good clean girl with no men-friends.' Jack repeated a quote from another newspaper piece they had found. 'Instant alarm bells. Perhaps she was having a secret liaison and Philip found out. If he suspected the man, that's a motive.'

They had sat up late in bed last night doing a trawl of the press archives on their phones. Stella was saddened that Enid Fleming had described Greta as her best friend. Did that mean neither of them had other friends? She doubted that her own mother, Suzie, would call Stella her best friend.

'If Philip Fleming knew who killed his sister, why not tell the police?' Stella always saw the police as first resort.

'To avenge Greta's murder? You stopped me killing my mother's murderer.' Jack added, almost to himself, 'Part of me wishes I had.'

'No, you don't,' Stella snapped. Jack would never get over being unable to save his mother. Stella got that. If she had given her dad her new mobile number, he would have reached her in those last days of his life and things might have been different. Whoever it was that sang about regretting nothing was kidding themselves. 'Would Fleming put revenge above their parents never knowing who killed their daughter?'

They returned to Yew Tree House through the churchyard. As they passed Captain Stride's grave, Stella noticed a bunch of flowers in the galvanised container. Ragged and wild, they were identical to the bouquet Rosa had given them when they arrived.

'Looks like Rosa and Stevie do remember their parents.'

'Father.' Jack was reading the headstone again.

'Odd, isn't it, that they're not buried together. The lettering is spaced to leave room for their mother, but she's not there.' Stella recalled her earlier thought.

'She probably is buried there, it's that the sisters never got around to adding her name. It's not cheap and they do seem short of money,' Jack hazarded. 'I guess there comes a point when it doesn't feel worth it if you're not far from death yourself.'

This idea silenced them both. Above them a light aircraft droned across the blue sky. As if shadowing it, and rendered the same size by the height difference, a buzzard flew past. Jack and Stella watched it until it wheeled out of sight behind the church spire.

'That badge Milly found might be a clue.' Stella returned to the reason they had gone into Newhaven.

'If it is, we'll get another ticking-off from Toni Kemp for Milly having snaffled it from the crime scene. *Whoa.*'

Diamonds are forever… The Shirley Bassey ringtone signalled Lucie. Jack read out the text.

Come to Prunella. Now.

Proving he could understand English, Stanley set off at such a scamper his lead slipped through Stella's fingers and streamed after him. Jack and Stella gave chase out of the churchyard and along Church Lane. The police had removed the outer cordon which had allowed Lucie to 'weigh anchor' in a shady corner of the car park.

★

'Hop in, strap up.' As soon as Jack, Stella and Stanley were strapped into seats that put Stella in mind of an aeroplane, Lucie started the engine and spun the steering wheel like a croupier.

'Where are we going?' Stella quelled the urge to ask to drive. Her secret childhood dream had been to drive the twenty-seven bus that ran along King Street in Hammersmith. Now, Lucie's motorhome would do.

'Ice cream by the sea, *yay!*' Lucie trilled out the window to an elderly man coming out of the lych-gate.

It was the Very Old Rector, Stella saw. What was his name? Snape? Snake? Snace.

'The beach?' Jack squawked. 'Let me out.'

'And me.' Stella was not in the mood for the seaside.

'Of course not, *you illuminated fools.*' Lucie accelerated up the road. 'That was to put that nosy parker off the scent.'

'That's the retired vicar.' Stella saw Jack's shoulders stiffen.

'Good that you did put him off the scent,' Jack murmured.

'He's a hundred and three, I think you could win an arm wrestle with him, Jackdaw.' Lucie cackled.

'Seriously, is he that old?' Stella had had a client aged a hundred. 'He must be the oldest man in Britain.'

'Not by a long chalk. Henry Allingham lived to a hundred and thirteen. Besides the oldest man never dies.'

'What?' Stella said.

'The king is dead, long live the king?' Jack muttered. 'Doesn't work with the Queen.'

'Oh yeah, I see. Very funny.'

'So three years over the century is young.' Lucie spun the wheel as they joined the A259. Stella gripped her seat belt. That Lucie was driving with supreme confidence was both reassuring and worrisome.

'Where are we going?' Stella forced the vicar and Lucie's vehicle handling out of her mind.

'To see an old friend.'

'What old friend?' Stella asked. She and Jack both knew that, apart from them, Lucie had no friends, old or otherwise.

'Our dead skeleton, as Milly – bless her – calls him, is a murderer.' Lucie glanced at the various mirrors and the TV-sized satnav map on the dashboard.

'How do you know?' It was Stella's turn to squawk.

'An intrepid crime reporter never reveals her sources.'

Stella didn't care how Lucie found out, she was only glad her promise to Toni not to tell Lucie had included the warning that Lucie might find out herself.

'Where does this old friend live?' Jack said.

'Esher.'

Chapter Nineteen

March 1945

The last years had passed in a blur of fundraising, getting Stevie through her matriculation exams, settling Rosa in at the village school and endless patrols with Mr Ridgeway and Mr Merry. Thankfully, the only injury to the ARP was Mrs Robertson's broken ankle when she was being a casualty during invasion practice in 1942. With Stevie turning into a splendidly capable young woman and Rosa a sparky seven-year-old, despite Greta Fleming's murder, Adelaide dared hope that her girls would survive the war unscathed.

As the bombings lessened and then, in a final hurrah, they were faced with the V1s and then the V2s, Adelaide found she appreciated what no longer felt like her new life. There had been no more damage to Rupert's grave and although she didn't believe that either Jimmy or Henry was responsible, she did wonder if they were protecting the person who did it. One of their friends, she guessed, although Rupert had been well loved so why desecrate his grave?

A lot of time had passed since then and Adelaide, with Rosa's help – Stevie was always too busy – kept the grave tended. If there was a blot in her landscape if was Snace. He had taken over all of the vicar's work and, to Pat's disgust, had moved in to live with the elderly man in the Rectory.

'Call me unfeeling, but the man's a chancer,' Pat said now when Adelaide came in to fetch her paper. Then, unexpectedly, since Adelaide had been in the shop chatting for ten minutes, 'It's lovely to see you, Adelaide.'

Adelaide turned towards Pat's horrified gaze. *Snace had entered the shop. How long had he been there?*

'They've printed the demob chart groups, I see.' Snace was hearty as he approached the counter. 'What group is your David in? He joined up in forty-three, didn't he?'

'Yes.' Pat reached behind her. 'Have you come for your cigarettes, Mr Snace?'

'Yes please.' Snace went on, 'Last in, last out seems to be what they're doing. Bit of a wait, but worth it I'm sure. You and Bert will be putting out the flag.'

'Of course.' Pat took the curate's coins. Crashing shut the till she handed him the change, which Snace immediately dropped into the orphanage collection box.

'Must be a hard time for you, Mrs Stride. Since your husband is *not* coming home.'

'I'm pleased for those men who are.' Adelaide snapped the stamps into her purse and turned to go.

'When would it have been? When was Captain Stride born, I think he was a little older than you?'

'I don't see—'

'Of course, it's on the headstone, 1898, and I know he joined up in January of 1940. Let me see…' The curate licked his finger and flicked through a copy of the *Daily Mail* on the counter. 'There we are, group fourteen. He would have been one of the first home. We shall make sure to pay you and your family due attention around the date.'

'Best not to dwell.' Pat Jordan took away the newspaper. 'Mrs Stride has much to look forward to.'

'Indeed, she has.' Snace rested his eyes on Adelaide for a moment then with a slight bow bid them good morning.

'You all right, Adelaide?' Pat Jordan asked. 'For a vicar, he's got the tact of an elephant. Better say nothing at all, my mother would say.'

'Rupert has been dead nearly five years. I find it easier every day.'

The women shared an arch look.

Snace was by the pond when Adelaide came out of the shop. She hurried past with her head down.

'Goodness, you are a hard woman to catch.' Snace appeared alongside her. 'I wondered if I might come back with you. I have something to ask.'

'The girls will be wanting lunch.' As if it were her enemy, the church clock began striking eleven.

'I just passed Stephanie with Rosa in the pushchair, she said they were going to the village hall.' Snace gave an exaggerated start as if this came as a perplexing surprise.

'I can't offer you a cup of tea. We've run out.' Opening the front door of Yew Tree House, Adelaide had no compunction about lying. Reluctantly she led Snace into the drawing room.

'I had one at the library with Miss Hall.' Snace made no pretence of believing her.

'Do sit.' Indicating Rupert's armchair, Adelaide took the sofa while Snace remained standing.

'I hope you won't take this amiss, Adelaide. After all this time I feel I can call you that. But over the five years since I came to Bishopstone, I have grown to respect you immensely. I would like to think it's mutual.'

'Stop, really, this is...' Adelaide struggled up. 'Mr Snace please don't say another word. I understand that last week you celebrated your twenty-fifth birthday. Do not make a fool of yourself. Or me.'

'A fool?' This seemed to cause Snace to baulk. 'War depletes the male population. Young men of prospect are a rarity and widowed ladies cannot afford to be—'

'Mrs Stride, I have... sorry, I didn't know you was busy.' Henry stood in the doorway.

'Henry, come in, come in.' Adelaide put out a hand. 'Mr Snace was just going.'

For a moment no one moved. Then came the sound of voices as Stevie and Rosa came into the room. Rosa rushed across to her mother and clasped her around the waist. Fleetingly, it occurred to Adelaide that Rosa often did this. As if she was relieved to find her mother unharmed. Maybe she wasn't unscathed after all.

'What's happening?' Stevie was on alert.

'Darling, would you see Mr Snace out.' Adelaide kissed the top of Rosa's head. The little girl looked more and more like Rupert every day. Even Pat Jordan had noticed it.

'May I dare correct you, Mrs Stride.' Snace left a pause which caused Adelaide to look up. His eyes were shiny as pebbles.

'I came to inform you.' Snace touched his cheek with a palm, the gesture with which Adelaide smoothed her own cheek with Pond's cream at her dressing table every evening.

'The bishop has seen fit to ask me to take over this parish. I am your new vicar. So, it is now Reverend Snace.'

Chapter Twenty

Present Day

The journey had taken two hours with a stop at the Cobham Services for the lavatory where they picked up the Big Macs and fries that Lucie had made Jack order in advance. Lucie had insisted there was no time to park and eat in the van.

'I don't want to be last.'

'Last?' Stella questioned.

'Late.'

Stella wasn't a fan of fast food but having missed breakfast with the fuss about the badge, she was ravenous. Never had a MacDonald's tasted so good.

Beyond saying that she had gone to school with the 'old friend' and what treat it was to have a 'luxury charabanc trip in Prunella with the gang', Lucie was unforthcoming. She'd put a stop to Jack's fishing attempts by singing along to Andy Williams' greatest hits on surround sound.

The luxurious motorhome – *'Prunella is not a camper van'* – put Stella in mind of the sort used by film stars on set. Seated high above everything except lorries, the panoramic curved windscreen gave the impression of an aeroplane cockpit. An illusion that, nestling into her sumptuous leather throne, Stella didn't want shattered. Despite Lucie and Andy watching the girls watching the boys, at some point she must have dropped off because she was awakened by the parking sensors going haywire as Lucie negotiated the van, a credit card space either side, through an entrance framed by laurel bushes. The sensors beeping, below her, Stella read a wooden sign that read 'Cosydene'. Another sign, unvarnished and written on cardboard attached to a cane, promised 'Honey for Sale'. Presumably a country thing. Jars and a battered tin money box were grouped on a camping table beneath an umbrella. It was one thing Lucie having a friend, but one who kept bees was pushing the bounds of plausibility. Glancing at Jack, seated behind Lucie, Stella saw he was thinking the same thing.

'Welcome to Ellesborough,' Lucie cackled. 'We're up the road from Chequers. Our prime minister's country seat.'

'I know what Chequers is,' Jack said. Less tuned into political news, Stella had needed the explanation.

Cosydene proved to be a nineteen-thirties, L-shaped building, the windows put in as if at random. As Lucie swept Prunella around a wide – thankfully – turning circle, Stella saw that alongside a hybrid Range Rover Evoque was a motor home of similar proportions.

'Geri has a free spirit. Like me.' Lucie narrowly missed a cartwheel that was leaning against the wall of a detached garage, the garish blue and red of the spokes suggesting it was ornamental. In keeping with the rustic aesthetic, two galvanised sheep troughs stood on brick plinths on each side of the front door.

'What's that about?' Jack pointed to the other end of the house where, dappled with sun, was a row of headstones. Slate, marble, black, white and speckled, lettering in gold and lead. 'Who in actual hell puts a cemetery on a suburban street?'

Before Lucie could answer – and Stella thought she looked as taken aback as Jack sounded and Stella felt – the air was split by a terrible scream. Rattled by the grave stones Stella took a moment to recognise the seagull's lament as Stanley's clarion call at the end of any journey. Too late she checked. 'Does this friend like dogs?'

'Loves them,' Lucie replied too promptly.

As they climbed down, Jack remarked that the horseshoe nailed over the door was the wrong way up.

'Their luck ran out aeons ago.' Lucie was enigmatic.

A woman in a pink tee, black jogging bottoms with pink piping and a pink zip jacket, emerged from the pitched tiled porch, arms outstretched in an apparently enthusiastic welcome.

'*Get off my property.* I'm calling the police.' She held up a phone in a pink case. 'Vultures! You are feeding off people's misery – as if this family hasn't suffered enough. Poor Greta would be turning in her grave.'

'Did she say Greta?' Jack turned to Stella.

Stella should have stuck to the facts. *Lucie didn't have friends.* 'I'm sorry—'

'You damn well will be. My husband will enjoy using his stupid gun. Believe me, he's a crack shot.'

'We're leaving, it's a misunderstanding.' Retreating to the van, Jack raised his hands as if he was at gunpoint. Which meant he let go of Stanley's lead.

Stanley raced past the woman, his lead – emblazoned with *Do Not Cross* whipping out behind him – and vanished into Cosydene.

Stella went to the door of the motorhome where Lucie was rummaging in her bag muttering, 'I've lost my effing pen. I had it—'

'*You tricked us,*' Stella barked at her. 'A friend, you said. We have come to the home of Greta's relatives.'

The next few moments were a blur of craziness. The woman pounced on Lucie. In the mayhem, Stella caught a flash of silver – *a blade.*

'Lucille *flaming* May. *God*, am I glad to see you.'

'Me you too, Popsicle,' Lucie crowed. The woman – the knife was a Pandora bracelet glinting with charms – hugged Lucie, rocking her back and forth like a baby. Lucie, who was usually horrified by hugging – in that sense Covid had worked for her – buried her face in the woman's neck and was mumbling something like, '*Love you, Gez,*' but surely she wasn't because Lucie wasn't that sort.

'I wonder if you'd mind if I...' With apologetic strides, Stella trotted into Cosydene. Stanley was lapping water from a dish on the floor holding the sort of plant that, Stella knew from clients, was supposed to replenish a room with oxygen. Panting, she berated herself: *bad owner* for forgetting to give Stanley a drink at the services.

'You should have rung and said you were coming.' Geri Gifford unpacked a tray of Emma Bridgewater crockery, the teapot decorated with the homily *There's No Place Like Home*, and gave them all hefty slices of fruit cake. Stella found herself deconstructing the well-worn words. Was there a place like home? Where was home?

Had she not known that Geri was Lucie's schoolfriend, Stella would have said she was in her early fifties. This must be down to the use of the gym visible through long windows in what Geri had referred to as her orangery.

'...to surprise you.' Seated in a white leather affair reminiscent of a seventies Elvis Presley, Lucie looked – *suspiciously* – beatific.

'Sure, you did, Doorstep Dorrie.' Geri Gifford gave a sniff as she folded into an 'S' bend chair that, designed to keep the back straight, Stella had always considered torture. 'Honestly, mate, if it wasn't you...'

'Better it *is* me.' Forever on an unnecessary slimming diet, Lucie dabbed a crumb and licked her finger.

'Better *what* is you?' Jack demanded.

Munching cake – Stella was all for Mr Kipling – she spotted a photograph in a silver frame in an alcove by the fireplace.

'Was Greta Fleming a relation?' A lump of Mr Kipling stuck in Stella's throat.

'Oh, OK, I get it.' Jack had seen the picture. 'I'm sorry. We thought we were meeting Lucie's friend. We should have known better.'

'If you know Lucille even just a bit, yes, you should.' Geri laughed.

Doorstep Dorrie.

'We'll go.' Stella put down her cake. Stanley let out a tirade of barks.

'It's all right, love, or you wouldn't have got past my gate,' Geri Gifford told her. 'Ever since that Inspector Kemp came, we've known Lucie would turn up. She's always ahead of the game.'

'How do you know each other?' Jack was eyeing a second slice of cake.

'Help yourself, love.' Geri glanced at an oversized watch on her wrist. 'Me and Lucille's sister were besties, as my daughter calls it. Bane of your life, weren't we, Luce, trying on your lippy and miniskirts. Oh God, and the day we – me actually – scratched your Frank Ifield LP…'

'Not mine.' Lucie avoided any pointers to a timeline.

'Have it your own way.' Geri did know Lucie.

'Did the police tell you the name of the man who murdered Greta?' Lucie was back on the chase.

'They don't know,' Stella said before she realised she wasn't supposed to know. Luckily, Lucie was too intent on quizzing. Stella felt relief as she listened to Geri telling Lucie everything Toni had told her at Yew Tree House the day before. At least she was off the hook for that.

'…as you obviously know, police found Greta's handkerchief in what had been the man's pocket. All a bundle of rags but they retrieved her DNA. Seems I'm a match.' She pulled a rueful face as if she was in some way wilfully responsible.

'Are you on the police database, darling?' Lucie looked lascivious. 'What *did* you do?'

'The police took my dad's DNA in 1986, a year before he died,' Geri said. 'Just for this reason.'

'How are you related to Greta Fleming?' Jack asked.

'Greta – God rest her soul – was my auntie, not that I ever knew her, since I was born in 1958. Same as Bette, your baby sister.' She flashed a smile at Lucie.

Lucie made sounds that might have been in vague disagreement. If, at sixty-five, Geri Gifford and Bette Lawson were 'babies' in relation to Lucie, it put a pin in Lucie's own self-indeterminate age. Jack and Stella knew she was in her mid-seventies, but the subject being strictly verboten, it was not discussed. By visiting Bette Lawson's best friend, Lucie had taken a clear-sighted risk that her age would become obvious. It hardly mattered to Stella, but she got Lucie's anxiety. In the media world, older women had ready-made scrap heaps waiting to welcome them.

'...never even knew she existed until Dad passed. He was her older brother. My mum told me. Mum said Dad couldn't even say Greta's name. Mum was desperate to share her own feelings, she loved Greta too. She and my dad, Phil, had just married when Greta was murdered so it was like Mum had also lost a little sister.' Geri paused and looked at the black and white portrait of the dead girl. 'Mum said Greta didn't have a bad bone in her body. She was Mum's bridesmaid, months later she's dead.' Geri splayed out her palms in a hopeless gesture.

'Did Greta catch the bouquet?' Lucie asked with grave intent.

'Yes.' Geri looked suddenly stricken.

'What's that got to do with it?' Jack said.

It would be to add what Lucie called 'colour' to her story, engage the readers with relatable details. Bring tears to their eyes. Thankfully, Lucie didn't pursue this.

'What do your children think about Greta?' Stella chipped in.

'We've not told them, it's not a nice thing to have in your past and Dean – he's a monumental mason – is dead set against it.' Geri indicated the end of the house where Stella had seen the grave stones propped against the wall.

Although Stella had been asked to clean gravestones and had over time visited many churchyards and cemeteries on her own account, it had never occurred to her that adding details of spouses, parents, children, to an existing headstone was made 'off-site'. It made sense; she'd often wished she could clean the stone in a less public place. What didn't make sense was keeping the headstones right outside the house.

'I see Dean brings his work home with him.' With an abrasive chortle, Lucie vocalised the thought Stella had considered best kept to herself.

'Thieves go for anything these days, can't be too careful.' Geri looked briefly pained. 'I'm hoping this will all blow over and we won't have to tell the kids.'

'Slim hope, popsicle.' Showing her teeth, Lucie looked genuinely concerned.

Families and secrets, Stella reflected. Would she prefer to know there was a murder in her past? On the whole, yes.

'I feel like I knew Greta. When we married, it was like I could see her, hovering on the edge in her dress. For ever the bridesmaid.' Geri Gifford was Lucie's kind of reader. 'She almost haunts me and like I say, it spooked Dean when I told him.'

From Jack, and other relatives of murder victims, Stella knew how a tragedy, even one handed down to younger generations, could blight lives. However, Dean Gifford, surrounded as he would be by funereal statuary, was surely familiar with death. Murder was a thing apart, Stella reflected.

'That's why you never told us at school. You never knew.' Lucie had abandoned the fruit cake for her notebook. Had Lucie known about Greta when she was at school with Geri, Stella had no doubt she would have splashed the story across the school magazine. Lucie was a paradoxical mix of fiercely loyal and ruthless. Geri had clearly clocked that Lucie was taking down her every word. Stella guessed Geri knew Lucie May as well as she and Jack did. Nothing got in the way of a story.

'To my dying day I will always wish Dad had told me,' Geri said. 'No one talked about Greta. Not even Nan and Granddad when they moved out of Esher to be near us. It was supposedly because they needed looking after, but Mum told me later it was because I'd started asking why we never went to Esher and Dad couldn't risk me finding out about Greta. It was like he was ashamed of her. Really, I suppose he couldn't bear to remember. He wanted to act like Greta had never been.'

'Where was your dad when Greta died?' Lucie was zeroing in.

'Mum said, but for Greta, Dad's family would have come through the war in one piece.' Geri sighed. 'He was training to go to Burma when it happened. He got two days' leave from the army, but didn't go to Esher. Mum went and stayed in a hotel near where he was stationed.'

'Was that Newhaven?' Lucie asked.

'Doesn't ring a bell. Wait.' Geri opened a teak cabinet on the wall above the teak stand where a huge television sat. Inside were ornaments and glasses. Geri handed Lucie an ashtray. Did she think Lucie still smoked?

'"Come to Sunny Seaford",' Lucie read out.

'That was where they stayed. Dad was cross Mum got this for Enid, my nan. Like she was a sightseer with his sister dead. Mum said she'd never seen him so angry. She never gave it to Nan. When Mum passed, I got it. Doubt our Lisa or Simon will want it. A small thing, but heavy with memories.'

'Seaford is a lovely little town.' Lucie sounded dreamy.

'Never been there.' Geri shrugged. 'Anyway, he could have got more leave than the two days, but he didn't want it. Mum said a seagull gobbled up her ham sandwich, she was laughing and saw he wasn't smiling. That's how bad he felt. Mum told me it ripped him apart that his parents had died without knowing who killed their baby girl. She said Dad never properly laughed again.'

'Did your dad ever tell your mum that he had guessed who killed his sister?' Lucie asked.

Geri took a bite of cake and put a hand in front of her mouth. 'He hadn't guessed, so how could he?'

'He must have had suspicions.'

'Why?' For the first time Geri Gifford looked irritated. 'Wait, do you know something you're not saying? If so, I'd be the first to know.'

'If I did, you'd be the first to know, yes.' Lucie was peaceable.

'Mum said if Greta had been seeing a lad, she'd have told her, if that's what you mean. Greta treated Mum like a big sister and told her everything.'

'If Philip had known the man, what do you think he'd have done?' Lucie sucked her propelling pencil.

'Gone to the police. Lucie, if you're suggesting—'

'Just considering everything. If it had been my sister, I'd have wanted revenge.' Lucie was sailing far too close to the wind.

'Then you'd have been hung,' Geri snapped. 'Mum said the detective on Greta's murder kept looking for the man until well after he retired. Then he had a heart attack, like they all do.'

Stella felt Jack move closer to her on the sofa. He'd be thinking that Terry, her dad, had been on the point of solving the case that had eluded him for decades when he died in the same circumstances. An idea that hadn't occurred to him when they'd been in the Co-op at Seaford days before.

'Greta was described as a "good clean girl".' Lucie liked to dot about.

'Naive, Mum said. Not like me, as you know.' Geri widened her eyes.

'You *are* kidding. You and my sister were all set to check into a nunnery.' Lucie executed what passed for a grin.

Silence as everyone heard the crunch and churn of gravel. A car door slammed.

'Oh God,' Geri groaned.

Moments later, a young woman burst in.

'Why didn't you tell me?'

'Lisa love, I—' Geri began to get up.

Lisa had the immaculate glamour of an Insta-influencer mixed with, Stella was shocked to see, an uncanny resemblance to her great-aunt, Greta Fleming. Her tee read *Gifford Pilates*, pink on sky blue.

Lisa saw Lucie first, then Jack and Stella. 'What, you let in reporters?'

'These are my friends. Lucie is Bette's sister, you know, from school.'

'Bette doesn't have a sister.'

'Yes, love, she does.' Geri must be wading in to the rescue.

Lucie had been estranged from her sister for years until meeting on a case Lucie had dubbed The Dogwalker Murder where they'd forged an uneasy truce. Seeing Lucie's dismay, Stella felt for her. As well as being Lucie's only friends, she and Jack were her family too.

'...we were going to tell you—' Geri continued.

'We didn't want to tell—' The tall burly man in the doorway behind Lisa somehow fitted Stella's idea of a man who dealt in marble headstones.

'Didn't want to tell me what?' Lisa jangled her car keys. 'That Granddad was a murderer?'

Chapter Twenty-One

Present Day

Meet churchyard in 30? DI Kemp – Toni

'I haven't talked to either sister,' Stella exclaimed. 'All I've found out is what Toni knows already. I don't know if she'll mind if you come too...'

'Let's not risk it. She likes that you're your dad's daughter.' Hunched on the sofa, Jack beamed over the top of his laptop. They were alone: Bella and the kids were visiting a place called the Booth Museum in Brighton. Bella had asserted that the gallery of floor-to-ceiling cases of stuffed birds shot by one man over his – Victorian – lifetime would be educational. Checking the website, Jack had said it looked like one big mausoleum and would give them nightmares. Bella pointed out that the twins were used to her drawing dead plant specimens – never mind they'd had a close encounter with a skeleton. Stella had noted yet again that parenting was a minefield.

'I'll get Lucie to make me one of her frothy coffees in her mobility home,' Jack said.

'Don't call it that in front of her,' Stella warned. 'It's a motorhome.'

'Hah, no. Wonder why Lucie calls it Prunella.' Jack wondered. 'Was that her mother's name?'

'Didn't Lucie dislike her mother?' Stella said.

'Don't you remember, Lucie did love her, but stories have always come first. When their mother was dying, Lucie let Bette, her young sister, do the caring. Bette said Lucie would pop in, fidget and bamboozle the nurse to know when her mum was going to die then fly out again. It's one reason Bette's kids are cool with Lucie.'

'Maybe Prunella is random. After all, why is Stanley called Stanley?'

'It was the name of your ex's father, remember.' Jack was trying to sound careless.

'Obviously I hadn't.' Stella grimaced. Stanley had been the one good thing to come out of that episode.

The previous afternoon, returning from seeing Geri Gifford, Stella had watched a rerun of the news conference on her phone. Toni Kemp had not explicitly said that Philip Fleming, Geri's father and Greta's older brother, was the killer of the man in the pillbox. Lisa Gifford was obviously given to dramatics. Although, even having her grandfather mentioned in the same item as a murder victim must be horrible. When Toni was asked if they had any suspects, she had said, 'It's too soon to rule anyone out.' Which didn't rule out Philip Fleming.

They had mined the internet for anything on Greta Fleming's murder late into the previous night. In the midst of war, with fatalities on the home front daily, it seemed that the fifteen-year-old's disappearance and then murder had stood for a loss of hope. Over eighty years later, Stella found her own mood lowered. Girls and women were still murdered, their deaths scarring their families' lives, as Greta's had.

Stella was shutting the gate opposite the Old Rectory on Church Lane when she saw she wasn't alone. From the angular elegance Stella recognised Rosa Stride. She hesitated then remembered that Toni wanted her to talk to the sisters. She was about to meet Toni empty-handed; this was her chance.

'Hello there.' Overly hearty, Stella was taken aback to see that the woman pulling out weeds from a grave was Stevie.

Not particularly curious by nature, Stella knew her skills lay more in cleaning than detection. But she had promised Toni that she would draw Stevie out and Stella always kept her promises. Despite this, she nearly turned tail. Stevie's expression told Stella she had crashed a very private moment.

'I'm sorry—' She began to retreat.

'I bet you are.' Stevie Stride manoeuvred to face Stella. 'A cleaner plays sleuth so she can nose into people's business and *drag out their skeletons.*'

'How did you know...' *Stella knew.* It was impossible to avoid an internet footprint.

'It's tempting to suggest you attend to your own family; we both know that Justin and Milly were lucky to return unharmed. I understand that your poor husband must lick his wounds, but it never pays to go back into your past.'

'He's not my—' Stella reeled. It had never occurred to her that Stevie and Rosa, having lived all their lives in the village, would have known Kate Rokesmith. If Jack had thought it possible, he'd never said. Stella had been so mindful of how the twins would react to hearing about their father's tragic past, she hadn't considered that she should have put herself out to make sure the twins were safe. She too could have played with them in the garden, then they wouldn't have been tempted to stray. It had taken a stranger to remind her.

'And here you are, sent to spy on me.' Stevie flicked the headstone with a damp cloth. *A woman after Stella's own heart.*

'I didn't expect to find you here.' Stella had always known why she preferred cleaning to detection. One brought out the best in you, the other made you a monster.

From the gate, Stella had assumed Stevie was fussing at her father's grave. Taken up by parrying Stevie's accusation of spying, she hadn't noticed Stevie was at an entirely different headstone. Now she read:

Adelaide Stride
1909–1963

'*Oh*, this is where your mother is buried.'

'I'm surprised you missed that in your investigation.' Stevie stood back and gazed at the stone. 'She died too young.'

'I only wondered... the other day when Jack took his twins to pay respects at Kate Rokesmith's grave, they watered your father's grave too. I hope that was all right. I did notice that your mother's name wasn't on the grave. I'm sorry, we were only interested because we're staying in Yew Tree House.'

'That's why I didn't want people there. I've always been a private person, as was my mother.' Stevie frowned.

'Listen, I'm sorry about that body in your pillbox. Not actually sorry because it's meant the police have found out who killed a girl in 1940. I don't suppose you remember when it happened?'

'Of course I do, she was the same age as myself and Henry. Mother was on tenterhooks as if it would be me next. I was more than capable of looking after myself,' she said. 'Henry would never have hurt a fly.'

'Henry?' Stella had seen Stevie's face briefly cloud as if at a painful memory. Her last remark was apropos of nothing they had been talking about.

'Nothing,' Stevie said. 'Greta Fleming probably thought she could look after herself too.'

'Greta Fleming lived in Surrey, which is hardly near here. Did your mother suspect Greta's killer lived here or something?' *Was this the link?*

'It's only the unimaginative who think a murder miles away has nothing to do with them,' Stevie said. 'When you expect to die on a daily basis, murder is just another way to die. Greta's beastly murder demonstrated to mothers all over Britain that the Germans weren't their only enemy. My mother knew that as well as any.'

'But she didn't fear for your brother?'

'What brother? I don't have a brother.'

'Henry. The children have been fascinated by the marks for yours and his height marks in the room where they're sleeping, we assumed—'

'Henry was the evacuee. We had three boys in the attic. Two went back because their mother wanted them with her, as I remember. After my father was killed, Mother felt it unkind for him to live alone up in the attic. She put him in that room at the end. Nothing more.' *Subject closed.*

'Where is Henry now?'

Jack could imagine the ghosts of the children who had clattered along the passages and staircase of Yew Tree House eighty years ago. To her surprise, and though ghosts were not her thing, Stella too could sense the lost children within the elderly women, Rosa and Stevie.

'How should I know? He didn't waste time returning to London when peace was declared. We were a drop in his ocean.'

'I'm sure not.'

'Stella, it's nice of you to reassure, but neither of us can know that. Life has moved on for us all.' Stevie drew herself up. 'I do feel I must apologise, Yew Tree House is really not fit for paying visitors...'

'I've been cleaning, if that's all right.' Stella was on the brink of saying that this made Yew Tree House a perfect fit for her.

'...I can't see the attraction of holidaying in a village. They are described as idyllic, but they are places of poison. Behind the façade of a pond, a green, a war memorial, lies cruelty and violence. You are a policeman's child, so like me, you will have learnt of the dark side from an early age.'

'Was your father a police officer?' Stella was keeping an eye out for Toni Kemp.

'A solicitor, but it's what a person understands that matters. I grew up in a war.'

'That must have been frightening,' Stella said.

'We got on with it.'

From her off-hand response, Stella wondered if Stevie had actually learnt her dark side from the war. Her answer seemed too aloof.

A robin alighted on Adelaide Stride's headstone.

'Rosa says robins are my mother watching over us.' When Stevie gestured at the bird, it flew off. 'Clichés are my sister's stock-in-trade, she sees life as a fairy tale – Disney, not Grimm. That Rosa is unscathed is Mother's legacy. She loved this scent.' Stevie tweaked off a sprig of rosemary and, with a transported expression, put it to her nose. 'It brings her back as if she'd never gone.'

Adelaide Stride had been dead about sixty years, yet Stevie's look of grief suggested she had died much more recently. Stella knew death could do that to you. Since arriving in Bishopstone, her dad's fatal heart attack felt like yesterday.

'Rosa seems fond of Reverend Snace.' Stella recalled Rosa's enthusiasm for the elderly vicar. If Jack's – and her own – feelings about the strange elderly man were not simply in their imagination, he could be a prime suspect for the murder. *Did True Hosts murder killers?*

'Rosa is too nice.'

'You're not so keen?'

'The man tried to take the place of my father. How dare he!'

'Did he have a relationship with your mother?'

'This has nothing to do with your skeleton, Stella. Snace is alive and well. He has not been mouldering in the Home Guard's pillbox all this time. I do think cleaning suits you better. It is very kind of you to tackle Yew Tree House, but no amount of cleaning can rid a house of phantoms.' Stevie sighed. 'Rosa is a dear thing, I should appreciate what she tries to do. The money you are kindly paying to stay here will indeed come in handy.'

'If you sold Yew Tree House, you'd be comparatively wealthy,' Stella said. 'It's definitely not my business, but if you have no heirs...'

'If only I could.' Using the headstone to turn, Stevie moved to the path and said, 'I can't help you solve this murder, Stella. I told Detective Inspector Kemp, I had little to do with the men in the pillbox. After the war Mother had it sealed. Does it matter? The man your children found killed Greta Fleming, hanging was too good for him. I am glad he got his comeuppance.'

'Miss Stride, can I ask you one more thing?' Stella surprised herself by asking.

'Stevie, please, Stella.'

'I got the impression that you knew Kate Rokesmith. I wondered if you could tell me a bit about her.'

'Kate Venus, as we knew her.' Stevie's face relaxed. 'I loved her, we all did. I'm sure if you had met her, you would have too, Stella.'

After Stevie had left, Stella stood for a moment. She had learnt nothing useful for Toni Kemp, but a cataclysmic amount for herself. Would she have loved Jack's mother? She snapped off a twig of rosemary and, as Stevie had done, breathed in the scent.

'You looked like you were the best of friends.' In a jacket like one worn by TV gardener Monty Don, Toni Kemp was sitting on Kate Rokesmith's bench by the flint wall.

'I wouldn't go that far.'

'Don't be modest, you were being Malcolm. I always end up as bad cop with him an angel on wheels.' Toni stretched out her legs, police-issue boots polished to a shine. 'It does stretch credulity that Stevie and Rosa didn't know the body was there. Are you any the wiser?'

'Not really.' Stella wanted to believe that Stevie was as ignorant as she had claimed. 'Stevie told me the box was sealed after the war.'

'She told me that, claimed not to know who cemented up the entrance and reinforced it with iron roofing and sandbags. Whoever did missed a gun hole. Didn't anyone notice a stench escaping as the body rotted? OK, Rosa was only seven in 1945, but Stevie was twenty.'

'The twins are seven.' Keen not to appear to be pointing the finger at Rosa, Stella went on, 'I got the impression from the news conference yesterday that you suspect Greta's brother Philip. Certainly, his family think that.'

'Yes, Geri Gifford told me that you and the roving reporter had been busy.'

'I didn't tell Lucie anything.' Stella felt herself redden. 'I didn't know it was Fleming's daughter when Lucie took us there.'

'Great that Geri's friends are there for her,' Toni breezed on. 'Anyway, you can stand down, things have cantered along since we last spoke. Want one? They've come from the fridge so won't melt all over you.' She offered Stella a Snickers bar from her jacket pocket. Although Stella baulked at eating chocolate before lunch, she needed a sugar rush so accepted it. This time Kemp had one of her own too. 'Last night the Crimestoppers' gods smiled upon us.'

'How?'

It seemed Toni liked to build suspense. Taking too much time to unfurl her Snickers, she then contemplated the chocolate bar like a treat in store. Finally, 'We have a match for Mr Skeleton.'

'You know who he is?'

'We can't do a briefing until we've got hold of the dad. He's flying in from Lanzarote – his home for half the year.'

'His *dad*?' Stella echoed.

'No, I mean the dad of the daughter who last night lost her licence to drink driving and assaulted the arresting officer. Her loss and our gain.' Toni crossed and recrossed her legs. 'Meaning we took her DNA.'

'Who is she?' *The sisters were innocent.* Terry had advised against getting close to witnesses in a murder investigation. But at the end of the day, she was a cleaner and it was OK to feel connection to those whose homes she restored to hygienic order.

'Ms Amanda Liddell, twenty-six, currently of Daddy's Sloane Square abode, headbutted the arresting officer. Horrible for the woman, but it meant they DNA'd Amanda and it turned out her great-grandfather was Greta's killer.' Toni got up and arched her back. 'He was one Alfred Liddell. Married Susan in 1940, one son called William born two months before VE Day in May 1945. Had Amanda not taken out a Belisha beacon and written off Dad's BMW, her great-grandfather might have got away with murder. Here's hoping Daniel Liddell skipped the angry gene or we should deploy a SWAT team for when Malcolm greets him off the plane.'

'Alfred didn't get away with murder,' Stella reminded Toni.

'This is when I have to believe in an after-life. I need Liddell to know we finally know what he did and that he will burn in hell.'

'Do you still think Philip Fleming killed Alfred Liddell?' Stella pictured Lisa Gifford, keys gripped in her fist, yelling, 'Granddad was a murderer.'

'What we don't know is if Alfred killed other girls or women. He could have other enemies. But we do now know that Liddell was a farmhand at an arable farm on the outskirts of Esher. Greta worked in a bakery on the high street. It's not inconceivable that Liddell came across Greta there. Had he struck up an acquaintance with her? Did she tell Philip? We'll never know.'

'I feel for the Liddell family too.'

'I wouldn't waste sympathy on Amanda; even sober she is one scary lady,' Toni said. 'And don't forget a person driven to murder through grief and revenge – which is likely the motive for whoever killed Liddell – can be as gentle as a lamb in ordinary life.'

Stella remembered Geri's description of her father. He hadn't wanted her to know about her aunt's murder and in turn Geri had kept it from her own children. Did she suspect her father?

'Liddell was forty-four in 1945. So far, we've had no luck tracking down his birth certificate. He was eligible for conscription, but didn't fight because agricultural labouring was a reserved occupation. His past is sketchy. Geri Gifford told Malcolm her mother recalled Philip Fleming believing Greta was sweet on some man. If he knew that, he never told the police.' Toni wandered over to Kate Rokesmith's grave. 'The story was that Greta wouldn't walk out with a fellow without telling her mum, she was a good girl, but who tells their parents everything?'

'Was Liddell questioned at the time?'

'He wasn't even in the frame. I *hate* sloppy police work.' Toni tssked. 'To be fair, during the war CID would have been at half strength.'

'We once worked on a murder which happened during the London Blitz.'

'That podcaster, yes. The boss loved that, he *hates* podcasters. Me, I'll take all the help I can get.' Toni whistled. 'What we do know is Alfred Liddell disappeared a couple of weeks before VE Day when his son was a baby. We don't know the time period between that and when he was virtually decapitated and dumped in the pillbox. Nor do we know if that was where he was killed.'

'I thought he was hit on the head?'

'Didn't I tell you?' Toni wove a blade of grass through her fingers. 'We're keeping it quiet so that it's between us and the murderer, but the pathologist thinks the bang on the head only stunned him.'

'What did kill him?'

'A slash across the throat so deep, it nearly severed his head from his body. Another reason why Fleming is a suspect. An efficient wound like that suggests a professional who'd been trained to kill. If they'd found his body at the time, as a soldier Philip might have been on the suspect list. Of course, with no DNA, police couldn't have found the link between Greta and Liddell.'

'What about that ARP badge Milly found?' Stella suddenly remembered.

'More likely it belonged to one of the ARP wardens, they were stationed at Yew Tree House. We checked out the members, all dead now, but nothing rang alarm bells. Now, as I said, with a clear link to Esher, we're not looking for a killer down here. The murder was classic overkill, which suggests the killer of Greta's killer was invested in the murder.' Toni looked grim.

'I remember from our research of a woman killed during an air raid that blacked-out streets were full of drunken servicemen, criminals, looters. Easy for a man to murder and get away with it. Even when the authorities knew the culprit, they needed men to fight so sent killers overseas.'

'That's terrible.' Toni waved her Snickers bar. 'Anyway, Stella, I'm here to say you can return to your bucket and spade. Now we know who killed Greta Fleming, the case is closed.'

'Closed?' Stella was dismayed. 'You said you don't have proof Philip Fleming murdered Alfred Liddell.'

'We don't have any which is why we're not saying he's definitively the killer.' Toni gave a wry smile. 'While I think of it, we did have a confession.'

'Who?'

'A ninety-five-year-old man who lives in the village, he used to run a shop here. I'll keep him anonymous if you don't mind. We've had a hard time getting him to stand down, he was quite insistent. But when I asked him why he'd killed Alfred Liddell, he went blank then offered that he did it with a poker.'

'A guess?'

'Yep, all a bit too Cluedo, if you ask me. I admit I sat up when he gave us a date: eighth of May 1945.'

'Wasn't that VE Day?' Stella was amazed she'd retained the fact.

'Bang on. But he'd shot himself in the foot – as it were – because Ji— whoops.' Toni dismissed the slip. 'It was his seventeenth birthday. His son showed us pictures of him with his sister celebrating. She's still alive and ticking in a care home in Shoreham and remembers that he stayed with the family all night.'

'Why lie?'

'His son says he's ashamed he was in a reserved occupation and missed the war. He's always coming out with stories of secret missions. Shame his mind is going, because the bloke is fit as a flea and all set for a telegram from the Queen.'

'Philip Fleming is the only suspect then?'

'There's not a shred of evidence it was him. Did he do it? We will never know for sure. If I were to charge Philip Fleming today, likely he'd walk.' Toni flapped back her hair. 'Worricker, my boss, doesn't want us wasting resources on an old murder. We found Greta Fleming's killer. End of.'

Toni bent down at Kate Rokesmith's grave and, looking at Stella, said quietly, 'Must be weird this being your partner's mother. I know your dad died in Seaford.'

'Jack wanted his kids to know about her,' Stella said.

'Good plan.' Toni nodded.

'You think?' Stella had expected – perhaps hoped –– Toni would voice concern if not be actually critical.

'Every time I solve a case, I visit my dad's grave.' Toni straightened up. 'He's buried in the cemetery on the hill above Newhaven. If I had kids I'd be taking them with me.'

'I'm sorry.' Stella was getting to like the detective.

'Don't be, it's a long time ago,' Toni said. 'This holiday is by way of a pilgrimage for you both?'

'More for Jack. I prefer to think of Dad where he lived and worked, not where he died. The main reason is for me to work out if I want to live with Jack and, when they're there, Milly and Justin.' Stella was surprised at how easily Toni had got her to open up. Or was it that Stella trusted Toni and had made the decision for herself?

'Wow, rather you than me,' Toni said. 'I need my space.'

'Me too.' Stella had a sinking feeling. She loved her own space.

'My dad was murdered too.' Toni nodded at Kate Rokesmith's grave. 'By our milkman. Over a pint of gold top.'

Toni seemed to be daring Stella to laugh. *No danger.*

'It's why I joined the police.'

'A good reason.' Stella felt lucky to have no such reason. And ashamed, since her reason for not joining had been partly to annoy her dad.

'I expect you were looking forward to working on a murder.' Toni aimed her wrapper, now a tight ball, at a nearby bin where it balanced on top of a heap of dead flowers.

'Not one bit.' Stella put Toni right.

Although it didn't sit right that the police were effectively letting people assume that Philip Fleming killed Alfred Liddell.

'...on the bright side, when the twins' ma – and the lovely Lucie – hoof it back to London, it leaves you and Jack to play happy families.' Toni had barely met Bella. *A good detective could read a situation.*

'Jack won't see it that way.' Stella spoke the thought out loud.

'Jack seems different to you, like he's off with the fairies.'

'That's why it works,' Stella said.

'Sorry, that was rude. Relationships have made me cynical. Maybe it's just me that prefers working a murder case to building sandcastles and scrubbing ice cream off kiddies' faces.'

'Not just you.' Stella smiled at Toni as the thought occurred.

'Wouldn't mind having you on my team.' Kemp turned to leave, then, in a classic detective afterword, she said, 'Got to say, Stella, your dad was a legend.'

Chapter Twenty-Two

Present Day

It was two days since Toni had met Stella in the churchyard and told her they were no longer investigating the murder of Alfred Liddell in 1945. Stella felt for Geri Gifford and her family. There was no proof that her father, Philip Fleming, had killed Liddell, but equally there was no proof that he had not. However much she tried, it was inevitable that Geri's memory of her father was tainted.

Jack had cried when Stella had told him Stevie remembered his mother and had thought her lovely, but to her surprise, he hadn't been round to ask the elderly woman if she had any memories to share. Stella, in the meantime, had been touched that Toni Kemp had confided to her that her father had been murdered. Whereas Kemp's experience had driven her to join the police, Jack had gone the other way. He preferred to go rogue. Not any more, thank goodness, Stella reminded herself.

She had been surprised when Jack had taken with equanimity the news the investigation was over and the police had handed back the pillbox. She was no less surprised by the enthusiasm with which they both took to sunbathing, swimming and taking trips to places like Lewes Castle and the Volk's Railway in Brighton. It was a proper holiday. Stella was also pleased to find herself enjoying getting to know Bella better. So much so she and Jack had discussed asking Bella to stay on, and while obviously pleased to be asked, Bella said she had already outstayed her welcome – much longer than her originally stipulated three days – and that she would leave the next day.

That evening, Stella had tried her hand at cauliflower cheese and for Bella's last night tomorrow, she'd up her game and tackle roast chicken. For a woman more adept at microwaving ready-meal shepherd's pies, this would be a stretch indeed.

'I was thinking I'd take Stanley for a walk.' Jack came into the drawing room after supper, the drying up cloth draped on his shoulder.

'Let me get my boots.' Stella had found a bit about lies in Piaget. Children, she had read, were told not to lie before they understood what a lie was. Stella doubted Jack, with a shaky understanding of 'moral realism', as Piaget put it, had sat his children down and explained they should stick to the truth.

'You stay and rest.' It was Jack's solicitous manner that alerted Stella. He could be considerate, but as a fellow workaholic, never had he urged her to rest.

Stella made a snap decision.

'Thank you.' Heaving a sigh, she tapped her Kindle as indication of being deep in a book. Jack's fleeting look of relief confirmed Stella's suspicion. *He didn't want her to come.*

Stella gave Jack a full minute then, abandoning Piaget and grabbing her head torch from a coat peg, she went after him.

Outside, she moved swiftly. Aside from keen hearing, Stanley might sniff her scent on the air. Jackie reckoned Stanley had a sixth sense because when she was minding him, he would start whimpering before Stella's van came into Jackie's street. On the other hand, the fact that Jack had Stanley was a last-ditch hope. If he was planning what Stella now suspected, an inquisitive animal in tow would be an impediment.

Growing accustomed to the dusk, Stella could see Church Lane was deserted. Following her own sixth sense, she crept along, avoiding potholes by keeping close to the wall of the Old Rectory.

All was still. It was as if Jack and Stanley had vanished.

Across the lane, Stella discerned deeper shades of black, gravestones and mausoleums set against the darkening sky. She was sure that Jack was not there. Her fear was not of ghosts drifting among the tombstones; her upbringing and recent experience had taught her that those of flesh and blood knew that a burial ground was an ideal deposition site for their murder victim. Stella dismissed the fantasy. Her mind was intent on playing tricks on her. She told herself that the only murderer she had to fear – the man who had killed Alfred Liddell – had been dead eighty years.

Stevie had said villages were poisonous places. Had she meant Bishopstone?

The gate to the Old Rectory was ajar.

The house looked even more forbidding at night. A mass of black, thin bluish moonlight tinting the windows made a face, ominous and threatening. Two words came unbidden into Stella's mind. *Death personified.*

Had the Old Rectory, once just the Rectory, ever been a sanctuary?

The curtains in the room where they had seen Reverend Snace were drawn back. Amidst monochrome shapes, Stella distinguished a desk, a wooden swivel chair and, her heart skipped, a crucifix above a mantelpiece etched in the meagre light. She gave a start, arrested by her own image reflected back, cadaverous and unfamiliar in the glass.

A sound that was barely a sound. Stella swung around too late.

'Don't speak or move.' A hand on her shoulder held her fast.

'What the—' Stella said as she moved.

'Ssssh.'

'Jack.' Stella's relief was quickly fury. 'You scared me.'

'Sorry.' He let go. 'But you could ruin everything and please, for heaven's sake, *whisper.*'

'Where's Stanley?' Stella didn't need an extra sense to tell that Jack wasn't clutching a dog on a lead.

'Stay close to me and don't say anything.' Jack went over to the front door and banged the knocker. Once, twice. They sounded like gunshots.

'It's late, he must be in bed.' Hardly the point. 'What are you doing? And where is Stanley?' Stella was insistent now.

The door swung open so quickly that it occurred to Stella that the Reverend had been behind it, listening to them. Absurd, the man was a vicar; Rosa had described him as a pillar of the community. Stevie hadn't been so keen. *Jack believed Snace was a True Host.*

The vicar hadn't turned on the hall light so it was impossible to see his face. Presumably he couldn't see them either. This was seriously odd.

'I've lost my dog.' Jack sounded incredibly upset suddenly.

'You've *lost* Stanley?'

'It's OK,' Jack hissed at her, then, to the vicar, 'We were walking up to the field and blow me if he didn't go and slip his lead. He rushed into your garden and I caught up in time to see him jumping in through one of your windows at the back. I'm terribly sorry, but could we come in and get him?'

'He's not here, I'm afraid.' The vicar sounded more nervous than when Stella had seen him in the churchyard.

'What?' Jack's astonishment was genuine. 'He must be, I—'

'He's *not*.' The vicar shut the door.

Stella stopped Jack knocking again.

'He said he wasn't there, we can't push it. What have you actually done with him?'

'That was true.'

'You are kidding.' Stella felt an uprush of anger and panic, it was all she could do not to yell at Jack.

'That bastard is lying.' Jack scrubbed at his hair.

'Which window, where?' Stella, too, thought that Snace was lying. 'He's got Stanley, he could kill him.'

'Don't jump the gun.'

'He's a *True Host*, isn't that what you said? Start with animals, work up to humans? He's old, maybe he's gone back to animals.' Stella was horrified by her own thoughts.

'It's not always as straightforward as that.' Jack's voice grated.

'Straightforward? Nothing about this place has been that.' Oblivious to tripping over a garden implement or crashing into a water butt, Stella stormed around the side of the house. Assuming Jack had followed she demanded, 'Which window?'

'Here.' Jack switched on his phone torch.

If Stella had called the Stride sisters' garden rewilded, she vaguely registered that the vicar had handed his back to nature. Caught in the light she glimpsed a monstrous jungle of trees, shrubs and brambles, a mass encroachment only halted by the flagstones on which they stood.

'That's it.' Sounding sheepish Jack shone the light onto a smallish casement just above their heads

'Stanley can't jump that high, it's nearly six feet. Even if he could, he'd never balance on the sill.' Essentially calm in a crisis, Stella was icy as reality dawned.

'In fact—'

'*In fact*, you prised open this window and posted Stanley inside.' Jack had promised to stop entering the houses of True Hosts – so named because Jack became their guest – instead, he'd devised another way in, one with a ghost of legitimacy. *The ghost was Stanley.* At least she knew for certain that Jack hadn't had a sit-down with the twins about why they shouldn't lie.

'I'm *so* sorry, Stella.'

'You should have known the man would lie. The vicar would want to destroy any evidence of whatever you think he's done.' Stella clutched the back of her head. 'Oh my God, *Stanley could be dead.*'

A terrible clang. Another. And another. The church clock struck ten, *no, eleven.* In between the chimes Stella caught something.

'That's Stanley.' Jack sounded jubilant. 'He's OK.'

'That was a "trapped" bark, quick.' Stella dug her fingers into a gap between the frame and the casement and pulled. This window wasn't open until you opened it, was it?'

'No, I er—'

'Bunk me up. *Now.*'

'It should be me going—'

'*Bunk me up.*'

Seconds later, Stella's knee balanced on the sill, she managed to manoeuvre her other leg over while trying to ignore the pain of wood compressing cartilage. With monumental effort, she propelled herself inside and onto the cold lino below.

She switched on her head torch and gasped. Heads sunk to drooping shoulders all in a row. *Dead vicars.* Daring to creep closer, the grotesque shapes morphed into cassocks hung on hooks.

Stella was in a storeroom, what her dad had called a glory hole, tall shelves filled with bric-a-brac, bowls, jugs, vases... presumably the unclaimed possessions, and gifts from grateful parishioners, to successive occupants now dead.

One vase with a pattern of roses on a trellis was familiar. But in the last thirty years she'd dusted hundreds of ornaments, doubtless a client had owned one like it. Feathery with fear for Stanley and horror that she was in the Rectory illegally, Stella didn't dwell on why good-quality stuff had been left to gather dust.

'You all right, Stella?' Stella had forgotten Jack was outside. Were it possible, her terror shot up several notches.

'Yes.' She was far from all right. 'I'm going to look in the house.'

'Go to the front door and let me in.' *That sounded nice and easy.*

'I'll get Stanley and get out.'

'Let me in, you shouldn't be in there by yourself.' Jack would be agonised that his plan had so dreadfully failed and with nothing to boost him up, he couldn't climb in after Stella. Anyway, she had to go, Stanley was her dog; she couldn't have stood around doing nothing.

To Stella's relief the door opened when she turned the handle, and with no noise. There was a key in the lock on the outside. She was in a brick-floored passage. Were they being idiots? The man was a retired vicar, a pillar of the community, as Rosa had said. Perhaps Stanley wasn't in the house. Stella concocted her justification for breaking in.

'*You lied when you claimed Stanley wasn't here, I had no choice but to...*

'*I am calling the police.*'

'*Please do. When they find I'm right...*' She ran out of words.

'Stanley?' she whispered.

The silence was too silent.

The doors in the passage were locked. Light from the head torch shimmered: it needed charging. Stella could hear nothing through the wood, no tell-tale whimpering. Rounding a corner, the light picked out a baize door. Stella had cleaned enough old houses still with original fittings to know that such doors absorbed the troublesome sound of servants and, swinging to and fro, enabled them to carry food through without having to turn a handle.

Stella pushed on the door and with a hiss, like a whisper, it swung out.

She found the switch on the head torch and turned it off. She didn't want to alert Reverend Snace to her presence. She could see the front door, the glass a square of moonlight suspended. A shadow filled the glass. Jack was waiting for her to let him in.

A weight hit her leg. Through a rush of adrenalin, she felt little paws, blunt claws cycling against her leg... and swooped down. She lifted Stanley into her arms.

Another shadow moved across the rectangle of glass in the door. *On the inside.* Her way to the front door blocked. *The vicar was coming.*

Aware that she must be more than a match for a man aged over a hundred, Stella was still terrified. She shouldered back through the baize door and, clutching Stanley close, raced along the passage. She shut the door in the storeroom and leant against it. She switched on the torch gain. There was no key. No point trying to sneak about now, Snace knew she was there. Stella found the light switch and flicked it down.

In the beam of her headtorch, she'd paid the objects brief attention. Now, illuminated by a central light with a tasselled silk shade, Stella forgot her panic. This was not junk awaiting a charity shop or church bazaar; there were statuettes, ashtrays, candlesticks, a silver rose bowl which looked of substantial worth. What were they doing there?

She heard a hiss. The baize door. He knew where she was. Stella snapped into action. Shunting Stanley further up her shoulder, she cast about for something to stand on in order to reach the sill. A hard-skinned suitcase stood by the door. Grabbing it with one hand, the other steadying Stanley, Stella vaguely noticed it was made by Revelation. She had found her family's suitcase, made by the same defunct brand, in the attic after Terry's death. *Stupid the things that occurred.*

Going by how light the case was, she knew it would provide minimal help getting her up to window sill level.

Stella stood the suitcase on end. The least stable option, but the only one that gave her the height she needed. As it toppled, Stella pushed herself against the narrow sill. Presumably expecting her to exit from the front door, Jack had shut the window. As if utterly aware of the gravity of their situation, Stanley gripped her shirt, the balance of his body right over her shoulder.

'Good boy,' Stella wheezed.

One wrong move and she would fall off the sill. Her nose pressed to the glass, Stella could see the yew tree in the front garden beyond the wall. Far beyond her reach. Cold air through a crack between the sash and the sill gave the faintest relief.

'Jack.' A hoarse whisper. Stella called twice more before she recalled *Jack was outside the front door.*

It was up to her.

Stella inched so that her hand faced the sash. She thrust it – fingers upwards – through the gap and hauled with all her strength. The sash slid up. Four inches. Stella elbowed through the widened gap and this time levered with her arm. A foot. She pushed herself through and with one leg on the outside sill, shoved the window right up.

Stella was sprawled along the short length of the window sill. Her position gave her no leeway, she couldn't jump feet first. Any effort to reposition herself would risk falling head first onto the path below. At the least she would break her wrists.

Suddenly Stanley launched himself off Stella and, with the speed of a whippet, he vanished into the darkness.

Stella had recurring dreams in which she was on a slope with water or a sheer drop below and all the while was slipping. *Down and down.* She always woke up before she fell.

Behind her, the door opened. *The light went out.*

Stella saw a negative of the mass of trees and shrubs.

'Grab my shoulders and jump.' *Jack.*

'Why did you follow me?' Jack latched the gate. Every limb hurting, Stella trailed after him around to the French windows.

Stella had followed Jack because she had not believed he was simply taking Stanley for a walk. That he had lied didn't justify that she hadn't trusted him.

They hadn't spoken as, clipping on Stanley's lead, Stella had hurried around the Old Rectory and along the lane back to Yew Tree House.

'Stella?'

'What? I wasn't—'

'How come you came to the Old Rectory?'

'OK, so I *was* following you.' Stella opted to go on the defence. 'I knew you were up to something. You didn't want me to come with you.'

'But you didn't say,' Jack said. 'If you had, I'd have told you.'

'And I would have stopped you using Stanley as a decoy.'

'That's the wrong word—'

'Call it what you like, you put him in danger to get into the Old Rectory. What did you expect to find?'

'Like I said, I think Snace is a True Host. He's living next door to my children – I have to be sure he can't hurt them.'

'That's ridiculous, why should he?' Stella thought the man was creepy and just now had been horrified that he might catch her in his house, but it helped no one to make him a bogeyman. Was it like Toni Kemp had suggested? That she and Jack wanted a murder to spice up their holiday?

'If I knew that…' Jack stopped by the French windows. From outside the drawing room was a homely tableau, pools of light warming the wood panelling around the fireplace. Only it was no one's home. The sisters didn't live here and for Jack and Stella, Yew Tree House had brought only strife and tension.

'You didn't trust me.'

'And rightly so.' Stella was good at being in the wrong, but tonight, there were more serious concerns. 'What if Snace calls the police?'

'He won't, True Hosts never do.' Jack's confidence brought back the terror she had felt in the Old Rectory. 'But if he bucks the trend, we'll say Snace knew our dog was in his house and refused to return him so we had to go in and get him. Seeing as Snace wouldn't answer the door, I got in through an open window and found Stanley.'

'That's not true.' Stella knew she was being pedantic.

'If you hadn't come along, it would have been.'

'If I hadn't come along, what would have happened?'

'Can we leave it now?' Jack said.

'The vicar has tons of stuff stored in there. Gifts from parishioners, I thought.' This was Stella's attempt at an olive branch.

'Or he stole them.' Jack gave a low laugh as he took her arm.

Chapter Twenty-Three

May 1945

Blackout rules had relaxed and at half past nine at night, a bar of light from the dining room window streamed across the lawn. It fell far short of the pillbox, now silent and empty. Blunt and Ridgeway were at the ARP post but for the second night running the planes that had roared overhead were the British heading for Germany. To finish them off, Blunt said.

Feet up on the sofa, Adelaide felt content. Hitler and Mussolini were dead. The war was nearly over and – not that she voiced it – her war had been luckier than most. Stevie seemed happy and Rosa was thriving. Since his failed attempt to propose marriage – she assumed that was what he'd been going to say – Snace was cold if they encountered each other. Thankfully this was seldom, not least because, no longer feeling she had to be the late Captain's God-fearing widow, Adelaide no longer went to church.

She would wait a suitable interval after VE Day, then she would put the house on the market. She would miss Pat Jordan. Adelaide paused to think how horrified Rupert would be that his wife was friends with the village postmistress. He had set a lot of store by class difference. But Rupert was dead and Adelaide could at last see a future. They could go abroad, America,

Canada, somewhere far away from here. Perhaps Henry would come. Perhaps she would adopt him...

Lifting her gaze from her novel, Anthony Trollope's *The Warden*, Adelaide imagined packing up the room. She would talk with Stevie about which of her father's things she wanted to keep, not that she cared about heirlooms. She must save some things for Rosa. Abruptly, Adelaide sat up straight in the chair.

Where was the carriage clock? Discarding Trollope, she crossed to the mantelpiece although it was blindingly obvious that the clock wasn't there. Rupert's roll-top bureau was open. Only an inch, but he had always kept it locked and, the dark wooden affair being akin to his coffin, Adelaide had avoided it.

Rupert had been secretive about his valuables, but Adelaide did know that he kept his father's coin collection in the bureau. She had caught him opening a secret compartment there. How cross he had been...

Unbelieving that she needed to check now, Adelaide pushed on a false column within the carved arches and drawers. The column loosened, allowing her to slide it out; it was actually a box open at the top. Adelaide held the wooden container up to the table lamp. Where she had seen Rupert depositing a velvet box that contained the coin collection – dating back to Roman times – was nothing. The box was empty.

Adelaide returned the box to the desk and pulled down the roll-top. She spotted the key lying on the tallboy opposite and, although there seemed little point in locking the bureau now, she turned the key and dropped it in a vase on the window sill. She stood in the middle of the room as if trying to get her bearings. Try as she might, she couldn't come up with a plausible explanation for where the coins had gone. Had Rupert taken them? Why would he want them when he was fighting? If he had, it didn't explain why the bureau was open. Or why the clock was missing.

There was only one explanation. *They had been burgled.*

The house was never locked, but although she couldn't bear Blunt, not for a minute did she think him a thief, and certainly not Nigel Ridgeway or Mr Merry. She disliked Snace, but being a vicar had to count for something. None of them had reason to steal from her and all of them spent enough time in and around Yew Tree House to have noticed a stranger. There had been no reports of burglaries in the village.

Henry. Adelaide clasped her throat in horror that the idea should even occur. A moment ago she had been mooting the idea to herself that she might adopt Henry as her son.

Last night she had found him making a drink in the kitchen at two in the morning. He had struck her as seeming guilty, but she assumed it was because he hadn't asked her first. She had hurried to reassure him that he must make himself anything he liked, this was his home. Henry had not made himself Ovaltine. Nor when she had left had she seen anything – a pan, the tin of dried milk – to suggest he was about to make some.

As much as Adelaide tried to convince herself Henry would never steal from her, something stopped her from calling the police to report the burglary.

Chapter Twenty-Four

Present Day

'Roast chicken? That's an effort, we could just get a takeaway.' Jack was peering in the window of an estate agents. 'Blimey, it's pricey here. If the sisters were to sell Yew Tree House, they could easily afford a perfect bijou cottage like that one.'

Jack and Stella had brought the twins with them to do a shop in the village. Stella was privately doubtful about roasting a chicken; at home it would have been another matter, but she suspected that the kitchen at Yew Tree House hadn't seen an upgrade since before the war.

'It's Bella's last night, we should do something special.' Stella peered at the property details. The cottage Jack had spotted looked twee. *Too perfect.* Stella preferred the rackety comfort of Yew Tree House. 'Stevie's mother wouldn't sell, and that's dictated her own decision too. She seemed very close to Adelaide.'

In the sunlight, the pond mirrored the turquoise of the sky. The church spire peeped over thatched roofs set around one side of the pond. A bright red Royal Mail van trundled past. It was August, but the village was practically deserted. People were going abroad for their holidays again. Ever since Stevie Stride's remark about villages being toxic, Stella was tempted to see cruelty and ugliness lurking beneath the scenic surface.

'I suppose she's also lived in the same house all of her life,' Jack mused.

'It's between a rock and a hard place. A bijou cottage with mod cons or a place that's familiar and reassuring,' Stella said. 'I'm back living in the house I grew up in. And now I'm thinking of leaving it.'

'I *love* roast chicken, you know that, just with what happened last night...' Jack was chatting on because the subject was cruising close to that of Stella moving in with him.

'All the more reason to get this holiday back on track. With salad, I thought. A summer meal. Don't you think I can do it?' Stella nudged him.

'No. I mean yes,' Jack said. 'But with a strange oven...'

'It can't be that difficult.'

'For a born liar, you messed that one up, Jackanory.' Lucie appeared with the twins, who were each clasping a plant that, in a fit of child-friendliness, Lucie had helped them buy for Bella from the florist across the road. 'All the same, I think you'd do better cooking in Prunella than in that clanky old kitchen. Oooh, fee fie foe fum, I smell the blood of a... *family butcher.*'

Chrismas and Son Ltd, Family Butcher.

'Let me buy it. It's the least I can do.' Lucie flew inside.

By the time the others joined her in the shop, Lucie was humming and hawing over two possible chickens, both of which looked the same to Stella.

'How many is it for?' The butcher, a grizzled man with glasses on the end of his nose, eyed Lucie as if he thought that – done up to the nines in her summer plumage – he doubted she would know.

'Us, that's four, with Bella and Lucie, six,' Stella said.

'Bet you two have *big* appetites,' the butcher said to the children.

'I do,' Milly agreed. 'Is this where Father Christmas lives? We've come to arrest—'

'And sausages please,' Stella cut in.

'Milly. Justin. Outside. *Now.*' With a rictus grin at the butcher, Jack hauled both the children out. Toni might have told Stella that the case was closed, but ever since Jack and Stella had explained this to the children, Milly had refused to believe it. They had brought the children into the village in the hope it would distract them, Milly in particular. Had she at some point merged the idea of a murderer with Chrismas the family butchers? Stella's heart sank; the children were as suggestible as she had feared.

While the butcher wrapped the sausages, Lucie was bobbing about the cold cuts cabinet.

'We're staying at Yew Tree House. What a to-do since that skeleton was found. Press – vultures more like – pitched outside the gate. I expect you know the Miss Strides? Such a sweet old couple of ladies.' Lucie dipped and swooped with apparent delight, despite her attempts to interview either sister having been stonewalled.

'Rosa Stride wouldn't say boo.' The butcher placed the card machine on the counter for Lucie. 'The elder Miss Stride doesn't suffer fools, now there's a woman who knows what she wants to the last giblet. Wouldn't say "sweet", but that's a compliment. Rotten business, this body being found in their garden. It's good for that girl's family. My dad seems pleased.'

'At least we have closure.' Lucie ran her finger along the tiled dado. It wouldn't be a finger-test, Lucie didn't care about dust. She was literally drawing a line. She had her story.

'The murder must have occurred while her family were living there. Yet one could almost suppose it's usual to find a skeleton in your pillbox. Astonishing that neither sister knows a thing...' Jack was fishing.

'Stevie Stride is like my dad – those that went through the war are a different breed.' Mr Chrismas handed over the bag with the chicken. He wiped his knife and laid it on a worn and bloodied chopping board. 'After Hitler, nothing fazes them.'

'Is your dad still alive?' Stella gave a start. *Father Christmas.*

'Ninety-five and still cycles around the village in his Home Guard hat on VE Day.' The butcher laughed.

'We know him.' Milly craned up to Jack. 'Do you ever listen to a word I say?' Another Bella-ism, Stella noted.

'If they've met Dad, you must have too. He's usually at his post by the pond, nabbing all and sundry to tell his life story.'

Jack made a non-committal noise. Now was not the time to say that the twins had met Mr Chrismas Senior (Father Christmas) when they had gone AWOL and now, it seemed, talked to strangers. Stevie was right: the children – and the adults – had been lucky to get away unscathed.

'...Talks nonsense but means no harm.' The butcher fiddled with the display of cuts in his window.

'Is your dear father at the pond now?' Lucie enquired.

'Yes, he's at his post ready with a tall tale.' Chrismas shook his head with obvious affection.

'Perhaps we might introduce ourselves.' Waving the bag with the chicken in farewell, Lucie was out of the shop with Milly close behind.

'Take what he says with several pinches of salt; like I said he talks a lot of twaddle. He was only ever in the Home Guard, but to hear him talk... still, as long as he's happy.'

Jack, Stella and Justin followed Lucie and Milly across the road to the village pond.

An elderly man, the cane on which his hands rested giving him the look of a sage, sat on a wrought-iron bench looking out at the pond. Although the day was hot, he wore a jumper. His gaze rested on two swans on the water. He must have been deep in thought as he gave a start when Milly flew up and blocked his view.

'I've told them you are the murderer,' she blurted, 'but I'm afraid they won't listen.'

'Milly, darling, you can't accuse people.' Lucie caught up. 'Even if this gentleman has committed murder, that's not the way to—'

'He must be. You must be.' Milly rounded on Mr Chrismas.

'Milly, *stop*.' Hands on knees, Jack's face was level with his daughter. 'You must not go about accusing people. I *do* apologise, Mr Chrismas. Lucie, *please* step back.'

'He's of the generation.' Lucie was gruff.

'Hello, I'm Stella and this is Jack.' Noting the polished brogues, Stella reflected that, regardless of possible dementia, Mr Chrismas senior cared about his appearance. Rarely rude and never rude to Lucie, she elbowed the reporter back from the bench and hissed at her, 'We need to wind right back here.'

'I always said I would say.' Chrismas's voice rumbled in his chest. 'I was a stay-behind.'

'Me too,' Milly squawked. 'We always have to stay behind. Daddy and Stella didn't want us to come today and if Mummy knew she'd be cross.'

'She knows we're here,' Jack said. 'Mummy is packing and we're getting her a special supper, remember?'

'Stella says everyone's a suspect at the start and you don't tell her to stop.' With the gesture of an over-burdened adult Milly pushed away a strand of hair off her face. Then descending to her default, 'It's not *fair*.'

'That's not—' Stella vaguely recalled someone had said don't work with children and animals. 'Not *everyone*.'

The man continued looking at the swans as if oblivious to the exchange. Just as Stella was going to say goodbye, Mr Chrismas said, 'I'm Jimmy Chrismas. Stevie says you're billeted with them at Yew Tree House.'

'We're not billit any*where*.' Milly scowled.

'Billeted means staying, Mills,' Jack said. 'Yes, we are staying at Yew Tree House.'

'We live in London.' Without a breath, at top speed and including the universe, Milly recited their home address which, Stella noticed, made Jimmy Chrismas smile.

'You remind me of baby Rosa, she was a little madam.' Jimmy lifted the stick off his lap and thumped it on the ground between his legs. 'This is safer than London, we only get the ones they drop before they cross the sea or miss Seaford.' He nodded. 'Mrs Stride will treat you like her own, she did Henry. Me too. She was a decent sort.'

'We do have to arrest you.' Milly probably felt they were drifting from the point. She plumped down on the bench beside Jimmy.

'Is your birthday in May? On the eighth?' From Jimmy's expression, Stella saw she had struck home. Toni had accidentally started to say the name of the man who had confessed to the murder. 'Ji'. Jimmy. *Had he told the children too?*

'How do you know?' Jimmy Chrismas was no longer friendly.

'It was VE Day. Your son said.' She could feel both Lucie and Jack looking at her. They knew that the butcher hadn't mentioned his father's birthday.

'I didn't hear him say that.' Milly stared up at Stella.

'You and Lucie had left the shop.' Stella dug deeper.

'By Mrs Stride, do you mean Adelaide who was married to Captain Rupert Stride?' Jack came to the rescue.

'*He* calls her that.' Chrismas was suddenly annoyed. 'As I said to him, she's Mrs Stride to the likes of you and me, and don't you forget it.'

'Adder-laide is *dead.*' Stella vaguely noted that Milly was becoming overfamiliar with the concept of death and dying. '... grave is next to Murdered Granny.'

'That's the captain,' Justin explained. 'Adelaide's not there. We like secret Stevie, she's one of a sort.'

'Secret...? Yes, she is.' Jimmy looked at Justin for the first time. 'Why do you like her?'

'I don't know.' Justin wasn't one for the limelight; clearly casting about for a reason, he announced, 'She gives presents to the old rector.'

'Presents?' Chrismas thumped his stick on the path, harder this time.

'Milly, Justin, we are leaving. Now.' Jack brushed the back of Stella's hand with his own.

'Sorry, Jimmy, we're obviously dredging up bad memories, we'll leave you in peace,' Stella said.

'It's a bad business. A very... please would you help me up, lass?' Jimmy asked Lucie.

'Of course.' Lucie would like 'lass'.

The butcher had warned them to treat what his father said with scepticism. He had referred to Jimmy telling wartime fantasies. For an understandable reason he would want it kept quiet that Jimmy had confessed to the murder in the pillbox.

Whatever reason Jimmy Chrismas had for falsely confessing to killing a man that Toni said he hadn't known, something about the Strides, and about that time, had rattled him. On his feet and swaying slightly, Stella could believe Jimmy was ninety-five. *Would he be cycling down the high street for the anniversary of VE Day next year?*

Jimmy let Lucie help him across the road and into the butcher's. Stella was surprised when Lucie came straight out again. Jimmy might not be a murderer, but he had been alive when someone killed Liddell and might have, as Lucie called it, given her colour.

'Calling people murderers is not only rude, it's unkind and can lead to all sorts of trouble.' Jack stood over Milly. 'This is not a game. You did not find the murderer of the man in the pillbox so please stop this now.'

'Father Christmas said he was.' Milly looked on the point of tears.

'You will learn adults sometimes say things they... that they don't mean.' Jack softened.

'Well, they shouldn't.' Stating an incontrovertible fact, Milly had the last word.

★

Stella knew she shouldn't have been surprised the Aga didn't work. Stiff with grime, the ancient contraption couldn't have been lit for years. Not for a minute had she imagined they could use the tiny oven and two-ring hob attached to the cylinder of Calor gas.

She gazed at the ceramic dish in which sat the free-range chicken, fresh from Salmon's farm and garlanded with a crown of rosemary (from the churchyard) as per the 'easy roast chicken' recipe on her phone.

'Looks like Lucie's camper van is the only option,' she told Jack when he stepped in from the garden.

'Bad news.' Jack grimaced. 'Lucie's grand offer was just that – seems she only has a microwave. What if we cut it up? They butchered a chicken on *MasterChef: The Professionals* in less than two minutes. Why don't I cut up the bird? We can fry the pieces in the skillet. It'll still be lovely.'

'With what, my penknife?' Stella reminded Jack that they had no knives.

'Lucie?'

'Her cutlery is wooden, saves washing up, she said.' Since they were having to pump every ounce of water they used, Stella now saw the advantage.

'What are we thinking? We have just the thing.' Jack rushed out of the room. Moments later he was back. 'Here we are.'

'I'd forgotten about that.' Stella gave a shiver as Jack opened his folded T-shirt to reveal the dagger Milly had found under the floorboard on their first day at Yew Tree House. He withdrew it from the leather holster. 'That's sharp enough to butcher more than a chicken.'

'It's perfect. Needs a wash though.' Carrying the knife across to the sink, Jack turned on the tap. It gave a cough, the water ran brown and then became a trickle.

'Damn, I forgot to pump it after Bella had her bath.'

'Milly said it was for murder,' Stella remembered. 'Alfred Liddell's throat was cut so deeply it nearly severed his head from his body.' Her mouth had gone dry.

'Yeah, don't remind me just as I'm about to sort the chicken.' Jack stopped at the kitchen door. 'Wait, are you thinking—'

'Why was it hidden?'

Jack came back to the table, and as he sat down beside Stella they peered at the exposed knife.

The hilt was engraved: 'Fairbairn-Sykes.'

'That bedroom we're in, who slept there when the family lived here?'

'Stevie said their evacuee Henry slept there after Captain Stride was killed. The boy we thought was their brother.'

'She told you she didn't know where he is now.' Jack nodded.

'I thought that upset her rather. I suppose he never kept in touch with the family after he went home. They were the same age, maybe they'd been friends.'

'We need to find out more about Henry. Not least, why did he even have a knife like this?'

'If he did. It might have belonged to Rupert Stride and he hid it in what was then a spare room. He probably intended to retrieve it but he was murdered so never did.'

'Maybe if he'd taken it to London, he'd have come back alive.'

'That rules out the knife belonging to Rupert Stride; he'd been dead five years by the time someone killed Alfred Liddell. Or this knife did belong to Stride and another sharp implement was used to kill him.' Stella tipped the metal handle with a finger, setting it on a ninety-degree turn. As it caught a beam of sunlight, the steel flashed as if with a light of its own.

There was a rap on the kitchen door. A shadow slanted across the frosted grass.

'Who would come around the back?' Stella jumped as if they had a reason to feel guilty.

'I would.' Toni Kemp was neither tall nor – despite the Snickers bars – overweight, but when she steamed in, it seemed to Stella that she filled the kitchen.

'I came to tell—' She looked at the table. 'Where the hell did you get that?'

'It was in a secret—' Jack started.

'I trusted you, Stella.' Toni let rip. 'I've given you inside information. I let you in on the workings of my investigation. I put my job on the line. Please tell me it never occurred to you this was likely our murder weapon. I can't bear stupidity, but I'll take it if it's all you've got.'

'Steady on.' Jack put up a hand. 'That's one hell of a leap. Stella has not kept anything from you. We've only just found this.'

Not true. Stella gripped the edge of the deal table. She had expected Toni to come to arrest her for breaking and entering. Or at least entering. Her guilt must be written all over her face.

'We found it hidden under the floorboards and were just thinking it could be the knife used to kill Alfred Liddell. There are pros and cons but whatever, if it was used, then Liddell's killer can't be Philip Fleming. He wouldn't have known where to hide it in the house.'

Snapping on gloves, Toni produced an evidence bag. She looked between them both. 'Apologies, shouldn't have flown off the handle.'

Sergeant Lane came into the kitchen and leaned on the Aga. Stella caught Toni's eye. Although still reeling from Kemp's tirade, Stella understood Toni hadn't told Lane she'd taken Stella into her confidence. *More secrets.*

'Listen, guys, I'm going to have to ask you both to come to the station and make a statement,' Toni said. 'Where you found this, when, how accessible it is. Have you been aware of strangers in the vicinity? For instance, the door wasn't locked. Where are the children?'

'They're in the van with Lucie.' Jack hadn't forgiven Toni. 'The door was unlocked because we're in the house. We lock it when we go out.'

'A bank card would do for a key.' Toni frowned at the ancient Yale in the door.

'Ma'am.' Sheena Britton, the detective who had received the ARP badge from them at the police station and implied that the 'Tooth Fairy' was tight-fisted, called Toni from the garden.

Stella and Jack followed Kemp and Lane outside. The detective was holding a plastic evidence bag. 'I think this is what we're looking for.'

'That's the same as the knife we found,' Stella exclaimed. 'Where did you get it?'

'Yes, where?' Grim-faced, Toni confronted her officer.

'It was on the floor of the pillbox where we... I'm absolutely certain we'd have seen it if it was there when we—'

'It *wasn't* there.' Toni gave a curt nod.

'It's likely whoever did it was in a hurry, they must have been desperate to get rid of it.'

'It was a sign,' Jack said.

Not now, Jack, Stella silently implored.

'A sign of what, mate?' Sergeant Lane's kindly tone might be tolerance rather than curiosity. Already one police officer had been rude to a member of the public.

'What if the person who put the knife there was continuing a story? You were meant to find it. Or rather, since the owner can't have known you would all be back, we were meant to find it.' Jack stopped. 'Thank goodness it wasn't Justin and Milly.'

'Why are you here?' Stella asked. Surely Kemp wasn't charging her for breaking and entering?

'We've got another murder.' Toni nodded towards the Old Rectory. 'Reverend Snace, aged one hundred and something and apparently with his faculties, has been found murdered. Could have lived longer, his doctor said. Stupid, but I'd like to think when you get to a great age, beyond a natural death, nothing bad happens to you. Yes, I said it was stupid.'

'Snace? What, the vicar who lives next door?' Stella felt dizzy.

'Who would kill a vicar?' Jack shook his head. Stella stared at him. Was that the point?

'Seems Snace was like a village elder. He was highly regarded for his pastoral work during the war. He ran the Home Guard that was stationed in your pillbox. I'm afraid you're going to have the media back on your doorstep,' Sergeant Lane said. 'And us, obviously.'

'Did the murderer know about—' Stella nearly gave away her knowledge of the 'stockroom' full of ornaments and silver in the Old Rectory. 'Did the killer know Snace, do you think?'

'Too soon to say. We can tell you there is no sign of the lock being forced. But Snace was a cleric and had lived here in the days when you left your doors open,' Toni said. 'There's one room jam-packed with bric-a-brac, some of it looks quite valuable. The housekeeper says Snace kept the room locked so she'd never seen inside. She can't tell us if anything is missing. That said, the viciousness of the attack suggests it was personal.'

'You don't suspect the housekeeper?' Stella waited until Lane and the Tooth Fairy had returned to the pillbox to ask the question.

'She's a suspect, but we think he was murdered last night, for which she has a solid alibi,' Toni said.

Alibi. When the Reverend Snace was murdered, Stella had *not* been reading Piaget in the drawing room.

'...Snace didn't want someone every day. As DC Britton just said, for a bloke over a hundred, he was remarkably fit.'

'Must be living here,' Jack said. 'The butcher said his father, Jimmy Chrismas, still rides a bike at ninety-five.'

'Show me where you found your knife.' Toni was official. Stella felt her stomach plummet. Wasn't Jack aware of the danger they were in? Was he so used to creeping about the houses of True Hosts that he'd forgotten he had let Stanley into Snace's where Stanley could have met the man's killer? *And that she...*

Jack led the way upstairs into the empty bedroom at the end of the passage. He had left the board up after retrieving the knife.

Putting on more gloves Toni crouched on her haunches and peered into the shallow cavity between the joists.

'Was the knife all you found?'

'Yes,' Jack said. 'My daughter Milly found it.'

'Milly's good at finding things.' Toni's tone was neutral. 'Was it your impression it had been lifted recently?'

'Hard to tell. Milly lifted it easily but she's strong. And its summer so likely the wood has shrunk.' Jack showed Toni the board.

'I wonder if it has military connections.' Toni got up. 'We know Adelaide Stride was in the ARP, but I don't think they carried weapons. I'll check on what the Home Guard were issued with. I rather think it was broomsticks and pan lids, but maybe that was just *Dad's Army*.'

'I was about to look it up when you arrived.' Jack opened his phone. *Not phone the police.* Stella followed Toni out of the room.

'Here we are. The knife was, quote, "a commando dagger, aka stiletto, designed in 1941 for use by a top-secret army called the Auxiliary Units". So, not the Home Guard. Along with the knife the men were issued with plastic explosives, Sten guns, and incendiaries. Conceived as a resistance army, their mission was to remain behind after the British had retreated and delay the invading army. Oh goodness look, this picture is identical to the knives we have.'

'What time was the murder?' Stella was preparing to put her head in the noose.

'Any time between yesterday evening when Jimmy Chrismas says he saw the Reverend Snace in the churchyard and ten when his housekeeper found him.

'...can you come in to give statements?' Toni was saying. 'Tick box thing. Anything you may have seen will be helpful.'

'Yeah, no problem.' How was Jack so nonchalant? Had he forgotten what they had done in the last twenty-four hours and that them giving a signed statement would be a very big problem indeed?

'Happy birthday, Stella.' The twins rushed in holding cards.

'They did them secretly in Prunella.' Lucie came in.

Jack muttered, 'Oh no.'

Then it dawned. Taken up with the murder – murders – and having to decide on her future with or without Jack, for the first year ever, Stella had forgotten it was her birthday. Jack had gone ashen. So, it seemed, had he...

Chapter Twenty-Five

Present Day

'Coffee, my pretty little suspects?' Lucie pulled shut the door after Stella had clambered up behind Jack into the motorhome. 'Or, seeing as it's Sherlock's birthday, a nippet?'

'We're *not* suspects.' Jack had hardly said a word on the way back from the police station where, in separate rooms, they had given statements. Jack had landed the Scottish tooth fairy, aka DC Sheena Britton.

Stella had got Toni.

'Just coffee please.' Stella sank onto the banquette beside Jack. While Lucie was slotting a pod into her coffee machine, he raised his eyebrows at Stella. *No, she was not all right.* 'Please, can we forget it's my birthday?'

'Some of us already had,' Lucie crooned at Jack.

'I am very, very sorry.' Jack seemed more upset about Stella's birthday than that he had been quizzed by – *and lied to* – the police. 'I had planned we'd all go out for the day. But that was before Alfred Liddell, Bella, Lucie...'

'Best present you could have given Stella.' Lucie cackled. 'A murder, not me.'

Fried chicken was off. Toni had taken the chicken to roast and share the spoils with the team. Bella had taken the children to the beach to get them out of the village, now filled with police stationed at the village hall and doing house-to-house enquiries. Outside the gate of the Old Rectory, a mountain of flowers was building up as parishioners came to pay their respects. As Toni had warned, the media were back. This time, parked outside Yew Tree House, Lucie was in poll position.

A plus point for Jack – and Stella – was that Bella had not suggested she take the children back to London. She still planned to leave in the morning.

'What did you both tell the police?' On the way there Stella had refused Lucie's advice that she and Jack agree on their 'story'.

'Nothing to tell.' Lucie took a milk carton from the fridge under the counter. Sloshing some in a mug, she slammed it into an overhead microwave. 'Boring old me and Prunella were here all night.' Lucie placed an espresso in front of Jack and glared pointedly at Stella. 'I told her I didn't move from this seat, which was actually true.'

'The murderer might not know that.' Stella had suggested Lucie join them in Yew Tree House that night. She might not be safe in the van.

'I told you, Prunella will keep me safe.' Lucie beamed. 'Did you two confess all to the Venerable Antonia?'

'Confess?' Stella knocked over the vase of stocks that Justin had bought for Prunella out of his own pocket money. The twins adored Lucie.

'We said the same as you – that we were in all night.' Jack passed Stella his hankie to mop up the water from the vase. 'We have nothing to *confess*, as you put it.'

'You might be able to pull the wool over the constabulary, but nothing gets past me, Jackanory.' Lucie looked severe. 'Lucky for you, Bella and her chicks slept like logs in my bedroom. It was only me who saw you both sneaking into the Old Rectory and then, precisely forty-six minutes later, sneaking back again.'

'Your blinds were down.' Later, Stella would rate listening to

Jack tell Lucie about their visit to the Old Rectory the previous night – *her* visit – lower on her list of bad memories than when he had told Justin and Milly that their grandmother had been murdered.

'Do you think that Prunella, cutting-edge of motorhomes, isn't kitted out with CCTV? That dish on the roof isn't just for the telly.' Lucie grabbed the TV remote from a slot below the small television above the table.

Moments later, ever the showman – she would have queued the footage – Lucie showed them a black-and-white film of first Jack hurrying out of the gate with Stanley, followed a minute later by Stella. The breadth of the lens put the Old Rectory gate at the edge of the screen.

'This bit is boring.' Lucie fast forwarded until Jack with Stella and Stanley reappeared. Jack closed the gate of the Old Rectory, and keeping close together – Stella had no recollection of taking Jack's arm – they sneaked – and sneaked was the word – back up the path of Yew Tree House. Lucie switched the picture to live which showed the same scene in colour.

'I checked the film, but no one else comes out or goes into Snace's house.'

'I was the one who went in.' Stella related what had happened. She was discovering that wishing the ground would open up and swallow her was a real thing. 'What if they find fingerprints?'

'You wore gloves,' Jack reminded her.

She had instinctively behaved like a criminal.

'Did Stanley have clean boots?' Lucie squawked. 'We haven't got Edgar Allan Poe to explain away pawprints.'

'Not funny, Lucie,' Jack said.

'I suppose Antonia et al could decide it was suicide?' It was rare for Lucie to try to make them feel better.

'They found a knife in the pillbox with blood on it, so that's not an option.' Stella tried to pick up her mug of coffee but her hand was shaking too much.

'Mr Harmon, you might think nothing of nesting in the homes of your True Hosts, but for Stella this is *beyond* hell.' Lucie was well-versed in Jack's obsession with True Hosts. Not averse to door-stepping, she admired that Jack used to dispense with knocking first.

'I'll tell DI Kemp I went in to get Stanley.' Jack hung his head. 'It will explain any paw marks.'

'Sorry, Stellagnite, but that riderless horse has cantered off. It will only expose that you lied.' Lucie was sipping her second – or fifth – espresso. 'Dear God, who would fluff out a vicar? Not you, I take it?'

'No, of course not me,' Stella barked. 'I'll tell Toni.'

'If forensics don't find anything incriminating then what will 'fessing up achieve?' Lucie said. 'It will only lumber that detective – who takes you seriously for yourself as well as your pa – with a new problem. Does she charge you or let you off with a wrist-slap? What we need to concentrate on is finding the killer. For instance, did you notice anything odd when you were in there? No sign of anyone?'

'I saw Snace crossing from the hall.' Stella rubbed at her temples. 'It stopped me leaving by the front door as I'd intended.'

'Or you saw the killer,' Lucie said.

'I'm never wrong about True Hosts,' Jack said. 'Snace was definitely a psychopath. Not everyone loved him. Someone hated Snace enough to kill him.'

'Maybe he was killed by another True Host?' Lucie ogled her eyes. 'They must collide at some point. What if one has cancelled another?'

'They are more likely to team up, like Hindley and Brady.' Jack scratched his two o'clock shadow.

'I still have Stevie and or Rosa Stride in my sights. Could either of them have sneaked around the back of Yew Tree House and then called on the vicar? My camera doesn't show the front door.' Lucie pointed at the live feed currently showing an officer guarding the scene and an elderly man laying some flowers on the heap that stretched across Church Lane.

'Snace kept the hall light off when he answered the door and lied saying Stanley wasn't there.'

'Are you sure it was Snace at the door?' Lucie said. 'As I say, it could have been his killer. Maybe by that time he was already dead.'

'If it was the killer that means Snace can't have been murdered by Stevie or Rosa.' Stella opened the door of the motorhome. 'I need some air.'

With no idea where she was going beyond the reach of Lucie's CCTV, Stella opened the gate into the churchyard.

'For a sleepy village, this one is wide awake.' Toni was on Kate Rokesmith's bench eating a Snickers. 'Granted, two murders in nearly eighty years shouldn't upset house prices, but it must be rare that the same man confesses to both of them.'

'Jimmy Chrismas killed the vicar?' Stella sat at the other end of the bench.

'No chance. Even if I didn't go on the word of his son and daughter-in-law that he was in all night, it's verifiably false. Jimmy lives with them up on Black Hill and even if he had the puff to sneak out of the house and do the twenty-five-minute walk – longer for him – he'd have been picked up on any number of doorbell cameras.' Toni offered Stella a Snickers. Haunted by her false statement earlier, Stella knew the chocolate would stick in her throat. 'And no, he didn't take his VE day bike.'

'If he was even ten years younger, I'd have him for wasting police time, but he really seems to believe it himself.' Toni shrugged and put the Snickers back in her pocket. 'Honestly, the place is bristling. Anyone planning a spot of rural crime, this isn't the village in which to do it.'

'Is there a camera on Church Lane?' Stella felt duplicitous for asking the question. If there had been Toni would not have been offering her chocolate.

'No, annoyingly it's a blind spot, perhaps Snace assumed God was watching...' Toni curled her top lip. 'It's very possible Jimmy Chrismas is protecting someone, but if the person did both murders that makes him the same sort of age as Jimmy. More likely this is a copy-cat murder and the killer has stolen stuff. It'd be a nightmare tracing all the stuff in the vicar's stockroom to establish if there is stuff missing. I bitterly regret making public that Alfred Liddell was damn near decapitated. If we released the information about the poker, would this person have stove in Snace's head? It's not often you get someone with the right credentials – age, a butcher, with no liking for the vicar – 'fessing up and you have to count him out. Worricker has done his best short of asking me to lie, to accept Jimmy's confession.'

'There's something—'

'One person is Stevie, I wondered— *oh*, you go first.' Toni smiled as they spoke at the same moment.

'The statement I gave you this morning, it, er... it wasn't right.' The words were glass marbles in her mouth.

'Wrong how?'

'I lied.'

'What, it's not your birthday?' Widening her eyes, Toni popped the last of her Snickers in her mouth.

'That was true, but...' Stella told Toni everything.

Chapter Twenty-Six

May 1945

He was out there. It was as if she could smell him.
Electrified with terror, Adelaide had checked that both girls were asleep. Henry's door was shut and she dared not risk waking him by opening it. There was silence above.

Adelaide kept to the hedge. Not being able to bear to use Rupert's greatcoat, she had donned one of the ARP black oilskins. The post had disbanded last week. *That was why he had felt safe to come.*

Since blackout was relaxed, Stevie never drew her curtains. Adelaide paused to check. The glass reflected clouds that swiftly crossed the sky. If Stevie was looking out, would Adelaide be able to tell?

There had been something odd about Stevie's behaviour recently. For a start, despite Adelaide's entreaties, she made no attempt to be polite to Snace. She wouldn't heed Adelaide's warning that the man was vengeful, he bore a grudge. Adelaide could not tell Stevie how she knew this. Nor could she curb her daughter's many ways of letting Snace know that she despised him.

If Stevie knew the truth, she would be very angry indeed.
'You took your time.' He shone his torch into her face.

'I had to make sure everyone was asleep.'

He snatched the paper bag from her and shone his torch inside it.

'It's all there, cufflinks, my rings, that necklace you—'

'It had better be,' he hissed. 'If you breathe a word to anyone, to that stupid old bore Blunt who sniffs around you like a rabid dog, or Ridgeway, wouldn't it be awful if that lovely little girl got hurt? She is turning out a beauty, isn't she?'

'How can you say these things? Have you no shame?' Adelaide knew too well there was no point in appealing to his nicer nature yet it was all she had left.

'I think you'd make a fine vicar's wife.' His laugh set her teeth on edge. What he laughed at was never funny.

'How dare you.' Adelaide had spent the last five years imagining things she could have said but her hands were tied. 'This is blackmail, I could call the police.'

'You could, but what exactly would you say?' He moved the beam around the pillbox and then to his own face. *Even good looks, perfect teeth.* No wonder women in the village had fallen over themselves to serve him. It was hard to be believe she had—

'Come here again and I will not answer for my actions.' She would kill him. Now she saw there was no option.

'God bless you, Addie, you have come on a pace.' He laughed.

He knew exactly how to get to her. *Only Rupert had called her Addie.*

Chapter Twenty-Seven

Present Day

'What are we being charged with?' Jack asked after Stella had returned and made the second confession of the day, that she had told Toni Kemp the truth.

'Nothing.' Stella slid along the banquette into the corner. 'Toni is classing it as a mission of mercy. I genuinely believed Stanley was in danger. She was more interested in the man who told us Stanley wasn't there. Although she was annoyed I hadn't told her.'

'You might have asked me first.' Jack had moved to the front seat in the motorhome which was swivelled to face the interior. 'Before confessing.'

'I think you chucked away your right to an opinion when, without a second thought, you posted poor little Stanley into a strange vicarage where you believed a murderer lived,' Lucie barked. 'Stella was true to herself. Terry would be proud.'

Stella had expected Lucie to be crosser than Jack that she had told Toni Kemp the truth. To be fair, Jack was mainly worried that Stella might get a police record. He didn't seem concerned that, although he had not actually gone into the vicarage, by going around the back and opening a window, he had trespassed.

'Shall we recap on the case?' Lucie flapped her hands as if to shoo away the subject from the motorhome.

'Bella and the twins are on their way back.' Right now, Stella would give anything for a bucket and spade.

'Then we better focus.' Lucie was strict. 'The police have their hands full with Snace's murder. As we know, they have closed the case on Alfred Liddell.'

'Do we care who killed him?' Jack said. 'Personally, if he was still alive, I'd want to shake Fleming's hand for, as Lucie put it, fluffing out Liddell.'

'I want to clear the Fleming name. It's the least I can do for my childhood friend.' Lucie joined Stella on the banquette.

'The police aren't actually saying it is Philip Fleming.'

'As you know, I think we should look no further than the family Stride. In particular Adelaide,' Lucie said. 'It defies common sense that they lived with a corpse at the end of their garden all that time. I refuse to believe it.'

'Toni said the entrance was blocked. By the time the sandbags had rotted and the concrete crumbled, the brambles had grown around it.' Stella felt an oblique need to defend Stevie. She had been genuinely shocked to hear that Alfred Liddell had been found murdered in the pillbox.

'Why block it? How does it explain numerous other pillboxes, of which I've examined two, near the hamlets of... let's see...' Lucie consulted her notes, 'Hamsey and Iford. I found three in all and not one of them sealed.'

'What about the evacuee? Henry, was it? He's a shadowy figure.'

'And the most likely owner of the dagger,' Stella agreed.

'I haven't eliminated him, but what motive did he have to kill Liddell?'

'Motive suggests premeditation. If Henry caught Alfred Liddell sneaking about in the grounds, perhaps he attacked him. Then had to hide the body.' Stella channelled her dad. 'Plenty of people could have a motive for wishing a person dead but they don't act on it. We have to follow the evidence.'

'Tell that to Toni Kemp.' Lucie did her gargoyle face.

'That's exactly what Toni is doing. Otherwise, why not simply arrest Jimmy Chrismas and be done?' Stella pointed out.

'What motive has he given?' Lucie said.

'None. After claiming he killed Liddell with a poker, he probably worked out that the less he said the more likely he would be believed. We said we'd recap, time is running out. Before we know it Milly and Justin will be wanting to join the meeting.'

'Let them,' Lucie said.

'Like I said, this is a story. It started when Alfred Liddell murdered fifteen-year-old Greta Fleming on Esher Common,' said Jack.

'Then he disappeared.' Stella picked up the baton, speaking slowly although Lucie was taking it down in shorthand at the speed of light. 'Toni blamed the police at the time for not making the connection between Liddell's sudden absence and Greta's murder. Although, she reminded me, they were incredibly short staffed with most officers having been called up.'

'Did Liddell's wife report him missing?'

'There's no evidence she did. After all, he was a grown man.'

'Can't blame the police then.' Lucie tapped her notebook with her pen. 'Moving on.'

She got up and turned to her coffee machine. 'More coffee, poppets?'

Jack refused, but hoping it would reduce the numb feeling after her interview with Toni, Stella asked for another latte. The aroma of fresh coffee filled the motorhome.

'All I can find on Alfred Liddell is he married Susan Abbey in August 1940. Their son William came along at the end of the war in March 1945. Liddell married Susan the day after he murdered Greta Fleming. The same day as your birthday, Stella, give or take twenty-six years.' Lucie handed Stella her latte and waited while the machine sputtered out an espresso. 'I'm trying to get hold of Daniel Liddell, the grandson, but since he flew in from Lanzarote he's gone to ground. Hot damn, if *The Sun* has him holed up in a spa hotel… I guess you can't tap Toni Kemp?' Then when Stella shook her head, 'Thought not.'

'What we still don't know is why Liddell came to Sussex and was murdered in our pillbox.' Jack slapped the leather arms of the throne-sized chairs.

'It's not *our* pillbox.' Stella snuggled deeper into her corner. She had never imagined living in a motorhome, but one as luxurious as Prunella rather appealed. If there was trouble, you could start the engine and drive away. Not like Lucie who always zoomed towards trouble. 'Since she didn't report Liddell missing, perhaps Susan Liddell suspected her husband had something to do with Greta's murder. Wives often have inklings when things aren't right. She could have been in denial.'

'If she had dobbed him in after he'd gone missing, what's the bet that the good people of Esher would have treated her as a murderer by proxy? Stevie said her mother was very upset when they found Greta's body. It had become a story that gripped the nation.'

'Liddell was a farmworker – didn't the farmer miss him?'

'Susan Liddell probably told them he'd got a better paid job elsewhere or maybe even that he had signed up.'

'And so he got away with murder,' Jack said.

'Hardly,' Lucie and Stella said together. In a sonorous tone Lucie added, 'The police didn't know until now that Liddell had murdered Greta, but someone did and they did something about it.'

'A stranger in the village would surely have been noticed.' Lucie sucked her pencil.

'It was VE Day, people were likely in a happy and generous mood and keen to share the celebration with all and sundry,' Jack said. 'What we haven't got near to answering is why he came here. The only link is that Philip Fleming, Greta's brother, was stationed here at the start of the war and, as a Royal Engineer, could have built the pillbox. It is hard to discount Fleming.'

'Agreed.'

Stella sat back as, reaching into an overhead cupboard, Lucie scattered several Snickers bars across the table with a, 'Tuck in team. Toni Kemp was buying some in the Co-op and I'm easily influenced.'

'What's your argument for saying that Stevie or her mother killed Liddell?' Jack was tucking into a Snickers. At the mention of Toni Kemp, still riddled with guilt, Stella stuck to coffee.

'Read that, I printed you one each.'

> *Interview with Stephanie Margaret Stride, 97, of Yew Tree House, Sussex.*
>
> *Q: Have you ever been inside the defence structure built at the bottom of your garden?*
>
> *S: As I child I would probably have entered it.*
>
> *Q: Did you go in there around the time the war ended, in 1945?*
>
> *S: I may have done. Before it was sealed.*
>
> *Q: Why was it sealed?*
>
> *S: After the war, the government had all such structures blocked up. No one would have gone in there, least of all my mother.*
>
> *Q: Did your mother ever enter the pillbox before it was blocked up?*
>
> *S: As ARP warden it's possible she did stuff for the Home Guard, but it wasn't their remit.*
>
> *Q: Was it mandatory to have the structure sealed?*
>
> *S: Yes, like I said.*
>
> *Q: How was it blocked up? Did the army do it?*
>
> *S: It might have been Henry, the evacuee who was billeted with us, I don't remember. I was a child at the time.'*

*Q: Doing the maths you were born in 1926, year of the gen-
eral strike, so I make you twenty so, definitely grown-up.
Yet you don't remember?*

*S: Those years were dreadful. My father had been killed,
men stationed in the house and in the garden. My mother
was a widow with two daughters. Reverend Snace tried
to propose to her. She shooed him off. She had a lot to
cope with.*

*Q: Snace wanted to marry your mother? He was surely
young enough to be her son.*

*A: Not quite, but that didn't deter him. He wanted her
money. We hated him.*

Q: You hated the vicar? Why?

*A: It's a mistake to suppose that men who work for the
Church of England are intrinsically good. Snace was an
ambitious man, out only for himself.*

*Q: I entirely agree. I can't find any evidence that the govern-
ment ordered pillboxes to be sealed.*

*S: My sister was seven in 1945. She was out and about.
Mother would have been worried she'd get trapped in
there and become frightened. Rosa was an anxious child
– she had known nothing but the war, of course. I made
her hide that from my mother, she needed to believe Rosa
had, as Mother told people, 'come through unscathed.'*

Q: Frightened because Alfred Liddell's body was in there?

*S: If Rosa had found a body, yes, she would have been fright-
ened.*

Q: You said Henry the evacuee blocked up the pillbox?

*S: I would think it was Henry. He helped my mother with
odd jobs when he could.*

Q: What was Henry's surname?

S: It was so long ago, I wouldn't remember.

'You've interviewed Stevie Stride?' Jack finished his Snickers.
'What changed her mind?'

'Nice old cat,' Lucie purred like an old cat herself. 'She wanted her side of the story told.'

'Did you pay her?' Stella said. Unless Lucie was waving a fistful of notes, she'd surely be the last person anyone, especially Stevie, would allow across to their thresholds.

'No. Not everyone wants their palm crossed with silver.'

'Lucie, she needs the money,' Jack protested.

'What do you take me for, Jackanory?' Lucie looked genuinely hurt. 'I offered, but she took umbrage. She only talked to me on the understanding that I didn't record her.'

'This is all from memory.'

'She didn't mind me showing off my speed of light Pitman's shorthand, though.' Lucie did her Cheshire cat smile.

'I can't believe Stevie was willing to answer these questions.' Jack was pouring a glass of water from the tap. He waved it at Stella. She took it. Unused to two coffees in a day, her heart was taking off. 'What about Rosa, did you interview her too?'

'I did, but she's like a butterfly, flit-flit and never on point. I think she's led a sheltered life,' Lucie said.

'You come pretty close to accusing Stevie of murder.' Stella ran her finger down the transcript.

'Stevie took it on the chin, she's a cool customer,' Lucie said. 'For all that, she gave herself away.'

'How?' Stella scanned the extract but couldn't see a slip.

'In almost every answer she employs the subjunctive.' Perhaps seeing Stella's face, Lucie continued, 'Stevie replies as if I'd posed hypothetical questions: *what if, supposing*, she never offers concrete information. Take the first one where I ask if she's ever been in the pillbox and she says "As a child I would probably have entered it." I ask who blocked up the entrance and she replies, "Henry might have done…" Every answer is wreathed in the fog of "may haves", "possiblys", "probablys" and "would haves", none of her answers can be confirmed or battened down. Even when I asked for the evacuee's second name, she claims not to remember – *a lie* – she predicates it as contingent on the time that's elapsed like "it's nothing to do wiv me, guv". Smart chick.'

'It could be how Stevie talks?' Stella did not feel ready to tell Lucie that Toni's attention – for both murders – had swung back to Stevie. Lucie would do more than run with it, she would take off. Stella needed the space to form her own opinion. To at least get over her utterly irrational wish that it was not Stevie. She needed to talk to Jack by himself.

'It's how a person talks when they're hiding something. Otherwise, why not dish up the facts? Answer me this: why doesn't Stevie Stride want to help get to the truth?' Lucie's tone suggested that this was all she wanted herself. 'Because it would lead us right to her door, that's why.'

'She agreed to talk to you,' Stella said.

'Only to mislead. She's a clever woman,' Lucie said.

'It is possible it's not a lie and she really doesn't recall Henry's second name.' Stella returned to Lucie's question about the evacuee. 'Rosa might know?'

'I asked. She said it was like the shelter and flitted off,' Lucie said. 'Are the police testing that knife Milly found under the floorboards for blood? What more evidence do they want that their double murderer is living in their midst?'

'Or Adelaide killed Liddell and her children had no idea,' Jack said.

'Yet they are sitting like hens on an egg refusing to sell Yew Tree House?' Lucie was like a tennis player smashing the ball back over the net before the bounce.

As a cleaner, Stella didn't want the killer to be Adelaide – or anyone who, but for fate, would never have resorted to murder. As a detective, she must keep an open mind.

Chapter Twenty-Eight

Present Day

After the Chinese meal in Seaford, Stella would have preferred a quiet walk through the village alone with Jack. After the day they'd had, she wanted to touch base privately. But when Bella insisted on getting another bottle of wine, it seemed churlish to refuse. She had offered to go into Bishopstone where they grabbed a bottle of Merlot as the Co-op was closing.

It was growing dark by the time they left the Co-op. The outward journey had been taken up with Bella talking about her children's reaction to the latest murder. 'Milly insists it's a man she calls Father Chrismas,' while noting that the picture of Lucie's foxgloves that Justin had done for Stella's card showed that, 'He's definitely got my genes.'

'Being with the kids is more exhausting than botanists,' Bella said as they left the Co-op. 'Nicer, obviously.'

'You find Justin and Milly exhausting?' Stella was astonished. She would rather solve murder cases than spend an afternoon in a museum of stuffed birds with two under-eights, but then that was why she'd been mugging up on Piaget. Until murder had taken over.

'Don't get me wrong, I love them. I never had much of a family until them. I'll miss them like crazy when I go tomorrow, but I've really appreciated when they're in bed and we're having adult chat. Even if it is about murder.'

'I thought you might want to take the children back with you, you know, with the vicar's murder,' Stella said. 'There's someone out there.'

'I have considered it, of course I have. But I trust you and Jack to keep them safe, Lucie too.' Bella looked at the pond, darkening now as the light faded. There was no sign of the swans. 'It sounds as if it was personal. I don't think the kids – any of us – are in danger.'

'We will keep them safe.' Given Bella's history of mistrust, Stella couldn't believe her ears. Maybe staying with Stella and Jack had made Bella feel more confident. Stella knew Bella had taken on an allotment – maybe it was communing with vegetables or whatever. Stella certainly liked Bella better.

LED lamp-posts casting pools of bluish light on the pavement made the pond look as if it had frozen over. The high street was deserted. Younger villagers would be on the Brighton train, bound for clubs where the night was beginning. In the village, it felt timeless. Eighty years ago, and the balmy summer evening in the present day, were as one.

If a murderer was on the loose, as the newspapers were saying, perhaps Stella's suggestion they take the shortcut back to Yew Tree House, literally off the beaten track, along the footpath behind the pond, was reckless.

'Lucie thinks it's Stevie.' The bottles clinked in Bella's rucksack as, in single file with Bella leading, they tramped along the footpath. 'They seem so nice.'

'Some murderers can seem nice. Anyway, I'm not so sure.' Stella trudged along behind Bella. 'It's just as likely to have been a robbery that went wrong. Perhaps the thief was interrupted.' Had she disturbed an intruder too late to save Snace from being murdered, but in time to prevent theft?

'Was this Adelaide ever burgled?' Thankfully, Bella didn't know about the debacle with Stanley at the Old Rectory. 'That's a reason to have killed Liddell. I wonder if we could ask Stevie. You don't tend to forget being burgled, it's such an intrusion. Although if she knows her mother killed Liddell she won't say. *That's it.*'

Stella just avoided crashing into Bella as she came to a sudden stop on the path. 'Adelaide kills Liddell because she caught him stealing. Snace knew about the burglary and when Liddell was discovered, he guesses the rest and is going to tell the police. To protect Adelaide, Stevie has to kill him.'

It seemed Bella could talk of nothing else but murder. Stella wondered if the change of heart was a good thing.

'What about Father Christmas?' Bella was off again along the footpath made narrow and darker by dogwood and blackthorn.

'I don't want it to be anyone we are putting in the frame. Fleming because, with Greta's murder, it's a double whammy that her brother killed even for revenge. And Stevie...' in the face of Bella's hawkish analysis, Stella felt soft, 'because I like her. The same goes for Jimmy Chrismas. With little to go on, I like the man.'

'Jimmy is safe, Lucie says he's got alibis for both murders. *Ouch.* Watch that bramble.' Bella stomped on a branch with a white Croc. 'Aren't you supposed to keep an open mind? Milly told me that.'

Toni had said Jimmy confessing might be to protect someone. If so, they were looking for a double murderer. Given the span of eighty years, the killer must be elderly, to say the least.

'Yes, that's why I'm a cleaner.' Stella sidestepped the bramble. Any minute now Bella would chastise her for Milly's familiarity with what it took to be a detective.

Instead, as an apparent non sequitur, Bella said, 'I wish I was as nice as you, Stella. You always see the best in people.'

'Do I?' Stella was confounded.

'Milly and Justin love you. I used to mind, but after this mini-break with you, I understand. *Tree root alert.*' Bella did a hop and pointed behind her. 'Me and Jack, the glass is more than half empty. Yours is brimming over!'

Bella's voice was disembodied, she was a vague shape in the gloom. For a while, the only sound was the clink of the bottles and, further off, the sea booming on the shingle. The air was strangely still, no birds sang.

'There's a storm forecast. It's not normally as dark as this,' Stella said finally.

'It's the *Hound of the Baskervilles*. There was a murderer roaming around in the dark then too, wasn't there?' Bella sounded hearty.

'We don't know they're—'

Something pushed against Stella's calf. A snuffle. *Stanley.* Feeling along his back, she established where the poodle started and ended and lifted him up. Immediately he nestled into her neck. *He was trembling.*

A growl. Stanley had sensed something. *Someone.* The thing about dogs was that they ostensibly offered protection while being akin to canaries in a coal mine. They signalled danger. Nine times out of ten, Stanley's warning growls were another dog or just a garden bag flapping in a breeze.

One time out of ten...

'Hate to burst your balloon, but I think we've proved Fleming could easily have killed Alfred Liddell. We haven't seen a soul since the Co-op.' Murder seemed to have made Bella positively cheerful.

They had reached the back gate of Yew Tree House; the pillbox on their left cast a shadow black as a chasm across the path.

'The village must have been rammed, it was VE Day.' Stella remembered the 'summit', as Lucie had called it, in Prunella that afternoon. 'For that reason, anyone could have killed him. Maybe we'll never know.'

Bella pointed at the pillbox. 'I haven't seen inside, what about a squiz?' She turned on her phone torch.

Stanley began to growl.

'Bella, you'd see more in the day.'

Too late. Bella darted around the external blast wall, which blocked her light, and plunged Stella into darkness.

'This is so creepy,' Bella whispered. 'Where was the skeleton?'

'There.' With one hand, Stella switched on her own phone torch and aimed it into the corner where the body had been propped against the wall. The police had also taken the tarpaulin that had covered the skeleton.

Bella raked her beam over the brick structure, moving deeper inside and around the 'Y' shaped blast wall; shadows crept and leapt. The brick walls seemed to swoop towards them and then away.

'Maybe we should go now.' Stella felt properly scared. Stanley began to mew.

A serious alert.

'I'm surprised they took the police officer that was guarding this place off.' Bella's voice was hollow as if from a deep cavern. 'It's an obvious place for the murderer to hide.'

'Too obvious.' Stella's tongue was rubber.

'Stella, come here, look,' Bella hissed.

'Bella, maybe—'

'These bricks are brown instead of pale terracotta and there's more sand in the mortar than the rest.' Bella swept her palm against one side of the blast wall. 'I reckon this is a repair.'

'Perhaps it got damaged in an air raid.' Stella put one word in front of the other. Facts were calming. 'In the daylight, you can see they used varying shades of brick to imitate dappled sunlight from the oak tree that partially shades it. Eighty years ago, it would have provided less shade than now. Stanley seems worried, I think—'

'But use different bricks inside?' Bella suddenly produced a penknife and, with what Stella supposed was a transferrable skill of the botanical illustrator used to handling a scalpel, dug into the mortar.

'Here we go.' The mortar gone, Bella shut the blade and, gripping the knife between her teeth, wobbled and tugged at the exposed brick. Stella thought of Milly working her tooth out. The brick slid out.

'There's something in there.' Bella reached into the gap. 'It's wedged at the back, I'll need to remove another brick.'

Stella felt the darkness pressing in on her. She moved back to the edge of the blast wall and, in a bid to reassure herself, pointed her phone to the space beyond. *Was that shadow caused by the movement of her light?*

'Stella.' Bella sounded odd. Like a different person.

'Shall I hold your—' Stella moved back around the blast wall and, her own light at mid-level to avoid blinding Bella, prepared to help.

A hand was around Bella's throat. Stanley's bark was so shrill it was a scream.

Sweat, aftershave, wet earth, the metallic tang of blood.

Chapter Twenty-Nine

Victory in Europe 1945

It was the amount of blood that shocked her. How could there be so much? She hadn't known her own strength.

When she had said he'd never dream of harming Rosa – or Stevie – he had laughed. *Remember Greta Fleming?*

It was all over the inner wall and the concrete floor. She had sluiced the floor and the walls with soapy water and covered him with the tarpaulin that had draped Rupert's Rover until she had sold it. She would block it up. She'd tell the girls and Henry that it was a government directive and they were not to go near it.

Her heart beat so hard she thought her head would burst and she pumped bucket after bucket, lugging it down to the pillbox. In the near distance came the shouts and cheers and car horns. The war was over. Stevie and Henry had gone into the village. It was young Jimmy's seventeenth birthday, too young for the pub, but they'd sit outside and no one was going to tell on him for having a pint. On this night of all nights.

Adelaide looked at herself in the bathroom mirror over the sink. No blood. She was clean. Would she ever again look at her reflection and recognise herself?

'Where have you been?' Stevie came out of her bedroom. *As if she'd been waiting there.*

'I was in there.' Adelaide indicated the bathroom. *Nubile*, he'd called her. 'I didn't hear you come in, I thought you and Henry had gone down to the village hall. Would you like some Ovaltine, darling?'

Adelaide could say she had found him stealing, that she was defending herself. *The poker would prove she had planned it.*

'I came back to see you, but I couldn't find you anywhere.' Stevie was staring at her.

'Perhaps that's when I popped out to Church Lane. You can see the fireworks over at Newhaven.' Adelaide led Stevie back into her room. 'I'll tuck you up. We don't want to wake Rosa.'

'I'm twenty,' Stevie snapped. 'Rosa sleeps through anything, remember?'

'You're never too old for your old ma to put you to bed.' Adelaide pulled the counterpane right up to Stevie's chin and kissed her forehead, confirming the kiss with the base of her thumb. 'There we are.'

'You're not old,' Stevie said.

'Sleep tight, sweetheart. It's a new world now.'

Not God-fearing, yet she knew everything had a price. What would she have to pay?

Adelaide would soon find out.

Chapter Thirty

Present Day

'Let go of her now,' Stella said. 'I've called the police.'

'Liar. I'd have heard you.'

Her mind ticker-taped. What had Bella found in the cavity? *Had they provided the murderer with a weapon?*

'...my daughter was framed, Nan loved him... can't have been all bad... no proof it was Alfred Liddell... *how much they pay...*'

The words swam in and out of Stella's consciousness.

'Well?' the man yelled in Bella's ear. She flinched but, held tightly, had nowhere to go.

'Did you kill the vicar?'

'What vicar?' Stella's question seemed to bring the man to whatever senses he possessed. He let go of Bella.

'The man who has been murdered.' Stella swore inwardly.

'I didn't kill anyone. What, you think murder runs in families?' He glared at Stella.

Too late, Stella channelled Terry: '*Never wind up a villain with no means of egress.*' She could rush out the way they had come in, but no way was she leaving Bella alone with this man. At that moment Stella spotted a long object on the floor. *A poker.* It must have been in the cavity. Without forming the thought, she dropped her phone on the floor, light bouncing around the pillbox. She grabbed the poker and held it behind her back. She felt a fizzing as her finger gripped the weapon. *One swipe and...*

'Who are you?' Bella was massaging her neck. She sidled across to Stella, who was poised to cross a line.

'You know who I am. You and your mates have made a fortune shopping my granddad to the papers.'

'Here's hoping Daniel Liddell skipped the angry gene or we should deploy a SWAT team for when Malcolm greets him off the plane.' Stella got it. Toni had no idea how close she had been to the truth.

'You're the man whose grandfather my kids found here.' Bella went from nought to sixty. 'The police got your DNA because your girl was off her head, crashed her car then bashed the arresting officer trying to breathalyse her. Exactly what twisted half-witted logic leads you to hold Stella and me responsible for your grandfather murdering an innocent girl back in 1940?'

'No girl walking on some heath at night can be innocent. Believe me.' Threat exuded from Liddell. 'My grandfather is innocent, he's the victim.'

Stella nudged Bella. If they made a dash for it, they might reach the entrance of the pillbox before Liddell. Or they could dodge back and forth around the internal blast wall. She hoped Bella had got the extrasensory suggestion.

'DNA has proved that your lovely Grandpa raped and murdered Greta Fleming on her way home from work.' It didn't help that Bella was not behaving strategically.

They had been gone longer than it took to buy wine from the Co-op, at some point wouldn't Jack come looking for them? Stella felt unreasonably annoyed that he had not already done so. But if Jack did look for them, he'd be more likely to go into the village along Church Lane. Stella's grip on the poker tightened.

'They get DNA wrong.'

'Straws in the wind, *matey*.' Bella using her best derisive tone. 'If you're looking for a woman to take out your misogyny on, start with your *innocent* daughter.'

'*Be quiet*,' Stella yelled at the top her voice. Surely Jack would hear.

'Leaving a poor defenceless girl with a kid and no money is worse than driving over the limit.' Daniel Liddell smacked his hand on the blast wall. '*Total bastard*.'

'You just threatened us because we – *accidentally* – exposed your grandfather as a murderer and now you're calling him a bastard? *Make up your mind*.' Stella smacked the poker in her palm.

'Out of interest, have *you* sold your story?' From over Stella's shoulder, Bella was chatty.

'I'm talking to a couple of guys,' Liddell muttered. 'For my grandmother. She never got justice, it's up to me.'

'Is your grandmother still alive?' Stella said.

'No, God bless her.'

'Tell you what, our friend Lucie is a reporter. I know she'd be terribly interested in hearing your perspective.'

Stella was horrified. Bella was inviting a man who hadn't thought twice about threatening two defenceless women into the motorhome where her children were sleeping.

'I won't say anything until I've signed a contract.'

'Oh goodness no. *Don't*.' Bella shone her torch into Liddell's face. As he blinked, she shoved Stella ahead of her out of the pillbox.

Stella held the poker as Liddell stumbled around the exterior blast wall into the garden. Her hands were slippery with relief.

As Stella recognised how close she had been to smashing the poker over Liddell's head, she would never know she shared this experience with Adelaide Stride who, eight decades earlier, had stood on the same spot.

★

'Margaret Rutherford's father was a murderer, that did her rep no harm.' Lucie stirred her nippet with her devil-headed swizzle stick.

'Who?' Liddell took a mug of tea from Jack.

'...makes me think of that thing on the telly that reveals celeb's ancestors. You could go on that.' Lucie jammed the devil end of her stick into her mouth. An ex-smoker, the stick was her latest cigarette substitute. Reminiscent of a lollipop, it rendered Lucie young and wide-eyed. 'You'd be a star.'

'No thanks. Since your skeleton, my girlfriend and me have been hounded by your lot. Course my ex snapped the offers up, she took me to the cleaners an' all.'

'So many smell the prospect of gold like a dog sniffs out a plate of liver.' Lucie waved the stick. 'Dan – may I call you Dan? – you have come to the right place. This is your story and we will tell it your way.'

The next hour passed in a blur. Faced with no choice, Lucie allowed everyone to stay in Prunella while she questioned Daniel Liddell.

Making the tea, Jack was furious that Liddell had been in the motorhome after his threats in the pillbox, and – uncharacteristically – had wanted to phone Toni Kemp. Stella made him hold off. Time enough for that. It seemed that offering the prospect of gold, as Bella had guessed, had neutralised the threat. Stella felt touched to see Jack sneak along the little passage to Lucie's sumptuous bedroom to make sure Justin and Milly were asleep. He was a good dad.

Stella was intrigued to watch Lucie at work. She soon agreed with Jack's muttered comment, it was 'not a pretty sight'. Lucie had the knack of bringing out the worst in the worst people.

'...like I told these girls, he left my nan high and dry with a new baby. At least Amanda was sixteen when me and the wife split. He bogged off just before VE Day leaving my nan with a nipper to manage all on her own.' Then, as if just now making the connection, 'My dad, that was.'

'He left after he had murdered Greta Fleming.' Lucie's tone was colourless as if she was remarking on the weather.

'To be fair, Nan was used to Alfie, as she called him, doing a flit. She said he was one for the ladies. After all, she'd been one of them once. She was sure he left another girl for her. She couldn't mind, she said, because he always came back. Except not that time.'

In the relatively bright light of the overhead lamp in the lounge, Daniel Liddell's Lanzarote tan accentuated receding grey hair. His attire was the leisure wear of Stella's quietly affluent male clients: chinos, polo shirt, loafers. She suspected his overly large watch with inset dials was a Rolex.

'...he always brought back presents and cash. I reckon he did jobs.'

'Jobs?' Lucie was filling her notebook with shorthand hieroglyphics. 'Like contracts?' Wide-eyed, she sucked her swizzle stick.

Stella knew what Daniel had meant which must mean so did Lucie. Her devil's headed naivety was convincing, though.

'Nan told me she was sure he was up to no good, as she put it. Going by some of what he brought back – old coins, cash, a carriage clock – it was likely he had a double whammy of seduced young widows who he stole from. It was the war, good pickings for a villain.'

'I expect it was,' Lucie crooned. As if panning for gold she stirred the contents of her sieve carefully.

'Ask me, he charmed them into giving him their valuables. Proposed to them, won their trust then got them to empty their accounts and give it to him for safe keeping. They'd withdraw their cash then he'd nick the lot.' Daniel's inexplicable grin betrayed a once handsome man.

'Is this speculation?' Lucie was rarely exercised over the difference between truth and imaginings.

'It's kind of what Nan said. It's what men do.' Liddell looked disgusted.

Did Daniel look like Alfred Liddell? Stella could keep quiet no longer.

'Did your nan think of reporting him to the police, since she knew what her husband was up to? What about the stuff he brought back?' As she stroked Stanley, nose tucked into his paws on her lap, Stella was dismayed to see her hand shake. Liddell had got to her. She caught Jack looking at her and attempted a reassuring smile. It couldn't have reassured, because, shifting closer to her on the sofa, he draped an arm along the back behind her, fingertips touching her shoulder. She nestled in.

'She'd never have shopped him, she loved him. He was taking care of his family. He loved to splash out on her, make her doll up and take her to the Savoy Grill. I tell my mates down the golf club, Dad was conceived at the Savoy. He knew how to show her a good time. I've taken after him.'

'They met at the Savoy?' Jack said. 'What did your grandmother do?'

'She wasn't selling sex, if that's where you're going.' Liddell shot Jack a nasty look. Stella was now strongly feeling that she should have Toni Kemp on speed dial.

'No, of course not.' Lucie slashed a line across the page as if deleting Jack's question and then, with the innocence of *Call the Midwife*, 'Had it occurred to anyone that Alfie had another family? I know some men do that.'

'If he did, wouldn't this whole thing have got them out of the woodwork to claim a share of the loot?' A cloud passed over Liddell's granite features. Was he lying?

'What loot?' Lucie sat up.

'What you're paying me.'

There was a silence. Stella hoped that Lucie wasn't planning on double-crossing Liddell. At least not in a – suddenly – cramped motorhome.

Secrets, Stella reflected, had no statute of limitation. But Liddell had a point – Amanda Liddell had been the only match on the database.

'Have you got photographs of your grandfather?' Lucie rattled the ice in her empty nippet glass. 'How fascinating it would be to see what he looked like.'

'Not even of their wedding. He said he was camera shy, but even at eighteen I knew that was a load of shit. Sorry, ladies.' Liddell waved a hand as if at flies.

'Don't mind us. It's being strangled that offends me,' Bella snapped.

'Yeah, sorry about that.' Liddell didn't sound sorry. Stella began to hope that Lucie was planning a double-cross.

'How nice you were close with your nan. Tell us about her.'

Lucie's best smile must have worked because, reddening beneath the tan, Liddell said, 'She thought the sun shone out of my arse, maybe because she said I was a spit of Alfie. My dad took after her. No one liked her, my mum said her life had made her bitter and twisted, the worst mother-in-law. Once Alfie dumped her for good, she couldn't parade around in glad rags lording it over the neighbours. For all she never had a good word to say about him, Dad splashed out on her funeral. Mum stayed in bed with sinuses. At least when Nan moved closer to us, she could pass herself off as a widow instead of a wife abandoned by her husband. There was a lot of shame in that, you know.'

'More shame in trying to strangle someone.' This time Bella slapped the generous leather arm of the swivelled driving seat where Jack and Stella had insisted she sit. Maybe it was now time to call Toni.

'It must have been so hard.' Lucie's look at Bella would have reassured Stella if she hadn't known Lucie's concern was less about Bella, more about whether this would endanger Lucie's own pot of gold. When she had talked about dogs and plates of liver, Lucie had meant herself. Stella didn't need reminding that it was pointless being friends with a tabloid reporter and expecting ethical purity.

'People are saying Alfie deserved to be killed.' Liddell fiddled with his Rolex. 'They forget how it was for Nan.'

'Sounds like you did too.' Stella felt Jack's hand on her shoulder. *Not here. Not with the kids just along the passage.*

Liddell was lying. It should be no surprise, but it was. He had never given a thought to how it was for Susan Liddell, his grandmother. Liddell was as good an actor as Lucie as she feigned concern for her interviewees in pursuit of her story. But where Lucie could actually care, Liddell's empathy was fake. He wouldn't know how to care. At that moment, Jack leaned in and whispered, 'True Host.'

Yet again, Jack had read her thoughts. Despite cooler summer air drifting in through the open windows of the motorhome, it felt thick with terrible possibility.

'Do you have anything from the stuff your – Alfie – brought back from his jobs?'

Lucie's detached expressions – 'Alfie', instead of 'your granddad', and her adoption of the euphemism 'jobs' was not good. Beyond ridiculous, given Lucie was in her seventies, Liddell could knock her down like a feather, but Stella had kidded herself that Lucie had him under control. Now Lucie too was being careful.

'Just a cigarette case. Since I stopped the fags, I use it for business cards.'

'Have you got it on you?' Lucie swooped forward.

'I didn't come here to network.'

'One should always network, I don't have to tell you that, *Dan*.' Lucie appeared as if scrabbling in her toolbox for the right wand. Stella cast about for a reason to leave and call Toni Kemp.

'It's got initials on it, one is an S, Nan used to say it was for Susan. Don't know why she kept it, it would have fetched a bob or two. I'll WhatsApp you the pics. It's all I've got of him.' Liddell's proud expression was genuine. 'It's not like I need the money.'

'I'll put the kettle on again.' Stella was a rubbish actor.

'Not for me, love, I've got to get back. Amanda and my girlfriend will be scratching each other's eyes out by now.' Liddell shook his head, presumably at the shortcomings of the two women.

Liddell left, silently gliding down Church Lane in a vast electric Range Rover. Doubtless he viewed his visit – resulting in the promise of cash and being holed up in a two-star Michelin hotel with Lucie to firm up his story – a resounding success. After he had gone, Stella was grateful to say goodnight to Lucie and Bella and retreat to Yew Tree House with Jack.

She checked all the doors were locked – flimsy though Toni had thought them – and on alert after Liddell's attack, pulled across the drawing room curtains, coughing as this released a cloud of dust. She had considered getting the curtains down to get them cleaned, but Jack had dissuaded her. There was no stepladder and likely the fabric would tear.

It was properly dark outside, but even so, she could feel the presence of the dark pillbox, the walls holding their secrets at the end of the garden.

'We'll call Toni in the morning.' Jack came over and looked at her with obvious concern, stroking Stella's hair from her face. 'Liddell's not getting away with what he did to you both, that was assault.'

'What can Toni do? We should have called her straight away. Instead, we let him into the house and made him tell us about his grandfather. If we charged him with assault, a defence lawyer could chew us up and spit us out. Bella said she'd rather leave it and it's her call.'

'That's how men like Liddell get away with it.' Jack's face was tight with anger. 'Unfortunately, they don't all end up dead in a pillbox.'

'I wonder if Susan Liddell knew her husband had murdered Greta Fleming. He lived in the area and could well have been interviewed,' Stella said. 'But surely not or she would have told the police.'

'That would have brought shame on herself and she'd also lose the money Liddell gave her.' Jack shook his head. 'Likely she closed her eyes to any suspicions.'

'And live with a murderer? She didn't have a child until the end of the war, why not leave him?'

'Maybe Liddell had some hold over her.'

'Oh, it's always so much more complicated than it looks in Lucie's articles.' When she had met Jack, Stella had tended to take refuge in black-and-white interpretations and divide humans into good and bad. Jack possessed a more nuanced approach to life. And murder.

The tension of the last couple of hours had made Stella cold, but it was over the top to put a match to the broken twigs and spills of newspaper gathering dust in the grate.

'I had no idea that Bella was so brave.' Stella ran her hand along the – now polished – mantelshelf. 'I was all set to hit him with this poker we found when she dangled the prospect of a story in front of him and he caved.'

'I can't see you hitting anyone with a poker,' Jack said. 'What poker did—'

'Believe me, I was *this* close.' Stella raised her thumb and forefinger, with barely a space between them. She wanted Jack to see her for herself and what, if pushed, she was prepared to do. Stepping back, she caught the rack of fire irons and knocked out the shovel. 'Oh, goodness.'

'What?' Jack reached down and hung the shovel back on its hook.

'The poker is missing.'

Chapter Thirty-One

9th May 1945

The corrugated iron caught on the grass and bounced out of Henry's hands. He went to grab it and caught his palm on the serrated edge. He swore.

'What are you doing? *Ouch.*' Jimmy ducked as Henry made to hit him.

'Henry, it's me. Jimmy.'

'What are you doing here?'

'Me?' Jimmy retorted. 'More like what are you doing? Suppose I'd have been a Nazi, I'd have got you before you had a chance to butcher and bolt.'

'It's not funny. Go before he comes.'

'Snace? It's all over now, mate, we're stood down and that bastard can't touch us.' Jimmy aimed his torch about the garden in a pantomime of checking the area, bringing it to a halt on Henry's chest. 'Good Christ, Morrison, what happened to you?'

In the torchlight, Henry's clothes were torn and streaked with mud. And something else.

'Is that blood?'

'I, I've...'

'Take a breath.' Jimmy clamped a hand on Henry's shoulder. 'Did you have a dust-up?'

'I *killed* him.' Henry leaned heavily against the wall of the pillbox.

'Tell me you're joking, I mean he's been asking for it, but no, mate, really not. Tell me you're having me on.' When Henry didn't reply, 'How?'

'What?' Henry appeared taken aback by the question.

'*How* did you kill him?'

'Slashed his throat. With, with my knife.' Seemingly unaware of it cutting into his skin, Henry held tight to the sheet of iron.

'Did he get you first?' With his other hand, Jimmy prised the corrugated iron from Henry and leaned it against the wall.

'He never knew I was there.' Henry straightened.

'What knife?' Perhaps something about the immediacy of Henry's response caused Jimmy to doubt him. He shook Henry's shoulder. 'What with?'

'The, er, Fairbairn-Sykes – you know. That knife.'

'Whose was it?'

'What do you mean? It was mine, of course.' Henry appeared to rally.

'Got you there.' A clap of mirthless laughter. 'You don't have your sodding knife.'

'Yes. I do,' Henry hissed.

'No, you don't. Because that's why I'm here. You left your jacket on the bench in the village hall, like a twit. I was last to leave and that Blunt asked me if I knew who it belonged to, he knew it wasn't mine. He was just checking the pockets for an ID card when I remembered if it's yours, you'd have your knife. Lucky for you I did or Busybody Blunt would have you court-martialled!'

Jimmy fished about in the bundle and passed Henry a knife in a leather sheaf, the exposed handle silver in the torchlight.

Henry didn't take it.

'Explain how you killed him with a knife that you don't have.' Jimmy was patient.

'It has to be me. It *has* to be me.' Henry coughed through tears, his voice strangled. 'She can't hang. Don't say nothing or I swear I'll kill you. *Don't make me.*'

'Get out the way.' Jimmy shoved Henry aside and pushed into the darkness of the pillbox.

Jimmy Chrismas had not truly believed his friend had killed anyone. They had both been dragooned into the unit, as much because Reverend Snace hated them as for their skills. Jimmy was trained in butchering flesh and had a close knowledge of the culverts, fields and trees of the surrounding countryside in which he'd spent all his life. Henry, brought up in London's East End, could look after himself, but soft as a lamb, hated the sight of blood.

'That's not— Henry, what?' Jimmy staggered out of the pillbox and leant against the exterior wall. For a moment it looked as if he might be sick, but after a few moments he raised his head and gulped in air. 'That's not... no.'

'He's dead.' It was Henry's turn to be calm.

'*Butcher and bolt.*' Jimmy cleared his throat. 'It's text book, we don't have to look far for who did it.'

'...I heard him going on at Mrs Stride a few days back and he threatened Rosa and Stevie. I thought I'd gone mad,' Henry said. 'He's been stealing from her.'

'Mrs Stride did this? Is it really—' Jimmy made to go back into the pillbox and visibly shrank back. 'It's... *like a ghost.*'

'It was Stevie. I heard a noise, she'd knocked over a flower pot, I goes and looks out of my bedroom window and saw her sneaking down to the pillbox. I saw her shifting this.' Henry tapped the corrugated iron. 'A few minutes later, she comes rushing out and goes like the wind back to the house. It was like she had the Devil behind her. I left it a bit and then went out and came here. That's when I found... found him.'

'If he'd been alive, what would you have done? He could have got you,' Jimmy said. 'And you didn't have your knife.'

'I didn't think.'

'Jesus, Henry.' Jimmy tutted. 'Where is Stevie now?'

'They're all asleep, that's why I waited.'

'Are you sure?' Jimmy looked up at the darkened shape across the lawn. 'Where are their bedrooms? We've made enough of a racket down here.'

'If Stevie – or Mrs Stride – had heard us, they would of come down.'

'You're prepared to say it was you? When you did nothing?' Jimmy said. 'You did that about the grave, are you trying to get yourself hanged? This is their business, it's nothing to do with you.'

'You're not listening. If Stevie is caught it's her who will be executed.' Henry paused. 'That can't happen, not with what he—'

'Better than it being you,' Jimmy said.

'Mrs Stride took me in. Even before he started on at Mrs Stride, she refused to send me back. I owe her. All of them.'

'I get that, she's a good lady, not like Mrs Blunt or the others who tell you off.'

For a moment Jimmy and Henry said nothing. The only sound was the distant hush and pull of the sea. At last Jimmy said, 'Listen, mate, I'll say it was me. I'm too young to get hanged, you're the right age. All that they'll do to me is send me to prison. One day they'll let me out.'

'You can't do that.' Henry slumped down against the pillbox. 'They'd never let you out. Not for this. The only way to make sure that no one gets arrested is to make sure that no one can get in there. But how? Why wouldn't someone go in? I did.'

'We'll do it properly. Come on.' Jimmy plunged back into the pillbox and, resting his torch upright on the floor, began hauling sandbags down from the sills of the gun embrasures. He panted, 'Take these to the door.'

'She must have used that too.' Henry pointed at a poker that lay in the gap between the external wall and the inner blast wall that divided the pillbox into three chambers. 'We'll need to wash it and put it back.'

'Better we hide it so it's not found.'

'Where?' Henry aimed his torch around the chamber.

Jimmy was looking at the roughly built blast wall. 'Leave it to me.'

Working in silence, the boys built a low makeshift wall just inside the pillbox.

'It ain't enough. My dad has some bricks on his allotment, I'll come back in the morning and see to it,' Jimmy said.

'How can we do that in broad daylight without Mrs Stride or Stevie seeing us? Rosa will ask to help.'

'You won't be here. You need to leave. You said your mum's started saying she wants you back to look after her baby, that's your excuse.'

'I won't go. Mum never showed any interest until now when I can do her a favour, it's always been like that,' Henry said. 'Even if I don't help you, what happens when Mrs Stride asks what you're doing?'

'I'll say I've got to go round blocking up defence structures, to keep out tramps and such. A government directive.' Wiping his hands on his jacket, Jimmy ducked out of the pillbox. He led Henry to the footpath that led to the village pond and looked at him.

'Except we know she won't ask, will she?'

Chapter Thirty-Two

Present Day

'Bingo! I said it was the Sisters Stride.' Lucie was triumphant. 'You find a poker in the pillbox and here, one is missing. You can count on murderers making mistakes, that's the only reason the police solve crimes. This is *huge*. They've only had eighty years to replace the fire irons. Arrogance, I call it.'

'I'm with you there.' It was rare for Bella to agree with anything Lucie said, but on this busman's holiday, much had changed. 'And we have a motive too.'

'This is conjecture.' Stella felt dazed with tension and exhaustion. 'Where are the kids?'

Last night Stella had agreed that it wouldn't be kind to rouse the sisters at midnight to show them what they already knew.

It had rained during the night and, unable to sleep, Stella had lain next to Jack, listening to water splattering onto the window sill from a leaky gutter. Eventually giving up, she had gone downstairs and stood looking out of the French windows at the dark silent garden.

The clouds had cleared. Stars pricked the sky. The brightest star, Venus or Jupiter, was like a dot of sunlight.

Stella had envied Jack that he could sleep. Like a film on a loop, the last hours replayed in her head. Two daggers, two murders, Daniel's innate brutality – all seemed to press down on her, forcing the breath from her lungs.

Now, dazed and headachy from no sleep, the question which still haunted Stella while she showered and dressed filled her with fresh dread. *Was it always right to solve a murder? Should they let sleeping dogs lie?*

'Playing nicely in their room for once.' Bella passed Stella a cup of tea.

It was the morning after Snace's body had been discovered in the Old Rectory. To avoid reporters trying to lure them out of Prunella, they had gathered in the kitchen of Yew Tree House for breakfast. Boxes of cornflakes and Shreddies along with fresh milk from Salmon's farm and a carton of almond milk – Lucie was on a health kick – stood on the table along with the stacked cereal bowls.

'Here's how I think it went. Alfred Liddell comes here, strikes up an acquaintance with the beautiful Widow Stride and worms his way in.' Lucie was playing with the handles on the Aga.

'How do you know she was beautiful? The only picture we supposedly have of her is under a cloth being a rock,' Jack objected.

'...don't be picky, Jackanory.' Lucie pulled a face at Jack. 'Liddell steals from Adelaide, and worse. This drives Stevie to kill him. Or perhaps Adelaide killed him herself. Either way, for some reason, Jimmy Chrismas is taking the rap. And for another reason, Stevie is letting him.'

'Why has no one in the village come forward to say they remember Liddell?' Stella said. 'If he got at all close to Adelaide, surely Stevie – even Rosa who was about seven or eight when Liddell was murdered – would have at least mentioned him.'

'There's no such thing as coincidence.' Jack intoned one of his favourite homilies, rather pointlessly, Stella thought.

'Rubbish.' Lucie came and sat at the table. 'With millions of sentient beings trotting about on the world as it turns, how could incidents not coincide? It's what we make of them that is fanciful.'

'That's interesting.' Against all odds, Bella seemed to have warmed to Lucie.

'My time with Terry Darnell wasn't wasted,' Lucie warbled merrily. 'Coincidence obfuscates; it's cause and effect that are your friends. You find a poker in the pillbox and there is one missing from the drawing room. Ergo, you have found the poker that used to be in the drawing room.'

'The cigarette case might also a clue,' Stella said. 'When he shows you at the hotel, send us a picture. If the case proves to be Adelaide's – or perhaps more likely Captain Rupert Stride's – then maybe there's something to your theory. Whatever, we should call Toni Kemp.'

'Stella, you're not going to like this,' Jack said. 'I'm wondering if we do call Kemp? Let's face it, what good will it do if she proves that Stevie and or Rosa murdered Alfred Liddell? Kemp and her team have closed the case. We have decided to nose about but wouldn't it be better to let sleeping murders sleep? Personally, I'd rather have it that Philip Fleming murdered Alfred Liddell. His daughter and her family will be OK. Who wouldn't feel sympathy for someone murdering the man who raped and killed their loved one? They won't be stigmatised. Unlike Daniel Liddell who, I hope, is dragged to hell and back.'

'Whatever, we do know that someone blocked up the pillbox and surely it had to be someone in this house. Whoever did it would have had to have known about Liddell's body.'

'Stevie thought it was Henry, the evacuee.' Lucie flipped back through the interview transcript. 'They could have bribed him to keep silent. Or he never saw the body, you said it was under tarpaulin.'

'Or they knew nothing about it and it was Henry,' Stella said. 'We can certainly cross off Rosa – like I said, she was about seven or eight.'

'People who are seven can do murders.' Milly stood in the shadow of the passage beyond the kitchen. Something, an umbrella or a walking stick, protruded above her shoulder.

'Milly, popsicle, what have you got there?' Lucie was endlessly interested in what Milly might do next.

'Stop.' Stella saw what it was a fraction before Jack got to his feet.

'Milly. Listen. I want you to… Carefully. Lay. That. On. The. Ground.' Jack inched towards her.

'Golly, Emilia,' Lucie said. 'Is that a gun?'

'Yes, and it's not a stupid toy and there's bullets.' Hardly taller than the rifle now pointing at her father, Milly soldier-marched into the centre of the room. 'It's mine. I found it.'

The four adults were utterly still. As if spoken through a loud hailer, Milly's words rang in Stella's ears:

People who are seven can do murders.

After Stella had got Milly to hand over the rifle – an Enfield – the little girl got over her annoyance because she could show the dumbstruck grown-ups where she had found it.

'We are not allowed in there.' Jack stopped outside the attic door at the end of the passage. 'Milly, did you forget?'

'I was looking for the new murderer,' Milly said. 'You have to look everywhere, even where you're not allowed.'

'True, o Queen.' Lucie's cackle betrayed that she was as horrified as the rest of them. To be held at gunpoint by a child of seven – a loose cannon – could prove to be extremely frightening.

Bella squatted on her haunches. 'Darling girl, did you think a murderer was lurking up there? If you were scared, you only had to come and tell us.'

'Scared?' Milly gaped at her mother, uncomprehending.

'Mummy means the murderer won't hurt you,' Jack said. 'Who did you think you'd find up there?'

'Father Christmas. *Obviously.*' Milly rolled her eyes. 'But he isn't there. I found his guns. Anyway, the man who murdered Snake man is on the loose, it said that outside the Co-op.'

'Darling, that's just the papers.' Bella put out helpless hands.

'*Guns?*' Stella caught the echo of what Milly had just said.

'There's loads and *loads*,' Milly chirped.

'Milly is right, Mummy. The murderah has been collecting them.' Justin emerged from the shadows.

If Bella wasn't thinking of taking her children back to London, Stella certainly was.

Lucie swiped open the attic door, slamming it against the wall. Wooden stairs wound up and around out of sight. A rope strung within iron hoops affixed to the wall did for a banister. In single file and in silence, their shoes clattering on the wood, they went up.

Bulkhead lamps made shadows of beams and rafters criss-crossed over the walls. A smell of damp with a hint of harvested corn hung in air warmed from the trapped heat of the day. Missing roof tiles had let in a flotsam of twigs and leaves, which lay scattered on the boarded flooring.

Stella had the fleeting thought that, although the building had survived two wars and decades of neglect, it would need more than Stevie and Rosa Stride returning to live in it to bring it back to life. If Lucie's theory was correct, and Stella credited Adelaide – a woman she had never met – with credulity, was a woman who had brought her children – and an evacuee – through the war, and had been an ARP warden, likely to be taken in by a roving chancer? It was all, as she'd said, conjecture.

'This must be where the evacuees slept initially, until Rupert Stride was murdered in the tube station. Bit gloomy, for sure.' Jack was examining a row of three camp beds neatly draped with harsh wool blankets.

'Breaks my heart to think of kiddies sent away from home with labels round their neck thinking they'd never see their mums and dads alive again. Just imagine if that was the twins.'

'I'd like to be evacuated. It would be like a holiday.' Milly did a hopscotch trip down the length of the attic.

'Yew Tree House has five bedrooms yet they shoved the children up here under the rafters.' Lucie snorted.

'Not they, it was Rupert Stride,' Stella said.

'Any*way*, this is my *guns*.' Milly stopped jumping and splayed her arms upwards to the rafters' apexed roof.

'"Are" not— *Jesus*, Milly. They are *not* your guns.' Bella grabbed Milly and held her.

The lamps attached to the vertical supports sent just enough light to make out long objects strapped to cross beams high above.

'Fifteen.' Lucie was counting along. 'Someone meant business.'

'Milly, how could you tell they are guns from here?' Stella asked.

'I climbed and saw,' Milly said.

'Haven't you seen our Milly swarm up a lamp-post like a kitten up a Christmas tree?' Perhaps recognising it was far from amusing, with a hand, Lucie wiped a grin from her face.

'Milly, did... did you have to untie the one you showed us?' Jack stammered. He'd be letting a dreadful 'what if' scenario that must grip every parent unfold.

'How did you know to climb up?' Had she just gone in and looked up, Stella was sure she wouldn't have seen the guns.

'They was where he said.'

'Who said?' Jack demanded. 'Stevie, Miss Stride? Rosa?'

'Father Christmas.' Milly folded her arms in saintly patience. Stella didn't believe her. So much had happened since they all arrived at Yew Tree House, Stella hadn't brought up the issue of the children's – Milly's, really – ability to smoothly swerve the truth.

'Jimmy, the man we met at the pond?'

'We met him first,' Milly said. 'He said they was in the attic.'

'Were. Were in the attic.'

'For God's sake, Bella, this is not the time for a grammar lesson,' Jack told her.

'These Enfields will have been up there since early in the war. Perhaps a secret stash for when the Nazis came.' Lucie rubbed the back of her neck, probably as stiff as Stella's was from craning up.

'Could they be a stash put there by the Home Guard?' Stella said.

'Why would they do that? Men in the Home Guard needed weapons for daily use.' Lucie batted away the idea. 'I would be surprised, too, if they got their hands on decent clobber like these.'

'What else can these be for?' Gripping Milly by the shoulders, Bella was keeping her fast.

'Jimmy Chrismas called himself a "Stay-behind",' Jack said.

'Like the people who had knives like the one Milly found,' Stella exclaimed. 'Is this a secret cache? If it is, Stevie and Rosa know about it. That's why they said the attic was out of bounds.'

'Since he was sleeping up here, isn't it likely the guns were concealed by the evacuee?' Jack said. 'Adelaide Stride could have known nothing about them. Any more than she may have known about the knife.'

'He moved down to the same floor as the family. And could the guns have been here all this time without either sister knowing?'

'It's all pointing back to Henry.' Jack was following a thought train. 'You told me that Stevie said he left suddenly and never got in touch again. Why not? Plenty of evacuees form relationships with the families with whom they were billeted that last the rest of their lives.'

'Perhaps Rupert Stride had them hidden up there but died before he could do anything with them,' Stella said.

'Like what?' Lucie said.

'I don't know, maybe he was in this Auxiliary Unit. It would explain the dagger under the floorboards.' Stella was flying by the seat of her pants now.

'They were set up in 1941, when invasion looked likely. Stride had been dead several months by then.'

'If Stevie knows, this is why she won't sell Yew Tree House in case the guns are discovered. She didn't want us staying and this is why. We might have found them. We *have* found them. What it does tells us is Stevie knew *nothing* about Alfred Liddell's body in the pillbox.' Perhaps more upset by the episode with Daniel Liddell than she'd realised, Stella was willing to snatch at any straw that could prove Stevie was not a murderer. She felt euphoric with relief. Had they found proof to the contrary that Stevie had murdered Liddell, she could not have buried the truth and not told Toni Kemp.

'I'm not sure it does, Stellagnite darling,' Lucie murmured. 'Guns in the attic, a knife in the bedroom and a body in the pillbox. Was Little Stevie Horner really able to get on with her curds and whey?'

Chapter Thirty-Three

Present Day

The house needed a shed load of cash to restore it. Stella's cleaning had failed to conquer the stale smell in the upstairs passage. Yew Tree House had survived two wars, but decades of neglect had overwhelmed Stella's air-fresheners. Stella tried to distinguish the different elements of the haunting smell, but for once, her olfactory gift was confounded. Mothballs? Vaseline and the rubber of gasmasks? Likely her imagination had taken over. So much for not believing in ghosts. The muffled quiet, held as if in aspic, conjured the sounds of over seventy years ago. Distant guns, the roar of bombers, the wailing siren. One day, when the sisters had died, new owners would do a 'Grand Design' on the house, gut the interior, crane in vast panes of glass held by suction and dig deep into the basement. Eradicate the ghosts.

'This is where Henry slept at first.' Stevie touched the walls of the corridor to steady herself as she led the way to the attic.

Stella had insisted they tell Stevie and Rosa that they had found the guns. Rosa had been making their breakfast in the little kitchen in the annexe. Stevie had said she was checking on something for the family and hurried Stella out. It was clear that she didn't want her sister to know. It had also been clear from her reaction when Stella told Stevie that she had already known there was an arsenal of rifles in the attic.

This time, Stella noticed a lump of metal under the nearest truckle bed; shrapnel, she hazily supposed. A discarded sock lay beside it. Stevie had seen it too because she said, 'Would you mind passing me those, please, Stella.'

When Stella gave them to Stevie, she dropped the sock and the shrapnel in the pocket of her cardigan. Less a vague attempt to tidy, Stella thought, than Stevie regarded them as precious mementoes.

'Was this Henry's bed?' Stella asked.

'I believe so. It's all a long time ago.' Gone was the brittleness, Stevie sounded only sad.

In the dim light from the bulkhead lamps, Stevie looked truly in her late nineties, somehow exhausted and hopeless. 'Father never wanted them, but as chief ARP warden he had to set an example. Mother and myself went down to collect them.'

'And then, Henry was moved to a bedroom below?' Stella couldn't remember if she knew this from Lucie's transcript, what Toni had told her or what she had learnt herself.

'That was after Father— Mother set Henry up in the bedroom where your children are sleeping now. As I told you.'

Nothing wrong with Stevie's memory.

'Mother thought of him like a son.'

'But you didn't think of Henry as a brother?' Stella did remember that Stevie had reacted sharply when she had assumed Henry was her brother.

'I never thought about it. There was a war on.' A stock phrase. 'In my grandfather's day this was where the servants slept. Until the war we had a housekeeper who lived where we live now, after the chauffeur went. My father liked to drive himself. A girl came in a few days a week and Rosa and myself had a nanny, they went when war started.'

'And you don't know where Henry is now?' Stella was pushing it.

'Long dead.' Stevie's memory had failed her, that was not what she had said last time.

However, it was probably true. While knowing virtually nothing about Henry the Evacuee, Stella's weight of sadness sat heavier still.

'How on earth did Milly get up there?' Stevie sounded impressed.

'She can swarm up lamp-posts. She's not afraid of heights. She has just confessed she got up that upright post and climbed onto the beam. She gives us kittens.'

'I was like that. I wondered if it was because my father had wanted a boy.'

'Do you know why these are here? Where they came from?'

'They were for if the Nazis came,' Stevie said. 'He shouldn't have told me and that's all I'm saying. Do feel free to call our lovely detective friend. I shall only tell her what I've told you. That I had forgotten they were there.'

'Did your mother put them there?'

'This has *nothing* to do with my mother. She was an ARP warden, the fiercest weapon she wielded was a stirrup pump.'

In the watery light the guns seemed to gain clarity. Cold metal. Solid. Their only purpose to end a life. Suddenly, Stella recalled Jimmy's words by the pond.

Butcher and bolt.

Everyone was assembled in Prunella. The twins in the front seats, Milly, with her back turned, pretending to drive. Justin, chin resting on a fist, looked out of the window. Bella and Lucie sat one side of the fold-out table, Jack and Stella the other. They had brought drinks and biscuits from the house.

At Farmer Salmon's suggestion, the harvest in and bales removed, Lucie had reparked Prunella in the field beyond the gate. Although Lucie had caused him no end of trouble driving into Bishopstone, the farmer seemed keen to help her. Again, the number of reporters had dwindled, but this new position gave them privacy. If anyone approached Prunella, they would be trespassing.

Through the cockpit-like windscreen lay a panoramic view, taking in the church and the graves to one side, Church Lane with the Old Rectory on the other. Far off, fields ended with a glistening line. The sea and then a blue, blue sky. It was not a day to be inside, but the beach had palled.

Stella had debriefed about her visit to the attic with Stevie.

'Did she give a reason for not reporting the guns?' Lucie said.

'She forgot they were there.'

'Someone removed the poker from the drawing room. Bashed Liddell with it and then walled it up in the pillbox. From what Jimmy Chrismas said, the killer slashed Liddell's throat, but of course, with no soft tissue, any evidence has gone. Not the act of an innocent party, and all this time, are you saying the family didn't notice it gone, or notice the body in the pillbox *or* this huge stack of guns?' Lucie had Stevie Stride in her sights.

'I found them.' Milly peered over the back of the driving seat. 'I'm going to tell the per-leese when they come when I tell them we found the murder-*rah*.'

'Leave everything to us, Mills,' Bella barked.

'You and the *de-teckertif* is wrong.' Exasperated, Milly vanished below the headrest.

'Why's that, popsicle?' Lucie's interest in the twins had a downside. Stella saw Bella and Jack each close their eyes.

'Father Christmas told us he murdered the man in the pillbox,' Justin said after there was a silence from the driver's seat.

'He lives in Lapland?' Jack went for a feeble joke. Mistake.

'Milly, for once and for all, if you want to play detectives, you have to listen to what is found. DI Kemp told us that nice Jimmy Chrismas had an alibi for when someone murdered the man in the pillbox. Your skeleton. I know it's disappointing, but please stop going on.' Bella might have been telling Milly that she couldn't have an ice cream because the van was shut. Except she was talking about murder not a Ninety-Nine. *There was nothing normal about the lot of them.*

Milly reappeared over the top of the seat and, goggling at them said, 'The *pleeese* are wrong. Ask Jimmy. That's all I'm saying on the subject.'

'I should be getting on the road.' Bella looked at her watch. 'Kids, do you want to help me pack?'

From everyone's faces, it was clear no one had remembered that, having stayed nine whole days, Bella was leaving for London today. Stella heard herself say, 'Why don't you stay?'

'No, really it's your holiday.'

'It would be great if you did.' Jack squeezed Stella's hand under the table. Stella hadn't planned to invite Bella, but after their nightmare in the pillbox the night before, Stella felt some kind of bond.

'That's really generous, guys.' Bella reddened as if she might cry. Stella recalled how, apart from her twins, Bella had said she didn't have family, a throwaway remark. Bella didn't have an ounce of self-pity.

Stella found that the prospect of Bella staying on lifted her spirits for the first time in at least twenty-four hours.

The rain of the night had washed everything clean. Grass around the pond, burnt light brown by the drought, was tinged with a haze of green.

After Stella had rung Toni Kemp, yet again Yew Tree House was filled with forensics and Kemp's team.

'*Did you remove the poker from this cavity?*' Toni's neutral tone had given away nothing. However, when she heard about Daniel Liddell's visit she said she would send Sheena to caution him. '*If you press charges I'll enjoy putting him in jail until some fancy lawyer gets him bail.*'

Stella could think of nothing she'd like better than to have Toni and her team cart off Liddell, he had truly upset them both, but Bella hadn't wanted any fuss. Like Jack had said, men like Liddell got away with it.

Toni was annoyed that she'd have to get Liddell's fingerprints to eliminate them from any found on the poker. She had seen Stevie and Rosa Stride, both of whom claimed to know nothing about the guns. Toni, like Jack earlier, said she believed them.

Jack and Stella had decided to walk into Bishopstone for a breather. Lucie had gone to a hotel in Arundel for the night to meet Daniel Liddell for photographs and personal information – colour – about his family and childhood. Bella had succeeded in persuading Milly that Drusilla's Park – a zoo aimed at children – might appreciate her patronage. Justin had simply looked pleased Bella was staying on.

When Jack and Stella saw that there was no one sitting on the bench by the village pond, they admitted to each other that they had hoped to run into Jimmy Chrismas.

'Let's go and visit him,' Jack said.

As they crossed the road and pushed open the plastic slats across the doorway of the butcher's, Stella admitted to herself that they had intended to come there all along.

'I told you not to take him seriously.' Bob Chrismas, his white apron streaked with slashes of bright red blood, was arranging cuts of meat in the glass display. The smell of cold flesh hung in the air. This time Chrismas sounded less welcoming. 'Is it you lot have had the police sniffing about wanting alibis? I'll tell you what I told them, Dad couldn't even kill a lamb. Luckily, in this job he didn't have to. He's an old man, can't you just leave him in peace?'

'We just wanted to ask a few things,' Jack said.

'You'd better not tire him. He's found this whole thing upsetting. That poor vicar, why would Dad want to hurt him? The man did only good, a dreadful way to die. Five minutes and that's your lot.' Bob Chrismas flapped another set of plastic strips aside and poking his head through raised his voice. 'You got visitors, Dad. I've told them not to bother you for long.

It's not the police.' Returning to the shop, 'I mean it, I don't want him upset. He's already had one visitor that upset him today.'

'How did they upset him?' Jack sounded outraged.

'Who was it?' Stella stepped forward.

'A stamp collector. Stayed a while, what there is to say about stamps, beats me. Bloke was even older than Dad, more mobile though.' Bob Chrismas slid a tray of spiced pork chops under the glass counter. 'I checked he wasn't here to grill Dad. We've had some reporters in from the papers. Being old doesn't stop you chancing your arm.

'And you missed your landlady. First time in sixty years she's come. Mum got it in her head they were sweethearts and was on guard. This murder has unsettled all the oldies. Reverend Snace christened me, that man was the heart of this village. Came for his mince each week without fail, a lovely chap. Remembered the names of my children and the grandkids. Hanging's too good for whoever did this to him.'

'Do you mean Rosa Stride?' Again, Stella recalled Stevie's remark about villages being poisonous place. Did she think the vicar a 'lovely chap'?

'*Miss* Stride to me, I used to deliver their meat as a lad. They're vegetarian now. No, the older one, she and Dad were apparently thick as thieves in the war.' The bell over the shop door clanged with a customer and Jack and Stella took that moment to go on in.

The room behind the plastic curtain contained several upright and one chest freezer. They walked down a stone passage past a 'cold cell', the name of which made Stella shiver, reaching, at last, a surprisingly cosy parlour with a view of a yard in which large plastic bins were lined in a row.

After the chill of the passage, the room was sweltering. Despite it being summer, all the bars of a ceramic electric fire placed in an iron grate glowed red. Covered with a crochet blanket, Jimmy Chrismas lay on a faux leather riser recliner.

Jimmy looked more his age than when they'd met him by the village pond. Far from the upbeat mood his son described, Jimmy looked depleted and diminished, a rag doll. Rather than coming to 'keep Jimmy company', they were there under false pretences.

'We should go,' Stella whispered to Jack.

For answer, Jack took one of the dining room chairs opposite the recliner and sat on it. This forced Stella to take the other.

Although Jack reintroduced them, Jimmy only showed interest when Stella reminded him that they were staying at Yew Tree House.

'It's lovely there.' It was as if he was transported to another time. Had it ever been lovely at Yew Tree House? 'Mrs Stride knew how to make you feel welcome.'

'My daughter found a load of guns in the attic,' Jack said. 'Stevie thought you might know about them? They must be from the war.'

'She only wondered.' It wasn't exactly how Stevie had put it; Stella felt bound to qualify.

'We didn't have a choice. He had me and Henry to ransom.' Jimmy plucked at the edge of his blanket. 'Your girl said they were investigating who killed... *him*... Plucky little thing. I told her – I told the police – it was me. Always said I would. I keep my promises.'

'Who did you promise?'

'He was top of my list. They had to be the first to go, but he would have got us first. You shouldn't have gone, lass.' Jimmy suddenly focused on Stella. 'You saw me? But—'

'The police say you had an alibi for Reverend Snace, your son says you were in all night.'

'I told him, I would and I have. He's had a life. More than...' Jimmy descended into a fit of coughing.

'Jack, we really should go.' Stella couldn't bear it. Even if Jimmy didn't have dementia, they should leave him alone.

'Are you saying you did kill Snace? That you got down here from your house without being seen on cameras or leaving the house?' Jack was persisting. 'And Alfred Liddell?'

'My mum loved the man on the wireless. She'd say if we have to have bad news, she'd rather hear it from Mr Liddell.'

'I don't think he was ever on the—' Jack said.

'You mean Alvar Liddell, the news announcer?' Stella was looking at her phone.

'That's a good little trencher girl you've got there.' Jimmy shifted gear again. 'Just like little Rosa Stride, for all she was a spit of...'

The fug from the electric fire was giving Stella a headache.

'I'm going,' Stella told Jack. Now, to her relief this time, Jack agreed. He pushed the chair back to the wall again and had shaken hands with Jimmy and thanked him for his time before she had got up.

As Stella bent to Jimmy to say goodbye, he clutched at her jacket, his fingers strong. He pulled her closer.

'Take this. You had to pay, they didn't want people knowing. I found it in the pillbox.' Jimmy wrapped something into Stella's hand and closed her fingers around it. He said something that she didn't catch.

'What was that, Jimmy?' Stella asked him.

'Bshhr n bowt.'

Her head fugged by the cotton-wool warmth, Stella still made no sense of it but wasn't going to push it. She met Jimmy's gaze, unblinking, as if he was trying to communicate something vital to her.

'Ste...'

'Stevie?' Stella said.

'...ook... afffte...' Jimmy's head dropped and his eyes shut. Falling into a stertorous doze, he let go of Stella's hand.

'Done with him?' Filling a plastic bag with wrapped purchases, Bob glanced behind him as, tendril strips trailing over their shoulders, Jack and Stella came back into the shop.

'He seems very tired. Like you said.' Jack waited for Bob Chrismas to finish serving his customer, a woman who looked annoyed that they had interrupted the sale.

'Take care, Mrs Barratt.' Bob hailed the woman as, the bell clanging, in a flurry of plastic strips she stepped out into the sunny street.

'What was the stamp collector's name? Jimmy couldn't remember.' Jack never gave up. Jimmy hadn't mentioned the stamp collector.

'If you are thinking I let in a conman, Dad looked like it was the King's telegram when the man walked in. Pleased as punch. He'd come all the way from Essex, all to see this blimmin stamp. Nothing special about it, as far as I could see.'

'Was he there long?' Stella said.

'An hour? Next thing I know Miss Stride was there too.' Bob Chrismas smoothed down a pad of wrapping paper.

'Did Miss Stride meet the stamp collector?'

'No idea – they both left the back way, couldn't face the smell of meat, apparently. What is this, twenty questions?' For the first time Bob Chrismas sounded guarded.

'I inherited my father's album.' Jack could be quick on his feet with a story, but Stella knew this was true. Jack's father, an engineer who built bridges and tunnels, had also collected stamps. 'You didn't say the name of the stamp collector?'

'Harold, I think,' Chrismas said.

'Just Harold.'

'He did give his surname, but I got a delivery from Salmon's Farm just then so had to hurry Harold through to Dad. Like a supermarket, maybe? No, it's gone.'

The only supermarket that came to Stella's mind was the Co-op.

'Earlier you said Jimmy hadn't spoken to Miss Stride for decades, so why now?' Jack pressed.

'We reckon she was Dad's first love. I liked the younger Miss Stride, classic blonde bombshell, men buzzed about her. She had the look of her dad – he was murdered too. Whenever I saw her in the village, she'd whisk me into Mrs Jordan's and buy me sixpennyworth of sweets. Because I was Jimmy's boy. Then my mum found out and went up to the house and tore her off a strip.'

'Your mother didn't like the sisters?' Jack said.

'Like I said, Mum suspected Dad was still sweet on that Stevie Stride. In the war Dad was in and out of Yew Tree House. The Home Guard was in their garden, well, you know that. Mum would say those Stride girls were no better than they ought to be.' Shaking his head as if the memory was amusing, Bob wiped down the cutting block. 'Breaks my heart that Dad's going daft. He's coming out with shocking stuff about that poor vicar. If people knew, they'd crucify him. That detective has been good at keeping it under wraps, but Dad's his own worst enemy.'

'He didn't like Snace?' Stella said.

'Not one bit. Snake, he called him.' Chrismas looked embarrassed. 'Dad wasn't a churchgoer, not like Mum; he got that from Stevie Stride, Mum said. He said Mrs Stride only went to church after her husband died to look the grieving widow.'

'Your mother must have been a girl too then?' Stella did the maths.

'She was sweet on Dad from a girl. He was the love of her life. To be fair, it went both ways. Dad wasn't interested in Stevie Stride.' Bob Chrismas gave a start. 'Has he been saying things about the vicar, is that why you're asking these questions? Are you reporters too?'

'No, certainly not. We really like Jimmy. What he has been saying is that he killed both Alfred Liddell in 1945 and now the vicar. We don't think that he did,' Jack said.

Didn't they? Stella glanced at Jack.

'He's fixed on that, but I swear he was at home with us all night.' Bob Chrismas rearranged his implements, putting them back where they were when he started. 'I'd hope I'd never lie to protect my family, not if they'd done something as bad as murder.

Before his stroke, Dad was the loveliest man, do anything for anyone. Hard act to follow.'

'He still seems lovely,' Stella said. 'What sort of things did he say he did in the war?'

'Reckons he was in some special outfit run by Churchill, they had to kill people, no rules, no fair fight. Get in and get out. I've told him, that's wrong, no prime minister would allow that, Churchill was a gentleman and he'd fought like one.'

'Has your dad said why he was in this army?' *The Auxiliary Units.* Stella looked at Jack. From his face she could see the penny had dropped.

'He said it was because he was handy with a knife; he started in the shop same age as me, fourteen. And always out on his bike, he knew every tree, hedge and culvert. Snace had them doing night patrols so that they could kill and disappear.' While doubting it was true, Chrismas seemed nevertheless impressed. 'Some of that will be true; as I said, Dad was in the Home Guard. However, he did not spend nights and some days in some underground bunker. He was in that pillbox where they found that monster.' Bob Chrismas waved a hand in the general direction of Yew Tree House. 'If Dad had killed him, I would shake his hand.'

'Why are you so sure Jimmy's stories are not true?' Stella said.

'Dad's war was humping bales for Jack Salmon, it was a reserved occupation.' Bob Chrismas began hacking chops off a ribcage.

One. Two. Three. He was as 'handy' with a lethal weapon as his father.

'My wife dates it to his stroke, like when people come out of a coma talking in a foreign language they never knew.'

'Or it could be true,' Stella said to Jack when they had left and were basking in the sunshine on the bench she thought of as Jimmy's by the pond. 'We know now Jimmy wasn't lying about the guns – suppose the rest is true?'

'You mean he could have murdered Reverend Snace?' Jack stretched out his legs. For a moment, Stella imagined what it would be like for the two of them to have an actual holiday. This time she didn't feel dread.

'We now know Jimmy disliked Snace and, alibi or not, the vicar was killed in the same way as Alfred Liddell. He was the leader of their patrol, perhaps Jimmy bore him a grudge for some unfairness or other,' Stella said.

'There *was* a Churchill's army.' Jack was swishing in Google. 'There's a *ton* of stuff about Auxiliary Units. The Stay-Behinds.'

'That's what Jimmy called himself when we met him here with the children,' Stella exclaimed. 'Milly said she has to stay behind, remember?'

Jack looked up from his phone. 'Jimmy Chrismas wasn't talking nonsense.

'Ooh, this is spine-chilling. The assailant approached from behind, encircled the enemy's neck with his arm and pulled him close. A slash across the neck instantly stops the victim breathing and he loses consciousness. They were left to bleed to death. The instruction was "Butcher and bolt".'

'*That was it.*' Stella sat up. 'That's what Jimmy said as I was leaving. Butcher and bolt.'

'You didn't say.'

'I wondered if I'd imagined it.' Stella could hear the words now as if Jimmy had shouted them. 'It's awful. Bob Chrismas said his dad feels shame for not fighting in the war, Bob sounded ashamed too, when all along, even though the enemy never did invade, those in the units signed up thinking they were going to. Jimmy was a hero, but people thought he was stuck at home playing soldiers like Private Pike in *Dad's Army*. How sad. Worse than that, it's outrageous.'

'The father of a boy in my school was a conscientious objector. I've never forgotten the history master telling him off as if it was his fault; he called the boy's father a coward.' Jack had hated his boarding school.

'That kind of shame gets passed down,' Stella reflected.

'Jimmy was involved in a braver war effort than many in the forces. When he was co-opted, invasion seemed certain and therefore they were signing up to die. And because it was a top-secret initiative, no one could ever know their sacrifice.' Jack looked misty-eyed. 'I'm inclined to believe Jimmy. After all, butcher and bolt is what someone did to Alfred Liddell.'

'And the Reverend Snace,' Stella said.

'Maybe he just didn't know his name.'

'It goes towards Lucie's theory – and Daniel Liddell's grandmother's assumption: Liddell was striking up relationships with single women of means and then robbing them.' Stella gave a sigh. 'I still go back to it, the way people describe Adelaide, she doesn't sound gullible.'

'Jimmy catches him nicking stuff from Yew Tree House and kills him? Maybe Liddell was stashing stuff in the pillbox?'

'Except how would Jimmy be there?' Stella slumped back on the bench.

'Bob Chrismas said Jimmy was in and out of the house. The ARP post was there, Rosa told us that.'

'Not in 1945 it wasn't.'

'Damn, no.' Jack got up and paced the path in front of the bench. 'Of course, Henry lived in Yew Tree House.'

'Jimmy said something about making a promise. Did Henry kill Alfred Liddell and Jimmy promised to take the blame? But why?'

'Maybe Henry was blackmailing him?'

'That doesn't ring true. Stevie – and Rosa – have spoken about him warmly.'

'Not true, Stevie seemed angry with him,' Jack reminded her.

'Because he left Yew Tree House after the war and never got in touch again.' Stella was watching the swans on the pond. Perhaps feeling the sun, they were in the shadows of the reeds. One swan was keeping a beady eye on Jack as he walked back and forth. 'If he had murdered Alfred Liddell, that would explain it. But the vicar too, that's a stretch.'

'Murder is a stretch,' Jack said. 'We need to find this stamp collector. Isn't it a bit fishy that in the midst of telling the police he's a double murderer, Jimmy entertains a philatelist? Like Clapham omnibuses, Jimmy gets two sets of visitors in one morning. That's fishy too, don't you think?'

'You mean number nine buses.'

From the reeds came a sibilant sound.

'That swan isn't happy, Jack, please come and sit down.' Stella patted the bench. 'If Henry was the same age as Jimmy, he'd be ninety-five. To be honest, the chances are that he actually is dead.'

'Jimmy Chrismas isn't dead.' Jack joined Stella on the bench.

'That's not an argument,' Stella said.

'It kind of is,' Jack said. 'We need to find out his surname and then we'll find him.'

'Neither Jimmy nor the sisters claim to remember. Rosa was little, but Jimmy *and* Stevie?' Stella paused. 'I can remember the names of everyone in my primary school class.'

The swan had stopped hissing.

'That's you. I can't,' Jack said. 'Apart from that boy Simon.'

They both grimaced. Simon had come back to haunt Jack in their third investigation together.

'*Henry is the stamp collector.*' Stella jumped up. *Sssssssss,* from the swan. Stella sat down.

'Stevie thought Henry was dead,' Jack said.

'I believe that she didn't know, but at some point today, after I showed her the guns, Stevie found out Henry is alive?' Stella felt herself revving. 'Stevie goes to see Jimmy, seemingly for the first time in years. On the same day a stamp collector called Harold comes to call. Oh, I forgot—' Stella felt in her pocket and then opened her palm. 'When we were leaving, Jimmy gave me this.'

In her hand lay a shield-shaped badge in two colours – blue and red – bearing the number 1, below that 202, and below that a 3.

'That's not the Home Guard.' Jack was on his phone. He pulled up a page about special forces.

'It's for Auxiliers.' Stella spoke in a whisper.

'It says unit men could apply for a badge after the war if they could prove which patrol they were in. Oh *wow*, they had to *pay* and they got no pension. They gave up their time for *no* money to join a crack resistance team that, had the Nazis got here, gave them a two-week window to wreak damage on the invading army before – *inevitably* – being killed. And they got no recognition.' Jack huffed. 'Isn't this an unfair world.'

'Not for everyone,' Stella mused. 'I remember that when we arrived, Rosa made a passing reference to the evacuee. She said his name was like a shelter.'

'Is anyone called Shelter?' Jack scrubbed at his hair.

'Maybe it sounded like it. Skelter, Skelton, *Skeleton*.' Stella gave a lop-sided grin. 'I was never any good at word association.'

'Let's ask Rosa again. Or Jimmy.' Jack got up and hands on hips wandered towards the pavement. He exclaimed, 'What's happening over there?'

Stella looked across the road. An ambulance, open doors revealing an empty interior, was parked outside the butcher's. The Closed sign on the shop door swung as if someone had recently flipped it. The street had gone quiet. There had been little traffic, now there was none. People were gathering outside the Old Post Office – now the florist – at a discreet distance. Some watching, others making a pantomime of choosing flowers.

'Jimmy.' Stella was across the road and at the periphery of the gathering crowd without being conscious of doing so. Jack beside her, they watched as paramedics wheeled out a gurney on which lay a long shape in a body bag.

Jimmy. As if in echo of Stella's exclamation, the name hushed around the group like a sudden breeze. Bob Chrismas came out and locked the door. Stella felt herself grow hot and felt a mix of shame and relief when, unseeing, he climbed into the ambulance. It could not be their fault that Jimmy Chrismas had died perhaps fifteen minutes after they had left him, but it felt like it.

Stella and Jack had reached Yew Tree House when the *Happy Valley* theme tune blared on Stella's phone. Lucie had set the ringtone herself.

'Ask Jimmy if he was in an Auxiliary Unit.'

'I can't—' Choked with emotion, Stella hurried Jack through the gate and up the path of Yew Tree House. She did not want to be caught on Prunella's state-of-the-art CCTV.

'Yes, you can, you're brilliant with people.' Lucie knew as well as Stella that this was untrue. Stella preferred the company of a portable floor polisher to interviewing witnesses.

'...him like a hawk when you say these words: "butcher and bolt".'

Chapter Thirty-Four

Present Day

'Jimmy Chrismas has died.' Stella blurted out to Toni Kemp once they were alone in the churchyard.

'You are kidding me.' Toni pulled a face. 'I know he was pushing a century, but still – how incredibly sad.'

'Even though he confessed to murdering Alfred Liddell?'

'How does that stop him being nice?' Toni was watering Kate Rokesmith's grave.

'It doesn't but...' Stella didn't even know what she'd meant. Although she had hardly known him – didn't know him – Jimmy's death had punched a hole in the holiday. The two murders were not water off a duck's back but, beyond hating a brutal death of any kind, Stella was able to treat the men's murders with cold consideration. In the few minutes they had spent with Jimmy so soon before he had died, he had gone straight to her heart.

'I didn't and I don't see Jimmy murdering anyone.' Toni did not disguise that she too was deflated by Stella's news. Watching her sprinkle water on the grave, Stella felt bad; she should have broken it to Toni gently.

'Have you had any more thoughts about the man who opened the door that night at the Old Rectory?' As if the question was of little importance, Toni kept watering. *Classic 'teccy ruse.*

'I suppose it could actually have been Snace,' Stella said after a moment. 'Or someone else.'

'A woman?'

'I'm sure not, or at least I don't think so.'

'Aha, you're a dab hand at the definitive answer.' Toni grinned.

'It was a risk for the murderer to come to the door.'

'Shame you can't give us a firm time as to when Snace was still alive.' *Toni must still be annoyed.*

'We didn't think—'

'You didn't anticipate having to tell me.'

'No well....' Stella gave up. 'Lucie found a booklet on the internet. It's written by an amateur historian and it lists the names of the men in the Bishopstone patrol. Jimmy Chrismas is there, it was led by Michael Snace.'

'Does it mention Henry the evacuee?' Toni asked.

'No.' Stella had brought up the booklet to leave the firepan of breaking and entering and instead was in the fire that was Lucie May. The journalist was, Stella knew too well, a red rag to a police officer. Stella had seen Toni in the window of the murdered vicar's study and waved. Toni had appeared only too keen to cross Church Lane and take refuge in the graveyard. The reporters had gone – again – but Stella hoped for Toni's sake that a residual photographer didn't think to snap a shot of the lead detective watering graves when she had a murder to solve.

'This Henry sounds like a unicorn.' Toni went over to the tap and refilled the watering can. 'Is there proof he ever existed?'

'Maybe it explains why there's no CCTV of Jimmy; auxiliaries were trained to move at night and make themselves invisible. If you're relatively fit – look at David Attenborough – then that skill might never leave you. '

'Even in his nineties, we don't see Attenborough climbing trees.' Toni embarked on Captain Stride's grave.

'The sneaking-about bit, not being a commando and crawling along ditches.'

'I'm not saying Jimmy murdered Snace, but both murders bear the hallmarks of a commando-style killing.'

'They do, yes, but there are plenty of men – and women – who have had such training since. They used it in Northern Ireland, for a start.'

Toni pulled out a weed from the grave. 'I suppose the sisters find it hard to keep this tidy now.'

Stella remembered the stamp collector. 'Someone visited Jimmy shortly before he died. He claimed to be a stamp collector. It might be worth seeing if he's caught on any footage. I know he left the shop the back way, supposedly because he didn't like the smell of meat, but that doesn't ring true to me. Jack and I were wondering if he was Henry the evacuee.'

'It would upset Worricker if we asked to spend dollars on footage, never mind get the media salivating. Are you suggesting this ancient Henry person killed Jimmy?'

'As you know he was billeted with Adelaide Stride during the war and we found the Fairbairn-Sykes knife under the floorboards in the bedroom that he had used. Stevie told Lucie May it was Henry who blocked up the pillbox. Or, she thought it was. If it was him that sealed it, he must surely have seen the body.' Stella remembered Stevie's 'subjunctive' answers in Lucie's interview. 'Or smelled it.'

'Look, off the record, I'll talk to a couple of shops. The florist has a camera, I noticed it the other day, but I'm promising nothing.' Toni put down the watering can. 'Are you saying you think this Henry murdered Liddell and now Snace?'

'It's odd Jimmy gets two visitors out of the blue on the morning he died, don't you think?'

'Not terribly. I'd like to think people were queuing up outside the day I was dying.' Toni launched into another Snickers. 'Give me this Henry's full name?'

'That's the thing, none of them can remember. Apparently, he left the village at the end of the war and never contacted them again. Stevie still seems upset about it. From something she said when we arrived here, she said it sounded like "shelter", but we've drawn a blank.'

'A bus shelter?'

'They don't have names.'

'A homeless shelter.' Toni seemed to be treating it as a game. 'Or hey, here we go, what about a bomb shelter?'

'No one is called "bomb".' Stella hadn't meant to snap.

'They are called Anderson. Some of the corrugated iron used to block the pillbox came from an old Anderson shelter in your garden.'

'That means he's called Henry Anderson,' Stella crowed.

'Or not.' Toni was the ever-cautious police detective.

'Jack, what are you doing?' Stella stood in the doorway to the kitchen.

'*Quick*, come in, shut the door. *Ouch*, that hurt.' Jack was holding an envelope over the spout of a steaming kettle.

'That's addressed to Stevie.' Stella caught the name through the envelope window.

'Ah-*ah*.' Jack had laid the letter on the kitchen table and, slipping a forefinger under the flap, peeled it open. Pulling out the letter inside, he peered at it.

'You shouldn't be doing that.' Stella heard her half-hearted tone. Gingerly she leaned against Jack's shoulder. 'Does that mean what I think it means?'

'We've found the reason why Stevie can't sell Yew Tree House,' Jack crowed. 'For the last thirty years it's belonged to an equity company.'

'The sisters released equity on the house.' Stella had to sit down. 'I have clients who have done that. If you don't have anyone you want to leave stuff to it makes sense.'

'It makes sense if the cash allows you to live in relative comfort for your remaining years.' Suddenly serious, Jack took a picture of the letter, put it back in the envelope and flattened down the flap. 'But as we know, the sisters don't have a bean to rub together.'

'How can they have spent all that money?' Stella gasped. 'A hundred thousand was a lot of money then and it's a fair sum now.'

Chapter Thirty-Five

Present Day

'I'm afraid we have very sad news.' Stella didn't feel able to sit down. She stood by the gate-leg table in the annexe. Jack stood in the doorway.

'I'd like to think that at my age tears have all been shed.' Stevie closed a battered-looking photograph album and passed it to Rosa.

'Nonsense.' Rosa laid the album on a table by the window. 'You cried at *Call the Midwife* last night.'

'Who has died?' Tense and wide-eyed, Stevie looked as if braced.

'Jimmy. I know you only saw him this morning.'

'Jimmy.' Stevie spoke the name as if trying it for size. 'Yes, I did. He was perfectly all right. Oh, idiotic thing to say since he isn't now.' She lapsed into silence.

'Jimmy's son told us that your visit put Jimmy in a good mood,' Jack said from the doorway. Stella wished he didn't feel the need to assuage feelings with downright lies. Facing reality was best.

'I am sorry,' Stella said. 'I gather you were once close, when you were children.'

'Jimmy and Hen—'

'Was it quick, did he suffer?'

'I don't know. I imagine not, when we left him—'

'You went to see Jimmy?' Stevie said.

'Did you know Jimmy confessed to the police that he killed Alfred Liddell?' Jack said. 'And the vicar.'

'Of course I did. Why do you think I went to see him?' Stevie said. 'Luckily the police have more sense.'

'We were just looking at these pictures.' Was Rosa trying to change the subject?

'Leave it, Rosa. Not now please.'

'I'm just going to show them you as a girl. Like you did for me when I was in hospital last year.' Rosa stood up for Jack and Stella. 'Stevie brought this in every day so that the nurses would like me. To show I'd been young once.'

'I'm sure they liked you anyway,' Jack said.

'Are you coming in or going out?' Stevie flapped a hand at Jack. 'When you are old, people overlook you. I'm glad now Mother didn't live to old age. She would have hated being patronised and treated as incapable. Like Jimmy.'

Stella sometimes felt that about Terry.

'You don't mean that, darling.' Rosa looked shocked.

'Did Jimmy Chrismas feel he was treated as incapable?' Stella asked.

'He was treated as barmy,' Stevie said. 'He was the fool in *King Lear.*'

'He was Romeo.' Laughing, Rosa held up the photograph. 'This is 1940, it could be yesterday. Oh, just you left out of them all now, Stevie.'

Three children in their mid-teens stood around a barrow piled with what looked like scrap, garden implements, a section of railing and an old geyser. Stella recognised the high street. A woman, hands in her apron, scowling at the camera, stood outside what was now the flower shop, but in 1940 was still the post office. The woman was blurred, the children were evidently the focus of the shot.

'Jimmy hadn't changed,' Stella said out loud. The latent force that Stella had felt radiate from the elderly man in the overheated parlour was apparent even in an old black-and-white picture. Stella pointed at a tall good-looking boy on Stevie's right who was staring directly at the camera. 'Who is that?'

'Henry. Him and Jimmy were inseparable. They're all collecting salvage for Spitfires. I wasn't allowed.'

'It was rather a waste of time,' Stevie said. 'The heap at the end of the village was still there after the war. The idea was to give the populace purpose.'

'Jimmy said Henry was there this morning,' Jack said airily.

'No, he didn't,' Stevie said. 'Don't overstep yourself, young man.'

'No, he didn't say. Yet Harold is "long" for Henry, isn't it?'

'Is this your father?' Stella pointed at a photo on the adjacent page. 'You look like him.'

'Yes,' Rosa mumbled. 'He was a hero. We will never forget him.'

It was a paraphrasing of Rupert Stride's epitaph. From Stevie's expression, Stella could see she noticed this. Perhaps over decades even real grief crumbled to cliché.

'Harry, Henry, Hal. Don't make castles in the air, Stella.' Stevie cut through the conversation. 'You have a dog, let it sleep.'

Stella again considered something that went against her grain. Should the truth always come out?

The photograph had got torn and been crudely mended so that Rupert Stride, standing at the end of the family group, was at a tipped angle to his daughters and a woman who must be Adelaide. Behind them Stella recognised the French windows in the drawing room. A carriage clock was on the now empty mantelpiece. Where had she seen the candlestick before?

'You look like him.' Jack had perhaps not heard Stella say this earlier.

'So people say.' This time Rosa beamed. 'That's the last picture of Daddy before he left for London. After that there are none. That's Mother in her ARP uniform.' Rosa tapped a photograph of a classic forties' woman, her attire giving her instant glamour, but not, Stella observed, the extra something – she possessed an energy, defying description, which was nothing to do with her looks – the same internal something she'd also seen in Jimmy Chrismas. Was that charisma? All the same, Adelaide Stride was no ordinary-looking woman and it was strange to put a face to the name. Although she knew from Adelaide's gravestone that she had been dead since 1963, Stella felt the same sadness that she felt for Jimmy, dead just a few hours.

'Stevie, you take after your mother,' Jack said. This time he wasn't just saying it to be fair, Stevie was the spit of Adelaide.

'Will there be a funeral?' Rosa was looking at the young Jimmy. 'Do they let murderers have—'

'Jimmy did not murder anyone. All I know is that now perhaps we can be left in peace.' Stevie noticed the envelope in Jack's hand. 'What have you got there?'

'A letter. It was delivered next door by mistake.' Jack passed it across.

'Have you read it?' Stevie said.

'Stevie, the very idea. It's nice of Jack and Stella to bring it round and to tell us about Jimmy,' Rosa said.

'It's the least we could do.' Stella knew they should leave the sisters in the peace that Stevie had requested, but she wanted to see Stevie's reaction when she opened the letter.

'Yes, we have read it.' Jack chose his moments to tell the truth. 'I steamed it open.'

'Then you'll be up to date with my private business.' Stevie looked at Jack.

'Yes, I'm sorry. Only me, Stella had nothing to do with it.'

'Naturally she didn't.' Stevie did as Jack had done earlier: folded the letter and, putting it back in the envelope, she pressed down on the flap. 'I would like you to both leave now.'

'I'm sorry.'

'Leave Yew Tree House?' Jack looked as pale as a ghost.

'Stevie means leave us now.' Rosa's stern tone left no room for doubt.

'I told Toni that Henry's name was like a shelter. She thought bomb shelter and came up with Anderson,' Stella said when they were sitting out on the patio, bruised and sad.

'Someone, was it Bob Chrismas, said it was like a supermarket.' Jack sounded listless.

'I forgot that.' Keen to recover Jack's mood along with her own, Stella began counting off shops on her fingers, 'The Co-op, Sainsbury's, Aldi, Lidl—'

'What is this, *Supermarket Sweep?*' Bella rounded the corner of the house.

Stella explained. Jack didn't contribute; staring blankly off, he might have been in a trance.

'The children are with Lucie in that Winnebago thingy, before you ask.' Bella clicked her fingers. 'Earth to Jack?'

'Good, that's nice.'

'I could see you were fretting.' Bella pulled a 'is he OK' expression at Stella who nodded. 'It must have been Morrison. Henry Morrison.'

'That's not a bomb shelter.' Stella hated to contradict.

'Yes it was.' Tossing her bag onto one of the dilapidated garden chairs, Bella obviously had no trouble with contradiction. 'The Morrison shelter was invented by Herbert Morrison after he took over from John Anderson as Home Secretary. The Morrison was basically a large rabbit hutch which doubled as a table with room underneath for a mattress. After the war, my grandparents put theirs in an outhouse. I would hide in it, not from bombs, but from my mother's tellings-off for existing.'

'That must have been tough.' Stella was acutely aware her response sounded inadequate.

'Not as tough as for my grandparents tucking in there every night as incendiaries dropped from the sky.'

'Perhaps differently so?' Jack came to life. 'Henry Morrison, you are a *genius*, Bella.'

'There's me thinking I'm a genius for being a prize-winning botanical illustrator when it's because I shop at Morrisons.' Bella changed tack. 'I heard Jimmy Chrismas died. Would you guys come with me to tell the twins? Breaking bad news isn't my thing.'

Chapter Thirty-Six

Present Day

If crowds at a funeral were a sign of popularity, Michael Snace had been as loved as Bob Chrismas had said. It was two and half weeks since the elderly vicar aged a hundred and three had been found murdered and the little churchyard surrounding the church where he had presided as first curate then a fully fledged vicar was packed, as if Snace had been a celebrity.

The grassy slope, dotted with graves, was a natural amphitheatre. Standing on the periphery, Stella had an uninterrupted view of the interment. In the hushed quiet, the words of the service carried as clear as glass.

Milly and Justin had been taken on a day trip by their parents to avoid the funeral. Jack had wanted them to be there: watching an interment might help them understand the meaning of death. Bella had said it was teaching them to be rubberneckers and anyway, hadn't this holiday taught them enough about death? For herself, Stella was concerned that the children had not yet grasped the fact that Jimmy Chrismas would never again sit on the bench by the pond where they could chat to him. This had been confirmed when Milly had wondered out loud if Jimmy would be there today.

One person who was, Stella was pleased to see, was Toni Kemp.

'Wayne Meekings cannot seriously feel the loss of Reverend Michael Snace, no way is he even a Christian.' Toni nodded at a man a few metres from them who was leaning on Adelaide's grave. 'GBH, house-burglar, out on licence, and more than half the occupants of houses in this village are right here, right now. You watch, Wayne and his jemmy will soon be creeping away.'

'Is Meekings a suspect for Snace?'

'He has an alibi, and really the murder isn't Wayne's style. He's more smash, grab, bash and flee.' Toni wandered across Church Lane to the Old Rectory. She looked up at the house. 'You left no fingerprints. If you had killed Snace, you'd have committed the perfect murder.' Toni was unlocking the door of the Old Rectory now. She grinned. 'Fancy a tour, for old times' sake?'

'Lucie saw me going through the gate.' Stella had made Lucie hand over her footage. 'You're not staying to look out for Snace's murderer?'

'We've got a few of the team there, watching for known villains and odd behaviour. I'd like to take this chance to have a tour of the Old Rectory with you.'

'I've never seen it daylight.' In the hall, Stella was assailed by the smell of a neglected house. 'Did you find any other prints?'

'Only Snace and his housekeeper's.' Toni pocketed the key. 'Whoever it was knew how to be invisible.'

This comment brought Stella back to the conversation with Toni at Kate Rokesmith's grave. She told Toni they now thought Henry was Henry Morrison, not Anderson.

'We'll check that out.' Toni scooped up junk mail from the tiled floor and squared it into a pile on a table.

'We did find a Henry Morrison had lived at an address in an Essex village called Tolleshunt-D'Arcy. He lived in a farmworker's cottage but, according to Street View, the cottage made way for a housing estate in the eighties.'

'Tolleshunt-D'Arcy, isn't that where Jeremy Bamber murdered his family in 1985?' Toni was obviously well up on criminal history.

'It was also the home of a crimewriter called Margery Allingham.' This fact had excited Jack, who had read Allingham's books. Stella was more interested to find that, going by the 1961 census, it had been where Henry, or Harold, Morrison lived. After that he had vanished off the face of the earth. He might after all be dead. They had hit a dead end.

'Have you asked Stevie why she visited Jimmy on the morning that he died?' Stella said.

'They talked over old times, she showed him a photo of her and him collecting salvage for the war.' Toni shrugged. 'Nothing to see there, Stella. Seriously, you don't think Stevie Stride killed Snace?' Toni unfolded a paper from her pocket. Stella saw it was the plan of the Old Rectory. Toni had marked up where Stella had found Stanley.

'She has the guts, but no,' Stella said. 'Did you get a chance to ask in the shops for CCTV of the morning Jimmy died?'

'I didn't, but I will.' Tapping the plan, Toni said, 'You were here when you saw someone cross the hallway?'

'It was dark, but yes.' Stella suspected Toni Kemp had never taken Harold-Henry as a suspect seriously. She would probably let it slide.

'It was about half ten, you said.' Toni also had a copy of Stella's second statement. The one where she'd told the truth. 'You've said here the figure seemed to flit across the hall, briefly blocking light from those panes in the door. That discounts an elderly frail man.'

'Could it be Wayne Meekings after all?' How simple that would be.

'He's still in my sights, his alibi is leaky, but the Reverend Snace's housekeeper reported nothing missing and I've never known Meekings leave a property empty-handed.'

'There was a suitcase in the room. That could indicate someone planned to fill it?' Stella remembered.

'It had Snace's name inside. The room is a kind of glory hole, a dumping ground.' Toni pulled a wry face. 'Helpful if you were a burglar.'

'You mean whoever I saw in the hall locked the room after I left?'

'Someone was around. You said you fled leaving the sash window up. We know from Lucie that when she went on a nose to see what you'd been doing, she found it closed.' Toni pushed on the baize door. 'Either at that point Snace wasn't dead and he closed it. Or his killer did.' Toni unlocked the room where Stella had entered the house and went in. Stella followed her.

The room seemed smaller with all but one shelf empty and the contents in boxes on the floor.

'We're storing all this while we look for Snace's next of kin. He died intestate. So far no one's come forward and no one here today is claiming he was their beloved long-lost uncle. Might be it goes to the church, including this house. Frankly I don't know how it works with deceased vicars with no relatives. Whatever, for a man you'd think would pass up on possessions, Snace seems to have been a hoarder.'

'Don't people hoard in situ, as it were?' There were even more ornaments, objects, knick-knacks or whatever than Stella had seen by the light of her torch. 'From cleaning hoarders' homes, they don't usually take everything into one room and lock the door.'

'Blimey, what hoarder wants you there cleaning? And how can you?'

'The relatives call me in. Generally, I accept a cup of tea and leave. There's no charge, obviously.'

'That's nice.' Toni returned to Stella's original point. 'Maybe Snace was trying to kick the collecting habit?'

'Doesn't the rectory belong to the church?' Stella said.

'Michael Snace bought it off the diocese ten years ago when they built a new vicarage, that cheerless bungalow that's on the coast road.'

'How come he could afford it?' Stella was astonished. 'I thought vicars lived on a stipend.'

'Single mother who took in washing, father unknown, so not family money. It could be a benefactor, like in *Great Expectations*. Thirty years ago he banked a large sum. Over a hundred grand in cash. That went a long way toward purchasing the house.'

'A hundred thousand pounds?' It was the same sum as Stevie had released in equity around the same time. She was about to say this when she remembered that it was due to Jack steaming open Stevie's post that they knew.

'This doesn't look like junk to me.' Toni held a silver candlestick, still with a stub of candle, up to the light from the window. 'Could be gifts from parishioners which Snace didn't feel he should use or sell.'

'That's what I assumed.' Stella looked at the candlestick. 'That looks familiar. I've probably cleaned one like it.'

'Your job must make you a bit of an antiques expert.' Toni returned the candlestick to the shelf. 'When I go into houses, it's often after a crime, so I'm looking at the gaps where stuff like this used to be.'

'Did Snace keep a register of his gifts? If they were gifts?'

'No one's come forward wanting something back since his murder. They'd have the cheek of the devil if they did. But plenty of people do.' Toni was holding a ceramic bowl decorated with flowers in golds and reds. 'It flies in the face of scant facts, but such a brutal and intimate murder feels personal. Despite his popularity, could the vicar have had an enemy who caught up with him?'

'Jimmy Chrismas called him Snake.'

Chapter Thirty-Seven

Present Day

After leaving the Old Rectory Stella had no stomach to return to the funeral. Parting from Toni Kemp, she returned to Yew Tree House.

Once inside, she closed the front door and leant against it. After three weeks, Yew Tree House felt very different to the damp unwelcoming place into which they had all piled nearly a month ago. Cooking had been minimal, but the warm air smelled pleasantly of toast, coffee, perfume, aftershave and bubble bath. From the open French windows – they should have been locked – came the trill of a blackbird.

Against a lot of odds, Yew Tree House had become a home of sorts.

The last weeks had been a roller coaster of events. Milly had used Stella's phrase 'take stock', because she'd heard Stella say it many times. On this busman's holiday, as Lucie had called it, Stella had not had a chance to take stock. After returning from the Old Rectory with Toni, she felt overwhelmed.

It would be a few hours until Jack, Bella and the children came back and after Snace's interment, Lucie would be in Prunella filing her article. Stella had time to take stock now.

She hurried upstairs, took her laptop from her suitcase and, setting up in the dining room, began what she liked next best to cleaning: creating a spreadsheet.

She listed all three victims, counting Greta in 1940, then populated cells with suspects, dates and locations of each murder and the method used to kill each victim. Motive had her stumped. Perhaps Liddell tried to rape Greta, she struggled so he killed her. Or he killed her to ensure she didn't speak. Stella reflected sadly that, had Greta lived, knowing she'd contravened her mum's instructions and gone across the common, it was unlikely she'd have told anyone what Liddell had done to her. Whatever, the result was the brutal end of a young woman's life.

Who had murdered Liddell? If it was Philip Fleming, it was revenge, but the only link was that as a soldier in the Royal Engineers he may have built the pillbox in 1939 when he was stationed in Newhaven. Flimsy, but it had satisfied Toni's boss. Jimmy Chrismas had confessed to both murders, but he had strong alibis, especially for Snace's murder. He was trained to kill silently and instantly, which matched the method used to kill Liddell, but what was the motive? Did Jimmy know that Stevie had taken out equity on Yew Tree House? Was it pure coincidence that around the same time, Snace had paid for the Old Rectory with cash?

Had Jimmy been protecting Stevie? Or her mother, Adelaide? It was some gesture. Jimmy was about seventeen at the time, would he really have risked execution? Even if Liddell had been stealing from Adelaide, it was still murder.

She had put Wayne Meekings on the list, but knew he was a red herring. Toni didn't take him seriously for a suspect. Stella thought again she wanted the murder to be the work of a nasty professional criminal. Not Jimmy, Stevie or the mysterious Henry.

Days ago, Jack had said Henry the evacuee held the key. They needed that CCTV.

Victim	Date of Murder	Crime Scene	Method
Greta Fleming 16 yrs Worked in Bakery Esher	Missing from August 1940 found November 1940	Esher Common	Strangled
Alfred Liddell Farm Hand married to Susan, son William born 1945	9/05/1945 approx.	Pillbox, Bishopstone	Stabbed
Michael Snace Vicar member of secret Auxiliary Unit / Home Guard	11/08/2023	The Old Rectory	Stabbed (same MO as Liddell)

Murderer	Suspect	Motive	Notes
Alfred Liddell	None	Prevent Greta reporting	Not solved at time. Greta's DNA on Skeleton.
Unknown	Philip Fleming Jimmy Chrismas A.N Other	Revenge for killing sister (if Fleming). Attack on burglar if JC	How Fleming know Liddell? How lure him to pillbox? Jimmy in Auxiliary Unit, *Butcher and Bolt*
Unknown	Jimmy Chrismas Henry Morrison Stevie Stride Wayne Meekings??? A.N. Other	Unknown, if Jimmy or Henry. Stevie hates Snace? (*Snake*)	Same MO as Alfred Liddell. Toni said Intimate, so personal? Jimmy had alibi and frail. *Butcher and Bolt*

She became aware of a sound. It had been happening for the last few minutes, but concentrating on her grid, she had ignored it. There were footsteps above her head.

Wayne Meekings. Toni had said he might be at the funeral to confirm that houses were unoccupied. Stella pulled herself together. Toni had said she had officers watching him. *The French windows were open.*

Stella's next move should have been to leave by the front door and from a safe distance call Toni Kemp, who would still be in the vicinity. It would have been her advice to anyone else and was underlined in her staff cleaning manual.

Instead, she did what Jack said was many people's first instinct. She crept up the stairs. Was it Jack who'd taught her to keep to the edge of the stair where, least likely to give, the wood wouldn't creak?

There was no one in the bedroom that had once been Adelaide Stride's, where she and Jack were sleeping. Her open suitcase looked undisturbed. Her laptop was downstairs. If she gave him that, would he go? Stella wasn't going to hand over her valuables. Wasn't that exactly how people got killed? Had Snace – and he had a lot of valuables – refused to hand his intruder the key to the 'stockroom'? Then she remembered that the key had been on the outside of the door. When she left the stockroom it had been unlocked.

The sound came from the twins' room. Not footsteps. A different sound.

Stella crept up to the door. It was ajar; she dared not open it wider in case it gave her away. She put her face to the hinge-gap.

Stella could have no idea that she was adopting the same method as Adelaide Stride had – from the other side of the door – to see who was beyond.

A man was crouched down by Milly's bed. Tufts of grey hair flopped over the collar of his mac. Stella pushed open the door. 'You won't find the knife there.'

Chapter Thirty-Eight

Present Day

'Where is she?' Jack stormed into Lucie's motorhome, striding past her kitchenette and shower cabinet and sliding open the door to the bedroom.

'Where is who?' Tapping on her laptop, Lucie didn't look up.

'Stella, who else? Is she with you?'

'She fell in the teapot.' Lucie gave the keyboard a final bash and sat back. 'Done and flippin' dusted. That'll have the readers choking on their cereal.'

'What?'

'Crowds turn out to bid farewell to much-loved vicar.' Lucie popped an espresso pod in her machine. 'Coffee?'

'Where is Stella? She was going to the funeral and then going back to Yew Tree House.' Jack spat out the words. '*She's not there.*'

'Have you tried the murdering sisters?' Lucie hadn't let go of her theory.

'She isn't there. Rosa said she saw her come back before the funeral had ended.'

'So, she's gone for a walk.'

'Stella can't see the point of walking without Stanley.' Jack was marching up and down Prunella. 'She didn't leave a note and three hours ago she saved a spreadsheet on our shared Dropbox.' Jack marched up and down the short corridor. 'The secret hole was open.'

'The what?' Lucie shut her laptop.

'The cavity where Milly found the Fairbairn-Sykes knife like the one used to kill Snace. Remember?'

'I'm not senile yet.' Lucie took her coffee and returned to the pull-down table. 'None of this is sinister though.'

'Who else knew the cavity was there?'

'Stella? Your children? Sussex police?' Lucie sipped her coffee. 'Have you called her?'

'For *goodness' sake*.' Jack scrawled his fingers through his hair. 'She's not picking up. Lucie, please. Whoever hid the knife in the first place had to be the murderer. Stella must have caught him opening the secret compartment to get the knife. Oh God, he could have killed her. *And where is Stanley?*' Jack ended in a shout.

'With Stella?' Lucie exuded a yogic calm. 'The knife wouldn't have been there, the police have it. I wonder if the person who put it in the hole came back for it?'

'Yes, I am wondering that too,' Jack bellowed.

'Clues?'

'Can we just stick to— What?'

'Has Stella left any clues in her spreadsheet, something to suggest where she might be?'

Finding the spreadsheet on his phone's Dropbox, Jack sent it to Lucie, and they looked at it together.

'Who's Wayne Meekings?' Jack said.

'There are three question marks by his name. He's in there because Stella couldn't leave him out. Not a serious contender.' Lucie washed and dried her cup and locked it in an overhead cupboard. She rotated the driver's seat to face the windscreen and tootled, 'Belt up, honey-pie.'

If Lucie or Jack had imagined a discreet trawl of the village as they scanned each side of the road, they would have been disappointed. Going at a funeral pace, shoppers and holidaymakers paused on the kerbs to watch the enormous motorhome pass.

There was no one on the bench and the butcher's shop had closed. There was no sign of Stella or Stanley.

'Drive to the police.' Jack slapped a hand on the dashboard.

'Deep breaths. Think.' Lucie slowed almost to a stop. 'Stella Darnell is a fifty-seven-year-old adult who has been gone from the house three hours max. The police – Antonia Kemp – will not thank you for reporting her as a Misper. Nor will Stella.'

'If you won't take me, I'll get a bus.' Jack unclipped his belt.

'What bus will that be? The service runs from Bishopstone once in a blue moon. Stop panicking.' Although Lucie had appeared to make light of Stella's absence, as soon as she turned onto the A259, she stayed at forty all the way to Newhaven police station.

'There she is!'

Lucie screeched to halt. Jack ejected himself from his seat.

Across the road, standing outside the police station, Stella was looking at her phone. Seeing them, she said, 'I've got thirty-three missed calls, *what's happened?*'

Chapter Thirty-Nine

Present Day

Lucie had parked Prunella parallel to the sea on a concrete apron on the beach at Newhaven. A sign warned 'No Campers', another 'No Fires'. There had been nothing to stop them buying chips and shandies from the pub at the mouth of the harbour and taking them to a picnic table that Lucie set up in front of the motorhome. Home from home, Stella felt, as she sat beneath Prunella's awning.

'Do you think Henry did do it?' Jack had asked this question twice already.

'Doesn't matter what Stella thinks.' Lucie dipped a chip in the squirt of mayo on their shared plate. 'It's whether Antonia thinks he's a double murderer that matters. I doubt she will.'

'I had no reason to disbelieve him.' Stella hadn't thought she'd want chips when Lucie ordered them, but she'd eaten most of Jack's share as well as her own. His appetite ruined by fright, Jack was pecking and he hadn't touched his shandy. 'He described the inside of the house, he knew about the donations in the small room. He knew where Snace's bedroom was and how he died. He even used the term "butcher and bolt". He claimed the medal was his.'

'What medal?' Lucie asked.

For answer, Stella showed Lucie the Auxiliary badge, which Toni had returned to her. Stella gazed out at the sea. White horses rode in on the tide, breaking into spume on the shore. A black square in the far distance must be the Dieppe ferry. 'It was given to Auxiliers in thanks after the war. They'd signed the Official Secrets Act, so could never divulge what they did in the war. He seemed a bit hesitant about the medal then was adamant it had been his and said how the MOD didn't give the medals, they had to pay for them. Nor did Auxiliers get army pensions, they weren't in the army.'

'That would make me murderous.' Lucie sipped at her shandy and pulled a face. 'So did Henry Morrison kill Liddell and Snace, and did he know he was second in the confession queue after Jimmy Chrismas?'

'Yes. He'd seen Jimmy the morning Jimmy died, hadn't he,' Stella reminded Lucie. 'Henry nearly cried when he confessed to me that Jimmy had made him swear to a pact. Henry started by saying he murdered Liddell – weirdly, since he killed Liddell but kept forgetting his name – because he had robbed Adelaide Stride. He'd blackmailed her by threatening to hurt Stevie and Rosa if Adelaide didn't hand over more and more money and valuables. Henry said he found Liddell in the pillbox waiting for Adelaide to bring the stuff and so slit his throat. A bit more probing and I got it out of him that neither of the boys had killed Liddell. Henry had left his jacket at the village hall and Jimmy decided to return it to him that night. He caught Henry in the act of blocking up the pillbox and Henry showed him Liddell's body inside. Jimmy insisted that if the murder was ever discovered, he would take the blame. At seventeen he would only get a prison sentence. Two years older, Henry would be executed.'

'Noble of Jimmy.' Lucie was tart. 'We believe this, do we?'

'Why not? It hardly puts Henry in a good light. Jimmy told Henry to leave the next morning. He would block up the pillbox to ensure the body was never found and 'fess up if it was. He told Henry it never would be.'

'And eighty years later, when the body was found, Jimmy did 'fess up.' Jack came out of his torpor. 'What a guy.'

'Henry told Jimmy he would contact the police. With capital punishment abolished, he'd get a prison sentence. He lives in a care home in Essex that feels like a prison so he might as well be in a real one. Jimmy wouldn't hear it. But now he's dead he can't stop Henry from confessing.'

Everyone stared unseeing at the three remaining chips.

'And Snace?' Jack said. 'Why did he kill the vicar?'

'Jack was right. Snace does sound like a True Host. As patrol leader he was sadistically cruel to Jimmy and Henry. He sent them out on exercises in the dead of night in storms and freezing weather and no matter how successful the mission, he found fault and hit them.'

'Couldn't he be sacked?' Jack said.

'I asked that, but criminals and thugs were recruited, blokes who would kill without flinching or remorse. For Snace it would have been heaven, he could bully and mete out violence with no comeback because to the outside world the patrol didn't exist. If Jimmy and Henry told anyone, they would have been shot as traitors, or so Snace told them.'

The sun had gone in; they retreated inside.

'It took Henry a long time to wreak revenge.' Lucie marvelled. 'I'm not into delayed gratification.'

'He was a bit hazy about that. Said he hadn't realised Snace was still alive until he read a mention of him after the skeleton was found.'

'So, he decided to kill two birds with one stone,' Jack said.

'Something like that.' Stella watched in awe as the ferry glided into the harbour mouth. Up close, behind other motorhomes and cars, it looked enormous. 'We should be getting back, Bella and the kids will be wondering where we are.'

'Justin said his bike misses him.' Jack was drying the chip plate.

'I'm sure Prunella misses me when I leave her.' Lucie looked dreamy.

'That means Justin is ready to go home to Hammersmith.' Jack stacked the plate with the others in an overhead cupboard.

'Both murders are solved and they're bored of the beach.' Stella could have said that the industrial-sized scrubber-drying polishing machine she had bought before they came away would be missing her. She was ready to go home, but wouldn't say so.

'I'm ready to go home,' Jack suddenly said. To Stella's surprise, for the first time since he and Lucie had picked Stella up from the police station, Jack was smiling.

Chapter Forty

Present day – two weeks later

Stella bent to admire her handiwork. The scrubber-dryer polishing machine was everything it had promised: the parquet flooring shone as if new. She bent down and touched it. The school gymnasium had been built in the sixties, the wooden blocks of wood, arranged in a herring-bone pattern, had each been set individually. It was a giant jigsaw. From a low angle the floor gleamed, not a speck of dust, even the grooves and scratches of decades added to the perfection. Yes, Stella decided, she was back doing what she loved best.

Not that she hadn't enjoyed their stay in Bishopstone. But when she'd seen a news bulletin announcing that police had charged ninety-eight-year-old Henry Morrison with not only the murder of Reverend Michael Snace, but also of Alfred Liddell in 1945, there had been no sense of triumph. The thought of Henry who, despite what he had done, Stella had liked, incarcerated in HMP Wormwood Scrubs didn't bear thinking about. In the last weeks, Stella had stuck to cleaning.

'There you are.'

Stella saw only the footprints of Lucie's knee-high leather boots marking a beeline to where she knelt.

'Your crew gave me the wrong directions for the gym, I've been all over this place. Then the headmistress tried to throw me out. *I should throw you out for masquerading, barely out of diapers, who's kidding who, kiddo.*' Lucie did her hard-boiled American accent. 'Luckily your stalwart cleaner Donnette rescued me.'

'What do you want, Lucie?' Stella knew she sounded rude.

'Dan the Man finally found it.' Pacing in busy circles, Lucie was leaving faint footprints on the parquet. 'I came straight to you.'

'Why?' Stella took a few seconds to realise Lucie meant Daniel Liddell.

'Why what?'

'Why did you want me?'

'All this cleaning is addling your brain. *Who else*, Sherlock? I tried Mr Jack on the way here, but he's driving one of his trains.' Lucie harrumphed.

'What did Daniel finally find?' Stella felt a stirring of interest.

'We have proof Shitbird Alfred Liddell was nicking stuff from Widow Stride. Here.' Lucie showed Stella a photo of a gold rectangular object.

Stella took in the letters in a curly script engraved on the otherwise smooth surface. 'RS'. 'Did it to belong to Rupert Stride?'

'It confirms why Liddell was there.' Lucie affecting modesty never suited her. 'He was nicking stuff off Adelaide. I doubt that he stopped there.'

'The murderer died twice.' Stella hardly made sense of the sentence that had popped into her mind.

'Prunella is panting at the bit outside, let's show this to Stevie and Rosa and see what they have to say.' Lucie spun on her heel.

The murderer died twice. As if in a trance, Stella repolished the parquet and packed her equipment in the van.

'Daniel Liddell said his nan told him she'd been seduced by Alfred Liddell's gift of the gab, and long words.'

'We are all fools when we are in love,' Lucie trilled. 'Your dad took me to a police fundraiser at the Dorchester. I tell you, if I hadn't already fancied him, the sight of him in white tie and tails would have done it. I went weak at the knees.'

Stella had never heard Lucie describe Terry as attractive before, and were she not subsumed by a sudden realisation of the truth, she would have felt uncomfortable.

'Lucie, I should see Stevie on her own.' Something in Stella's tone must have convinced Lucie, because she didn't protest.

All the time it was staring them in the face. Literally the face – it wasn't only her father who Rosa looked like.

'I don't need to ask if you recognise this.' Expecting Stevie to say she'd never seen the cigarette case before, Stella was appalled when Stevie literally shied away from it and refused to as much as touch it.

Rosa had said that Stella would find Stevie in Yew Tree House. *She's been there every day since you all left. Almost as if she missed you. I certainly do.*

Stevie was huddled in the corner of the sofa, a shrunken creature. She held the hidden-mother photograph on her lap. Before Stella could speak, Stevie said, 'You can prove nothing.'

'But you can,' Stella said softly. 'Jack questioned that Henry waited a long time to murder Snace. All those years he had hated him and did nothing. Henry told me he'd been prompted to kill Snace after seeing the news report that Liddell's body had been found in the pillbox. He confessed to that too. It sounds too pat to me.'

The gold case – more like a bomb – felt warm in Stella's hand.

'Jimmy told Henry that if Liddell was discovered, Jimmy would confess,' Stella said. 'Because already twenty, Henry would hang. Jimmy made Henry leave the next day. They agreed never to contact each other again. Jimmy walled up the pillbox, as you said, claiming it was a government initiative. Your mother never questioned it.'

'Why would she?' Stevie's voice was dull, toneless. 'We were inundated with strictures from the government.'

'You know the answer to that.' Stella paused, but when Stevie said nothing, she continued, 'When the body was discovered, Henry was going to confess; with no capital punishment any more, there was no need for Jimmy to claim the murder. But the police gave out that Philip Fleming, the brother of Greta, was a likely suspect. Philip was dead. Henry decided to say nothing.'

September had not seen an Indian summer. The air was chill.

'I expect Henry was always amiable and kind. One reason your mother didn't send him home, even when she suspected he had stolen from her, was she couldn't really believe it. She was right not to, wasn't she?' Stella could see that every word she said was like torture to Stevie, but now she knew the truth, she could not stop. 'It surprised me that such a nice man could let an innocent man – a dead man with no comeback – be labelled a murderer. Not many blamed Philip for avenging his sister's violent death, but he hadn't killed Liddell, had he?'

There was a movement near the pillbox. A rabbit broke cover and shot across the garden. Stella could not know that a rabbit chased by Stanley, followed by Justin and Milly, was the start of a chain of events which had brought her back to Yew Tree House today.

'Henry would not have let Jimmy go to his grave as Liddell's supposed killer.' Stella came into the room. She rested a hand on the mantelpiece. 'So why was Henry prepared to let Philip Fleming be blamed?'

'Jimmy was like a brother to Henry.'

'They hadn't seen each other for eighty years, no bond is that strong.'

'How would you know?'

'You're right. I don't know.' Stella felt daunted by the length of time so many secrets had been kept.

'When we arrived, I put the lack of ornaments and valuables down to Rosa storing them to avoid breakages.' Stella patted the mantelpiece. 'A silver candlestick stood here. There are two, but you can only see one in the family photo Rosa showed us. The last one with "Daddy", as she said. The one where Adelaide stands so close to him it made me wonder if she knew she would soon be a widow.'

'There was a war, everyone expected tragedy at any minute.' Stevie hugged the picture, perhaps more as defence than from affection.

'There were two candlesticks identical to the one in the picture in a room at the Old Rectory. A rack of shelves crammed with valuables. DI Kemp and I concluded they were gifts from grateful parishioners which Snace hadn't felt he could use or sell. A bowl decorated with a pattern of flowers in reds and gold looked familiar and so did a candlestick, but I supposed I'd seen similar objects over thirty years of cleaning.'

'You left the house looking lovely.' Stevie twitched as the words escaped.

Stella smiled, although in the dimming light, Stevie wouldn't see. 'I know now where I had seen it. It was on a table in the family photo, just to your father's left. The photo's black and white so the bowl didn't catch my attention when I was in the Old Rectory during the day.'

'As you said, you must have seen it when you were cleaning.'

'Why not say you gave it to Snace?' Stella was surprised that Stevie hadn't opted for the obvious get-out.

'That would be a lie,' Stevie said. 'Neither my mother nor I gave that Snake anything.'

'Living a lie all this time must have been a torture,' Stella said quietly.

'You use the word lightly.'

'Jack and I commented on how alike Rosa and your father were. But it was when I read Lucie's interview with Daniel Liddell that something struck. A fleeting impression I couldn't hold on to. Only when Liddell finally sent a picture of the cigarette case that Alfred Liddell had given his wife did I get it. That, and Liddell's threatening behaviour with Bella and myself in the pillbox.'

'What did he do?' Stevie's eyes blazed.

When Stella explained, ending with that she had wondered if violence ran in families, Stevie was vehement: 'It does not.'

'I agree. We are not Victorians.'

'You can talk all night but I won't help you. I cannot break my promise to my mother.'

'Which was?' Stella felt like Lucie May. Not in a good way.

'To protect my little sister from trauma or harm. Mother strove to give Rosa a good war and to come out unscathed.'

'Is Rosa unscathed?'

'None of us are,' Stevie said. 'I will not let Jimmy down. Nor will Henry. If you have friends as special as Jimmy and Henry, you will understand.'

'When we saw Jimmy on that last morning, he gave me this.' Stella passed the Auxiliary badge to Stevie. 'Bob Chrismas had warned us that Jimmy was less coherent since his stroke. I caught Jimmy's last word to me in retrospect. Lucie found a training manual – disguised as a fertiliser catalogue – where it said that a key instruction which all members of the commando unit had to undertake without hesitation was to creep up behind someone and slit their throat. "Butcher and bolt."'

Stevie knew the words.

'Jimmy found out from Rosa that you had been meeting Snace in the churchyard. It seems she bears a grudge that, as she sees it, you stopped her marrying the love of her life. She was under the impression that you had feelings for the Reverend Snace. Jimmy knew that wasn't true. So why were you meeting Snace?

Where had all your money gone? Rosa told him you had taken out equity on the house and that you'd asked Snace to mind it.'

'I would never…' Stevie began.

'Of course not, but Rosa was trying to make sense of what didn't make sense. She had co-signed forms releasing a hundred thousand pounds thirty years ago. But it had made no difference to your lives. You had earned your living as a teacher, Rosa had temped as a typist. She had no pension and although yours is good, it never seemed to be enough. Jimmy got you to admit that Snace was leeching off you.' Stella stopped. 'Bit by bit he was taking the contents of the house he had already effectively stolen from you. Blackmailing you. He'd been trained to lead a commando unit, he knew how to torture. It wouldn't have worked if he had taken it all at once, would it. What hold would he have had over you then?'

The day had been dogged by cloud. Now a premature dusk had descended, light in the room had diminished Stella and Stevie to vague shapes.

'Nothing of what I will tell you can be proved,' Stevie whispered.

Stevie talked softly, as if she intended to hypnotise Stella. She certainly caught Stella in a spell.

When it became properly dark, Stella considered switching on the lamp, but confronted with tangibility, Stevie might not say another word.

'Please come with me to the police and tell them what you have just told me,' Stella said after a few minutes in which neither of them had spoken. 'Everyone deserves the truth.'

'Your Jack understands that some truths belong in the past. Leave us with our secrets.'

'How can you protect your father? He was a murderer and a rapist.' Stella switched on the light. 'The man lying in his grave in the churchyard – forever loved – is *a stranger.*'

'As you said, you have no proof.' Stevie got up and seemed to glide out of the door and into the back garden. 'Stella, please would you lock the French windows when you leave? It's a long time since we felt safe enough to leave doors and windows open. These days, anyone might come in.'

Pools of bleak LED lamplight lit the pavements. Inside the family butcher's, a blue light from the insect-catcher gleamed on metal meat trays. On the coast road Stella made a call.

'Are you busy, could I see you?'

'I'm always busy, but yes you can,' Toni said.

Chapter Forty-One

Present Day

Jack and Stella were sitting on an old concrete mooring block near well-trodden river stairs known to locals as the Bell Steps. Stella had remembered that at the end of a case Toni Kemp went to her father's grave and told him about it. She suggested that, as they were no longer in Bishopstone, perhaps they could go to the place where Kate Rokesmith had been murdered. A scrap of beach – when the tide was out – they would reclaim Kate and the place for themselves.

Three weeks had passed since Stella had gone to Yew Tree House. She had finally given up hope that Stevie would tell the truth about her father. Stevie had protected her mother for eighty years, why should she change her mind now?

In the middle distance, Hammersmith Bridge – closed for repair or demolition – reflected in the Thames and formed a complete oval. The smell of river mud, cloying and yet comfortingly familiar, hung in the air.

'Toni confirmed that, without proof, she can't do anything.' Stella sent a stone skittering along the shingle. It stopped short of the water. 'Don't reckon she believed me anyway. I bet she thinks I have a need to investigate murders to feel real.'

'Did she say that?'

'No, but it was obvious. And she disapproved of me making Stevie talk. She said none of it would stand up in court unless Stevie gave a statement. Otherwise, it's hearsay. She actually laughed when I suggested she apply to have Rupert Stride's body exhumed.'

'It's hard enough to get a disinterment when there is proof.' Jack was only confirming what Stella knew. She had hoped pigs might after all fly. 'Since Stevie Stride won't give her DNA or let Rosa do it, why not show Daniel Liddell a photo of Rupert Stride and see if he recognises him?'

'He never knew his grandfather and there are no pictures of Alfred – he was supposed to be camera shy, remember?' Stella got off the concrete block and, choosing a likely stone, walked to the river's edge and sent it leaping – one, two, three, four times – across the water. Terry had taught her how to skim stones. Doing it now made her feel obliquely cheered. 'Toni won't ask herself to tea and steal a toothbrush.'

'Did you ask her?' Jack looked impressed.

'Of course not.'

Although it was why Jack and Stella had come to the Thames, neither had yet acknowledged that metres to their right had been where, in 1981, Jack's mother, Kate Rokesmith, was strangled.

'It's a very big bubble to burst and to what end?'

'Rupert Stride was not murdered in the Blitz, as Daniel Liddell said, he was a... he was a True Host. Stride killed a soldier in the street, dressed him in his clothes, being careful to disfigure him so that he couldn't be recognised. Then, either wearing the soldier's clothes – although I expect only for a short while – he changed his name to Alfred Liddell and started again. Before he "died" the first time, Stride subjected Adelaide to domestic abuse. Unknown to Adelaide this was witnessed by not only Stevie but Henry too, although neither knew the other had seen it. As Alfred Liddell, Stride strangled Greta Fleming, ending her young life and ruining her family's lives for ever.' Stella heaved a breath. 'To *that* end.'

'So basically, Stride was dubbed a hero for being murdered. But how come no one recognised Stride when he came to Bishopstone?' Jack said.

'He came at night and went straight to Yew Tree House. By 1945, the ARP as well as the Home Guard had been demobilised. Only Adelaide, Stevie, Rosa and Henry were there. It was relatively easy to catch Adelaide on her own.' Although Stella had told Jack what Stevie had said, paraphrasing it now engulfed Stella in a wave of inchoate rage. She couldn't hurt Stride, he was long dead. The wounds he had inflicted were now deep scars. What would she do if she encountered him now?

'It's odd Henry and Jimmy were prepared to lie to protect Adelaide. And now, when her mother's been dead nearly sixty years, Stevie in turn is prepared for them to take the rap.'

'She could be protecting her mother's reputation?'

'But at the expense of Henry, who is alive now?'

'Unless she is protecting someone else,' Jack mused.

'Herself, do you mean?'

'I was thinking of Rosa.'

'Rosa was *seven* in 1945.'

'And, as Milly was quick to remind us, seven-year-olds can murder.'

'Milly hasn't murdered anyone.' Stella snapped. But she knew, not least from a case they had solved – which Lucie had dubbed The Playground Murders – young children could murder children. Still...

'Whatever, it seems that Henry, aged ninety-eight years, will be spending the rest of his life in prison for a murder that he may not have done.'

'His age is irrelevant were he guilty.' Stella wandered over to the spot where Kate Rokesmith's body had been found in 1981. 'Those flowers we planted have taken.' She pointed at a plant growing out of a crack in the supporting wall of the back gardens in Hammersmith Mall above them.

'I never knew what my mum's favourite flower was.' Jack had never got to know his mother. Time had stopped for Kate when he was three. When did it stop still for Stevie and Rosa Stride?

'Someone's calling.' Stella scrabbled in her pocket but got there too late. '"Possible fraud."'

Up on the street beyond the Bell Steps, a passing car played Madonna's 'Holiday'. Glancing at Jack, she saw he had clocked the irony. They had sung it on their way down to Sussex two months ago. He said, 'It was sort of a holiday.'

'Busman's holiday.' Stella linked her arm through Jack's and rested her head on his shoulder.

A text pinged. *Toni-Police*. The telegrammic words danced.

SS's DNA. Positive for Liddell. Stride grave exhumed tomoz 5.3oam. Tx

Chapter Forty-Two

Present Day

From the tent came the clink of spades. Shadows flickered on the canvas as the diggers moved towards and away from the lamps inside in a macabre shadow show.

Arc lamps as bright as day lit a path between the graves. Stella trudged along the path, the brick herringbone indistinguishable beyond the reach of lights, passing the mausoleums that had become familiar by day, but were now great slabs of stone. When they reached the tent, the first thing Stella saw was the uprooted headstone leaning against a buttress.

Rupert Stride
Forever Mourned

Fleetingly, she recalled the headstones beside Geri and Dean Gifford's house. If there was an after-life, was Greta watching them now?

'In here.' Toni Kemp kept her voice low.

Negotiating around guy ropes, Stella and Jack followed the detective into the tent and stood where Kemp indicated, behind a heap of earth supported by boards of plywood.

A scrape. Murmurs. Spades were discarded on the edge of a cavernous hole.

They had reached the coffin.

A smell of earth and *something else*. Stella was grateful for the barrier of Vaseline that went some way to blocking the stench. It was particulate, she dared not breathe through her mouth. Without waiting for the coffin to be disinterred she stepped out again. Jack signalled he would stay.

It took a moment to get her bearings. When she did, as if to a lodestar, Stella stumbled out of the area of unremitting light and shadow and made for Kate Rokesmith's bench. From across Salmon's field behind her she could smell the ploughed soil in the cool autumn air. It felt aeons since the long summer days on the beach and walking on the Downs. Over the distance of time, despite all that had happened, their month in Yew Tree House had taken on the aspect of an idyll. Stella closed her eyes and became aware of the dawn chorus.

'I didn't have you down as squeamish.' Toni handed Stella a cup of takeaway coffee.

'I can handle anything that I'm there to clean up.' Stella sipped the hot liquid, appreciating the sensation of warmth travelling down her gut. She didn't correct Toni but it had not been revulsion that drove her from the tent. The scene had been too sad to bear. Taking another sip she said, 'You'll be hoping for a DNA match, I suppose?'

'Only if the body in the coffin, like Liddell né Stride, has relatives who broke the law. More likely this will mean good old-fashioned leg-work. Churchill announced an amnesty for Second World War deserters in 1953. There should be a list.'

'You're not treating him as a deserter?'

'No, of course not. But the Defence Office will have. A soldier goes on leave in London and never returns to base. Whereas the poor man was murdered by Rupert Stride, who swaps his clothes for the soldier's uniform and leaves him a disfigured – therefore unidentifiable – corpse carrying Stride's ID. Stride called himself Alfred Liddell and, 'washed clean', began a new life.

'He took not only the man's life, but his reputation too.' This was why Stella had not been able to watch the disinterment. The outrage done to the 'unknown soldier' was beyond words.

'Malcolm said there were around ten thousand soldiers who deserted. At least with the publicity – some of it to do with your mate Lucie – the powers that be have had to commit to it. The job itself is OK, we've had to search larger haystacks.' Toni was one of those who took the lid off a takeaway cup to drink. Stella kept the lid on to preserve the temperature. Crushed by the enormity of what Milly finding the skeleton had set in train – *lamps, tent, forensics, an innocent buried under his killer's name* – Stella took refuge in prosaic observation.

'Where are Stevie and Rosa?' she asked.

'I thought you knew.' Toni looked surprised, 'It was entirely down to Lucie May that Stevie gave us a DNA.'

'I did know that.' Stella had been shocked to discover that Stevie had talked to Lucie.

'Her paper paid for the sisters to be put up in a posh hotel while this is happening. Stevie wasn't keen, but Rosa jumped at it.'

'I refused,' a voice said.

'She's a braver woman than me. Given the chance to hang out in a spa versus a chilly graveyard, I know which I'd have chosen.' Corncrake cackle.

Stevie Stride leaned on Lucie's arm. Toni and Stella jumped up to give them Kate's bench.

'I'll get you coffees,' Toni said.

'Goodness, don't bother,' Stevie said. 'I've had a full English in Arabella. Far nicer than a hotel.'

'Prunella, darling.' Lucie gave a little hop.

'Excuse me, ma'am.' Malcolm Lane appeared beside them. He shone a torch on an evidence bag dangling in his other hand. 'Jack Harmon noticed this poking out from the soil. It's a—'

'*Jesus, Mary and Joseph*,' Toni seethed. 'I can see what it is. Another of those knives. How many more can there be?'

'It was a top-secret army, there would have been no weapons amnesty,' Lucie chirped.

'It was about a foot below the ground. We kept soil samples from the area to confirm it wasn't buried recently,' Malcom said. 'Soil is impacted into the handle.'

'My guess is it's the knife which killed Stride.' Jack appeared from behind a gravestone.

'The killer buries the knife in Rupert Stride's not-grave to make up for Stride dying under a different name?' Toni said.

'More likely it's a symbolic stabbing by someone who didn't get the chance to actually kill Stride,' Jack went on. 'Only a handful of people knew the body in the pillbox was Rupert Stride. Stevie,' Jack was looking at the elderly woman, 'Jimmy Chrismas, Henry Morrison and well, I think your mother, Adelaide?'

'Adelaide wasn't in the Auxiliary Unit, she can't have killed Stride.' Coffee had thawed Stella's brain. She disliked that Stevie was party to their discussion. If Stevie was protecting her mother at Henry's expense, this wasn't the time and place to confront her. If there was such a time and place.

'She could have used Henry's knife.' Toni lowered her voice. Perhaps she too was thinking of Stevie. 'Just when you think it's all over.' Toni groaned. 'If this knife was used to kill Stride and you guys found Henry's knife under the floorboard in his old room, whose knife was used to murder Snace?'

'Three knives, two victims.' Stella tipped back the last of her coffee; it must have been strong because already her heart was going ten to the dozen. *Or was she close to the truth?* 'Who else had a Fairbairn-Sykes knife?'

'You are all forgetting Snace.' Stevie's voice grated. 'My mother only stunned my father with the poker from the drawing room. She hadn't meant to kill him, it was spur of the moment. She would have been horrified by what she did and, I would think, set about hiding him. As he always was, Snace was creeping about and he would have found my... Rupert Stride and, well, finished him off. Snace was trained to kill silently and swiftly, you see.'

Stella caught Jack's eye. Was Stevie going to tell Toni the truth?

'Could this knife belong to Snace, Miss Stride?' Malcolm Lane's gentle tone reminded Stella suddenly of her dad.

'I would think so,' Stevie said. Stella realised suddenly that Stevie was using the subjunctive now as she had in Lucie's interview, not to hide something but because she didn't know the facts. She had, over the last eighty years, pieced a likely story together.

'Wait, are you saying Snace murdered Stride?' Obviously taken aback, Toni spilled some of her coffee. *Another reason for keeping the lid on.* Stella dismissed the irrelevancy.

'Mother told me that Snace threatened to frame her. She didn't say what it was for. I knew he had a hold on her, I wasn't clear what it was, she said it was better that I didn't know. But what you don't know, you make up.'

'Do you think your mother found the knife and buried it in your father's grave?' Lucie said.

'I would think it was Jimmy. He sealed the pillbox. If he found the knife, what better place to hide it than in the grave of the man who made my mother's life a misery.'

'Except it wasn't your father's grave.'

'I didn't know.' Stevie hugged her coat closer. 'I knew little of this. If I had known I would have killed Snace long ago myself. Arrest me too, Detective Inspector Kemp.'

'If we arrested people for wishing other people dead, our prisons would be more crammed than they already are.' Toni shook her head. 'Did Jimmy and Henry know about the abuse your mother suffered at the hands of Rupert Stride?'

'I thought I was the only one who knew.' In the dawn light, Stevie Stride seemed to have lost years. She was as beautiful as her mother had been. Now Stella knew why Stevie had appeared upset when she and Jack had compared Rosa to her father. Rosa must have been a daily reminder of a man who had brutalised his wife.

'Jimmy and Henry saw me ripping up the plants in Stride's grave. I won't call him Father. They were returning from a late-night top-secret Auxiliary mission, not that I knew that then. I was terrified they had seen me and upset that whatever they'd been doing, they hadn't taken me. We were the Three Musketeers until they joined the Home Guard. When they said nothing I assumed I'd got away with it, until the next day when Snace caught Jimmy putting the grave to rights. Henry rushed out of the house and said it was him. Mother didn't believe either of them. She told Snace to leave them, it wasn't his business. I couldn't admit it was me, that meant explaining why. Mother didn't know I'd seen the man who was my father hit her, insult her, drag her around the kitchen by the hair. All those times I never stopped him.'

'You were a child,' Toni said. 'He would have hurt you and that wouldn't have helped your mum, believe me.'

'I couldn't say I was overjoyed when Stride died.' Stevie looked across to the tent. 'I suspected Mother knew I'd desecrated his grave. Putting everything together she would have guessed I knew the truth. That Rupert was a violent deceitful husband. Given time, he would have been violent to us, his daughters too. It appals me now.'

'Why does it? It seems pretty understandable,' Jack said.

'It's not his grave, is it?' Stevie looked distressed. 'It's some poor chap that Stride killed for his own ends. Everything he did was for his own ends. Favours for villagers, contributions to the church; for generations my family's generosity has been motivated by the need for power.'

'Most generosity is.' Toni pulled a face.

'I want to see Henry, please,' Stevie suddenly said.

'Of course, Miss Stride.' Malcolm Lane stepped forward.

'I'll take you, Stevie.' Lucie had been remarkably quiet, no sign of a notebook.

'Not this time, Lucie May.' Toni was firm. 'Let us do our job.'

'For eighty years Snace had Adelaide, Stevie and, without her knowing, Rosa, in his power.' Jack was watching Malcolm lead Stevie out of the churchyard.

'And before that they were at the mercy of Rupert Stride,' Stella said. 'If only Adelaide had told the police. It was self-defence – she might not have been hanged.'

'Hard to argue that when she had hit him with the poker that she'd obviously taken from the house to the pillbox. She came equipped for murder.' Toni was grim.

'Think of Edith Thompson: she didn't know her erstwhile lover was going to shoot her husband in the street. She was executed on the basis that she'd wished her husband dead in a bunch of letters and the misogynist judge treated her words as louder than actions,' Lucie said.

'Greta and this poor man were murdered by a self-serving psychopath. Then Stride himself was murdered by Snace—' Toni crushed the coffee cup in her fist. 'Who in turn was murdered by Henry.'

'You believe him?' Stella said.

'No, but he will stick to his story.'

'Snace killed Liddell. A True Host killed a True Host. It can happen, Jackanory,' Lucie murmured as she got up from Kate's bench and linked arms with Jack and Stella.

In silence the little group watched as the body of the murdered man was carried to the morgue van.

'What about the ornaments in that room in the Old Rectory?' Stella said when the van had rounded the bend in Church Lane towards the coast road. 'Some of them definitely came from Yew Tree House.'

'Stevie and Rosa have confirmed that everything came from there,' Toni said. 'All of it belonged to Stride's family and has terrible associations.'

'I persuaded them to let me sell it,' Lucie said. 'They should at least have the money. Stevie said it was "blood money", but gave in when Rosa agreed.'

'Hopefully it will go some way to paying the bills on Yew Tree House,' Jack said.

'Oh, they're not going to live there.' Lucie looked appalled at the idea.

'But it's not like they can sell it, or rather get anything from it if they vacate,' Stella said. 'Doesn't most, if not all, of it belong to the equity company?'

'Yes, but the cash that Stevie released and passed on to Snace can now come back to her. I've given Toni here sufficient evidence of blackmail and dirty doings to ensure that the girls get more than enough to live on once the Old Rectory is sold. I'm taking Stevie and Rosa away.'

'What? Where?' Stella said. 'Taking them how?'

'In Prunella, of course.' Lucie gave a low cackle. 'We're having a road trip. It was Stevie's idea.'

'For a story?'

'No, *not* for a story, what do you take me for?'

There was no answer to that.

'Martin was right, you two are the A team,' Toni said as, standing by the lych-gate, they waited for Jack to bring round the car. The sun had risen, it would be a fine autumn day.

'Martin said that?' Stella was surprised and, she realised, rather pleased. Then her mood changed. 'Is Stevie going to get Henry to retract his confession to Snace's murder, do you think?'

'She may well try, but Henry's told us special knowledge we didn't release to the public, including that he shut your dog in the Old Rectory kitchen before answering the door and telling you and Jack that your dog wasn't in the house.'

'Oh my—' *Henry had left that out when they talked.* 'It didn't sound like Henry.'

'Maybe he disguised his voice?'

'Maybe.' Stella couldn't remember the voice properly. Had it even been a man? Stella was reeling. Who had killed the Reverend Michael Snace? The strength of loyalty between the three friends, Stevie, Henry and Jimmy, was beyond her experience. A police officer's daughter, she would not break the law for anyone she loved. *Or would she?* 'Henry agreed reluctantly to let Jimmy take the blame for Stride's murder in 1945 rather than take the blame himself. I guess because he never had to follow through with their agreement that if the body was found and hanging had been abolished, he would say it was him. And that's why he's confessed to Snace's murder.'

'Jimmy couldn't have murdered Snace, we established that, the logistics don't work. The lack of forensics is a stumbling block. We've searched Henry's home and found no bloodied clothing. It's my hunch that at trial, Henry will be found not guilty.'

Silence as they watched the old BMW putter down Church Lane towards them. Stella, for one, was hoping that Toni was right.

'I meant to ask, did the holiday work?' Toni said.

'Sorry?'

'Wasn't the idea of you going away for a month in the country to see if you could live with Jack and his kids? Try being a family?'

'Oh...' Stella realised that with Henry on remand – he'd been granted bail – and Lucie away with the sisters somewhere in Scotland, she and Jack hadn't discussed it. It was up to her because Jack would never be the one to bring it up. 'Yes, I shall move in with him.'

'Bet Jack's over the moon.' Toni nodded towards Jack, who had parked a couple of metres up the lane. He nodded back.

'I only decided I would this second,' Stella admitted.

'Oh, my days! I didn't have you down as a spur of the moment girl, we have more in common than I supposed.' Toni gripped Stella's shoulder. 'Maybe you should tell Jack kind of soon? Put the guy out of his misery.'

'I will,' Stella said. Guessing that Toni, like herself, was not a kissing type, Stella proffered a hand.

'Break a leg, mate.' Toni grasped Stella's hand. 'Keep catching the bad guys.'

When Stella turned to wave, there was no one by the lych-gate.

Any indecision about when Stella might tell Jack was taken out of her hands when they were caught at the Newhaven swing bridge and Jack had to turn the engine off.

'Best news ever.' Jack leaned over the gear stick and hugged her. 'I love you, Stell.'

Stella had intended to tell Jack she loved him too, but instead she said, 'I wondered, what do you think to the idea of us getting a camper van?'

Acknowledgements

The idea for *The Mystery of Yew Tree House* comes from long dog walks with my partner and our dog. Roaming the Sussex countryside, we see countless red-bricked structures dating from the early years of WWII, there to defend the coast and waterways from Hitler's army. These 'pillboxes' are now over eighty years old and many are engulfed in foliage and, as intended, blend in with the landscape.

Readers local to Sussex wishing to visit the village that features in this story will not recognise Bishopstone. While the village in my story is fictional, it owes something to Bishopstone and to Lindfield, both in Sussex. As, fabulous places that they are, do I.

My novels arrive fully formed only through the support and advice of friends and the professional skill and attention of the team at Head of Zeus.

My thanks to my fabulous long-term editor, Laura Palmer, for her initial thoughts and guidance and then to my wonderful editor Bethan Jones for advice and feedback that was cogent and inspiring. Peyton Stableford was, as ever, a forensic – and endlessly *patient* – force. Thanks in awe go to copyeditor Liz Hatherell for ensuring my characters do what they're meant to at the right age and in the right year. On proofing with the sharpest of eyes was Nicola Bigwood, thank you! My thanks too to Ben Prior for the stunning cover design.

I am grateful to Georgina Capel at Georgina Capel Literary Agency. Thank you.

I've loved Stevie Smith's poems since watching the film *Stevie* with the late and great Glenda Jackson when I was twenty. I am thrilled that Faber in the UK and New Directions in the USA granted permission to use 'Advice to Young Children'. This poem – from my forty-year-old copy – expresses the essence of this novel. In homage to Stevie, one of my characters has her name.

As ever, Elly Griffiths and William Shaw were beacons of encouragement and are the best examples of how to be a crimewriter that I know. Special thanks to Dom for advice, road trips and rock cakes on the beach.

To the mates who cheer me on Philippa Brewster, Moya Burns, Jonny and Kathryn Burton, Gill Butler, Marianne Dixon aka Vikasini, Juliet Eve, Nikki and John Gower, Gill Hamer, Flis Henwood, Lisa Holloway, Miranda Kemp, Andy Maxted, Cat Murphy, Sarah Price, Tina Ross, and Joann Weedon.

Warm thanks to my lovely family, Tasmin and Simon Barnett, Peter and Lynn Nelson, Katherine Nelson and William Nelson. Melanie Lockett, to whom this novel is dedicated, lives with my novels as they take shape and indeed makes them possible.

Big thanks to Liam Baker, Jesse Roberts, Tony Roberts and Bill Roberts, who literally worked alongside me as I wrote(!). Thanks, guys.

About the Author

LESLEY THOMSON grew up in west London. Her first novel, *A Kind of Vanishing*, won the People's Book Prize in 2010. Her second novel, *The Detective's Daughter*, was a #1 bestseller and the resulting series has sold over 750,000 copies. Lesley divides her time between Sussex and Gloucestershire. She lives with her partner and her dog.

Visit her website at www.lesleythomson.co.uk